Found Underneath

Finding Me Duet #2

K.L. KREIG

Found Underneath

Published by K. L. Kreig
ISBN-13: 978-1-943443-26-0
ISBN-10: 1-943443-26-2

Cover Art by Kellie Dennis of Book Cover By Design
Interior Formatting by Author E.M.S.
Editing by Nikki Busch Editing
Cover Model: Assad-Lawrence Hadi Shalhoub
Cover Photographer: Christopher John

Published in the United States of America.

Found.

Sometimes you find yourself in the middle of nowhere and sometimes in the middle of nowhere you find yourself.

~ Unknown

Author's Note:

This is NOT a standalone. If you haven't read LOST IN BETWEEN yet, close this book immediately and read that one first. FOUND UNDERNEATH is the conclusion of the Finding Me duet and must be read in order to understand and enjoy the entire story. If you've read LOST IN BETWEEN, then I suggest you grab a few tissues and buckle up. It's going to be a bumpy ride! (Insert evil author laugh here.)

Prologue
One day before meeting Willow Blackwell

REGARDLESS OF WHAT THE FEMALE population thinks, simply because a man chooses to remain single does not mean there is something wrong with him.

Take me for example.

I am not broken.

I am not damaged.

I'm not a sociopath, a narcissist, or a recluse.

I don't have a black soul or a shattered heart.

Life hasn't beaten me down to the point where I don't think I'll make a sufficient mate.

I haven't had a bad relationship or met a woman who "ruined me" for all others. I am not pining for the "one that got away."

I'm a normal, down-to-earth guy who has made a *conscious choice* not to be tied to one woman for life.

From the time I was four and the smell of success pulled me under her seductive influence, I knew having a wife and family would only interfere with my life, not enhance it.

And I don't mean to sound like an asshole, but why settle for a single entree when a whole buffet is at my disposal?

I work hard. I play harder. And I like the little gig I've set up for myself. It works well, and you know what they say about things that aren't broken.

No, I'm happy just the way I am.

Free and unattached.

A self-proclaimed bachelor for life.

My life is perfect the way it is, and there is no woman I will ever meet who could possibly change that.

The cursive title "Shaw" is set above the skyline image.

Shaw

Chapter One • Present Day

MY HANDS ARE TREMBLING. MY stomach is a wreck...knotted and churning. Acid made purely of anxiety eats me raw. It keeps crawling its way up my esophagus and I keep shoving it back down.

I'm trying not to overreact. I want to give Annabelle the benefit of the doubt, but...*should I*? She's not exactly Snow fucking White and four years ago, she was as far from a Disney princess as a girl could get.

Drug abuse strung her out, changed her, almost stole her from us. If I hadn't saved her when I did, if *she* hadn't decided she'd reached rock bottom, I've no doubt she'd be long gone. Living in a crack house or resting peacefully beside my younger brother who died two days after birth.

I replay words over and over from an asshole who wants my woman, wishing they were different. Praying they're wrong.

"Am I playing, Shaw?" he sneers. "You picked up your sister that night from the police station. Miraculously got her off on coke possession charges. Wasn't she soaked to the bone? Distraught? What bullshit story did your drug addict sister

feed you that you bought with the gullibility of a five-year-old?"

A loud horn to my right jolts me. I yank the wheel to the left, realizing that I've drifted into the right lane.

"Watch what you're fucking doing," a woman with three kids lined in the back seat yells out the window she's rolled down specifically to berate me. She flips me the finger before tearing off through a yellow light that turns red halfway through, while I stop.

Good role model, that. *Don't follow in her footsteps, kids.*

While the engine idles, my mind drifts, and I reluctantly remember the night that's etched in my memory forever.

"Merc, you need to get down here."

"What is it?" My stomach churns. I already know the answer.

"It's your sister. And she's pretty out of it."

Fuck. Annabelle, what have you done now? *The second I hear Bull's words, I grab my keys and head out the door. I slide into the driver's seat and start the car, the engine quiet. The Bluetooth kicks in. "Did you call my parents?"*

"I should have but..." Bull hedges, his throaty voice ringing through my speakers.

Relief swarms me. "Thanks, man. Be there shortly."

I immediately call Noah and we arrive at the Seattle PD half an hour later. When we step inside, soaked due to the downpour, we're greeted by Captain Ryan. Captain Cade Ryan, or Bull, as we affectionately referred to our best defensive linebacker in high school, also happens to be a good friend of Noah's and mine.

"What's going on, Bull?" I ask, trying to keep my shit together.

He shakes his head and starts down the hall to our left. We silently follow corridor after corridor until we stop at a closed wooden door. Only then does Bull address us. Well, me.

"Your sister needs serious help, Merc. Professional therapy.

Detox. I could book her on Schedule 1 CDS possession right now and get it to stick. That's up to five years if convicted."

My eyes close as despair makes it impossible to hold my head up. "What did she have?" I ask, glaring at the matted carpet flooring that probably used to be light brown twenty years ago. Now it's just a snarled sea of mud, bad decisions, and ruined lives.

"Cocaine."

"Fuck," Noah and I curse loudly at the same time.

"Look, I'm not even sure it was hers. She says it wasn't, of course. A baggie was in the bushes beside the vehicle, and there were three other girls inside, but it's obvious she's been using something."

"Where did you find her?"

"Holsteen Road. She and three other girls. She wasn't driving but it was her car. They were picked up for speeding and erratic driving."

I pin him with a desperate look. Annabelle is just shy of her seventeenth birthday, and a conviction will ruin her future. Kiss scholarships and college good-bye. Generally, a drug possession charge would only result in probation…if it was your first run-in with the law, especially with the best lawyers, which I happen to have access to. But this isn't her first. And this is a hell of a lot worse than a few dime bags of weed. She could be in real trouble here.

"What now?"

The air is weighty with indecision at my unspoken and unfair request of a fucking police captain. How do I make this shit go away?

After making me wait what seems like an agonizing amount of time, he finally offers, "She goes right from here into inpatient rehab. No less than thirty days."

"I can do that." I almost weep at this gift Annabelle's being given, but she probably won't see it that way. She'll see it as worse than a prison sentence.

"Get her help, Merc. I see her in here again and there's

nothing I can do. And any of you breathe a word of this to anyone, it's my badge."

Emotion clogs my throat. I nod but can't respond. Noah does instead. "We understand. Thanks, Bull. We got you covered."

When Bull opens the door, I'm momentarily frozen at the tiny, fragile thing sitting in a metal chair at a matching shiny oblong table. Cheeks streaked with tears and mascara. Red-rimmed, haunted eyes. Disheveled blond hair. A swollen cut on one side of her lip. Her clothes are askew, her top ripped. She has scratches up and down one arm. All one hundred pounds of her is soaked to the bone.

She looks like she could shatter with a simple breath.

"Bluebelle, what have you done to yourself?" I choke, unable to keep a tear from leaking.

In slow motion, she looks up. My breath catches at deadened icy blue eyes that latch on to mine. It takes her several seconds to realize it's me and when she does, she launches herself from the table and runs into my arms like she used to when she was a little girl. Every limb winds around me and she sobs uncontrollably.

"What happened, Belle?"

She won't answer. Her tiny body silently shudders against mine.

I distinctly remember it took me half an hour to calm her enough to remove her from the PD without bringing attention to ourselves. While I worked to pacify Annabelle, Noah worked on finding a place to take her. When we left, he had everything arranged for a small, boutique facility in Portland. The last thing we needed was to keep her in the city and have the press find out.

Annabelle never told me much about that night, and even to this day, I don't know the particulars. Whenever I pushed she withdrew, so I decided it wasn't worth rehashing because for quite a while there she was on the brink and I didn't want to throw her over it with the third degree. She relapsed once in the middle of treatment. Left, then came back. She pulled through, though. Managed to stay clean until last year when she slipped and returned to rehab on her own.

Drug addiction is a soul-sucking experience for everyone involved, including the addict. Hope disintegrates, faith is destroyed, trust erodes to nothing. Less than nothing. It takes a lifetime to earn those back once they're gone if it's even possible. And one mistake...*one* mistake can have everyone backtracking to square one on the game board, aggravated at having to start over.

Even though she's been doing well, I have no shame admitting I've never made it much past square one with her. As I now stand at the mouth of Allen Library, watching my sister with her nose tucked in a book, looking all scholarly and happy and youthful, I freeze.

Can I trust a word out of her mouth?

Will I find answers to questions I don't even know if I want?

My entire future rests on my baby sister and isn't that fucking ironic? Her entire future rested on me only a few years ago. For once in my life, I need something from someone else and I feel as if I'm going to be hung out to dry. My chest physically constricts at the thought of not having Willow in my life.

Maybe I should be knocking on Bull's doorstep instead to see how the hell Reid "fuckface" Mergen even knows about a case where the paperwork was supposedly "misplaced." Perhaps I should be attacking this problem from an entirely different direction, burying Reid Mergen so far underground in the process he'll never again see the light of day. Slander his reputation so no one believes a venomous word he drips.

Yeah. New plan.

I'm halfway to my car when Annabelle's melodic voice floats from behind, "Hey, where are you going?"

For a split second, I consider pretending not to hear her.

Just get in my car, drive to the PD, and ferret out who Bull's rat is. If I turn around and acknowledge her, if I let the accusation settle hard between us, I can't take it back. Once the cat is out of the bag, I'll never be able to shove that hairy monster back inside.

Maybe this is exactly what Mergen is after? Fracture trust. Weave doubt. Set the trap, letting me set myself on fire while he stands on with a fire extinguisher he has no intention of using.

But I think back to his taunt, and I know there was something there I didn't want to acknowledge when I was contemplating choking the life from him.

Confidence.

He was so goddamned certain what he was saying was the truth.

Stop being a pussy, Merc. Even if I want to run from this, I can't. I need to know what happened that night, now more than ever. And if something did...figure out how the fuck I'm going to mitigate the fallout without losing anyone I love in the process.

Shaw

Chapter Two

"YEAH. JUST FORGOT SOMETHING. IT can wait," I answer when I turn back around.

"You sure? You look"—her eyes narrow and she cocks her head, scrutinizing me a little too closely—"weird."

What? The panic swelling inside me like high tide is seeping out of my pores? Tightening my cheeks? Tingeing my eyes wild with fear? Imagine that.

"Always looking for something that's not there, Bluebelle."

Her lips thin. My diversion falls flat. Once again, I briefly contemplate making a run for it, but fuck it. Delaying this conversation isn't going to make it any easier. And it's certainly not going to make this shit go away.

Grabbing her gently by the arm, I direct us to an unoccupied park bench underneath a large oak alongside the sidewalk. Fall is finally upon us and nature is helpless to resist. Leaves are already turning shades of copper and yellow. A few have dried and fallen early. They crunch beneath our feet as we silently walk.

I take a seat, relishing in the warmth of the metal seeping through my suit pants. In a mere moment, I'm afraid my entire body will feel as cold as dry ice instead.

"What's up, Shawshank?"

I let her irritating childhood nickname roll off. Staring ahead, I watch the flurry of life on campus. I remember camping out like this between classes, watching the freshmen skitter by virtuous and unaware. Easily weeding through them to find the shameless so Noah and I could play with them later.

Back then had Willow walked by, she would have immediately been rejected. Too sweet, too tame. Far too innocent. And what a shame that would have been. To never touch her supple curves or her silky hair. To never feel her melt under the touch of my hand or hear the hitch of her breath when she's coming undone under the weight of my body. Jesus, the thought of never hearing her whisper or moan my name is unfathomable. She's twisted me in ways I didn't know I could bend. She's apparently the one I've been waiting for and I would have discarded her with a passing glance for the very thing that draws me to her today.

"What were you doing the night you got picked up for coke possession? And I need the truth this time, Bluebelle."

I didn't even look at her when I blurted out a question that slammed into her from behind with the force of a Mack truck. I know it did because I heard the breath whoosh from her lungs right before the sharp intake of air to refill them.

I turn my head to gaze hard at my sister. She's staring at me with this shocked look on her face. I know why. This is a taboo subject between us. Hell, with the whole damn family. We all walk on eggshells, hoping they don't crack beneath the weight of our steps. *Never discuss how Annabelle spiraled out of control. It may upset her.* It's as if we're all supposed to forget she is a recovering addict. Will *always* be a recovering addict.

But I've never forgotten. Neither should she. Neither should anyone who cares about her. And apparently neither has an outsider who is now hell-bent on taking what's mine by using my love for my family against me. Little does he know it's exactly my love for my family—and that now includes Willow—that will fuel me to steamroll right over him.

"Answer the question, Bluebelle." I soften my tone only marginally, but the hoarse rasp in it gives away exactly how wound up I am. She's keeping something from me. I see the secrets plain as day in her striking blues. They're trying to dive below the surface, remain hidden.

Well, I'm dragging them back up to the top. It's time to unearth old ghosts no matter how loud they howl.

"Why…?" She stops to swallow, and that guilt I always feel for upsetting my baby sister swells when her eyes gloss over. I fight my instincts to give her an out. I need this fucking answer. For me, for Willow, but honestly…mostly for her. That campaign asshole has something on her, and I need to find out what it is and make it go away. Maybe I can even bury it before Willow ever needs to know.

"Why are you asking now?" she husks.

The weight of what she didn't say is so fucking heavy, the muscles in my neck give and my head drops. Clasping my hands together, I let them hang between my legs while working to control my breathing *and* my temper.

I'm at one of the biggest crossroads of my life here. Do I tip my hand and simply ask straight out or do I lead her with questions, like some goddamned cross-examination and hope she trips herself up enough for me to catch her in a lie?

This is excruciating.

I've never been a beat-around-the-bush kinda guy. I drill straight to the point, no time for bullshit. With everyone except her, that is. My emotionally fragile baby sister who I'd lay down my life for. But that ends today. It has to. I have to know what I'm facing. I can't grapple in the dark and hope to blindly catch a lifeline.

Straightening, I turn to face her. The well of tears in her eyes is about to give way. "I'm asking now because it matters now. Were you on Schultz Bridge that night?"

The color in her cheeks fades and the dam holding that water back breaks. Tears streak down her pale skin as she continues to stare at me, unblinking.

And now I know.

My sister had something to do with the untimely death of Charles Blackwell.

Jesus fucking Christ.

My sister played a part in the night that ended a man's life: the father of the woman I love. My gut feels full of rocks. My lungs constrict as if someone's wrapped a thick cord around them and yanked with all their might. I am utterly sick.

When she responds softly, "I don't know," I fucking lose it.

"You don't *know*?" I roar, causing people to slow as they pass. "Or is it that you just don't want *me* to know that you caused an innocent man's death when you were coked up?"

"What are you talking about, Shaw?" she chokes.

Oh fuck no. We are not doing this here. I should have never started this line of conversation in a public forum.

Grabbing her by the elbow, I pull up her up and guide her to the car. By the time I seal us both inside, she's a blazing mess of hotness.

"I didn't kill anyone, Shaw," she exclaims, her eyes wild. She's unconsciously picking at a scab on her arm, making it bleed. "I swear it. I swear it." She keeps mumbling those three words under her breath.

She's breaking apart right in front of me.

I still the hand digging into her flesh, warm blood smearing underneath the pads of my fingers. She's trembling. Her frightened eyes bulge and lock on me so tight it almost hurts. Pinching the bridge of my nose, I close my eyes and inhale nice and slow, exhaling the same way, thinking on what comes next.

"Tell me everything you remember about that night."

She blinks a couple of times before dragging her attention out the front windshield. With each second that passes, I'm not only losing my patience, I'm losing my goddamn mind.

"Annabelle," I growl.

"I don't remember much," she says without inflection.

"Define *much*."

I give her fingers a gentle squeeze, hoping to jump-start her since she now seems lost in her own head. I tick off the seconds, one by one, ready to crawl out of my skin.

When she speaks at last, it's monotone as if she's disconnected from those events. "I was out with Hannah, Emily, and Lia. We got a little high before we went to a party in the Valley." I keep my eye-roll internal. Rainier Valley isn't one of the most desirable parts of Seattle. "It was still pretty early, but by the time we got there, the place was buzzing."

If by *buzzing* she means it reeked of cooked meth, greasy hair, and day-old orgies, then I have a pretty good idea of what she walked into. I had to pull Annabelle out of one of those parties once when she was fifteen. It makes my stomach roil to think of her in a place like that, flushing her future down the toilet.

"When I walked in, someone handed me a woolie along with a beer. We vegged and listened to a couple of guys on their guitars." She pauses a few seconds, before softly adding, "They were good. One was cute."

My patience is waning. Fast. "Can we maybe get to the part you don't remember? Because it sounds as if you remember a helluva lot."

She shoots me a glare before the corners of her mouth lift slightly. They flatten out so fast I could have imagined it. With her free hand, she starts methodically plucking her jeans, and I know shit's about to get bad.

"I had to hit the loo, so I was winding my way down the hallway when I heard him. Eddie," her voice trails off.

Fucking Eddie Lettie. Her pusher, her supposed boyfriend, the bane of my sister's existence.

"I knew I shouldn't look. I knew I should just keep walking and forget I heard anything. But I couldn't. It wasn't the first time he'd cheated on me with some coked-out skank." She stops to lick her lips. Her voice holds absolutely no emotion when she says, "He had a little old train going, getting pegged in the ass while he was fucking some whore."

"Jesus, Annabelle."

She's my little sister. I changed her diapers, fed her bottles. Bandaged up her scrapes and wiped her nose when she was sick. I let her paint my nails bright pink and crawl into bed with me when she had bad dreams. I sure as shit don't want to hear the words "sex" or "fucked" or "pegged" coming out of her sweet mouth. And I sure as hell don't need to hear about Eddie's sex life.

"What?" she says, finally looking at me with glistening eyes. "You wanted to hear what happened that night. *That's* what happened."

"He's not worth those, Bluebelle." I wipe away a tear streaking down her cheek. "Don't give him that."

"I know," she answers, running her fingers along the same spot. "I know that now, but that night I'd gotten into another fight with Mom and Dad. I felt so alone, and I needed to be needed by someone. Anyone." She blinks a few times and lowers her voice a degree. "God, he was such a smug bastard. I should have just walked away then, but I didn't."

Her gaze darts over my shoulder. I wait it out while she sorts through her memories.

"I stood there like an innocent little girl, who didn't know what she was witnessing. He saw me watching. He was strung out, I could tell. He laughed; pounded into the girl he was banging until she cried. Then he choked her until her eyes rolled into the back of her head. He told me I was up next. That it was time he broke me in good because he liked it rough and hard and painful. He told me to go do a bump and I'd be good and pliable by the time he and his sidekick took turns fucking my ass, making me bleed. He told me he wanted me to cry and beg for my life while he choked me until I came."

The more she says, the more my vision hazes. It's dark. So fucking dark I think I'm going blind with rage. I work to swallow but can't. My throat feels swollen with violent thoughts of revenge. Did he do it? Did he follow through? Did he violate my baby sister with his sick and twisted threats? Is that why she was out of sorts that night?

If he did, if I get even a hint that he laid a single finger on her that night, Eddie Lettie is dead. Fuck that. He's dead anyway for even thinking it.

"What else?" God, it hurt to push that out. Please, for the love of Christ don't say he did something or I will call on every single person I know until I find one who knows the right people to gut him in his sleep, then make his body permanently disappear. Noah probably knows someone.

She chews her lip raw before looking at me with unease. My gut feels like it's bleeding out. "Then he told me he knew I'd love it because he heard kinkiness ran in the family."

That's it. That motherfucker dies. Slowly, painfully. He'll be tortured until he cries like a little pussy for his momma.

I've never given it much thought until recently, but my proclivities for sharing women with my best friend, Noah, have had a much further reach than I could have possibly imagined. They *have* hurt my family, tainted their reputations, even fed into deviances so depraved and disgusting it reached my baby sister at a time when she should have been enjoying football games and worrying about midterms.

"I'm so—"

"No. Don't." She waves her hand in dismissal. "He was talking about more than you anyway." *Lincoln. She means our brother who we both revere.* "I stayed. I know I should have left, but I stayed and snorted a few lines until the euphoria set in. But I started to feel weird…weirder than usual. Like I was disconnected from my body. And I was scared because…"

Jesus, I don't want to hear this. I don't want to ask. I don't want to know. But I have to get to the *after*. I have to understand how she ended up on Schultz Bridge.

"Because what, Bluebelle?" I prod, gentler this time, belying the red-hot frenzy of hate and fury scorching its way through my veins.

When her eyes shift to mine, the look in them absolutely kills me. She tries to hide it. She always tries to hide it, but unlike Willow's impenetrable shroud, I see right through my sister's. Her soul is complicated. Ripe with self-loathing and shadows of demons I don't understand. How I wish she were still little and I could protect her. She could climb on my lap again, painting my lips with my mother's ruby red lipstick instead of painting my heart with this twisted inadequacy she clings to.

"Because I thought: maybe I am like them. Maybe I am twisted and fucked up and that's what's really wrong with me. Because I was actually thinking of letting him do everything he told me he would."

"Fuck me," I mumble, not able to hold her gaze any longer. She's waiting for me to judge her. I am, and I don't want her to see it. And I can't possibly ask the question balancing on the edge of my teeth because I can't stomach her answer.

"You don't understand, Shaw. I was in some really bad headspace then," she continues in that irritatingly even tone. "I just wanted to be loved, even if it was by some asshole who only pretended to care."

"Annabelle…" My heart is twisting in agony. "You were loved. You *are* loved." I grab her face between my hands and wipe away the tears wetting her cheeks. I want to shake some sense into her.

"You don't need a worthless piece of shit like Eddie Lettie to feed your self-esteem. All guys like that do is feed *off* of it until there's nothing left."

"I know."

Does she, though? She says all the right things at the right times, but most of the time I don't think she believes a word of it. She's still as confused and tormented by whatever started her down this destructive path, to begin with.

"Eddie came out of the bedroom awhile later with his jeans on but the zipper undone, and he…"

"He what," I barely breathe. I loosen my fingers around her jaw when she winces. It's hard. All I want to do is punch something until my knuckles split.

"He eyed me with this look that meant keep my mouth shut, then he grabbed me from the couch. The sick thing is...I went willingly."

I have to let go of her then. I have to grab the steering wheel and wrap my fingers tight around it, fighting like hell not to pick up my phone, call Bull, and demand he put out an APB on this low-life fucker, holding him until I can personally choke the life from his rotten soul.

"He pushed me against the wall even before we got to the bedroom. He tore my blouse while telling me all the vile things he was going to do to me. But the whole scene faded in and out, like I'd accepted my fate and checked out of my body. I knew I didn't really want what he was telling me. I knew I needed to fight but I couldn't make myself do anything about it. He may have hit me. I may have screamed. I don't know. It's all pretty hazy."

Jesus fucking Christ.

"I get these snippets of fighting and yelling and glass breaking. The last thing I remember was stumbling down the steps outside and after that, it's all black until I woke up the next day in rehab. If I was on that bridge, I honestly don't remember. I don't even remember you picking me up from the police station, Shaw."

She stops talking. I'm not sure how long we sit in stone silence. She's waiting for me to say something, *anything* I suppose, but I've got nothing. My heart is heavy. Breaking for her, breaking for what's been done to her, for everything she's been through in her short years already. But mostly it's heavy because this conversation didn't fucking help at all. I know little more than I did before, except I have another to-do to add to my ever-growing list.

"I'm sorry I don't remember more."

"Don't be. It's fine," I lie.

She swallows hard. I hear it over the two feet that separate us. "Why do you think I killed someone?"

I look at her then. Her eyes shine. Her face looks sallow. Her lips are trembling. She's picking at that damn cut again because she's nervous about what I'm going to say.

"I don't think you did, Bluebelle."

"Then why did you say that?" Her voice is shaky and shrill and I feel as though I'm one-half step away from losing her to that sordid world again. I don't want to lie to her, but I don't know how honest I should be either. I have no idea how close she is to that invisible ledge or what will make her tip over it.

"It's just a misunderstanding is all."

Her spine straightens. "I don't believe you. Something made you think that. Someone brought up that night, specifically Schultz Bridge, or you wouldn't be here quizzing me."

"It's nothing," I offer again, hoping she'll leave well enough alone until I can figure this the fuck out. I'm already trying to plot my next course of action.

"I want you to tell me the truth, Shaw."

My sigh is long and drawn out. She can't handle the truth right now. Maybe not ever. "Annabe—"

"I'm stronger than you think, Shaw. Everyone always acts like I'm a baby and I'm stupid, and I'm sick of it. 'Be careful what you say to Annabelle.' 'Annabelle won't understand.' 'Annabelle's too young,'" she mocks. "I'm a grown-ass woman now. Start fucking treating me like one. Whatever you tell me isn't going to send me back there. I promise."

"Isn't it?" I challenge, turning toward her. Only minutes ago, she was falling apart. Now she's suddenly strong as an ox? In about five seconds I'll wish I hadn't let her petulance goad me. "What *if* you were responsible for someone's death that night and you don't remember? What *if* that person happens to be the father of the woman I'm in love with? What *if* someone else knows that and is using it against me? Against our family to get what he wants?"

At the horrified look on her face, I reach for her hand, hoping my touch soothes the sting of my tirade, but she yanks it back.

"Is all that true?" she croaks.

Every fucking word of it, I want to say. Right down to the part where I'm in love. Jesus...I. Am. In. Love. Three months ago that was laughable. A big part of me wants that oblivion again because if this is what being in love makes you feel inside—unholy panic at every turn—I am in for a world of hurt.

"That's what I'm trying to figure out, Bluebelle."

Her hand flies to her mouth, stifling a sob. She looks every bit the young naïve twenty-one-year-old she is instead of the mouthy, carefree one she tries to be.

This time I don't let her recoil. I set my hand on the back of her neck and force her to me, throwing my arm around her in comfort.

"I'll fix it. Whatever it is, trust me to fix it," I declare. I don't know how. I only know I have to.

Her small body shakes against mine. I feel like a heel putting her through this, but honestly, better me than the cops. I wouldn't put it past that cocksucking campaign twat to try stirring up legal trouble for us as soon as it suits his purpose. And I hear that countdown clock ticking. It started the second I stepped outside his office doors earlier.

He didn't throw out some idle threat. This I already know. All the pieces fit together too perfectly. A little *too* perfectly, if you ask me. He has to know I have connections. He has to know I'll turn over every rock I can. He has to think I'll find something and walk away from Willow, leaving him to scoop up the pieces of her broken heart. What he doesn't know, though, is how deep my well of pure grit and determination runs when I want something badly enough.

He's about to find out, though. I want Willow, and I won't let him, or anyone else, take her from me. I decided on my way here that there's something to be said about the adage *keep your friends close, but your enemies closer.*

I'm not saying a word about this to my father, something I think Mergen banked on. This news would absolutely crush my father's heart. It would ruin his chances of reelection. Mergen knows that. The fucker thinks he can get away unscathed with everything he wants.

Only he won't.

He will not threaten my family.

He will not steal my girl.

He *will not* take a single thing from me that is mine to protect.

Willow

Chapter Three

I'M HAPPY.

Skipping in the rain, unicorn believing, rainbow chasing, chocolate-doesn't-make-your-ass-fat deliriously happy.

I beam, remembering every detail of the past three glorious days I spent wrapped up in everything Shaw. Our weekend together was nothing short of magical. I didn't want it to end.

What I'd had with Reid felt warm and comfortable, like a smolder. There was heat, but we never truly caught fire. We could have grown old together. I would have been happy if I let myself. Content, not fulfilled. I loved him, but there always was a pause with us. That something I knew was missing yet could never quite put my finger on. In retrospect, I think it was the reason I left him. I used my father's death as an excuse and at the time, it was valid, but the real reason started long before that.

I didn't fully understand that, though, until I met Shaw. What I have with him is unmatched. Unparalleled. It's—*he's*—the serenity and peace I didn't know existed, let alone the kind I'd find. He fits me. He *sees* me. He makes my blood boil, my heart sing, and my soul crave something I haven't in a long, long time, if ever.

To be truly, openly, terrifyingly vulnerable.

This habit I've perfected of staying bulletproof is a hard one to break, yet of any man I've ever met Shaw Mercer makes me want to try. He makes me want to shed old skin, leaving the fresh stuff pink and raw and ready to be scarred again.

The thought gives my heart real palpitations, but I shove away the cynical side that whispers happiness is fleeting and tragedy lurks around every corner. Today I'm walking on sunshine and I'm going to let myself enjoy this remarkable feeling of pure and utter bliss and hope that, for once in my life, it's not merely a glimpse on the horizon but an actual reality I only have to reach out and grasp.

Because if Shaw is willing to try, then—*deep breath*—so am I.

For the fiftieth time, I look down at the text he sent this morning and grin like a lovestruck fool.

I didn't like waking up without you in my arms this morning.

God. The things that string of words does to my heart is insanity.

"You're glowing. You knocked up?"

I reluctantly rip my gaze away from my phone to face Sierra. It's just before noon. She's up earlier than usual and I can immediately tell she's in a mood, but the sunshine beneath my feet feels balmy and fluid. Neither dynamite nor Sierra's snide comments will wipe this grin off my face. So I decide to play. Sierra knows I'm sleeping with Shaw anyway.

"What if I am?"

I'm not, but damn...the thought it's not entirely *impossible* I could be carrying a life Shaw and I created feels so good I need to slam the brakes.

"Then you're going to have to pack up your shit and move out. There's no way I'll be able to get any sleep with a crying baby in this cracker box."

"You're all talk. You wouldn't kick me out."

"The hell I wouldn't," she deadpans. I watch her tug open

the cupboard and grab her favorite oversized black mug with gold knuckle-dusters as the handle. An old boyfriend gave it to her as a gag, but the joke was on him when she used it as a weapon a few days later after catching him making out on his couch with his ex. Trust me…you do *not* want to get on Sierra's bad side or she will cut you. But beneath her crust, her heart is solid twenty-four-karat gold.

"What if my baby and I didn't have anywhere else to go?"

"You have a rich baby daddy. You'd be his problem."

"What if he didn't want us?"

"Then sue his fucking ass for everything he has," she retorts, not kidding in the least.

"What if I made you the godmother?"

She stops pouring the thick black tar she calls coffee midstream and stares my way. "You would want that?"

I cock my head at her disbelieving tone. "Of course I would. Why wouldn't I?"

Her thin, still painted-on brows rise. "Look at me. I'm not exactly role model material, Lowenbrau."

She's right. She'd probably have to get rid of a few piercings or they'd be ripped out by tiny, searching hands. She'd need a different job because you can't leave a baby all night long four or five nights a week. And she'd have to find that politically correct filter pretty damn fast so the baby's first words weren't fuck or tits or ho.

Shrugging, I answer sincerely, "If my baby didn't have anyone, there's no one else I'd want to raise them other than you."

Her eyes water.

"Hey, what's wrong?" I ask reaching across the island top.

"Nothing," she sniffs, skirting my touch before turning away. "What the hell makes you think something is wrong?"

I bite my tongue. I know this Sierra. Another guy is plaguing her.

"I'm not pregnant," I tell her softly, feeling stupid my heart dropped a little.

Her mouth turns down. I see it from the side. She takes a deep breath in and I wait for it. It doesn't take long. When her now dry eyes meet mine again, they're filled with concern. "What are you doing, Willow?"

"What do you mean?" I mentally brace for it. Sierra doesn't use my full name all that damn often…only when she wants to get a point across.

She sets down the coffee pot and pushes her mug away, facing me once again. "You know exactly what I mean. I thought this thing was supposed to be temporary. You insisted you didn't fuck your clients and yeah, after seeing him I maybe get the curb appeal. But not only are you fucking him, now you're spending the weekend with him and suddenly talking about a fictional baby you're now trying to saddle me with."

I'm not sure which part to be incensed about more. I decide to go with the fictional baby comment since that feels easier than addressing the other stuff.

"You were the one who brought up said fictional baby. I just played along." I try to hold off my snarl. I'm not successful.

A corner of her mouth ticks up. "Yeah, okay, sure. But are you going to sit there and tell me the thought you were baking his kid didn't get your lady parts wet?"

"Jesus, Sierra."

"Are you?"

No. "What's this really about? Because it's not about my imaginary baby." Or the sudden fluttering in my womb.

Setting her palms on the Formica countertop, she leans toward me, widening her already large whiskey eyes. "This is about a playboy who won't think twice about discarding you at the end of four months when he's had his fill. This is about yet another person cramming you in behind *their* needs, Willow, instead of making you a priority. You deserve to be a priority and you are *not* a priority to him. This is all a lie for fuck's sake!"

I'm stunned silent as anger churns and festers. For what seems like forever we stare at each other.

She's wrong. It started out that way, yes, but she hasn't seen the way Shaw penetrates my heart as if he's always been there. She hasn't felt the tender way he caresses my skin or plants tiny kisses along the length of my neck. She hasn't heard the reverence and sincerity in his tone when he says my name. He's protected me from the media. He's taken countless hours away from his company for me. He's sat outside my house just to apologize. He's worried about my safety in a less-than-safe vehicle.

He *has* put me first. At every turn, so far. And as much as I love my family and at one time Reid, they didn't. But Shaw has.

She's wrong.

Isn't she?

Where's that goddamn sunshine I was walking on a minute ago? Damn her.

"You were the one who told me to sleep with him!" I shriek, throwing my hands in the air. "'Break the rules,' you said. 'Let him scald your insides,'" I mock in her low-pitched voice.

"Yes. I told you to *fuck* the hot coffee," she says, "not fall in love with its exotic taste. That's it!"

I glare daggers, ignoring the *love* comment. "I think I like sugarcoated bullshit better."

She smirks. "I'm not Dr. Seuss."

That's funny but I can't even laugh because what if she's right? I look down, suddenly interested in the flecks of gold smattering the weathered countertop. I think back to the weekend, Friday morning, in particular, and Shaw's heartfelt words: *Well, the truth is...you captivate me like no one else has before, Willow, and what I feel for you is...new for me.*

Was I too caught up in the moment and every subsequent moment after that? Was I naïve enough to think a zebra can change its stripes—that *I* would be the incentive for him to do so? Do I honestly believe a man who doesn't "do relationships" would suddenly want to be loyal and monogamous? Is being "captivating" enough? Is "new" all that bad?

Shit.

I don't know.

But he came to the club for me.

He took the day off for me.

He spent the entire weekend doting on me.

He wanted to meet my *mother.*

Why should I doubt him?

Damn Sierra and her sunshine-stealing gloom. This is usually my gig. I talk myself out of anything good that comes my way, believing I don't deserve it. I shared a part of me with Shaw that only Sierra knows about—how I feel responsible for my father's death—and he still wants me. Still thinks I'm worthy of him. I deserve Shaw, dammit. I deserve this. I deserve happiness, love. A *chance,* anyway.

Don't I?

"I didn't think you did relationships."

"I'm not sure I do, Willow, but I...I want to try. I'm trying to be as honest as possible here."

He's been up front. I trust Shaw. He's given me no reason not to. From the time we sat outside his parent's house and he told me he wouldn't feed me lines only to get between my legs, I've believed him. He hasn't promised me shit. No condo together, no diamond on my fourth finger, no golden wedding anniversary. No future. He simply said he wants to *try*. And shouldn't that be good enough for now until it isn't anymore? Until he proves to be untrustworthy?

"You're wrong about him, Sierra. This is more than a binding agreement now."

The corners of her mouth turn down. "He's thirty-some years old and views commitment like the black plague. Why now? Why you?"

Snap. That was cold.

I know Sierra's simply trying to protect me, but that hurts a little. Okay, a lot. I raise one shoulder. "You don't think I'm worth it?"

"Of course you're worth it. You're *more* than worth it." She sighs. "That's not what I meant and you know it. This is about him. Not you."

I take in my friend. I love her to the ends of the Earth and back, but sometimes I think we're not doing each other any favors. We protect the other too fiercely. We fan the flames of past pains hot enough to burn the good threatening us with real happiness to nothing but ash. We're our own worst enemies.

So I could let that comment—which I know was said with the utmost love and concern—bring me down or I could fight back the urge to do just that.

I choose to fight. Worse than falling in love and getting hurt would be to let this incredible man slip through my fingers because I'm scared to let myself feel something good. Or feel at all.

"I think that's exactly who it's about, Sierra."

She takes a quick, deep breath in and blows it back out. At least she looks contrite. "I'm just worried, that's all. I mean...you and me? We don't exactly have the best track records when it comes to men."

"I know, but this is different. *He's* different."

"If you say so." She turns her attention back to the pungent-smelling brew, announcing nonchalantly, "You had a visitor Saturday."

"Who?" I never have visitors. Not that I'm a recluse, but I also don't have a lot of friends. Certainly not ones who stop by without calling first.

"Reid."

"Reid?" I breathe in confusion. I saw him briefly at the club Thursday night when a fight almost broke out between him and Shaw, but I haven't talked to Reid in almost a week—when he sat here on my couch, forgave me for the unforgivable, and told me he still loved me. Six days later, I'm still not sure what to make of that night. Or his declaration. Or how I should feel about it. All I know is that everything has changed. In those six days, Shaw and I have morphed from a partnership into a relationship. A real one. Not one for public deception.

"What did he want?"

"Don't know."

"Well, what did he say?" I press, wondering why he didn't call instead of stopping over or why he hasn't called since.

"Not your answering service, Lowenbrau," she clips before taking a long sip of her supposed coffee and sighs with her eyes closed. She takes a few more large gulps before refilling her cup. She drank it so fast I'd be surprised if she didn't scald off the first layer of skin on her tongue in the process.

"Better?" I ask, my brows now up to my hairline. I should have known better than to carry on any type of conversation with Sierra before she's had at least one cup of coffee. She's angrier than a momma bear defending her cubs before her first injection of caffeine.

A self-deprecating smile appears. "Getting there."

"Bad night?"

She shrugs. "Same old bullshit, you know?"

"What happened?"

"He looked like a lost little puppy."

Huh? "Who?"

"Reid."

I let my mouth turn down slightly at her blatant change of subjects. Guess we're done talking about her and her own life. She'd much rather pry into mine.

"He's still into you."

I know. I sigh, but keep it on the inside.

"What makes you say that?" I ask, trying for lighthearted.

I didn't disclose much to Sierra about the other night when Reid came over, and I certainly didn't tell her he admitted he's still in love with me. She stood by my decision to call off the wedding. She held me when I cried myself to sleep at night for months afterward. She didn't say a word when I repeatedly refused to talk to him or see him, but she genuinely liked Reid, and though it was one of the few times she held her tongue and supported me unconditionally, I don't think she agreed with *how* I handled things with him.

"Oh, I don't know…could have been the look on his face when I told him you hadn't been here since Emfest, or maybe it was when I mentioned your boyfriend's name." Boyfriend is said with a little derision. I choose to ignore it.

"What look?"

"Let's just say I thought he was going to go all Yosemite Sam on me and I would be staring down the barrels of his smoking guns."

I laugh. "He did not."

"Did." She takes another drink, watching my reaction over the rim. I hold my face neutral.

"So he just got pissy and left? Nothing else?"

Her lips purse while she pretends to think. "Pretty much."

"Huh."

"Huh," she mimics. "Something you're not telling me?"

"What would I not be telling you?"

She sets down her cup and crosses her arms. "I don't know. You tell me. I just think it's awfully coincidental that when you start dating"—she puts dating in air quotes—"a fake boyfriend, who your ex unknowingly set you up with, by the way, that he's back in the picture. And I don't believe in coincidences."

I don't generally either, but in this case, that's all this is: a bizarre set of flukes. Shaw rear-ending me. Noah—Shaw's best friend and business partner—rescuing me from Paul Graber's less-than-honorable intentions. And even though he set all the dominos in motion, there is no way Reid could have possibly known Shaw would have picked me, out of millions of women in this city, to be his girlfriend. I don't buy there's anything else to it, though, but sheer, weird coincidence.

"Just goes to show how small the world really is," I offer.

"What does he want?"

"How would I know?" I feign.

She shakes her head and smirks. "You're playing the player here, Lowenbrau."

I let my shoulders rise and fall, pretending I don't know

what she's talking about. "I think he just wants closure, Ser. I mean, we didn't part on the best of terms."

But even as I say it, I know it's not true. His tirade at the door plays through my head: *I'll call you, and fuck him. He doesn't need to know. And even if he finds out, I don't give two shits. I'm happy to take him on.*

He said we were past tense, but after the bashing on Shaw and the almost kiss and forgiveness I'll never earn, I'm not entirely sure he believes that. *Oh, Reid.* The last thing I want is to hurt him again because we can't be what we once were. It didn't work then. It definitely won't work now.

"No. Someone who just wants closure doesn't get crazy jealous over the mention of another guy." She tips her glass in my direction, almost spilling the contents when she announces, "He wants you back."

I'm saved from responding when my phone rings. I swipe the buzzing piece from the counter hoping it's the man I haven't been able to get out of my head since I left him last night, but my hopes die when I look at the screen.

Reid.

I flick my eyes back up to Sierra who has a smug grin plastered on her face. Mug in hand she strides out of the room to give me privacy, mumbling as she passes, "Closure, my ass."

Willow

Chapter Four

"My God, Willow. This is just as good as I remember."

"I can't believe you still like it," I tell him, sliding a glance his way. I take a bite of my own sandwich, relishing in the childhood memories it brings back. This used to be my father's favorite Saturday afternoon lunch.

"Fat and grease. Best combo ever," he'd tell me every time.

Reid is holding two slices of bread that house bologna, potato chips, and a generous helping of mayo between both hands. He leans forward, allowing the crumbs to fall onto the deck instead of his lap. His eyes close in bliss with every bite. It makes me a little wistful, remembering better times.

"I haven't had one of these in years," he announces after shoving the last of it in his mouth.

"Really? Why?" I set my three-fourths-eaten sandwich down on the table beside me and wipe my hands on my napkin, my appetite suddenly missing.

I recall the first time I ate this concoction in front of him. We were on a quick lunch break during play practice. He gave me endless shit, telling me how disgusting it looked. Only when I made him try it, he promptly changed his mind and asked that

I make him one for the next day. Whenever we'd picnic on the grassy banks of Lake Union, I would bring two BC&M's, as Reid nicknamed them, four pickle spears, and a box of the cheapest wine I could find.

Reid laces his fingers together and sets them on his stomach before fastening his gaze to mine. It's both plaintive and hopeful, making me wonder why the hell I agreed to let him come over for a late lunch when I should have said no instead.

But for some reason, I don't feel like I can—or *want*—to say no to him. While he still makes my heart beat fast and stirs those familiar flutters low in my belly, I don't want a romantic relationship with Reid. That spot is taken by a commanding, powerful, beautifully bullish man who stirs the other half of my soul whether I want him to or not.

"What was the question again?" he asks with a quirky smirk. It always made my heart stutter when he did that. Still does.

"Did you really forget or are you deflecting?"

His mouth curls, making those liquid green eyes of his pop and sparkle. "No one ever got me like you, Willow. No one before you. No one after."

I look away and breathe heavy, not knowing how to respond.

"Why are you here?" I ask the empty air in front me, suddenly feeling awkward.

"I'm here because I'm working on Preston Mercer's reelection campaign."

"No," I reply, now swiveling my head his way. "Not in Seattle. Why are you *here* here? On my porch? Eating bologna and potato chip sandwiches and making conversation like I didn't crush your heart and ruin your life?"

He unwinds his fingers and leans forward, his hands hanging loosely between the open space of his legs. His muscular thighs flex underneath his well-worn denims, but I focus my attention on his face. His gaze stays attached to mine when he says, "You crushed my heart. I'll give you that. But you didn't ruin my life, Willow. You…" His pause is long, his stare so searing I start to heat up. "…gave me perspective."

My huff comes out as a snort instead. "Perspective? How?"

He turns his attention to the backyard and I feel like I can breathe again. I don't understand where he's going with this. I don't understand why I care about the answer so much either.

Because I hurt him terribly and I don't want him to hurt again.

"When I walked into the theater for that audition and caught sight of that messy blond hair piled on top of your head and your trim waist and that perfectly heart-shaped ass, it was immediate lust."

I watch him talk, a faraway look on his face. He's never told me this story.

"But when you spun around and caught my eye and smiled that fucking mind-altering smile of yours, Willow…" Rotating his head slowly to me, I'm frozen. My lungs scream for air. "You knocked the very breath from my lungs. I knew you were The One."

My head starts shaking. The ache in my chest intensifies. "I'm not, though," I tell him softly.

A reticent smile passes his lips. "But you are. And I fucked it up."

I can't look at him anymore. I zero in on two squirrels chasing each other around the yard before shooting up a tree and disappearing out of sight. Confused under his intense gaze, I pop up and go to the railing, leaning over it as I think about how to respond without hurting him.

The creak of the chair reaches my ears a second before I feel the warmth of Reid's body heat. He turns me toward him and cups my face in his hands. Breathing quietly, he searches inside me. Whether I want it to or not, the past sticks between us, still tying us together.

"You needed more from me." His voice is low, raw…vulnerable. "I didn't get it at the time, but I do now."

"What do you think I needed?" I ask foolishly, berating myself for letting the question slip. This line of discussion will only wound him more because whatever he's asking for now, I can't give. It belongs to someone else. I realize it probably always has.

His thumb starts a slow circle over my cheek. He watches it go around and around before his eyes track back up to mine. "You tell me, Summer. Tell me what you need and I'll give it to you. Tell me what to be and I'll change. Tell me what to do to win you back, because so help me God…I may have hated you for a while, but I have *never* stopped dreaming of a life with you."

My breaths are choppy. He's asking me to choose him. I stare into the pleading eyes of a man who will forgive the unforgivable. Who is ready and sure and absolute in his feelings, and I wonder why I can't take what he's offering.

I mentally tick off all the reasons I should.

He's offering me a future, while Shaw is noncommittal.

He's not afraid to tell me he loves me or readily show me his emotions, while Shaw is cautious and holds back.

With Reid, I know I'll have security and certainty.

Or I could put everything on the line, taking a gamble with a man who has a big fat zero in the commitment column.

One road is paved, the other untraveled.

There is no choice, though, regardless of the outcome.

I need someone who *already* holds the key to those hidden parts of me, not someone who is asking where to find it.

My hands come up to curl around wrists. "I don't want you to change, Reid. I like you just the way you are."

His handsome face falls. The sides of his mouth tip down as he studies me, listening to the unspoken. When his hands float away from me, I'm momentarily sad, but I know I'm doing the right thing. Leading him on in any way would be far worse than what I've already done.

As he sits back down, his soulful eyes snag mine once again. I grab on to the wooden rail behind me for support. Or maybe it's so I don't drop to his feet and beg for forgiveness for not being the person he wants me to be.

Running his hands along the smooth arms of the chair, he proceeds to ask, "This is about him, isn't it?"

"No," I tell him honestly. Because it's not *just* about Shaw. It's about me. It's about who I am with Shaw versus who I am with Reid.

"I call bullshit."

I shrug and lick my lips before sighing. "I don't know what you want me to say, Reid." *Don't do this. Please don't do this. Don't make me say things that will only hurt us both.*

He takes in a deep lungful of air and blows it out quickly. "Well, what I want you to say and what you're saying aren't exactly lining up."

I smile then. It's slow and deliberate and draws one from him, too. But then I flatten my lips back out, the heaviness on my heart weighing them down. "I'm sorry."

He waves his hand as if it's no big deal, though I know it is. "Don't be. But I want you to know I'm not going anywhere either."

He's earnest and sincere. I want to ease the ache I hear in his voice, but I don't know how. Instead I ask, "Does that mean you're sticking around after the election?"

And do I want him to or will things just be awkward? Is it truly possible to be friends with someone who wants more? I don't think so.

"I haven't decided yet. Possibly. There may be something here that holds my interest."

His underlying meaning is crystal clear. He's biding his time. He's done his homework on Shaw and he thinks the same thoughts that have plagued me: that he'll leave me behind the second his father is reelected.

And that was always the plan, wasn't it? It's what I willingly signed up for. It's why I already have $150,000 sitting in my fund with Randi. From the beginning, I was a pawn. A diversion. A strategically planned campaign move.

All the balmy sunshine dancing on my skin earlier turns icy and slick. A horrible feeling settles in the pit of my stomach that I want to ignore. It's the same one I've been pushing away this entire time.

Shaw is going to break my heart the same way I broke Reid's. It's inevitable. I know this yet I can no more stop the feelings I have for him than I can stop blinking. I'm in far too deep to turn back now, the shore merely a speck on the horizon. I'll never reach it in time.

Deciding it's best to change subjects, I ask, "What have you been doing all this time?"

The way he eyes me means my not-so-subtle diversion is transparent, but I don't care. I can't talk to him about the man who kinks my insides but feeds my soul. Reid pushes himself up and walks my way. Stopping beside me this time, he leans his forearms on the banister and stares ahead. I spin to my side, setting my hip against the wood and watch him.

"I moved in with a buddy in Minneapolis for a while. He was in the same Poly Sci program with me and was working on the gubernatorial campaign that year."

Reid has been involved in politics since he was in high school. By the time things ended between us, he'd already worked his way up to managing several fairly big campaigns in a three-state area. He loved the frantic energy, the ball busting, the games. And he was good at it, too. It's no wonder he was recruited to work on Preston's campaign.

"They were already in the thick of things but with my experience, I slotted nicely into a junior position, though everyone quickly found out I could be far more useful than someone who knocks on doors or organizes speeches. Turns out the acting governor, whose campaign I was on, had a little piece on the side who threatened to out his perfect façade of a marriage when he tried to cut it off with her. It didn't take me long to uncover her three previous abortions by three different men, including the governor's, which he didn't know about by the way. So I buried her. I got so much fucking dirt on her she would never see the light of day. If she as much as breathed a vowel of their affair, she'd be blackballed. No one would believe a word out of her mouth even if it was mostly true."

"You sound proud," I reply, finding the story oddly disturbing. I don't like to think of the man I used to love sinking down into the gutter with slimy politicians. I like to think that he's helping put the good ones in office instead.

He straightens and turns toward me. "I am proud. Governor Browning is a good man, Willow. He made a mistake, yes, but he is one of the smartest, savviest politicians I've known. He deserved that job, that title, that respect, and power. He shouldn't have been ousted from office for good because he made a mistake."

"And do you think that about Preston Mercer? That he deserves his job?" How did my former fiancé *really* end up on Preston Mercer's campaign?

He's thoughtful before replying, "I'm at the point in my career I can be somewhat selective. I don't take on campaigns where I don't believe in the candidate."

"But?"

The corner of his mouth ticks up. "You think there's a but?"

"Yes. I heard it."

Bringing a hand up, he runs a finger from my forehead down the side of my cheek, tucking some hair behind my ear. It's gentle and soft. And longing. It leaves behind the smallest of fires, which quickly burns out. "Well, for a number of reasons it will be a challenge getting him reelected, but I'm up for a good challenge right about now."

There's so much innuendo buried in that single statement I don't even know where to begin. "What challenges?" I ask, trying to take the safest route.

Instead of answering, he squints, asking a question of his own. "How much do you really know about the Mercer family, Willow?"

My spine straightens, locking my defenses squarely in place. The Mercers are not my family. Hell, they may *never* be my family, but I will defend them as if they are. The way a real "girlfriend" would. Maybe I'm not a real one, maybe I never will be, but after this weekend it sure feels like I *could* be. Once again, I choose to ignore the incessant whispers of doubt about Shaw Mercer that echo between my ears.

"I think you should stop right there, Reid."

He crosses his arms and mirrors the way I'm standing. "You're dating a Mercer. It's a fair question." Yeah, I heard the way *dating* was layered with disgust and jealousy.

"It's none of your business."

"Everything about the Mercers is my business, Willow. Everything, including you. I *make* it my business because that's how I win."

The hairs on my arms stand up. "This is not about you. Or me. Or us, or whatever it is you're trying to make it out to be. It's about Preston Mercer and doing your job."

He purses his lips and shakes his head. "No, babe. This is politics. And like a court of law, in the court of public opinion, anything and everything can and *will* be used against the candidate. It's my job to bury that shit before it happens. That's why I was hired. Everyone has skeletons they want ten feet under. *Everyone*."

His statement knocks me straight in the gut. What dirt does Reid have and on who? What if he digs into what *I've* been doing the past couple of years? Is there anything that links me to La Dolce Vita and to Randi? Have there been any photos posted in the paper or on social media sites that he could rummage through and start connecting the dots? As careful as I've always tried to be, the answer has to be yes. Nothing is foolproof. Every interaction, every transaction leaves a trail; you just have to be savvy enough to follow the crumbs.

And, *oh my God*, what about the money Shaw has already paid me? It's not in a traditional bank account, but is it at all possible it could it be traced back to him? There has to be an electronic footprint somewhere.

Oh *fuck*.

This could ruin everything. Shaw hiring me to help reelect his father could ultimately bring this entire family down if what I do and how we hooked up is exposed. But would Reid do that when he is supposed to do anything to help the mayor win? Would he hide this to save the mayor or exploit it to try to drive a wedge between Shaw and me instead? At this point, I'm not sure.

And if Reid could find it, the man vying for Preston's seat could too.

Double fuck. I'm kicking myself for not asking Shaw more questions before I signed on the dotted line. I have literally run into a pack of wolves blind and weaponless.

"It's your job to bury the competition, not the other way around," I remind him, hoping my voice sounds as steady to him as I thought it did in my mind.

His eyes narrow a bit.

Damn.

"It's my job to protect my candidate by any means necessary. Even from those who think they mean well." The way his mossy-green eyes flare with passion and conviction would be enthralling under any other circumstances. Now, though, all it makes me feel is a horrible sense of foreboding.

"What is *that* supposed to mean?" I press. Jesus, my stomach is churning.

Reid steps into me, running his palms down my arms. Both his voice and eyes soften considerably. "It means nothing, Willow. It means that I'm worried about you, is all."

"Now I call bullshit." Oh, how I want to throw in his face that Shaw taking a girlfriend was *his* idea. How we're only talking about Shaw in circles now because of him. How Reid and I only reconnected because of the train he started down this windy, treacherous track that could possibly derail us all. But I can't. Because I'm not supposed to know. "What do you have against Shaw?"

His jaw clicks shut and that fire banked in him flares hot. "This isn't about Shaw." He spits Shaw's name with contempt.

"Isn't it? Because I think it is. I think you're trying to warn me away from him for some reason. But you're beating around the bush, hoping I'll just ask so you can have a clean conscience when you tell him you told me."

I'm right. By the minuscule widening of his eyes, I am right. He parts his lips. Something sits on the tip of his tongue. He wants to say it, he's *dying* to tell me, but he won't until I push him.

I won't do it. Whatever Reid is doing is for selfish purposes only. He's jealous, he wants me back, and he'll do anything to win. He said so himself.

I take a step back. "It's time for you to go."

"Willow—"

"No, Reid. I'm with Shaw now. Regardless of what you're trying to make me think, he's a good man. I trust him and I don't need you trying to sabotage what we have. It's good. It's *more* than good, and you just need to stop right now."

He stands there, stony, obviously angry. Maybe deciding how to proceed now that I've left the taunt he threw hanging idly between us. I cross my arms and give it right back.

"Okay," he says somewhat regretfully. Scrubbing his hand over his face, he repeats *okay* again, only this time, the tone resembles resignation. He starts toward the stairs of the porch, intent on going out the back gate when he stops three steps down and looks over his shoulder. "If I promise politics and your boyfriend are off the table can I see you again?"

I swallow hard, conflicted. "I'm not sure that's a good idea."

It's the same line I used last week, only now it's a far stronger feeling than it was then. He's trying to undermine my relationship with Shaw and I don't think Shaw and I need any help in that department. We both brought our own issues into an arrangement that has turned out to be far more than either of us thought.

Reid's grin is sheepish, bordering on boyish. It's the laid-back, easygoing Reid I remember and it tugs hard on those good memories we shared. "Not even for a Milky Way latte?"

He knows how much I love Milky Way lattes from Frankie's, an old staple three blocks from the theater. He brought me one every day. I don't flat-out tell him no but I don't quite shut the door all the way either. I can't make myself do that yet.

"I gave up chocolate."

His smile morphs into a smirk. "I'll talk to you soon, Sum—Willow."

He rounds the corner out of sight. I hear the gate click behind him, signaling he's gone, and I'm left to wonder what in the hell just happened and why that niggle of doubt he successfully embedded about Shaw stayed right here with me instead of following him as it should have.

Shaw

Chapter Five

HAZY REDS.

Various shades of them—some darker than others—swirl in my periphery as I rap my knuckles on Willow's front door and wait.

I replay him backing out of the driveway.

I see the shock in his eyes that quickly morphed into victory as I slammed my car door shut.

It's hard to swallow my hatred as I relive him throwing one last pointed look at Willow's house before he guns the engine and flees down the street like the pussy he is.

I envision Reid fucking Mergen's neck between my hands as I steal the life from his slimy soul if he uttered a single word of his fucked-up story to Willow. One I still don't know how I'm going to validate or refute.

But what makes me nearly shake with rage is wondering what the fuck he was doing here in the first place. Appearances would suggest he's not wasting any time trying to snag her out from under me, but is that why he was here? To spread his unfounded poison? Did he show up unannounced or did Willow invite him? How long was he here? What did they talk about? Does she understand he's trying to slot himself between us? Could she possibly want him back? Would I even blame her?

I've made no commitments to her. I've not told her how strong my feelings are. I've not told her how much she's altered my life or how she utterly consumes my every thought. In just a few short weeks together this frustrating, secretive, perplexing woman has decimated every plan I laid out for my future.

When she asked me the other morning *why her, why now*, I didn't know how to answer, mostly since I had no idea how to explain it. When I told her she captivates me like no one else has, that I feel something new for her, it was true. Every word of it.

But how do I tell her she's the one I never saw coming? That she's moved in. Taken up residence inside me without my knowledge, without my permission. Without even trying. How do I make her understand I see something in her I've not seen in another woman? Hell, it's something I never *wanted* to see in a woman before.

Me.

What started out as a desperate need to sink my cock between her thighs until neither of us could move has twisted into something unexpected and fragile.

I love her.

I fucking *love* her.

Wholly unimaginable, yet here I am. Ditching yet another set of business meetings because, after my disturbing conversation with Annabelle, I needed to see Willow. Be with her. Soak in her sexy voice. Feel her skin against mine and relish the rapid beat of her heart pressed against my chest after I've fucked her hard and dirty. I need to solidify that shaky connection between us. The one that only grows stronger on my side but seems to fray apart on hers whenever she's out of my sight.

Frustrated I'm still standing outside her closed door alone, I pound on it again and push the doorbell a few times in quick succession. I know she's in there. Her car is in the driveway. Finally, I hear heavy footsteps. A moment later, the door flies open but instead of gazing into the sensual Caribbean seas I wanted, I'm staring into the fiery hickory ones of Willow's roommate.

Last time I saw her, she had bright pink streaked through her midnight-black hair. That's now gone, replaced with brilliant lavender tingeing the ends. Her face is makeup free, and without all the crap lining her eyes, she looks as though she could be somewhat approachable. But I know better. When the side of her lip quirks up into a slight sneer, she looks exactly as she did last time: protective and boorish.

"Sierra." I nod, trying to catch a glimpse inside.

"Braveheart," she quips. My junk shrinks at the blatant threat she made to dismember me the first time I met her. Leaning against the frame, she throws a glance over my shoulder where she has a direct line toward the street. When her eyes meet mine again something unspoken passes between us. "Interesting timing."

Or not.

"Where's Willow?" I demand, already tired of her not so indirect taunts.

She pins me with a heavy glare before sighing and stepping aside. "Porch. Through the kitchen."

I breeze on past her, torn between wanting to set my starved eyes on Willow or demand she tell me if she has something against *me* personally or the entire species that wields a third member.

It's a no-brainer, though. Willow wins. She will every time.

Quickly, I'm through the kitchen and, pushing my way out the screened door, I see no sign of her. But her surprised voice drifts from my left.

"Shaw? What are you doing here?"

When I swivel, she's rising gracefully and starting toward me. For some reason, my eyes fall to the table beside her chair. Sitting there, like another goddamn insult, are two plates. One is empty, save for some crumbs, and one still holds the leftovers of a sandwich.

I know in the whole scheme of things it's nothing, but he *ate* with her. He shared a meal and a conversation and I can't even see straight right now with the feelings of jealousy that stirs in me. An emotion I was completely oblivious to before her.

Her gaze follows mine until together, they collide again midair, violently exploding.

"I think the better question is what was my father's campaign manager doing here?" I know I growled, but *fuck* I am seething with fury. And I purposely didn't use that asshole's name. I'm not sure I could stand the pungent taste it would have coated my mouth with. When she doesn't answer fast enough, I bark, "I'm waiting."

Those usually warm waters of hers ice over like the Arctic. No doubt an iceberg is building below the surface. "You talk to me like that again and you'll be waiting a hell of a long time for anything. Especially an answer."

Possessiveness rages inside me. He has parts of her I want. Lazy conversations. Inside jokes. Secret looks. Seemingly insignificant details that relationships are built on. It makes me crazed. Reckless. And decisions based on wild, thoughtless, rash intent never, *ever* end well.

She goes to scoop up the plates, but I'm faster. In a move I couldn't have orchestrated ahead of time, I simultaneously kick the plastic chair out of the way, grab her, and spin her, pushing her against the outer wall. The dish she'd barely had between her fingers clatters to the table and I don't even look to see if it broke. The irrational and out-of-control part of me hopes it did. And that it was Mergen's.

Her chest is heaving. So is mine. Being this close to each other unleashes both of our beasts. They're hungry, starved for what the other offers that neither can satiate with anyone else. I have to remember that as the haze of selfishness sits as heavy and encumbering on me as a wool blanket.

I open my mouth but she speaks over me. And god damn if

it isn't full of fire and scorching heat. I go from soft to raging hard before she finishes her sentence. "This feels very déjà vuish, Shaw. And I have to say I don't like the way you're acting like a jackass any better this time than I did the last."

Shifting my stance, I cage her in completely. Her wrists are now trapped in my hands, shoved above her head. My legs are on the outside of hers, my thighs flexing to hold her in place. And my pelvis, thick with ferocity, is pressing into her soft middle, making her gasp.

My attention falls to that intricate necklace she always wears, resting in the concave of her slender throat. It stokes my ire up a thousand degrees when I remember how that bastard's face looked when he took it in. Surprised recognition. Knowing it's yet another link between them, I want to rip it off and replace it with something of mine. Something that ties her to me instead of him.

My mouth turns up. It's wry and surly. Full of contempt for that motherfucker who's trying to step between us. "Yes. I turn into quite the prick when I see another man blatantly coveting my possession."

I did it. I used her words against her. Words she flung at me at La Petite last month when she told me to own her is to possess and that I would never possess her. Except I do. And she knows it. I possess her just as she now possesses every last shred of me, including my sanity.

I expect her to roar. To twist and squirm or try to ram the family jewels with her knee, but she stays still and steady, using that snarky mouth I love so much instead. The one I'm now aching to fill with my cock.

"Wow, Drive By. You run out of people to bully at the office, did you?"

"Why was he here?" I have no intention of letting this go. The need to know what he said is as sharp as the tip of a knife digging painfully into my chest. Did he tell her? Would she let me touch her if he did? Doubtful. "Besides to ogle my woman and eat a free lunch, that is."

"Ogle *your* woman?" She edges her chin up and cocks a brow high, punctuating each word with force. It would be cute if I weren't so damned angry. And horny. So fucking horny.

She left me last night around nine. I've been away from her not even twenty-four hours, yet the time between yesterday and now has seemed like endless minutes of torture. Spending the weekend with her was both a blessing and a curse. I'm into her so deep now there is no way out without emotional ruin.

"Wasn't he?" I challenge, knowing full well I'm right. And truth be told, scared shitless.

"Am I?" she fires back.

She *has* to know she's wound me tighter than a child's plaything. That I'm totally out of sorts because of her and how much she's transforming me, more and more every single second.

My forehead drops to hers and I breathe in her titillating scent momentarily before gruffing, "You know you are, Willow. You're mine. I thought we'd already established that."

"Because I signed a binding agreement."

Her reply is soft and torn, proving I was right to come when I did. She's already trying to slam those fucking shutters closed again, no doubt by some not-so-subtle seeds planted by that fucker. And it pisses me the hell off. In fact, it ignites a volcano of unfounded emotion inside me so scorching I develop an instant case of verbal diarrhea, attempting to purge the foreign feeling.

"No. Because I'm in l—" I freeze, choking on the confession she almost wrenched from me. *Say it, say it,* my mind screams. *Tell her you're in love with her. Tell her Mergen can't have her because she's yours. She'll be only yours from now to forever.* But saying three words I won't ever utter to another woman while we're talking about another man feels sleazy and wrong. It feels manipulative.

"Because you're…what?" She's panting. Waiting. She knows I'm holding back, and the way skittishness and eagerness clash to brighten her eyes, I think she knows what I was about to declare. But once I say it, I can't take it back. And while I'm sure what I'm feeling for her can't be anything *but* love, when I tell her, it's going to be on *my* terms. When I'm buried so deep I wrap her spirit in mine. When I'm making her scream *my* name. When I'm sure she won't crush me.

So I do what I do best instead. My hold on her wrists tightens. I press them harder into the siding of the house as I shift my pelvis lower and thrust against her sweet spot until her eyes drift shut, a light moan escaping her lips. "This isn't about the contract, Willow. This is about your ex wanting you back. Something you specifically told me would not happen."

At that, her gaze slices back to me. The hurt now floating around the rims almost knocks me over. "I already told you this was sheer coincidence. He didn't come *looking* for me."

"Maybe not." I know she's right. He couldn't fake his surprise any more than she could. "But now that he's found you again, he's figured out what a fucking idiot he was to let you go in the first place."

Looking to my chest, she licks her lips, sucking the lower one inside that hot little mouth. Another nervous habit she does when I bring something up she doesn't like.

"Why was he here?"

Glancing up from underneath those naturally spiky lashes, her tone is meant to lacerate when she snips, "To get a free lunch."

"Mmm. Funny girl." One I want to punish with a few orgasms withheld.

Tactical change. I'm pissing her off when all I want is her concession.

Dipping my head, I nuzzle her cheek until her head falls back against the house in heavenly surrender. "He can't have you," I whisper harshly against the shell of her ear.

"I don't want him."

Wrists still pinned between a palm, I draw my fingers lightly down the inside of one arm. I cup a breast, running my thumb over her now pebbled nipple until her breaths are choppy. Nibbling my way along her neck, I inhale her heady perfume, murmuring, "I don't want him near you."

"He's just a friend," she says in earnest.

Slipping my hand inside the front of her tiny gray gym shorts, I ignore her breathy "What are you doing?" because I'm both shocked and turned on when I find her bare pussy underneath the pads of my fingers.

My blood boils at the thought there was no barrier between her and campaign asshole except a thin layer of terry cloth. If he knew that, he would have been on his knees begging for a taste. Maybe even was.

I should turn her over my knee right here and blister her ass for that stunt, and I'll probably do that later when I have her naked and spread-eagle. For now, though, I plan to punish her in other ways that may or may not get us arrested if the neighbors look out their back window.

"No, Goldilocks," I push into her ear while sliding two fingers back and forth through her drenched slit. Spreading her arousal around smooth lips, I delight in the ragged whoosh that leaves her lungs when I plunge them inside without warning. I start to finger-fuck her right out in the open, uncaring who sees. "He wants to part these long, supple legs of yours and drive his tongue inside this dripping wet paradise until you're coming on his face, your addictive juices sliding down his throat."

I curl the tips of my fingers toward me and round her clit with my thumb, bathing in her full-body shudder.

"God, Shaw," she pants as she scoots closer to climax. Her pelvis rolls back and forth with abandon, same as it did that first night I fucked her this way in my kitchen.

Clamping her fleshy lobe—hard—between my teeth, I soothe it with gentle sucks before continuing. "When he's wrung you dry, trust me, Willow, he wants to shove his cock so far in you, he moves in. Makes your sweet pussy his permanent home. He wants to brand you with his seed and take your heart prisoner. He wants to lock it up and throw away the fucking key so it's his forever."

Jesus. The thought of that is excruciating. Almost debilitating.

I want those things. The same ones he does.

I want her body. Her soul. Her divinity. Her love and devotion. I want to dominate her mind, rule her soul, eat her cries every morning for breakfast.

Leaning back, I watch her sex-hazed eyes blink open, settling to where they're hooded and glazed and begging with the need to come. Her pussy is clenching hard now. My dick pounds relentlessly against the zipper of my dress slacks. I need to adjust the metal so it's not piercing my hard flesh, but I'm not about to stop the momentum.

"But he can't have that, Willow," I tell her pointedly, taking her to heights I know only I can.

She doesn't speak. She can't. She's long gone in that empty space right before euphoria hits. But she's listening. Hearing every word I'm saying.

"He can't have any of those because they're all mine, you hear me? They're mine, aren't they? Say it," I demand, now wanting a reply. *Needing* it.

Just as she's cresting, I stop dead in my tracks. She whimpers, forcing herself against my rigid hand, trying to take what she needs. But it's mine to give and I'm not handing it over until she tells me what I want to hear. I let go of her wrists and grip her hip, halting her. It's rough, probably bruising.

"Answer me, beautiful."

She nods, lips parted slightly.

"Every fucking one of those things belongs to me, doesn't it?" I demand at the same time I put the slightest amount of pressure back on her clit. Her arms fall to mine, nails deliciously digging in.

"Yes," sails out on a wispy breath.

"Has he ever made you feel this way, Willow? Strung so tight you think you'll snap in two? Simultaneously stretching for that goal but never wanting to reach it? Never wanting the pleasure to end because it feels that fucking good?"

She's so close I can taste it. That honeyed flavor floats up and lands on my taste buds. I lick my dry lips, trying to catch more of it. Wishing my tongue was buried in her pussy instead of my hand.

"Has he?" I prod.

"Never," she mumbles, knowing I won't let her fall without it. Her hips fight against my hold, but her soft beseeching does me in. "Please, Shaw. God…please."

Part of me wants to string her out. Drive her to the ledge of bliss, stop and watch her fall back toward me before doing it over and again. She's so beautiful when she's completely at my mercy. Malleable, needy, and wild. But I think my control of her in the bedroom is merely an illusion. Willow holds all the cards and can get me to do anything she wants by simply asking, whether it's with her sassy mouth, her bewitching eyes, or this tight pussy that's currently squeezing the blood to my wrist.

This time our needs happen to align, though. I want to watch her lose the battle and dive headfirst into an explosive release *I* created. I move faster then, press harder and command her, "Come now, beautiful. Come for *me*. I want your scent to soak into my skin so I smell you for days."

She looks straight into my eyes, into me, and does as I ask.

She soars. Flies right in my arms. She cries my name. Shakes and convulses until her muscles weaken. Until she sags, spent, between my body and the wall she's still pinned against.

It's beautiful and brilliant.

It's awe-inspiring.

Sacred.

It's a precious gift and one I will not walk away from in this lifetime, or the next.

Chapter Six

MY BODY IS LIMP AS Shaw carries me through the house and up the stairs. I barely get to enjoy the strength of his hold or the flex of his muscles as he takes them two by two and slams the door to my bedroom shut with his foot. My blood still buzzes delectably with the effects of the orgasm he gave me less than thirty seconds ago when he drops me onto the twisted, unmade sheets of my bed.

He looks nowhere but at me when he unapologetically husks, "I need to be inside you, Willow."

He tears at his tie until it's hanging loosely around his neck. He rips the buttons on his dress shirt apart with vicious jerks. He shucks his dress pants with efficiency and, having thrown everything haphazardly over the edge of my dresser, stands before me in nothing but his tight, sexy-as-sin navy boxer briefs. When he reaches inside and strokes himself, my whole body liquefies.

Holy shit, he is a male specimen to behold. Swagger. Presence. Looks. Cut lines. Sway. A calm edge that's innate not learned. He has it all. And he's eyeing me as if *I'm* the queen he needs to secure his kingship, his rightful place on the throne. As if I'm his next and only breath.

I swallow a thick knot of desire as he eats every inch of my still-clothed body alive. With every pass he makes my nerve endings flare. My skin feels more sensitive.

"Lose the clothes. All of them."

Oh, how I want to smart back. Make demands of my own. Like, finish the sentence you left hanging outside. You take risks every day. Take one now. Put your heart on the line, because mine is already there, waiting. I want to believe it was love and jealousy warring in his eyes instead of crazed possessiveness.

"I'm waiting," he tells me, his voice piqued.

By the way his brows almost kiss his hairline, I'd say I'm waving red at the bull by disobeying. I should do as he asks—I want to even—but that little internal war I battle when he orders me around starts raging, and it wins instead. The need to push him so he'll pull me along screams so loud I can't ignore it any more than I've been unable to help falling in love with him.

This is what we do, who we are. Why we work.

I lever on my elbows and with a straight face start pressing buttons. "You can't just walk in here, act like a jerk, and boss me around like you own me, expecting me to strip on command."

The gradual smile that tilts his lips up is nothing short of wicked sins and promises made.

"I had other plans for you, Goldilocks, like a good spanking until your ass was so red you couldn't sit for the rest of the day, but I think that clever mouth of yours needs something to keep it busy for a while instead."

God of all the Gods. He makes me burn.

I go hot everywhere. Blistering flames of iniquity lick my skin, sweetly caressing every inch of it, arousing each nerve ending. Coaxing the dormant vixen out to play his dirty games.

He knew exactly what I was doing and he one-upped me. He also knows he has me exactly where he wants me when I don't respond.

"This is how it's going to go, Willow," he says while dragging his underwear down his muscular legs. When he straightens back up, his cock stands tall and proud, the tip beading with need. "Eyes up here," he barks, and I have a hard time breaking my stare from his hand's slow up-and-down caress as if he has no care in the world but driving me out of my fucking mind. Which he's doing splendidly.

"Willow." His voice is low, commanding. Irresistible.

I cut my eyes up to his and catch fire at the voracity lining his face. His need is urgent and acute. He's not playing around. And I love it. God, how I *love* it.

"You're going to take off those fucking short shorts and show me how wet that pussy is right now."

I am. He's right. My hands are already pushing them down.

"You're going to lose the shirt, the bra, and that sassy mouth and suck my cock until I'm good and ready to sink it home and fuck you until there is no other thought but how good I feel filling and stretching you."

Oh yeah. My shirt is over my head. My bra is unclasped, falling down my arms behind me.

Remembering how I sucked him and left him hanging in the hotel room on Thursday night makes my stomach flip. I want to take him in my mouth. Drive him to his knees with lust. Finish him off until he loses every ounce of that cocky self-control he clings to. I squeeze my thighs together to hide the moisture now coating them. Shaw doesn't miss this because that devilish grin of his turns smug and cunning.

"On your back."

I obey, my snark lost with my clothes, wanting everything he just guaranteed.

He swings me around so I'm sideways on the bed, grabs a pillow, and tucks it under my hips. He sets my feet on the edge of the mattress and presses my knees open. They lay wide, an exhibit for his viewing pleasure. He takes a step back and lets his eyes run the length of me until I feel thoroughly exposed but incredibly worshipped.

By the time his gaze slams back into mine, my entire body vibrates with raw electricity. *Please, please, fucking please* is perched on my lips, ready to free-fall. He reaches out and draws a single finger through the heavy dampness between my legs before he dips just the tip of it inside and all that comes out instead is a long, broken mess of a moan.

"Fuck, so ready for me," he whispers, more to himself than to me.

My hips involuntarily tilt in open invitation, needing so much more than Shaw's giving me but he is already on the bed, crawling up my body. Dipping between my legs, I jolt at the first touch of his tongue against already swollen tissues. An appreciative manly groan rumbles from him as he tastes me far too briefly before laving his way straight up the center of me. He drifts to the left for a nibble around my nipple, then tastes the tender flesh behind one ear before swirling his tongue in the hollow of my throat. I'm barely breathing as he erotically bites his way across my shoulder and down the ticklish innermost part of my arm before rising above me like a deity. He exudes power and sex appeal, raw and pure.

Burning gaze on me, he places his knees on either side of my head. I moan when he circles his thick length and sweeps his thumb over the tip, wiping away the drops of pre-come that have formed. He runs himself over my lips repeatedly until I open wide, silently urging him to end his merciless teasing. He torments me with his display of dominance until I'm nothing but sharp need. And when he slips his cock inside on a ragged rush of air, I feel all the power he held shift to me.

"My God, you look so right beneath me, your lips wrapped around my dick like that." He praises me through gritted teeth, making the energy in me pulse and surge. I curl my fingers into the sheets, resisting the urge to grab him by the base and go to town.

Feral eyes latched to mine, he twines his fingers through my hair and leisurely pushes in and out of my mouth. His free hand comes to my throat, gently circling it, holding me the way he wants so he can drive as far in as I can handle.

He searches my face for fear or hesitancy, especially when the ends of his nails slightly pinch into my tender flesh. Only finding compliance, he pushes farther every time until he starts hitting the back of my throat. I never miss a beat, trying to relax my muscles, though I've never given head quite like this before.

The way his eyes darken at my submission is positively heady. "Oh yes, beautiful. Just like that. Suck me just like that."

Thrusting slow and steady and oh so deep, he swells with each pass. He tests how far he can push me, sinking low enough that I feel my throat bulge under his hand at one point. I only encourage him to do it again.

"Men would wage wars over this mouth," he tells me, his composure slipping faster than a mudslide.

Ecstasy tugs at his eyelids. He fights against it, but I fight him harder. With only my mouth and sheer grit to make him unravel above me, I flick his slit each time he pulls out. I massage him with the flat of my tongue and scrape ever so lightly with my teeth on every descent back in.

"You're trying to make me come," he accuses in that growly tenor that means he's on the verge of losing it.

I can't smile because my mouth is busy, just as he wanted, but I know the rest of my face must show it because his fingers clench, stinging my scalp. "If you want me to come down your throat, Willow, then I want something back."

Oh, you'll get something, all right, Drive By. A mind-melting orgasm that will disintegrate your will and crumble your dominion.

"Agreed?" he asks, but it's breathy and hoarse. It fills me with pride to know *I'm* doing this to him. That I can get him to cave to his wants, giving me mine instead. I hollow my cheeks until I feel them rubbing against him as his thrusts start to pick up pace.

"Oh shit. *Fuuuck.*" His surges are coming faster and with far less finesse. His fingers around my neck grip hard and I gag. He lets up, only for a moment. "Blink twice if that's a yes," he croaks.

In five seconds he's mine, whether I agree or not. But I find I don't care what he wants. What he asks. All I care about is ruining him for anyone else but me. I need his mastery. I need the way he gets me, breathes me in as if I'm his air, his life. I want the way he's looking at me now, as if he loves me, to be another pocket of time stolen for my memory banks.

So I blink twice...and that does it.

Every muscle he has tenses and I watch his resolve crumple under the force of mine.

He comes.

Hot.

Hard.

So thick, so much, so fast I can hardly keep up.

I never stop studying him as he lets himself go completely. The strain around his lips and eyes is painful. Breathtaking. He's utterly beautiful, yet even in this most vulnerable state he still looks formidable and commanding. It's easy to see how he rules both his world and now mine. I bask in the power shift a little longer, knowing it will be short-lived. Understanding I'm okay with that, too.

Struggling to catch his breath, he still pulses slightly, is still so damn hard I'm convinced he could go again right now. And when the gaze that grabs me and holds me hostage every single time latches on to me again, I melt under it.

I want everything I see in it to be true. Oh, how I want that.

"Hey," he says sweetly, cupping my cheek before withdrawing.

"Hey," I give back, wondering how stretched my mouth looks.

"Did I hurt you?" He uses his thumb to wipe around the edges of my lips. I feel saliva, likely mixed with him, smear under it. His gaze falls to my throat, which didn't feel sore until this very moment. Not that I'll let him know that.

I try my hardest to make my voice sound normal when I

respond, "Not hardly. I mean, you are squeezing the very air from my lungs with your bulky weight, but no biggie."

He moves so fast it's comical. It was true—somewhat—but I would have drawn in shallow wisps of air through a bruised neck all day if it meant I got to see more of this softer side of him he rarely shows. I start to laugh when he runs his hands over my body, inspecting me for injuries. When he sees I was only messing with him, his eyes sparkle right before his fingers dig into my sides. He tickles me until I'm squealing and begging him to stop.

"Tell me you're sorry for scaring me like that."

"I'm not, I'm not," I keep crying over and again.

"So many punishments coming, Goldilocks," he whispers in my ear at one point. "You're just digging yourself in deeper with every lie."

I love this carefree side of him, but finally I can't take any more and I give. "I'm sorry!" I yell.

I'm breathless, still gasping for fresh air when he stretches out beside me. He's panting and we both lie still for a second, catching our wind. Then he slides his arm underneath my limp body and tucks me in close.

"You're very ticklish."

"You're very mean," I say, poking him in the chest. He quickly grabs my hand, trapping it between his. He places it against his heart, palm down, his on top to hold it in place. The gesture is sweet and unexpected, especially after he just fucked me like a man exorcising demons. It makes my eyes prick.

"So I didn't hurt you, then, right?"

I tip my head up. He's waiting expectantly. His concern is genuine and unnecessary, but for some reason, it only endears him to me more. He loves me. I know he does. He may not be able to say it, but I see it. I *feel* it. He's as scared to put sound to it as I am.

"It was incredible," I tell him honestly.

One side of his lip curls, just a little. At first I think it's his signature cocky move, but I quickly realize it's not. It's relief.

My words seem to knead and soothe his muscles as he slowly relaxes. Blowing out a short breath, he whispers, "Good."

There's no way I could suppress my grin, even if I wanted to. I'm over the moon in the middle of the day. The sunshine Reid stole is back and it's warm and balmy. I'm sure I'm glowing.

And as much as I hate to dampen it, I'm wondering what the hell he's doing here. It's not even 2:00 in the afternoon. He told me last night he had a full day, especially since he took three days in a row out of his schedule to focus exclusively on me.

I push up to my elbow, resting my cheek in my palm. He's watching me with avid interest. Drawing little circles around the hard planes of his chest, I try for lighthearted when I ask, "So, Drive By...playing hooky again? This is becoming a nasty habit."

His face instantly darkens, as if a thundercloud suddenly swept in.

"Not that I'm complaining," I add quickly, leaning in so our lips barely graze. "A girl could get used to afternoon delights like this."

I realize that he's been here for nearly forty-five minutes, and two orgasms later, I've yet to have his mouth on mine. Before he can respond, I remedy that.

Setting my lips to his, our kiss starts out tentative, me doing most of the work. He's stiff, resistant even, but I won't let him deny me this. Clamping his lower lip between my teeth, I bite down and pull back, opening him up to me. He tastes of authority with a hint of desperation.

But the second our tongues touch he takes the kiss over.

Then I'm on my back, my head between his strong hands. Firm lips press to mine, his tongue frantic, searching. His length is hardening against my belly so fast I start to ache. He's dominating and controlling and my whole being sighs at the feeling of warmth flooding through it.

I start to writhe under him, trying to position him where I need, when he breaks our lip lock and leans back. I reach up for him out of instinct, but he holds me still and I know it's time to make good on the promise I made only minutes ago. My heartbeat, which had already soared, reluctantly comes back down. He parts his lips, readying to say something, but before the question is even out of his mouth, I know what it is.

"What was he doing here?"

I almost want to laugh at the way he never says Reid's name, but the thing he doesn't understand—because I haven't told him—is the way I felt about Reid pales in comparison to how I feel about him. He has nothing to worry about, though if I were in his shoes I'm sure I'd feel the same way.

"Are we going to have this conversation with you restraining me?"

"Do we need to?"

"Shaw." I sigh. "It's not what you think."

"Isn't it? Because I'm pretty fucking sure it's exactly what I think."

"Which is?"

His lips thin out and when he talks again, his exhales feel like sharp, angry arrows when they fall on me. "Cut the shit, Willow. I want to know why he was here and I want to know now."

I can't help it. It's the wrong thing to do because I see how fast his thread is unraveling, but he looks so dark and serious and I've never dealt with such an overpowering presence like his…that a giggle escapes. First one. Then another. The stormier his face becomes, the harder I laugh.

"Answer the question," he demands.

I roar with laughter. His hold on my wrists tightens in warning, which has the opposite effect he wanted.

"I—" I gulp air, trying to calm myself. I can't.

"What is so goddamn funny?"

"You," I manage to wail through fits of giggles.

Shaking his head, he growls, "God, you are one frustrating woman."

It takes me another few seconds but I eventually pull

together some measure of composure. "You only find me frustrating because I don't bend over backward for you like everyone else."

He regards me for a few beats. "You're so wrong, Willow." He says that with such gravity, I feel weighted down. Dipping low, he runs his nose lightly along my cheek. Placing his lips against my ear, his simple sentence about does me in. "*That's* what I find fascinating about you."

Goo.

I feel like a mound of sticky goo.

Turning my head slightly, I place my lips to his cheek and rest them there for a few moments. "You're right. He does want me back," I confess softly, knowing it will make him angry, but also knowing I can't keep it from him either. He's not blind. Or stupid. He remains perfectly still as I continue. "But *I* don't want *him* back. Even if I wasn't with you, there was a reason we didn't make it. That reason hasn't changed."

"Did you tell him that?"

"Yes. I made it very clear I am with you."

"It makes me crazed," he mumbles against my neck, laying wet kisses along my collarbone.

"I know," I breathe. I want to apologize, but I'm not sorry. Not in the slightest. I'm glad he's jealous. Casual leaves no room for crazy.

"Willow." My name is thick and textured with longing. "I don't want to lose you or what we have."

My heart surges, pushing against my breastbone in the most deliciously painful way. It's not in Shaw's personality to be so insecure.

Crazed. I'll take it.

Wrapping my arms around his broad shoulders I run my nails along his roped back muscles, enjoying the flex and sway of each one. "You won't." I add, "I know you don't want to hear it but if it wasn't for him, we wouldn't be together right now."

I expect him to deny it. To tell me he would have found a way for us to be together regardless of Reid's involvement, but he doesn't. And I love him even more for being honest instead of trying to feed me a line.

"I know. I fucking hate it and rejoice in it at the same time."

He moves restlessly on top of me, kisses turning hungry and feverish. His lips roam liberally, sucking and licking and nipping until I'm edgy and out of my mind with need. Deft fingers pluck at my nipples and play between my thighs, testing my readiness briefly before he's back on me. Spreading my legs. Pushing inside. Driving us both up fast.

We are wordless, nearly soundless, our bodies moving in perfect synchronization until we both reach the crest and peak together. As his hazy gaze struggles to remain glued to mine while we navigate our passage through pleasure, I know there is no gray area between us. Everything is crystal clear.

I am his.

He is mine.

There is an us.

It's love, without a doubt, no matter if we say it or not.

What started out as a job, a way to earn enough money to care for my ill mother has completely changed my life in ways I wasn't expecting.

All weekend I questioned myself and what I was doing. I doubted me. I doubted him. I doubted we had a real future ahead of us. I let others feed it. Because how can a foundation cemented in lies and deceit not eventually crack under the power of them? But after this afternoon, I don't doubt anymore. We've turned this into something far, far more. Somehow over the past two months, we've both unconsciously been laying new groundwork, this one layered in truth and honesty.

Now I just have to figure out how to navigate this foreign territory I've found myself in because as much as I want us to work, I know stripping down to the bare bone will be the hardest challenge I've ever faced.

Chapter Seven

"THAT'S FUCKED UP, MAN," NOAH says, taking a swig of his Yuengling.

"Which part?" I ask, sipping my Hennessey 250 more slowly than I'd prefer. But getting drunk won't solve a damn thing. I'm not sure what will, quite frankly.

"All of it. Does your father know about this?"

I wondered the same thing, but my father would never have been able to keep his surprise hidden when I first introduced Willow, so no. Mergen hasn't said a thing to him about this. I'm not sure what to make of that either.

"I don't think so."

I take in a heavy breath. Leaning forward, I let the tumbler hang between my legs. I stare off into the inky night, listening to the constant rippling of the lake not fifty feet away from my backyard. The sound of waves gently crashing against the shore usually lulls me to a place of inner peace that's hard for me to tap into, but tonight I'm wound so tight it's a nit. Another irritant.

Noah stormed through my front door about half an hour ago on the warpath. Can't say I blame him. I left him to deal with an important meeting today. We need a new president to run our private equity division and we've been secretly whisking one away from our biggest competitor. We had a full afternoon of interviews scheduled for him, and I bailed without a single explanation, leaving Noah to deal with it.

Not that he's incapable, but we work best as a team. Always have. He respects my input, as I do his. He sees things I don't and vice versa. We are a well-oiled machine, in the bedroom and the boardroom alike, and this is a big decision. This guy may be the shits, but he needs to fit in with Wildemer's culture and values.

Last week getting him on my payroll seemed like the most important thing on my agenda. Now I honestly couldn't care less.

Once Noah stopped screaming profanities at me, I beered him and ushered him out to my fire pit for an account of today's events, starting with my morning meeting with that campaign fuckhead.

Jesus, that seems like a lifetime ago already. I wish it was. I wish it was dust in my mirror and I was sitting here enjoying the cool fall air with Willow instead, knowing my sister is safe and sound, happy and remains drug free. But it hasn't even been twelve hours since my carefully constructed world started cracking so damn fast I can still see the void widening.

Twelve hours and I'm *still* in no different position than I was when I left his goddamn office.

No answers.

No idea of what comes next.

Nothing except confirmation from Willow of what Mergen told me earlier.

He's waiting for me to fuck up.

He's working to win her back.

The only good news is he hasn't said anything irreparable. *Yet.* But I know that's only a matter of time.

"I need to bury this fucker. Far and deep," I growl.

"Then we will," my best friend replies evenly. "We're pretty good at burying shit."

"Apparently not good enough," I mumble, still wondering how the hell Mergen found out about that night.

"What size shoe does he wear?"

Noah hasn't even asked the most important question of all: did she do it? Did Annabelle have a link, direct or indirect, to Charles Blackwell's death? And he won't either. Instead he goes full bore into problem-solving mode: let's make this shit go away.

I shift my attention to him then. He has an ankle casually thrown over a knee, an elbow hooked over the back of his chair, a brown bottle bottling dangling from two fingers. His demeanor is relaxed. Lazy even, but I know he's dead serious. There's no doubt in my mind that he could get all sorts of sordid shit done. I only have to ask.

But I don't want Mergen at the bottom of the Puget or eating through a straw for the rest of his pathetic life. Although neither option would make me lose a night of sleep, that's not how I operate. I simply want him gone. Out of Seattle and the state of Washington. Out of my hair, out of our lives.

Our lives. I still can't believe I'm thinking in those terms. It feels equally intoxicating and scary as fuck.

At my silence, and with one brow cocked high, he asks, "You sure she's worth it?"

Under any normal circumstances, that question would cause my spine to steel and my temper to fire. But tonight it doesn't. Noah's not asking to be antagonistic. He's asking out of genuine curiosity. No one threatens my family and fares well.

Only Willow is not an outsider. She's not collateral damage or some interloper. She's become the sun I revolve around. I'm not willing to risk her, but I'm not willing to risk my sister either. Once again I am at a dead end.

"Yes," I answer simply. That tells him all he needs to know.

"First time in my life I've seen a woman on equal footing with your family."

"A miracle witnessed, never to be repeated." She's it for me, I leave unsaid.

He gives me a clipped nod. "Okay, then. We'll figure it out. Whatever it takes."

My relief is there, but marginal. A shitstorm has kicked up and it's going to take a deluge to quell the dust.

"I need to ask you something." Easing back in my chair, I throw the rest of my pricey cognac back and set my glass gently on the concrete pavers beside my chair.

"Shoot."

"Is the money you've been putting in Willow's account traceable?"

The time I should have been asking *that* question was about two-and-a-half months ago when Noah and I sat in a bar and I watched him get our waitress off right at our table. The night I agreed to this charade in the first place. Not now, when everything's rigged to blow up in our faces.

After Willow begged me to give her a respite this afternoon, she pressed her naked body to mine and spilled her worries about Mergen digging into both of us. She was particularly concerned about the money. Easily traceable if not done right. But she was more worried for me and what this may do to my father's campaign than how it would reflect on her.

Fuck, I love her. She's selfless and humble. She's loyal, when I'm not sure I deserve it yet. For not the first time I'm kicking my own ass about that contract. It was necessary to get her but it's undermined the basis of our relationship. And why wouldn't it? There was never supposed to *be* a relationship. And now? What the three of us have engaged in? It could bring us all down in a plume of flames if it's discovered.

"Don't worry, Shaw. I wouldn't do anything that would finger either of us."

I eye him. "How is that exactly? These are large sums of money we're talking about. Deposits that are reported to the feds and terror watch lists. How are you keeping it under the radar?"

Noah brings the bottle to his lips and tips, sucking the last of the liquid dry. He throws the empty behind him. It lands in the grass with a dull thud. He grins when I scowl.

"Don't worry, lover boy," he pokes in jest. "I won't litter your perfectly manicured lawn."

"You annoy the shit out of me sometimes," I huff.

His teeth are so white they glow in the dark. "It's what endears you to me. Admit it."

"I need to know how you're keeping this covered, Noah." I need to know his little scheme isn't going to put our entire lives under a microscope.

Noah sobers, losing his cocky bravado. "We don't need to keep it covered. It's all legit."

I scoff. "Somehow I don't think Randi Deveraux is paying quarterly estimated taxes to the IRS."

His smile is slow to return. I wish I knew how well he knows this woman. How much we can trust her. "The escort side of her business, maybe not. But she runs a legitimate public foundation, and that foundation gives grants for those in hardship."

"Hardship?"

"Yeah."

"What kind of hardships?"

"Financial ones."

Suddenly I wonder how much Noah knows about Willow. What did Randi tell him? What does *Randi* know about her? Do they both know her secrets? And why does that send my blood pressure through the roof? *Because you want them all, that's why.*

"Financial ones?" I prod, needing more goddamn information. "You'd better tell me everything you know, Noah. I'm not fucking around here."

He barks a laugh, throwing his head back for good measure. "Your bite won't work on me, Merc. Save it for your woman."

"Fuck you," I say with a hiss.

"Gonna be a hard pass. I like fucking *with* you, but pussy is my cuppa tea."

When I start winding my fingers through my hair in frustration, he finally gives me what I need. "She's a shrewd businesswoman, Merc. She has a foolproof, legit process for funding these types of transactions through the foundation. There's an application from Willow on file for audit purposes, but because it's a public foundation, they don't have to disclose any grant information to the government. Donations," he quotes, "are a write-off—"

"A write-off?" I interrupt incredulously. "You think I give a shit about a fucking tax break when everything I love could be on the line?"

I realize what I just admitted when Noah's grin eats up his whole face. Well, fuck him. I don't care.

"I paid in cash anyway, anonymous donation, so it's untraceable to either of us. And before you ask, there isn't a wad of unexplained bills sitting somewhere in Willow's account that can be questioned or uncovered either. Randi holds the funds in a foundation account."

My knowledge on public foundations is limited, as the foundation we run through Wildemer is private, but once again, I have to trust Noah used a fine-tooth comb on this before he dragged me into it.

"You're sure?"

"I'm sure. I wouldn't put you or your father or Randi into that situation, Merc."

"Yeah," I agree on a long exhale. "Yeah. I'm sorry I questioned you."

He shrugs like it's no big deal.

I push up and head over to the outdoor fridge, snagging two beers. I'd prefer my Hennessey, but I'm too lazy to walk back up to the house to get it. Popping the tops on the under-counter remover, I let them plunk into the garbage below and head back to Noah, handing him one, which he takes with a "thanks."

Settling back in my chair, nighttime sounds fill the absence of noise that falls between us. Cicadas sing. Water laps. The faint hum of an occasional car engine can be heard even though I'm set back from the main road quite a ways.

My mind frantically races after answers that remain elusive.

Drumming his fingers against the lift of his chair, Noah breaks the silence. "We need to talk to Bull."

"Have an appointment with him tomorrow at three." I'd planned to swing over to the PD after talking to Annabelle, but I had a visceral need to see Willow first. Then I ended up drowning in her for the rest of the day, unable to make myself leave until she kicked me out, saying she needed to work or she was going to be late with a recording for a client.

"I'm coming."

"Fine by me," I reply after I swallow the beer in my mouth, wondering who the fuck is going to run our multimillion-dollar business while we're both out playing detective.

"I think we need to pay a little visit to Bluebelle's friends, who were with her that night."

It feels as if I'm pushing two tons of air from my chest. "Scaring the shit out of girls who are barely out of their teens is not my idea of a good time."

"We don't have to scare them. I'll use my quick wit and wieldy charm."

That makes me laugh. Breathe a smidge easier.

"I'll also have someone quietly start looking into this tool."

"That would be much appreciated."

"So it's settled."

"That it is."

"So," Noah starts slowly, "I guess sharing her is off the table then?"

My head snaps toward him in disbelief. Envisioning Willow sucking his cock the way she did mine earlier, as if it were her source of life, makes each muscle in my body tense for a throwdown. I want to pound his face into the cement beneath my feet until he eats the bitter words he dared speak.

In typical Noah fashion, he's scrutinizing my reaction, staring at me with this unreadable look on his face. I can't tell whether he's screwing with me or serious as a heart attack.

I'm going with the latter. "You lay a finger on her, I'll castrate you."

That low chuckle is back. Grating down each nerve ending until they're sensitive to the touch.

"I mean it. She's off-limits, Noah," I warn. "No flirting, no propositioning, no trying to charm the pants off her. You so much as think about her naked and I'll rip your eyeballs out. You got it?"

I've discovered something about myself over the last few weeks. I'm an irrationally jealous he-man when it comes to his woman. Another label I never thought possible but will own with pleasure.

Noah's casual, "She's the one, huh?" throws me for an upside-down loop after the calculated goading he just did.

I break my death glare, loosen my grip, and let my head fall back against my chair. "She's the one," I admit, after taking a long drink of the cold beverage in my hand.

"Have you told her you're in love with her?"

I want to. I told my sister this morning, and I certainly left Mergen with the impression I loved her. Yet being that vulnerable with her? The thought twists my gut into so many knots it hurts.

But if I *don't* tell her, where does that leave me?

On the outside looking in, that's where.

I've no doubt Mergen is vomiting his emotions all over her, and even though she told me earlier she didn't want him, I can't help but wonder what I'd do in her position. We're both on our knees, hanging on to her for dear life, but only one of us has bared his soul. Only one man wins.

And what if my sister was somehow involved in her father's death? Then what? Christmases and Sunday meals will be mighty uncomfortable. She would end up leaving me. I'll have bared my very soul to her, only to have it flayed if she walks.

Yet if I don't make myself vulnerable, I risk losing her.

"Not yet."

Silence stretches between Noah and me for such a long

time, I swing my gaze back his way. He's staring out at the lake, blinking slowly. Contemplating.

I wonder what he's thinking. If he's envious or feels slighted. Or maybe he's just upset our uncomplicated encounters have finally run their course.

His eyes cut to mine, his head barely turning as if he can't be bothered to angle it all the way. "You should. Don't let her get away. She's good for you, Merc."

I know.

"You think?" He's never put that string of words together.

This time his smile is genuine. "I don't know how I knew it when I first saw her, but I had this feeling. About her. About you. I won't bullshit you. I wanted her. I wanted to—"

"Don't fucking say it," I threaten through gritted teeth. My hand curls tight around my beer bottle. I'm surprised it doesn't shatter.

One side of his lip twists up wryly. It's his trademark. Women rip off their panties when he drops that look right there. "But the second she opened that brassy mouth…Christ." He shakes his head, remembering. I tamp down envy, knowing it's unnecessary. Having a hard time with it anyway. "All I heard was Shaw Mercer's demise."

I'm speechless and surprisingly emotional at that. "Thank you," I tell him, choking a bit on my sincerity. Knowing if he tried hard enough he might have had her that night causes a sharp pain in my chest. And I'm not sure I could have sat here and acted like that didn't bother me. Because it would have.

For once in my thirty-six-year friendship with Noah, I selfishly want a woman's taste and moans of pleasure to belong solely to me.

Chapter Eight

"ARE YOU SURE I CAN'T help?" I offer again for the umpteenth time.

We arrived at the Mercers' less than twenty minutes ago, but well ahead of the rest of the family. Shaw said he had some business matters to discuss with his father and wanted privacy before the evening turned chaotic. "Maybe I can set the table?" I add, anxious for something to do.

"No, dear. It's all set. You just sit and relax. Enjoy your wine," Adelle Mercer replies. She reaches for the plump hothouse tomato next to her and slices the top off before dicing it into perfect wedges for the enormous salad she's creating. It's a masterpiece. It looks so delicious it could be photographed for a spread in *Martha Stewart Living*.

"I'm afraid I don't sit and relax well." I fidget with the glass in front of me, twisting and turning the stem so the wine inside swirls in arcs that leave long red legs racing back to the liquid below.

"Well, that's a problem. Everyone needs to unwind more instead of go, go, going all the time." Her eyes find mine. "You seem the type who takes the world's problems into her lap and makes them her own, never finding time for yourself."

Her intuition strikes me mute for a few seconds. God, am I *that* transparent? "I've always had a lot of responsibility." It's lame, but I don't know what else to say. I can't spill my entire sad story to my "boyfriend's" mother. And maybe it's time to stop thinking of Shaw with those caveated quotations? It's just another way I keep him out. Or me trapped. It's all the same.

I expect Adelle to pry, ask questions I'm not prepared to answer. She doesn't. She simply nods her head as if she understands and picks up the next tomato, cutting into that one, too.

A deep boom of laughter from the other room catches my attention and I look up from Adelle's impressive knife skills, my gaze landing straight on Shaw. He's perched on the edge of a plaid wingback chair, leaning forward, legs wide, pointing to some papers on the coffee table in front of him. His father sits on the edge of the couch, his position mirroring Shaw's, intently listening, a smile on his lips.

From my angle, I can only see Shaw's profile, but my God in heaven the man is handsome. That nose. Those lips. The muscles that jump in his strong jaw when he's thinking intently or when something winds him up tight are so damn sexy I'm breathless just thinking about it. The natural sexuality oozing from him is potent and dizzying. The way he affects every part of me is unnerving.

He must sense a weight because he stops talking and turns his head my way. Our eyes connect across the distance. The moment slows. He's probably twenty feet away but I feel as if he's standing right in front of me. Looking so far into me I can't escape.

For a moment, maybe two, I let it all go. Every guard. Every wall. Every reservation. For those few stolen moments, I let him in all the way. I let him see that I don't want anything between us but real and reckless, no matter if it hurts one, or both of us, in the end. That it's too late and I'm already madly in love with him. Then, in the next breath, I beg him to handle me with care. To keep me if he thinks he can try, to let me go if he knows he'll crush me.

He sees it.

He sees *me*.

I think he has from the day he stared into my wild eyes behind his mirrored aviators.

And in him, I read everything that's in me. The fear of heartbreak. The trust needed to put your heart in someone else's keeping. The unknown we're about to plunge headlong into with wide eyes.

I release a breath I didn't realize I was holding and the corners of my mouth draw up slightly into a soft smile. He does the same, blinking slowly, not looking away. Right now, there's just us.

The more he stares, the more a rightness I won't be able to undo snaps securely into place. That lock I told him only my future could pop just did. I felt it, more than heard it. It hurtled to the bottom of my belly where it sits heavy, quaking with the fear roaring inside me that I don't have a clue what the hell I'm doing.

Whether he realizes it or not, I just handed him the last thing I have to give a man.

My complete and total trust.

He breaks into a slow, sexy, promising smirk. It says: *I know exactly what you did. I know how hard it was. I'm going to reward you later, but rest assured, we're in this madness together.*

The need to tell him I love him right this second bubbles up, but I pop every one of them before they pass my vocal cords. Now isn't the place or time.

"I've never seen him like this, you know," Adelle says so low I almost miss it.

I blink a few times, embarrassed to be caught staring. I desperately try to tear myself away from the man who has come to mean more to me than I ever wanted.

It's hard. When I succeed and face one of the few women

who means something to Shaw, she's smiling this goofy motherly smile that makes me want to smile too. So I do.

I know what she's telling me, but I ask, "Like what?" anyway, shifting in my stool toward her. I'm interested to see how much insider information Adelle Mercer is willing to give me.

She holds her chopping knife still in one hand and glances at Shaw. I follow her line, but quickly return to her when I see Shaw's attention has refocused on his father and their conversation.

"Spellbound. The way he looks at you..." She says this absently, not finishing her thought. I'm not sure if I'm supposed to respond or ask another leading question, so I don't, even though I'm dying for her to finish that sentence.

Scooping up the tomatoes she cut, she places them carefully on top of greens and takes the cutting board to the sink. She picks up her wine and sits on the stool next to me. "Shaw told me he's met your mother."

I nod. He spent the afternoon with us only yesterday in fact. My mother was unusually engaging. At one point, they got into a deep conversation about football, but she talked about the Steve Largent days like the present. The hall-of-fame wide receiver hasn't played for the Seahawks since 1989. Then she told him she'd like him to come back and meet my father. It crushed me but Shaw took it all in stride and handled it with ease.

"She has Alzheimer's," I tell Adelle.

The corners of her mouth turn down in sympathy. "Yes, I know. Shaw talked about it at length with me."

"He did?" I don't know why that surprises me, but it does.

She turns contemplative. "I can honestly say he's never told me that much about any woman before, let alone her mother."

"I..." I chuckle nervously. I'm speechless. "Huh."

With a sparkle in her eye, she says, "I already told you he's not brought many girls home to meet us."

I nod, remembering, still stuck on the mother comment.

"Even when he was in high school or college. He would date, of course, and he's had several girlfriends who lasted more than a date or two, but I can count on one hand the number of times he's brought a woman to the house." She takes a sip of her white wine, eyeing me over the rim. "You're number four."

Four? They've met *four* women in thirty-six years?

I give her small, tense smile. "Why do you think that is?"

She quickly throws her eyes Shaw's way again. When they come back to me, I nearly tear up at the genuine kindness I see. I can easily see myself sitting in this exact spot with Adelle Mercer, engaging in relaxed chitchat while our kids—Shaw's and mine—fish off the dock or play in the other room.

I have to force myself to check this fake family before I get carried away. We haven't even uttered those three important words to each other yet, and because we haven't discussed a future, I have no idea what Shaw sees in his.

Marriage? Kids? *Me*?

I don't know. But I want to.

"My son has always had a singular focus, you see. Shaw is headstrong and passionate. He has vision and a business savvy that Preston never did." She laughs. It's light and soothing. "At the age of five, he was already following Preston around, wearing little button-down shirts with pens tucked in the breast pocket. And not just any pen. No. It had to be a fine-tip felt one. Black. I had to throw away so many of his dress shirts because he'd forget to put the cap on and the ink would seep through and stain."

I realize I'm smiling ear to ear, hearing about a younger version of him. I can only imagine a little Shaw running around with a pocket protector and a TI calculator in his hand. "That sounds like something he'd do."

"He'd spend hours by his father's side when he came home from work for the day. He had his own little setup in Preston's office. A desk and a rolling chair with a bamboo chair mat underneath. He even insisted that he have his own phone, and we finally caved thinking it couldn't do much harm. When he made a long-distance call to one of Preston's business contacts in Thailand, we took it away. I think he was maybe seven or eight then. If I remember the story right, it was a small company Preston was looking to acquire and Shaw told the man he'd be a fool to pass up the offer. Three weeks later Preston closed the deal."

With each word she says, I laugh harder and louder, drawing Shaw and Preston's attention. Shaw's left brow ticks up, silently asking what we're giggling about and I grin wide, waving him off. Wanting to hear more.

"He is something else. Always has been." Her voice holds nothing but unconditional love and pride for her child, now a grown man. It warms my heart to witness the close relationship Shaw has with this family, with his mother. It's charming. It makes him irresistible.

"Shaw is a great man, Willow. He has the love and loyalty of his family, the respect of his employees and peers. He has success and wealth and any material possession he could want. But the one thing he's missing is the love only a soul mate can offer. He doesn't think he needs it, of course, but intangibles are often a hard concept to wrap our minds around. None of us really understands what we're missing until we find it, do we?"

My smile falters as I swallow thickly. Is she saying *I'm* that woman? That Shaw didn't know he was missing me until he found me?

"He just needed the right woman to come along and show him that the one thing he was incapable of understanding is suddenly the only thing he can't live without."

What am I supposed to say? Anything? Nothing? I don't know. Butterflies batter my insides.

She leans close to my ear, whispering conspiratorially, "And you, my dear, have opened his eyes. He's thoroughly taken by you. I wasn't sure I would ever see that day. Kudos."

She holds her glass in the air and I instinctively raise mine to clink with hers, my hand trembling. I feel like Shaw has changed so much in the two-plus months we've been together, but hearing it from someone who knows him inside and out…

"I'm scared he'll hurt me," is out of my mouth before I can stop it. Oh fuck, how I wish I could have chewed that up before confessing it to his mother of all people.

But Adelle takes it in stride. Reaching over, she places her hand atop mine. I keep my eyes glued to her sun-spotted, aged skin until I'm forced to look up when the silence becomes too much. She raises the corners of her lips, cocks her head, and floors me with, "So is he. The best kind of love has a healthy dose of fear attached to it, Willow. And once you feel that fear burning holes in your belly, *that's* when you know you have found something rare and special, worth holding on to."

I blink, digesting her words. Does she think her eldest loves me? Can she see it in my eyes, too? I never felt the fear she described about Reid, but I do about Shaw. My gut is raw and tender. I don't know exactly how I'm supposed to respond, but I'm saved when Shaw's low voice hums, "Hey, what are you two plotting in here?"

"Nothing," I croak at the same time Adelle chirps, "Girl talk."

His eyes hood, turning sort of predatory and I take a nervous sip of wine while I watch him amble around the island toward me. Stepping up behind me, his strong grip lands at the base of my neck, flexing a few times. I feel the heat of his body at my back when he leans over and whispers in my ear, "You're not in here planning our wedding already now, are you?"

I choke on the liquid that was sliding down my throat, sputtering and coughing as Shaw and Adelle take turns slapping my back, asking if I'm okay. As soon as I can take in a breath without feeling moisture drag back up each time, I whip my head around to face Shaw.

I can't decipher the look on it and stammer, "God, no." It was defensive and sounded as if the idea was sour in my mouth, but it wasn't. It was a delicacy that tasted too damn good, actually.

"I was kidding." The words are smooth, but the way he says

them feels forced. Almost as if he didn't actually *hate* the idea if we were.

"Were you?" I ask before I can think better of it.

"Were *you*?" he counters, and I'm not sure which question he's actually asking. Were we talking about a wedding or am I opposed to the idea? His grip is back around my neck. It tightens as his eyes bob back and forth between mine, intent on dredging an answer from me, even though he won't reciprocate.

Instead of fighting, I decide to give in—my armor lying in a heap at my feet anyway—and answer both questions honestly. "No."

I know it's the right one when his eyes turn molten at the same time his entire body relaxes into me. "You continue to surprise me," he says huskily.

"So do you," I tell him, my voice thready.

His gaze drops to my lips and I lick them. He groans. It's barely a noise at all, but it's become as familiar to me as blinking. *Desire*. He dips down, his lips almost on mine when a shrill voice screeches, "Unca Shaw!"

Shaw has no sooner stepped back from me when a rambunctious five-year-old scrap of a girl jumps two feet off the ground straight into his arms.

"Coraboo," he coos, swinging her around until she giggles uncontrollably.

"She had a juice box in the car," Gemma warns, kissing me on the cheek as she passes by as if we're already sisters or something. I reach up, running two fingers over the spot. "You're on cleanup duty if it comes back up."

Shaw doesn't let that faze him at all. He's now holding her above his head, blowing raspberries on her belly, making her squeal and squirm. It's not until Cora makes this god-awful burping noise that Shaw stops and gently sets her on her feet.

"You okay, Boo?" he asks with concern, squatting down to her level. It's so darn cute, I can't help but picture him doing that with our children.

Willow, good God, get a grip...

She hiccups a few times before answering, "That was fun!"

"You're not going to ralph, are you?" Shaw's brows are now tugged inward.

"What's ralph?" she counters, all guileless and wide-eyed.

"It means you throw up your guts until they're all gone and they're lying on the floor in a big giant blob of nothing but rotten gut parts," her brother, Nicholas, chimes in, miming exactly what he means, noises and all.

Then chaos descends.

"Nicholas," Gemma chastises at the same time Cora screws up her face before crying, "Mommy, I don't want to throw up all my guts. I like my guts. I don't want rotten guts."

Behind me, a baby starts to wail and I turn to see Gemma's husband, whose name escapes me momentarily, try to calm the little boy in his arms, whose name I do remember: Eli. And I guess three years old isn't quite a baby anymore.

"Here, I'll take him if it's okay," I offer, holding my arms wide.

"You sure?" he asks, toggling back and forth between a now howling Cora, who's carrying on about her guts, a taunting bigger brother, who's only making it worse, and the crying little one in his arms.

"Yes, I'm sure. We'll be just fine, won't we, big guy?" I slip my hands around Eli's torso and press him against me, bouncing him as we head into the other room, away from the anarchy.

"Want to play?" I ask, trying to wipe away the tears that have wet his chubby face. Last time I was here, I noticed Adelle had a Little Tikes toy box in the corner of the main living area. We head over there and I gently sit us on the floor. I open the top, pulling out the first thing I see that may interest him. He stops crying immediately when he sees what I have.

"Squigz!" he exclaims, his voice still watery. He grabs the container from my hand and dumps out these multicolored silicone pieces that look like giant molecules with suction cups on each end.

"Wanna see how to do it?" He looks up at me with bright blue eyes, full of life and curiosity and an innocence you can't find anywhere else but in a child. I know he's only Shaw's nephew, but I see a lot of Shaw in him. My imagination starts running wild and free again wondering if Shaw's son would have the same dimple in his left cheek or the same mischief burning inside.

"I'd love to." I smile, trying to focus back on Eli and not this made-up family I keep returning to.

He starts sticking the pieces together, making a random pattern. He stops and hands me a piece. "Youw tuwn."

"That's very nice of you. Can I put it anywhere?"

He nods excitedly, and I attach a blue piece with four suction cups to an orange piece with only one. He picks up a yellow one and sticks it to my blue.

In the other room, it sounds as if Cora has calmed, but Nicholas is now in trouble, being marched upstairs. He's pouting, his bottom lip stuck out. He's trying hard not to cry. I watch him stomp out of sight, giggling to myself.

Eli hands me another piece right as a shadow in my periphery catches my attention. At some point, Shaw came in and sat in that wingback chair. He's casually leaning back, fingers laced and resting on his stomach, watching us. *Me, actually.* His eyes are nowhere but on me. And he looks the same way he did when he saw me sitting in his chair during our first meeting at his house.

As if he's in awe and struggling to understand why.

I feel as gooey now as I did then.

"Hi," I say. A tiny laugh tries, but fails, to contradict my nerves. "I—" I stop. Swallow hard. Maybe I overstepped my bounds? "I hope this is okay?" I motion to Eli, who is now ripping apart his masterpiece in order to start again.

He nods in slow motion. That's it. That's all I get.

I try giving my attention back to Eli, who is now chattering about a kid named Sid but I'm not following him at all. All I can feel is Shaw's gaze on me, over me, stitching its way through my heart until I start to panic a little at how damn good it feels to have 100 percent of this man's attention.

"You look good," his baritone voice practically sighs. The ordinary compliment drizzles down like a gentle rain shower, but instead of cooling me, my entire being goes hot with desire, whether that was his intention or not.

I slide my gaze to his, expecting it to be fiery and hungry. It's not. It's soft and warm and so damn sweet my stomach falls right out of me.

"You were born to be a mother, Willow." He stares right into my soul as he tells me this.

Shit. I am on fire. Lava crawls through my veins, burning me from the feet up. I've started breathing again, but it tastes of hot air and repressed wants.

He extends his hand toward me and without even thinking I hop up and walk over to him. I step between his legs and lace my fingers with his. He studies our joined hands for a long time, twisting and turning them to various angles. His thumb rubs the outside of mine hypnotically until I feel that single place he's touching me over every inch of my skin.

Everything fades away when he slowly walks his eyes up my body and latches them to mine. He says nothing. And it's okay. Nothing needs to be said. We just breathe, both our lives not so subtly shifting and whirling around us with each inhale and exhale. We stay like this until we hear a female voice call, "Five minutes till dinner," shattering the spell that had opened a place where only we existed.

Shaw never lets go of my hand as he stands, but once he's on his feet, he drops it to my side and takes my face in his stronghold. Uncaring that someone's waiting for us, he lowers his mouth to mine and gives me the sweetest kiss I've ever had in my life. It brims with reverent purpose and burgeoning love.

We break apart, laughing when Eli's little voice drones, "Oooooo, gwoss. Unca Saw and that giwl awe kissing." He runs out of the room, leaving us alone.

Shaw rests his forehead against mine, saying so low I have to strain to hear, "I'm having a hard time keeping up with how fast you're changing me, Goldilocks."

Be still my beating heart.

I feel as though the moments between us are becoming more honest and real by the second. I wrap my arms around his waist and close my burning eyes, emotions threatening to overwhelm me. "So am I, Drive By."

His lips come back to mine, moving just as leisurely and focused as before. With every firm press of them, I crave him more. With each twist of his tongue against mine I feel more lost, but also as if he's found me underneath all the masks I use to hide behind.

Between unhurried kisses, he murmurs my name over and over and I forget where we are. Then he simply rests his lips against mine for a moment before starting gruffly, "Willow, I—"

"Hey, lovers, Annabelle's here," Gemma interrupts.

At the mention of his other sister's name, Shaw stiffens and pulls away, dropping his hold on me entirely like I'm a conductor for electricity.

"What's wrong?" I ask, stepping closer. I want to touch him. I raise my hand to his arm but drop it before it makes contact. He snags it on the way down. Clasps it tight and clings to me, some sort of desperation now emanating from him like a groundswell. For a beat or two, he looks torn, as if maybe he wants to get the hell out of here. But I know how much he loves his sister, so that makes no sense.

At last, I see her out of the corner of my eye. She's standing in the entry between the front foyer and the living room watching *me* closely. I would recognize her anywhere. She's a slightly older version of the girl littering Adelle's Steinway.

She's exquisite. Porcelain skin. Dainty features. Thin, reedy. A snow angel, only with jet-black hair streaked in sapphire ink. Her black-rimmed blue eyes sparkle like glitter falling through a floodlight. Her lips are stained a cross between currant and mahogany. She's wearing a pair of shredded black jeans paired with a black V-neck tee that says in big gold letters "Solemnly swear that I'm up to no good."

I believe that's true.

Shaw hasn't talked much about this sister, Annabelle. He's only alluded to the fact that she's in college and "a little wild." Now I see what he means. She's got that same mischief I saw in both Shaw and Eli's eyes. Must be a character trait of a Mercer.

But there's also something else about her. I can't quite put my finger on it, yet it jumps out and grabs me with such force, I can't dismiss it. Or ignore it. It draws me to her. It's a pull I can't stay away from.

Instinctively I break out of Shaw's hold and head toward her. Her eyes widen, and I swear I hear Shaw's breath hitch. It's not until I'm about five feet away that what I was seeing across the room comes into focus.

She's suffering.

Her young soul has taken a beating but she powers on, trying her damnedest to forge her way through a darkness only she thinks she can see.

I know it's a crazy thought having just met her but it screams at me so loud I can't disregard it because I've witnessed it firsthand.

Sensed its immense power, fingered its implacable grip.

Looked directly into its cavernous eyes and felt just as helpless as I do right now.

Annabelle Mercer's soul holds the same shadowed, haunted look I've seen in someone else before. Someone who I still feel a connection with no matter how much space and time part us.

Someone I couldn't save.

As I stare into the otherworldly eyes of this tiny beauty in front of me, there is no mistake. No shred of doubt. No hesitation or uncertainty at all.

Shaw's baby sister is battling the same unknown demons as my dead sister, Violet. And I have to wonder if her family knows it or if they're choosing to ignore it instead…the way my family did until it was too late.

Shaw

Chapter Nine

I DIDN'T EXPECT HER TO show.

She's invited, of course. Always is. But it's a toss of a coin whether she'll walk through those front doors, gracing us with her presence or whether her place at the table will remain empty, while everyone pretends not to notice.

And it's not that I don't want her here. I do. It's not that I want to keep her from Willow, either. I don't. But this whole fucking murder mystery thing is killing us both. It's been more than a week since Mergen dropped this Hiroshima bomb in our laps and like a bad rendition of hot potato, we're trying frantically to figure out where to throw the fucker that will result in the least amount of carnage.

It's been a week of nothing but dead ends. Maddening dead ends. One after the other.

A visit to Bull didn't glean much. He swears on his dead mother's grave that he implicitly trusts every single person on his staff. And why wouldn't he? Officers put their lives in each other's hands every day in the field. You don't trust those who walk by your side, you're dead. But someone knew something, said something to someone else in casual conversation over beers and ribs. No other explanation makes sense.

And the friends—and I use that term loosely—with her the night in question are scattered to the wind. We tracked down one in Seattle, but she was so fucking strung out it was like talking to a zombie. One is in jail in Portland on drug possession charges, and the other has moved out of state, presumably living with a grandparent who is trying to help straighten her out. We may be able to track her down, but it will mean an unplanned road trip. More time away from the office. Time away from Willow.

So as I stand here, tethered to the carpet, and watch Willow walk toward my little sister, I stop breathing.

What will Bluebelle do? Will she crack and confess all or will she act flippant, effectively isolating herself with that protective coating I'm used to seeing on Willow? I'm holding my breath because I have no idea which Annabelle has shown up today. Or what will happen when she opens her mouth.

Annabelle's eyes track Willow all the way. My usually well-composed sister is on the verge of losing it. I see it plain as day. Her blood-red lips tremble slightly. She's balancing on the heel of one boot, the toe of that foot shaking back and forth fast enough to make fire. I think I might even spot water glassing over those baby blues of hers.

Fuck. I see the fissures splitting open. When she sinks her bottom teeth into her upper lip I know she's on hysteria's edge.

I'm about to whisk her out of here when my generally unaffectionate sister shocks the shit out of me by lunging forward and throwing her arms around Willow's neck.

Willow's reactions are a bit more sluggish. In slow motion, I watch her snake her arms around Annabelle's waist and when Willow returns that affection, my baby sister's eyes bolt to mine and she lets go of a tear she's been trying to hold back. She surreptitiously reaches up with a single finger, wiping it away before drawing back from the hug.

"Hi," she says to Willow, sounding a little sheepish.

Willow hesitates only a second before returning a "Hi" that's riding on top of a light chuckle. She sounds confused over Annabelle's display, especially since they've never met before. She's not the only one. I slide my gaze to Gemma who's watching the entire scene unfold, her brows fixed together and her mouth agape.

"I'm sorry, I, ah…I got a little carried away there." Annabelle now nervously bounces from foot to foot.

"No apologies needed. I'm a hugger, anyway. Annabelle, right?"

Bluebelle's lips round up at the corners. "Yeah, that's right."

"Well, it's nice to finally meet you, Annabelle. Shaw's talked a lot about you."

Her eyes flash to mine, panic quickly rising from the bottom of those lake blues.

Does she know? they ask.

I shake my head, subtly.

"You can't believe a word out of his mouth, you know," she jibes, quickly reverting back to her insolent self in an attempt to cover her swelling anxiety.

Willow laughs and turns to gift me with a smile that makes me hard as a fucking rock. "Yes, I'm well aware of that." She replies to my sister but is saying it to me. Except I know she's bullshitting. Every word out of my mouth to her has been nothing but honest.

"Time for dinner," my father's deep voice calls from the kitchen.

"Well, that's our cue," Annabelle proclaims, threading her arm through Willow's, tugging her along. "We need to be sitting down in under sixty seconds or I'll be blamed when the lasagna is cold."

"Annabelle," I caution, my voice gruff as I catch up to them. "That's not true and you know it."

Her face falls before popping back up. She says nothing but drops her hold on Willow and forges ahead of us. I snag Willow's hand and we walk to the formal dining room table together. I pull out her chair, push it back in for her when she starts to sit, and take the place next to her.

My father sits at the head of the table with, as usual, my mother opposite him. I'm to his right with Willow next to me. Gemma is next to her, followed by Cora and Nicholas. Directly across from them is her loser husband, Evan, and little Eli. Annabelle rounds out our small family sitting opposite Willow.

Each of us is in the exact same spot we are usually in; only there is one thing out of place tonight. An extra place setting I know is not for Linc because he's stuck working. Again.

"Are we expecting someone else?" I ask my father, nodding to the empty spot as the doorbell rings.

"We are," he responds, not making a move to answer it. Two seconds later I know why.

"Apologies for being late, Adelle." The recognizable male voice drives nails into my skull and fire ants through my veins.

What the ever-loving fuck is *he* doing here? And he simply walked into my father's house as if he owns the place? My blood is boiling fast and hot.

I look over to my mother to see that slimy motherfucker, Reid Mergen, kiss her cheek before shaking Evan's hand as if they're old high school buddies or something.

"How are you doing, little man?" Mergen says with unnerving familiarity as he playfully ruffles Eli's hair on his way by. Apparently he's spending more time with my family than I realized. While that wouldn't bother me under any other circumstances, because it's him, because he's threatening everything I love in this room, it enrages me to the point I think I'm going to blow.

"What's he doing here?" Willow whispers at the same time Mergen greases me with a smug grin.

"I have no fucking idea," I grit. But I'm not saying it to her. I'm addressing my father. "Why *is* he here? This is a *family* dinner."

"We're sewn at the hip these days. Hell, I'm practically blood," fuckface interjects, rubbing the dig in with his searing gaze.

Every muscle in my body readies to bloody his face. "I wasn't talking to you, asshole."

"Shaw Andrew," my mother scolds, doing that clacking thing she does with her tongue when one of us disappoints her.

Well, fuck that. If she thinks I'm going to sit by and cower while this poseur tries to undermine my family, mother or not, she has another thing coming.

My fingers coil into my palms, my dull nails piercing fiercely into the skin. I ignore everyone else, biting out, "Leave, before I throw you out."

Willow lays a palm gently on my forearm, trying to calm me. I let out a smug grin of my own when Mergen's eyes drop to it and flare.

"Shaw." This time my father chimes in. "I invited him."

My father nods to Mergen, whose eyes now dart between Willow and me, and while I can't see the look on Willow's face, whatever it is must be enough to give that bastard pause. He has the chair pulled halfway out, a slight hint of indecision now sitting on his previously haughty features.

"Sit," my father commands. He does but won't meet my hateful gaze. "As for you," he addresses me. Dresses me down, is more like it. "Reid is a guest in *my* house, at *my* table, and while I have some idea what's going on between you two"—his attention slides to Willow, then back to me—"you will act civil to *my* guest while you're in *my* home."

I don't respond, not verbally anyway. A diatribe sits round and heavy on the end of my tongue, clawing to get out. I fear if I open my mouth, though, I may do irreparable damage with my parents and no matter how many insults I want to hurl, that fucker right across from me is not worth it.

Willow surprises the hell out of me by caressing her lips against my cheek before whispering, "I can do this if you can."

Running on some primal instinct I have no control over, I grip the back of her neck and hold her still while I kiss her breathless right at the dining room table with everyone watching.

When I lean back, Willow blinks a few times. Her eyes are dreamy. Her face is flushed the delicious hue of longing. I thought maybe she'd be pissed, but when one corner of her mouth tips up, mine does the same.

"Well, this should be entertaining," Annabelle spouts, clueless that the man within a finger's length is the man who could very well be this family's demise. *Her* demise.

"Can we say grace now or is there more boundary marking yet to do?" my father asks, to which nearly everyone snickers. Except for Mergen, that is. His eyes flame with the same firestorms of hate I imagine fill mine when I think of him with Willow.

There's a part of me that knows I should feel bad for him, but if it's there, I can't find it. I don't know what happened between him and Willow, and I'm not sure I want to know. All that matters is she's mine now.

"Oh, there's more marking to do." I slide my hand high around Willow's upper thigh and squeeze, all the while never taking my eyes from my new enemy. "But that will be done in private."

"Oh my goodness," my mother gasps.

"Jesus Christ." My father's head drops forward as he shakes it.

"Mommy, Gwandpapa said a naughty wood," Eli chirps.

"Oh, this is getting good," Annabelle chimes in, a broad grin splitting her face.

Mergen and I lock wills. *You want to challenge me, campaign boy? Fucking bring it. I eat weaklings like you for breakfast.*

The tension at the table mounts to uncomfortable proportions when a comment out of the mouth of babes dissolves it. At least for me. "Mommy, is that girl Unca Shaw's kissing his girlfriend?" Cora asks.

Fucking A right, she is.

"Yes, sweetie. Yes, she is," Gemma replies, a smile in her voice. Way to go, sis. "And her name is Willow, remember?"

"That's a pretty name."

"It sure is," my sister answers.

"Are they gonna get married and have babies?"

Gemma stutters, "I...ah...I..." and when I flick my eyes to Mergen, his jaw is cinched so tight you'd think it was wired shut. One can dream.

I rescue my sister and find myself answering my niece's question with tremendous ease. "It's a definite possibility."

Next to me, Willow takes in a sharp breath and you could hear a pin drop with how quiet the room has gone. I'm sure my family is in about as much shock to hear me say that as I am, but I tune everyone else out and turn to face her. She's staring at me, her mouth parted, eyes slightly bugging.

Did you mean that? they ask.

I'm pretty sure I did, I answer.

Her entire face lights up. Glows. Where has this woman been all my life?

"Can we eat now? I'm hungry." Cora's tone borders on a whine. In about three seconds she'll go into drama queen mode.

"Best idea I've heard in the last five minutes," my father says dryly.

It takes a few seconds before I'm able to break my gaze from Willow's. I find myself wishing we were alone so I could tell her everything I'm feeling inside, even though I'm not sure yet how to voice it. After the prayer, I hold on to her hand longer than necessary. I take every opportunity during the meal to touch her, not because I'm trying to piss Mergen off, although that's a nice side benefit, but because I feel grounded in a way I never have when her skin is pressed to mine.

In the most interesting twist, I find myself ignoring Mergen and his not-so-subtle glowers at me. His lame attempts to rein in the longing he has for Willow should set me off, but I only find them pathetic now. I can do it only because of her. Her focus is solely on *me* even when she's interacting with my family as if they are already hers.

And when I walk out the door a short while later, my arm tight around her waist, the only thing I'm thinking about is burying myself so far inside her we both find the very soul of the other. And it's not that I feel the need to erase another man or stake my claim. It's because I realize that's the only time I feel as though I've truly come home. I never realized I was missing that feeling until I met Willow. I am so in love with this woman, and more and more I'm embracing it. Not running from it.

I only pray I can keep her.

Willow

Chapter Ten

I WAKE UP WITH A dry mouth, thirsty. My eyes slowly open. I blink a few times to clear the haze of sleep, even though my brain tells me it's not morning yet. It takes a few more seconds before I realize where I am.

Shaw's bed.

I twist my body, reaching for him, only to find his side of the sheets cool as if he's been gone for a while. I sit up, look around the room, and note the air is still. The bathroom is black. No sound drifts through the dark.

Throwing the covers back, I swing my feet over the edge, letting them sink into the plush carpet. I sit still for another few beats, listening, wondering if maybe he's on an overseas business call. Hearing nothing, I push myself from the mattress and pad quietly out of the bedroom, into the hall.

It's not until I'm halfway down it that I shiver, realizing I'm naked. We barely made it through the front door after dinner with his parents and Reid when he had me up against it. In three blinks of an eye, my clothes were off and he was kneeling at my feet, spreading my legs, shoving his tongue inside me until I trembled on the verge of an orgasm. But before he let me fall, he was carrying me through the entry, into the living room, and bending me over that chair. *His* chair.

He took me from behind with beautiful ferocity, in a way I've not been taken before. It was territorial but devout. The whole act was unhinged, but filled with such raw passion I felt his emotions bleed into my pores as he came inside me, whispering my name while he pounded me sore. Hours later, I'm still tender between my thighs, feeling the skillful way he owned every inch of me with every step I take.

I make it a few more feet and come to a stop. The hallway spills out into Shaw's open living space and from the mouth of it, I scan the entire area, not seeing him here either. Snagging a chenille throw from the couch as I walk by, I wrap it around me, heading toward the opposite end of the house where his office is, fully expecting him to be sitting behind his large maple desk burning the midnight oil.

But when I round the corner, it's empty. Dark. He's clearly not there. A quick perusal of the other rooms in this this wing, including the gym, finds them just as vacant.

"Where the hell are you?" I mumble, making my way back to the center of the house. Did he leave? Should I check the garage? Try his cell maybe? The glimmer of the moon off the water catches my attention as I stand there, stumped, racking my brain on what comes next. Where would he go at three in the morning?

Only then do I spot him, lounging on a chaise outside on the deck to my far left.

He doesn't see me. He's staring ahead toward the bay, which looks especially picturesque tonight. He brings something to his mouth and takes a bite before setting it back down on the table next to him. I edge closer to the window, attempting to remain unseen, not wanting to interrupt him if he wants to be alone. But when I get close to the glass that separates us, I see something in his posture. The tense way he's holding himself. The contraction of his jaw. The squinting of his eyes. This isn't a relaxing midnight snack while breathing in the fresh night air.

Something is bothering him.

I stand there for seconds. So many of them I lose count. Should I go back to bed and pretend I never woke? Or should I go out and see if I can comfort him? If he wanted comfort, though, wouldn't he have woken me, even under the guise of sex?

I know what a girlfriend would do. What I *want* to do.

As the sound of the sliding door breaks the silence, he turns his head toward me. His irises glimmer under the night sky as he takes me in, head to foot. His eyes run down me leisurely and when they connect to mine again, even in the dark, I can tell they've heated considerably.

I stay still, letting my gaze run the length of him, too. He's shirtless, wearing only low-slung army green pajama pants with a white drawstring that's tied in a bow, sitting right below that exquisite line of triangle-shaped muscles that point straight to the most glorious cock I've ever experienced.

Not knowing what I should say, if I should even stay, my attention falls to the small stand beside him. I see an open jar of something dark, a dirty knife lying across a plate and what looks to be a half-eaten...*cookie*?

"Didn't get enough for dinner?" It's a stupid question, but the only one I can come up with. I'm losing that *under-pressure edge* I'd perfected as Summer, having spent so much time with him. I'm not sure I like that, though I wouldn't change it either as that means never meeting him in the first place.

His eyes follow mine down and he reaches over to pick it up. He takes a bite, chews slowly as he watches me, and sets the remainder down once again. Then he smiles that brilliant megawatt smile of his, rendering me stupid. Suddenly I'm glad I came out.

"It's an Eleanor special," he says.

"A what?" I ask, edging ahead, struggling for a closer look. The air is crisp and I try to forget how it's slipping through the bottom of the blanket I've draped around me. I pull it tighter, hooking it under my chin. How is he not freezing?

"Come here," he says softly when he notices a tremor rack my body. Glad I'm invited to stay, I rush to his side and crawl into his lap when he indicates that's where he wants me.

I bring my knees up to my chest and snuggle into his chilly skin, hoping I can warm him. "It's cold out here."

"I know. Been out awhile." He brings a hand to my crown, twists a few strands of hair between his fingers, running them through to the ends. He does it a few more times until I stop shivering.

Relaxing into him, I drop my head back to watch him talk when I probe, "What's an Eleanor special?"

"Hmm...well in simple terms, it's a waffle with jam."

There's more of a story here. A memory that makes him happy. I see it. I want it. Every last detail. "And in not so simple terms?"

His face brightens. His arms squeeze me closer. "This is one of the things I love about you, you know?" My breath catches at his word choice, but I don't acknowledge it. It makes my stomach flip to even think of acknowledging it. Days ago—hell, even hours ago—I wanted this. Now the thought suddenly puts the fear of God in me. He continues as if he hasn't upended my world in the most frightening way. "You don't take what I say at face value. You never do. You hear things others don't."

"It's a curse." God, I'm breathy. Breathless. All the breaths are gone.

"It's a gift," he counters quickly. The compliment makes my blood buzz even more than it already does. By the way he eyes me he's not oblivious to the way he's affecting me.

"In *not* so simple terms, these remind me of my grandmother. My mother's parents lived in Maine, and we didn't get to see them too often, but for two weeks every summer, Gemma, Linc, and I would to stay with them and wander around the quaint village of Castine."

"Sounds lovely."

"It was." He sounds so wistful he infuses me with it. And when he describes it in vivid detail, I feel as if I'm there experiencing it right along with him. "I don't think I appreciated it enough at the time, but grand-mère Eleanor used to let us run wild. I mean, wild. We'd leave at sunup and not come home till sundown. We'd be a dirty, sticky, stinky mess. We'd wander the streets down to the Maritime Academy to watch the cocky college kids try to navigate the *Bowdoin* schooner. Eat ourselves sick on ice cream from The Mill. We'd kayak and bug the fishermen until they took us out for a spin, letting us cast a line or two."

I laugh. "That sounds dangerous."

"Nah. It was just good old-fashioned fun. A small New England village that was safe and harmless. Everyone knew everyone. All the locals were friendly. I even kissed my first girl there. They were some of my best childhood memories."

"So when does a waffle with jam come into play?"

His lips touch my forehead briefly before he continues. Part of me wants him to forgo the rest of the story and just leave them there.

"Grand-mère was a master jam maker. Any kind of jam you can think of, she'd make it. Jalapeno, blackberry, currant, peach, pepper. She tried hundreds of different kinds. But my favorite by far was her blueberry jam. I ate it on everything. And when Gemma and Linc would fall into bed exhausted, we'd stay up; sit on her porch, which overlooked the river; and eat homemade waffles slathered with blueberry jam."

"That sounds amazing," I tell him, a lump now clogging my throat. "*She* sounds amazing."

"She was."

Was.

Guess we've both had our share of loss.

For the first time, I have the urge to talk to him about Violet. To tell him how much I loved her. To share how her senseless death created this blank space inside me I don't know if I'll ever fill and how he needs to protect Annabelle from the same demons that took Violet because if they do, he'll never be whole either. And I simply couldn't bear that.

But that conversation seems too heavy, too complex for the moment and besides, I think he needs lightening up, so instead I ask, "Who makes your jam now?"

He smirks. "Remember that first kiss I mentioned?"

"Yeeesss." I may be a teensy bit jealous.

His smirk widens. He sees the green-horned monster behind my eyes. "Her grandma Bessie was my grand-mère's best friend. Bessie still makes me a few jars and sends them at Christmas. Enough to last all year."

"That's nice."

"It is. Want a bite?"

I nod. He brings the remnants of the waffle to my mouth and I open. "Sorry, it's cold now," he tells me as I bite down and moan.

"It's delicious," I say once I've chewed and swallowed. And I mean it. It's the most delicious jam I've ever tried. Even better than my momma's apple butter.

"Not as good as my grand-mère's, but pretty damn close." With that, he pops the rest in his mouth and finishes it off.

We go quiet, the one thing holding our conversation together now gone. And as the seconds tick by, I build up the courage to ask what I really want to ask.

He's not out here by himself to enjoy his grandmother's best friend's jam. Something is on his mind. Has been for days.

This is the stuff I've never been good at. Sharing. Opening up. Trading vulnerabilities. I've kept a lot of shit inside throughout the years thinking it's better served there than out in the open weighing other people down. I've done this with my father, with my mother. I most certainly did it with Reid. I've done it with nearly every person in my life. I even do it to a certain degree with Sierra. I keep myself closed off and I've always thought it's been for good reason.

Only now I'm not so sure.

I realize I don't like the way it feels when I'm on the outside and I want someone to let *me* in.

Setting my palm over Shaw's heart, I let the tips of my

fingers graze his smooth skin back and forth. "What are you doing out here all alone?"

"Couldn't sleep. It's my thinking spot." He says this soft and thoughtful.

"Do you want me to leave?"

"No." It's a short waft of air more than a word. When his grip squeezes my arm, I know he means it. He wants me here. Maybe he just didn't know how to ask? God, we're two peas in a pod, aren't we?

"Everything okay?"

He takes awhile to answer. When he does, though, it's not much of an answer at all. It's the exact same thing I would do. One recognizes expert deflection when she is an expert herself. "Just some things on my mind, beautiful. It's nothing."

I keep moving my fingers in a circular fashion, my touch light, all the while working hard to squelch the hurt feelings his evasion stirs.

Let me in.

It's completely hypocritical, I know. I want it anyway. Being on the outside sucks ass.

"Does it happen a lot? This witching hour thinking?"

He lightly chuckles and his chest expands as he inhales deeply. Is it as hard for him to talk about what's on his mind as it is for me? "A little more often than I'd like lately."

I tip my head back again. He tips his down. We stare at each other, neither making a move to do anything else but let this moment catch us up in it. I'm terrified of being this happy. I've never felt more protected yet so exposed in my life.

"Anything I can do?"

He fingers a piece of my hair. "You're doing it right now. You in my arms like this? In my home? My bed? Honestly, not a better feeling." His voice is gruff, heartfelt. Sincere. It settles those nerves inside that *I'm* the one who has him so twisted.

"You could have woken me up," I offer. *I wish you would have.*

His lips turn soft, rounding faintly at the edges. He runs his thumb over my bottom lip before he whispers, "I think if I had woken you, I would have lost myself in you, Willow."

I have no idea what malfunctions between my brain and my mouth, but something misfires when I say, "Maybe you can find yourself in me, instead."

Silence. How is it you never notice how high-pitched that void is until you're trapped in it? Until you wish you could take back whatever it is that made it descend in the first place.

In my mind, the silence lasts long enough for me to replay those words a hundred times, but in reality, I think a half second elapses before Shaw fists my hair and tilts my head back severely. His mouth brushes mine when he confesses, "I already have, Goldilocks. I've found so much more in you than I ever expected. Than I ever wanted."

He seals his lips to mine, making my head spin anew. I expect the kiss to be hard and unforgiving. Desperate based on his tone, his confession. It's not. It's tender and sweet. Languid. A 180 degrees from the last several times we've come together, which have been frenzied and all consuming.

"God help the man who tries to take you from me, Willow Blackwell." That hot, fervent declaration is pushed smoothly into my ear a second before his tongue starts a path down my throat. His avowal soaks in, drugging all my faculties until I feel sluggish and pliable.

"No one is taking me from you," I assure him in a whispered voice, moaning his name when he dips to continue his wicked trek downward.

My free hand goes to his head to hold him to me but he pulls back, locking his eyes with mine. Fire and blood oaths dance in them when he growls, "Damn straight they're not."

He's talking about Reid, that much is obvious. Yet it's so much more, too.

Cupping his face, I place my lips back on his. The move causes the blanket covering me to slip from one shoulder, exposing my flesh to the cool night air. A tremor runs through me, followed by a coat of goose bumps.

"You're cold." He runs his hands over my arm when he notices something else. "Fuck, I love this," he groans, skimming the backs of his knuckles over the sensitive tip of my peaked nipple.

I think he's going to tuck the blanket back around me but with a grin that's nothing short of sins promised, he reaches over and dips a finger into the open jar of blueberry jam instead.

Balancing the sweet on the tip of his finger, he starts at the top of my breast, draws a line straight down until he reaches my pebbled areola and, moving clockwise, scrapes his way around it, making sure I feel the bite of his nail as he coats every inch of me.

"Oh my God," I mutter, my blood now running hot.

He circles me again and again, watching me while he teases, studies, bends, and adapts, adjusting his technique for maximum impact. He concentrates on his task of driving me mad, rolling the sensitive tip between his forefinger and thumb until I gasp, letting my head fall back in sublime pleasure. When his wet mouth covers me and his teeth clamp down, a wash of white-hot desire flash fires through me.

It's cold out. Mid-fifties, probably. I should be shivering. Instead, this serene calm spreads over me while Shaw pays homage to my body as if I'm some sort of sacred place he hasn't visited before.

"I'm only eating this off you from here on out," he growls, sucking hard before releasing me with a pop. He licks me clean, drenches his finger again, and goes after my neglected breast, painting me with the sticky substance until my breaths come in small bursts of anticipation. Once he's satisfied, he lifts me to his mouth, his tongue and teeth making me dizzy.

"I fucking love your body, Willow."

He nips on the fleshy parts of my breasts. The bites are hard. They sting. They'll leave marks. *This* is the Shaw I know. The one I need. The one whose will makes mine graciously bow and obey.

"I love the smell of your skin, the curve of your ass, the taste of your pert nipples," he says, shifting me to my knees until I'm straddling him.

He reaches over and dips a finger in the jam one more time. Hand closed around my hip, he pushes me up until I'm hovering over him, thighs tense.

Smiling mischievously, he brings his sugary finger between my legs and circles my clit, already swollen and ready. My eyes drift shut as he paints my outer lips, one side after the other, taking care to avoid my opening, before drawing a line along my perineum, stopping just short of my sweet spot.

I'm panting, heart literally galloping in my chest because I know what comes next. He reaches back and drops the back of the lounger flat. He lays down and with his hands clamped around my hips, motions me forward.

"I love the taste of this pussy." That panty-dropping smirk of his grows.

Positioning me over his mouth, my knees bracketing his head, he urges me down. I'm helpless against his mastery. So weak and needy and solely focused on the eroticism of the moment I forget about the cold.

I gasp at the first touch of his mouth, open and probing. He sucks, he moans, he devours me as if I'm a new food he's never tasted.

"Shaw," I cry out when his tongue circles that sensitive puckered area, and when he opens my cheeks and pushes the tip slightly inside, it feels dirty and wrong and so absurdly fucking incredible I almost sob. Nerve endings blaze to life as if they've been dormant for all of time.

I reach back and grab the arms of the chaise for something to hold me to Earth as he takes me places I've never even dreamed of. I moan his name. God's name. I curse. My mumblings are encouraging but make no sense to anyone outside of us.

"That's it. Fuck my mouth, beautiful. Take what you need."

That's the detonator. That, and the suction on my clit and

the fingers diving inside my pussy, which is already convulsing with my release. I'm coming long and loud, uncaring who may hear or see.

He allows me only a slight reprieve before he reaches between us and yanks down his bottoms. He fists his erection, thick and veiny, pumping a few times while I salivate. Scooting me down his body, he circles my clit with the head repeatedly until I'm a trembling mess, nearly upon another orgasm. Then he replaces his hand with mine and directs, "Use me to make yourself come again. Just like this."

"God," I murmur, feeling hedonistic. His palms cover my breasts, kneading, fingers plucking at my tight nipples as I work him against me, watching him watch me, until I soar once more, humming his name. With near desperation, I place him at my opening, mid-climax. I need him inside me. Now. I start to sink, tremors of pleasure still racking my muscles, as he takes over and seats himself completely. I gasp, that fullness pressing against my walls never feeling so right before.

We haven't used a condom since that day in his parents' bathroom. I would say I'm not sure what to make of that, but it would be an out-and-out lie.

"I love the way you feel hugging my cock," he grits, sucking in a harsh breath.

Gripping both hips hard, he directs, as usual, moving me up and down his shaft, my only job to feel. My boobs bounce, my skin becomes slick, and that unholy pleasure he expertly plaits gathers energy at lightning speed in my very center. It's fast. So fast. *Too* fast. A third orgasm is already upon me.

Shaw palms my neck and pulls me forward. Leaning his forehead to mine, his thrusts are steady and powerful as he gruffs, "I love the way you move on me. I love the way you scream my name and weep for me to fuck you harder. I love how your pussy strangles me right before you come." He pulls my ear to his lips, whispering more filthy words that make me explode. "I love the feel of you milking every last drop of my seed like you're going to starve without it, Willow. I fucking *love* that."

That euphoria I crave barrels through me. My inner muscles clench hard and I crest a third time.

"Oh fuck, yes. So beautiful." His voice is so gravelly and sexy, my release doesn't die; it grows stronger. I'm gone. Flying high in that utopia of warmth and unmatched ecstasy, wanting it to last forever when his next sentence rips me back to Earth so violently I feel the thud of it in my bones.

"But I also love your broken heart and that tattered soul you guard with enviable strength, Willow."

That euphoria I was riding screeches to a halt.

"I love that obstinate backbone. God, that's a fucking turn-on."

His movements are harsher now, more erratic, and he's growing inside me indicating his own orgasm is starting to barrel down on him. But all I can concentrate on is how my heart pounds at his repetitive use of that word.

Love.

"I love your siren voice and your secretive eyes. I love your character, your satire, the power you don't think you hold over me but do."

True blistering panic unfurls until all the air seems to squeeze from my lungs. I thought I was ready to go there. I thought I wanted him to take that risk. I did, days ago, but now…now I'm scared shitless. I'm not ready.

His face pinches. He's going to come. It doesn't stop him from talking, though. "I love—"

That's it. I slam my mouth to his, silencing him. Eating those words until they're gone and the taste of regret that I did lines my mouth like lard, but still I don't stop. He tries to separate from me but I don't let him. I set my hands around his jaw and hold tight, twining my tongue with his. I grind my pelvis into him, squeezing my pussy with everything in me until I pull a guttural moan from him that's base and raw. Until his fingers dig painfully into my sides.

"Come inside me," I whisper against his lips. "I want to smell like you. Feel you drip down my thighs when I get out of bed in the morning."

"Jesus fucking Christ, Willow."

And that's all it takes. A few well-placed suggestive words to turn a controlling male into a primal being with a singular focus: the need to stake a claim, mark, brand what's his.

He pulls out and flips me over onto all fours. My blanket is long gone, but I don't feel the bite of the air as he spreads my cheeks and enters me roughly from behind. I don't feel the bruise of his fingers while he holds me in place and fucks me with undisguised vehemence so I'll feel his words instead of having to listen to them. I don't feel the numbness that sets into my knees as he reminds me that he owns every single inch of me, inside and out, even the organ now beating madly for him.

But I do feel his intense pleasure when he throws himself over the edge of bliss, scalding my insides with his virility, just as I'd begged for. I do feel the love he was in the middle of professing as he gently lifts me into his arms and carries me through the house and back to his bed. And I sure as hell feel his disappointment when he spoons me from behind, gruffly telling me to sleep.

Yeah. I feel *that* sting acutely.

Chapter Eleven

I REREAD THE PROPOSAL ON the expansion of our knowledge center in India for the third time. I try to absorb the insights an analyst spent hours researching and documenting. I attempt to put into context the cost of investment, including the additional experts we'll need to hire in our risk-management unit, and weigh that beside the value we'll bring Wildemer and its investors. I try to do my job as the co-CEO of a company my family founded ninety years ago.

I try and I fail.

All because I'm distracted by a leggy blonde with captivating eyes the color of fresh summer rain and a fucking two-inch steel levee completely encasing her heart, which I'm trying to find a single chink in.

Not only do I have to fight Reid fucking Mergen for her, I have to fight *her* for her as well. It's exhausting.

And I thought *I* was the one scared shitless. I've got nothing on her.

Frustrated, I toss the fifty-two-page report on my desk and turn toward the wall of windows behind me. I drift back to last night when the mere sight of Willow standing in that open doorway eased this awful tension festering inside me. I felt it all release the second she slipped onto my lap and set her head on my shoulder. When I was buried inside her tight, wet heat, I found myself in her just as I'd confessed.

The words I said came easily. I'm more and more convinced the excuses I was using to hold back are unfounded. I just need to prove that. So I wanted her to know exactly how far I've fallen into her and how there's no hope for escape. Her essence is tangled so deep inside me I'll never be the same.

She's scared, though. I get it more than she understands, but if she thinks I'm walking away from her, she has another thing coming. Willow Blackwell has blown up my entire world as I know it. Now that the dust has cleared and the pieces have settled around me, all I see is her. The angle I view it at doesn't matter, either. Top, bottom or upside-fucking-down. Everything before her is blank, empty. Everything after her is life.

"Mr. Mercer," Dane's voice squawks through the speaker.

For a half second, I think about not answering. I need to solve the puzzle that is Willow. I need to get all the pieces perfectly aligned and superglue them together to secure a future that now looks colorless without her. But I remember how I've been skirting my duties of late because of the distraction that is a five-foot-five package of sexy-as-sin spunk and I swivel, punching the button that's lit on my phone a little too hard.

"What is it, Dane?"

"I have Jack Hancock from Aurora Pharmaceuticals on line two."

"'Bout damn time," I mumble. I've left Jack Hancock three voice mail messages over the last two days, each one getting progressively pissier. I have been hitting wall after wall in my quest to put Mergen's threats underground and the weight of continued failure is getting unwieldy. I need at least one damn win in my corner. Picking up the handset, I push line two.

"Jack, how nice of you to return my call."

The bastard chuckles. “Sarcasm doesn’t suit you, Mercer.”

“Really? It was tailor-made and everything.”

Still chuckling, he says, “What can I do for *the* Shaw Mercer today?”

“Charles Blackwell.”

There’s a brief hesitation before, “What about him?”

“I want a copy of his entire personnel file and all policies concerning his compensation. Retirement plans. Incentive plans. Life insurance contracts. All of it.”

Silence.

Jack is a client of Wildemer’s. An important one I personally worked my ass off to land. He took a chance on us when we were building up our specialty consulting business. *He’s* the one who gets to make demands of me, not the other way around.

So this move of mine is risky. Jack Hancock has a short fuse. He doesn’t like to be *told* to do anything, not that there are many people in our positions who do. But I’m also successful because I’m savvy at guiding people where they need to be. Where I want them to go.

And while I should have put all that experience and finesse to work with my request to vet out whether Aurora Pharmaceuticals fucked over the Blackwell family, the thing I’ve come to learn about Willow is she makes me completely lose my head.

“Jack?” I prod impatiently.

I fully expect him to tell me to pound sand. He probably should. I’m asking for documents I have no business having access to. But if he tells me no, things will get ugly. Fast. And all the work I’ve put into growing our pharma consulting division over the last several years will be on the line. Aurora Pharmaceuticals is the linchpin client of that division. We lose him, we’ll take a hit not only to the bottom line but to our reputation as well.

Our shareholders will have my ass in a sling. Hell, Noah will have my head.

Yet I'm not even blinking an eye. Willow is worth that risk. She has quietly slid into the number-one slot in my life, above everything else, and I wouldn't change a thing about it.

Jack clears his throat, his voice now pitched low and concerning. "What's this about, Shaw?"

"Justice."

"Justice?"

"That's what I said."

"Justice for who?"

"His family, that's who."

Another pause. "I'm sorry, Shaw. I'm not following at all. This is old news. The death of my top scientist damn near killed this company. You know this."

"Yes, I do."

"Then why are we talking about it?"

I think about deflecting, but the fact I'm dating Willow is public knowledge. We've already been in the papers. Twice. In fact, at the moment, I'm staring at a picture taken of us last week leaving a cozy Italian restaurant; it's in the social section of the *World Herald*. The light in her eyes as she looks up at me is blinding, even in black and white.

"I'm dating his daughter."

"You're...the woman in the paper? *That's* his daughter?"

"Yes."

"Jesus," he breathes.

I stay quiet, let him absorb what I'm telling him. Willow is mine. Jack and I may only be business partners, but we've known each other for many years now. He knows I'm rabid about protecting what's mine.

"Those files are confidential, Shaw."

"Don't bullshit me, Jack. I'm not going to ask again."

Jack's voice is harder when he tells me, "I think you have our roles confused here, Mercer."

I'm sure my sneer comes through the phone line perfectly. "My role in life has never been clearer."

This time the pause is endless. We're in a Mexican standoff, neither of us wanting to blink. I would think he hung up on me but the solid yellow light on line two indicates otherwise.

"What are you looking for?" he finally asks with a heavy sigh.

Muscles I didn't realize were knotted start to unwind. Leaning back in my chair I once again spin to gaze out the wall of glass. My eyes drop to the window across the street, one story down. A man rises from his desk when a redheaded stunner enters his office and closes the door. I see the play of her lips clearly from here. Daring. Taunting. Her hands move to the buttons on her blouse while he quickly moves to close the blinds that face the rest of his office, leaving the ones facing me open, as usual.

"I'm..." I take a breath, making sure what I'm about to say isn't taken out of context.

Do I think Aurora screwed Charles Blackwell's wife and daughter? Maybe. Do I think it was intentional? I hope to hell not or, linchpin or no, I will see Jack Hancock slapped with a lawsuit that will sink his ship before it ever leaves port.

"In all the time we've known each other, Jack, have you ever known my hunches to be off?"

"I have not," Jack answers evenly.

"Then trust me. I'm not out to cause harm to you or Aurora. You're an important client."

"Why do I feel like if I don't agree to this I'm going to get fucked up the ass?"

"Because you trust your instincts, just like I do."

There's a long bout of silence. "This is highly unusual."

"I understand that, Jack. I will use the utmost discretion and confidentiality."

"I want an NDA signed."

"It's totally unnecessary, but if it makes you feel better, not a problem."

The sigh that reaches my ears is long and resigned. "My HR VP is going to have my head."

"I appreciate this trust you're placing in me," I say, trying to give him some comfort I'm not looking to fuck him over. And I'm not. I only want Willow to get what's owed her.

"Trust runs both ways. I trust if you find whatever it is you're looking for I will be the first to know."

"And I trust if I find something that's off you'll honor your obligations."

I hear a knock on my door a second before the click of the latch. Only one person generally walks in without permission. When I slide my gaze away from the woman across the street, who is now melting into a puddle of pleasure, my eyes land on Noah striding over the threshold.

"Charles Blackwell was not only a pioneer in this field, Shaw, I considered him a friend. Based on what you asked for I can only assume you're looking for compensation not yet paid and I assure you I trust my HR team implicitly. They don't make those kinds of mistakes."

I feel Noah stop beside me, his gaze following mine. A low curse ensues.

"Sometimes mistakes are just mistakes. Nothing nefarious intended, I'm sure. A second set of eyes can't hurt."

"I can have Sandra review everything again." Sandra is his Human Resources VP, I assume.

"You can. But if it's all the same, I'd still like the documents couriered over as soon as possible."

"You'll have the NDA within the day. Sign it and they're yours."

Noah moves around me, getting a better look at the show across the street. He leans his hip against the glass, his eyes glued to the exhibitionist couple.

"Thank you."

"How about eighteen next week?"

Well, that's a good sign I haven't fucked up too bad, I guess. "Sounds great. Have Dane and Peggy set up a tee time. We'll talk soon." I push myself up and reach over to cradle the handset.

"That Jack?" Noah asks absently.

"Yes," I answer, stopping to his right. I stuff my hands in my pants pockets and spread my stance slightly, rocking back on my heels.

"He give you a hard time?"

"Nothing I couldn't handle."

"I'm jealous as hell you have a front-row seat to this every week."

I stare at the woman, whose glossed eyes beg us to join in on their little fun and games, the same as she always does. Her skin is pale. Her breasts are perky. She's beautiful and alluring. But she's not tempting in the least. She's not Willow. I hit the button that closes my blinds as ecstasy washes over Red's face.

"Show's over. I have work to do," I bark. I plunk down into my leather chair and pick up the report I've been trying in vain to get through, forcing myself not to snag the cell mocking me from the corner of my desk. Three quick moves of my finger and a couple of well-timed commands is all it would take to have Willow here. Waist bent. That pretty ass in the air. Pussy swollen and dripping.

Hand to God it takes every bit of restraint not to make that call.

"Two things," Noah says, his face now serious. Taking a seat, he throws one leg over the other.

I drop the papers in my hand, every bit of attention drifting away from my insatiable desire for Willow, now honed in on my best friend instead. "You hear something?"

His lips turn down before straightening back out. "Not exactly, but I have a lead."

"On?"

"The missing friend of Bluebelle's."

I narrow my eyes. "The one who moved?" The only one we haven't been able to find.

"Yeah. She lives in a small town a couple of hours outside of Charlotte. I was thinking we could take a road trip. Pay her a little visit."

"Road trip?"

"Well, you know," he says with a smirk. "Take the corporate jet. We'll be in and out in twenty-four hours."

I let that roll around a few seconds. We need to do this. See if she knows anything about that night. But twenty-four hours without Willow? Not gonna happen. If Mergen gets wind I'm out of town, he'll be all over her like white on rice, spewing his lies. Poisoning her mind.

Maybe I can take her with me? We'll stay at the Ritz. I'll book a spa package for her. She can be pampered while I hopefully get what I need from the girl to refute all this crap and then I'll spend all night celebrating as I bury myself in her repeatedly.

Yeah. That may work.

"Let's do it. The sooner, the better."

Noah nods. "I'll make the arrangements. Saturday work?"

"Fine."

I'm preparing to ask him the second reason why he's here when I hear Dane's high-pitched voice again. "Mr. Mercer, Mr. Wilder, they're ready for you in the boardroom."

I smile a slow smile, my gaze floating down to Noah's not-quite-deflated woody. It's time to tape our quarterly state-of-the-union address to Wildemer associates, and he's wearing a fitted charcoal suit today. If he was filmed in his current state, you'd better believe no one would give a rip that we've increased profits by 11 percent quarter over quarter. They'll be focused on one thing and one thing alone.

"Better get rid of that or people will think you've developed some unholy attraction to me." I rise and grab a manila folder so I can refocus on business on the walk over.

Laughing, he flexes his thigh muscles to stand. "Nah. It just adds to this mysterious allure I've got going on."

I can't help but chuckle. He's right. Noah Wilder is a mystery that most women are desperate to solve. I'm not sure anyone will, though.

"What's the second thing you wanted?" I ask as we make our way out of my office and down the hall.

When we pass by his admin's desk, she jumps up and scrambles around the short partition, practically running to keep up with his long stride. She hands him three small pink pieces of paper, which he quickly flips through and tucks in his leather binder, leaving her huffing behind us.

"Is it *really* necessary to bring a date to this fundraiser on Friday night?"

I sigh. We go through this every year. And every year Noah shows up to the Angels Among Us fundraiser alone, bitching about the lack of available pussy at the end of the night. "Do whatever you want, but to keep doing the same thing and expecting a different result is the definition of stupidity. And I know you're not stupid."

"Why do you do this to me? Every fucking year?" he hisses.

Whatever. He'll bitch, he'll come, he'll donate a hefty amount to support the families of children waging war against things that are truly important, like life and cancer, then he'll go home, call one of the dozen women he keeps on speed dial, and I won't hear anything about it until next year.

We take a right. I nod and smile to several people as we walk by. "You have a bevy of women at hand, Wildman. Surely you can find one who wants to spend a few hours with you outside of the bedroom."

We walk into the boardroom, side by side, where there is already a flurry of activity. Lights, makeup artists, film crew. These next few hours, while we're reporting on a serious topic to the people who have made Wildemer what it is today, is always filled with a fair amount of fun and smooth banter. Noah and I play off each other perfectly, our passion for our jobs and our company equally matched by our playful attitudes.

"That's just the thing. I don't," he tells me, smiling at Carly before taking a seat to have some stage makeup applied.

I wait for the chuckle, but it doesn't come. Narrowing my eyes, I see he's serious. Suddenly I wonder if Noah isn't as sick of our bed hopping as I am but that he's afraid to acknowledge it. It's all we've done. All we've known for eighteen years.

An idea starts to form and the more I think about it, the more I like it. Slapping him on the back, I give him a vague, "It will all work out," before I take my own chair.

But what he thinks I mean and what I actually mean are two different things. I've never tried my hand at matchmaking before and this may very well blow up in my face, but what the hell. At least it will be good entertainment for a night.

Chapter Twelve

THE HAIRS ON THE BACK of my neck prick. Uneasy, my eyes track around the room again, wondering who's watching me yet seeing no one. It's the same feeling I've had since I stepped foot into the grand ballroom of the Sheraton two hours ago.

At first I thought maybe it was Paul Graber. My stomach lodged in my throat when I saw him here. He stared for a good long time, clearly noting I was with Shaw, before fading back into the crowd. Shaw noticed I was edgy but I never told him about Paul Graber, and I don't want to, so I said I had too much caffeine today instead.

But Graber left. I saw him walk out the door with a redhead who towered above him. That was an hour ago and the eerie feeling I'm being stalked has not dissipated.

"They seem to be getting along okay." Shaw's lips graze the shell of my ear, causing a shiver of desire to run up and down my spine. Tonight's live band is playing a great rendition of Michael Bublé's *Home* and with Shaw's body pressed to mine, his arms encasing me from behind, I've honestly never felt happier.

I take another quick look around and, seeing nothing, decide I'm being ultraparanoid. Seeing a former client, especially *that* one, has thrown me for a loop. Instead, I focus my attention on our two best friends across the crowded room and laugh. "Really? Is that what you see?"

Sierra's fingers are clenched together in front of her, her claws barely leashed. She stands shoulder to shoulder with Noah, his arm secured firmly around her bare midriff. They're talking to an elderly couple. Actually, Noah's doing most of the talking; Sierra's lips are drawn into a thin, tight smile.

It's been utterly comical to watch Noah parade her around like a prized shih tzu at a dog show, his hand at the small of her back. He's barely stopped touching her all night long. I still can't believe Shaw sweet-talked her into coming to this stuffy event. And not just to donning a ball gown and unsteady sling backs, but to being Noah's date. *Date.*

"Well, I don't see blood under her nails or scratches up and down his arms," he jokes.

We shuffle ahead a few feet. We've been standing in line for a cocktail for ten minutes. Seems as if everyone had the same idea at the same time. "Yet."

I feel the warmth of his breath a second before his lips land on my temple. They're soft and soothing. They linger. A smile creeps across my face.

"I'd like to be covered in scratches," he murmurs for my ears only.

I'm suddenly hot and tingly all over. All the diabolical techniques he uses to master my body fly through my head at lightning speed and I croak, "Yeah?"

"Oh yeah." He chuckles. It's shameless and sexy, with endless possibilities attached.

A finger gently presses against my jaw until I'm forced to turn and look up at him and, *oh God*...the devotion, undisguised want, and absolute love I see treading in his dark blue depths make me breathless. These crazy feelings I have for him start firing off all at once.

"Shaw..." His name is weighted with so much. Unparalleled longing. A plea not to break me. Fear that he will.

"I know, Willow." He presses his lips tenderly to mine, mumbling, "I know."

He spins me and wraps one hand around my waist. Placing the other around my head, he settles me into him, my cheek on his chest. My palms smooth up his back, my fingers curling around the slick fabric of his expensive suit jacket. I am one microscopic step away from handing everything I am over to him, reservations be damned.

"God almighty, I need two seconds away from this pretentious bullshit."

Shaw makes a noise close to a grunt before releasing me. Before I face Sierra, Shaw tips my face up and smiles a lazy smile, drawing the same from me. "If I haven't told you already, you are heart-stoppingly beautiful tonight."

My grin widens. He's told me this no less than a dozen times already. He makes me feel beautiful. Desirable. Makes me believe every word he says is true.

Then stop doubting him, Willow.

"Blah freakin' blaaah," Sierra complains behind me. Fingers pinch my biceps and she yanks on me. "You can stroke your own cock for five minutes, can't you, Mercer?" Dragging me with her when she starts to walk away, she stops to bark at Noah, "Top-shelf whiskey. The best they have. Double. Neat. Make it fast. I want it here when I get back."

For a moment or two Noah stares at her with awed fascination before quirking his mouth into that panty-melting smirk. "Your wish, milady."

Sierra huffs and rolls her eyes so far back they're in danger of getting stuck. Noah barks a laugh at our backs as we wind our way toward the back of the ballroom through the heavy crowd.

"Noah seems enthralled with you," I say as we break through the throng of bodies, making a beeline for the ladies' room.

The noise she makes is a cross between a snort and another huff. "I've never seen so many puckered assholes congregated in one room in my life," Sierra drawls with disdain as she shoves open the restroom door hard enough for it to bang off the wall.

I laugh nervously, looking around to be sure we're alone. She may not care, but I do. Said puckered assholes donated a hell of a lot of money tonight, according to Shaw. Luckily I see no one by the row of sinks.

"You didn't answer my question."

"I didn't hear the question mark."

"Do you like him?" I press.

She slaps down the small gold handbag she has tucked under her arm and jerks it open, lifting out a deep red lip pencil.

"Like him? He's an egomaniac and a whore."

She likes him. Noah Wilder may be the atypical man for Sierra Wiseman but her eyes don't lie. And what's not to like about him? He's sexy, charming, and suave. And not in a smarmy, *I've got swampland for you* way, but in a genuine one that draws you in closer with each breath he takes. He's a ladies' man, clearly, but there's something more underneath that cool demeanor. If I had to guess, I'd call it loneliness, though I'm sure he'd never admit it.

She takes off the cap and starts meticulously lining her full mouth, catching my gaze in the mirror when she pauses. "Tell me why I fucking agreed to this again?"

Sobering, I tell her lowly, "You know why."

Sierra and I may be unconventional friends, but we share an unbreakable bond no friends should. We both lost sisters. Mine to overdose, hers to childhood cancer. Only she doesn't talk about Sammy, the same way she doesn't talk about anything else. She's a veritable cask of internal suffering like me. And I don't like the way it looks on me anymore.

Ignoring me, she takes a deep breath and goes back to painting her lips the color that makes men's thoughts turn to what it would look like staining their cocks. When she's satisfied, she throws it back in her purse and snaps it shut. Then she stands there, fingers wrapped around the counter, seemingly looking at her reflection. But she's not. She's far away. I know this is hard for her. My heart aches because I've walked so many miles in her shoes my soles are fraught with irreparable holes.

I set my hand over hers and squeeze. "Thanks for coming. I know this is hard."

Her eyes snap to mine in the mirror. They clear, then calcify, emotions back under lock and key. Girl talk is over.

"I made your boy toy promise a donation so big it would give him hemorrhoids."

A smile tugs at the corner of my mouth but I bite my lip. Somehow I doubt this "date" Shaw orchestrated has anything to do with a donation. He sits on the board of the Children's Hospital and has a soft spot for kids, so he probably already had a big check penned before he even asked her. No. This is something else entirely. A setup. And with the unwavering attention Noah has been paying Sierra all night, I'd say something unlikely might be brewing between them.

"I'm not surprised. You're a good negotiator, Ser."

I spin on my heel and head for a stall as that smile I've kept at bay breaks loose.

"I want proof," her voice drifts through the hollow metal as I close it.

"If he made a promise, he'll keep it. One thing I've come to learn about Shaw Mercer is he's good to his word."

I hike up my ankle-length, pale pink pleated skirt and tug down my barely there nude thong. The one I know Shaw will go crazy over later.

"He'd better be. I'll have his left nut if he doesn't."

"Wow. Just the left? That's generous of you." I unwind some toilet paper and wad it in my hand.

"I figured I should give you a shot at the fake baby you were talking about."

God. That sends a jolt of electricity through me.

The squeak of hinges reaches my ears, signaling someone else has entered our domain. Sierra calls, "I'll meet you out there. I need a drink in the worst way if I'm going to make it another hour in these medieval torture devices some male bastard created thinking it would get him laid."

"Ha! Couldn't agree more." My own feet are screaming for mercy. But Shaw's eyes widened like saucers at these gorgeous silver shoes with slinky straps that lace several times around my ankles. And when he whispered how he couldn't wait to feel them scrape his ears as he devoured me later, I knew I'd endure any pain to feel that pleasure.

I finish, wash my hands, and dig my MAC See Sheer lipstick from my purse, applying a fresh coat.

I find myself thinking about the words I just spoke to Sierra. How Shaw's good to his word. He's never lied to me. Not once. He's an honorable man. Good and loyal. He makes me feel comfortable and understood, and isn't that what every human being wants? Freedom to be yourself? To be accepted for who you are, not who you have to pretend to be sometimes? Someone who strengthens you simply by their sheer presence and nothing else?

That person is rare. One many of us never succeed at finding.

Suddenly, all that anxiety I have of telling Shaw I love him and hearing him say it back falls to pieces at my feet. *I've* found that person. The one who makes me stronger. The anomaly I didn't think existed, but does, and I would be a fool to continue keeping him at arm's length.

I've not risked a damn thing in my life. I didn't risk anything with Reid. I held it all back, afraid. I don't want to be afraid anymore. I'm tired of fear ruling me. I'm tired of others ruling me. For once *I* want to rule me. I want to risk it all, even knowing what pain may be waiting for me at the end.

With excitement and a healthy dose of nerves now pumping through my veins, I exit the bathroom with every intention to head straight into Shaw's embrace and make my confession. I attempt to throw my makeup back into my purse but miss and it falls quietly to the carpeted floor. I bend my knees gracefully, scoop up the lipstick, and make it into my bag the second time around.

It's not until I stand and take one step forward that my eyes land on *her*.

Voodoo Eyes.

The gorgeous brunette from the fundraiser I attended with Paul Graber a few months back who stared me down. The same one I saw pictured on Shaw's arm several times before he started dating me.

Those hairs on my neck rise again.

She's been the one watching me all night long.

I want to keep walking, but for some reason, I'm frozen stiff. She stares at me intently. Gives me the once-over, slow and deliberate. She still hasn't said a word. Neither have I.

Coming to my senses, I start to move but her provocation paralyzes me again.

"So you're the flavor of the month, huh?"

I say nothing. I'm not about to get into a trivial catfight with a woman spurned. I tell my feet to go. They do. I'm practically beside her when she taunts me again.

"A word of advice, little girl. Don't get caught up in his selfless gestures and sweet words. He'll use you until he tires of you, then cut your heart out with a spoon. He'll let you fall in love with him and walk away, leaving you to wonder what in the fuck just happened. Because Shaw Mercer doesn't do love." Her fingers curl, air quoting the last two words.

I say nothing as she watches me, not dropping my guise for a second. But saliva has flooded my mouth and my heart has plummeted to my stomach, bouncing back up to lodge in my throat. My skin has tightened and I'm definitely clammy.

She's looking for an outward reaction and I refuse to give her one. My years of acting couldn't have come in handier.

"Sounds suspiciously like a woman scorned to me."

Her cool green orbs flit down my body before connecting again to mine. She smiles. Not one that says *let's get our nails done next week* mind you, but one that lets me know she thinks I'm as unworldly as Laura Ingles Wilder.

"Have they shared you yet?"

"Excuse me?" I spit incredulously, spinning toward her. Two women skirt around us quickly, very much aware this isn't a long-lost reunion.

Her cocky smile slips a little. If I'm not mistaken, I see bits of sympathy bleeding through her hateful glare. "You are so naïve I almost feel bad for you. Shaw Mercer and Noah Wilder are known as the famous Wonder Twins, or haven't you been let in on that little secret yet?"

Anger sits hotly in my stomach, its smokiness swirling and thickening until I feel it crawling up my esophagus in bitter waves. I force myself to be cool and unaffected by her goading, but inside it's a whole different story.

"I have no idea what you're talking about."

"Debauchery, dear."

I know my look is pure confusion and in about five seconds, I'll have wished I'd just played along or walked away because the next thing she says steals my breath.

She sighs and rolls her eyes. "Threesomes. Orgies. They are very *practiced*. It's their specialty, actually. Been doing it since college, I hear. See"—she crosses her arms and taps her witchlike nails against one bicep in an efficient, irritating rhythm—"Shaw lures you in. Convinces you it's *your* dream come true. I mean, what woman hasn't fantasized about two gorgeous men fucking her brains out? Not any that I know of. And let me tell you, Shaw and Noah not only do it, they do it very, *very* well. But here's the thing...the second Noah Wilder sets foot into that bedroom is your kiss of death. When he slides inside of you while Shaw watches and encourages him on, you're already a fading memory."

My lungs seize. I don't think I'm blinking. Pretty sure I'm not breathing either.

Is what she says true? By the flush of her skin and the slight heave of her chest, I would say yes. Plus, she was extremely...*descriptive*.

Jesus Christ. Tomorrow I'm boarding a private plane with Shaw and Noah. Shaw said they had quick business in North

Carolina and that he didn't want to be away from me for even a day. He said we'd get a hotel room and he'd do things to me I never imagined I wanted.

Is *that* what he meant? A threesome with Noah? Was this all just a game? Is he upset about the other night? Noah is every woman's fantasy, but he's not mine. I know I have a lot of walls and when Shaw tears one down, I throw another one up. I know I haven't even talked to him about my most painful loss: my sister. But is *this* the way he'll end us?

Nausea stirs up all those doubts and fears I thought I'd just buried. My legs wobble under my skirt, and my throat feels like it's closing. Weakness momentarily conquers strength and I set two fingertips against the arm of a nearby chair to steady myself. And to think I was about to rush into his arms and tell him how I've fallen in love with him and can't imagine my life without him.

Now the smile she gives me is genuinely sad and full of heartbreak.

"From one woman to another, get out before it's too late. Find a man who's capable of loving someone besides himself, his family, and his twisted partner in crime. Shaw Mercer doesn't do commitment. He's like the wind. Uncatchable."

Uncatchable. That's what I've thought all along.

My heart feels sluggish and weak as this incredible sadness tries to take me under. For long blinks, we size each other up, quiet. She's waiting for a reaction, a fight, a naïve rebuttal maybe. But what would be the point of that? I believe every word she says is true and it crushes me.

After I take a moment to recapture the breath I lost, I do the only thing I can. What I excel at. I ease back into Summer's skin and become someone else. It's the only way I'll get out of here without falling apart. Or scratching the bitch's eyes out. "Well, then it's probably just as well I'm looking for a great fuck instead of happily ever after. H-E-As are for suckers and romance novels."

I don't spare her another glance as I turn on my heels and

flee. On unsteady steps back to Shaw, though I feel her eyes boring holes into my back, I keep my head high and heartache buried in an abyss that seems bottomless. The plastic smile is back in place as I slip into his strong arms and I work double time to keep my muscles from shaking with tremors of despair.

I'm generally the master of disguise. It's become as natural to me as taking a breath. Only this time, as Shaw whispers, "Are you okay?" quietly in my ear, I genuinely wonder how I'm going to pull off the greatest act of my life.

How do I pretend nothing happened when I felt the world split open right beneath my feet?

Shaw

Chapter Thirteen

I GLANCE OVER AT HER again, seemingly engrossed in a paperback, wondering what in the hell is going on. She's been quiet and distant ever since she came back from the restroom last night.

Oh, she slid into my arms easily enough. Kissed me back when I kissed her. Even danced with me until I took her back to my place and made love to her until she begged me to let her sleep.

But not once did she melt for me. Her muscles weren't soft and pliable. Her sighs were hitched, but not the sweet kind that has her coming around my cock. It was as if she was working overtime to hold all her emotions inside that vault she deadbolts watertight. Her mind was anywhere but on me and what I was making her feel. It simultaneously pisses me off and terrifies the hell out of me.

"Is it good?" I ask, drawing those detached eyes up to mine.

"Is what good?" She uncrosses her legs and tucks a bare foot under her opposite thigh. She kicked her shoes off the minute we boarded the plane, grabbed that damn book, and hasn't said five words since. Her other foot swings back and forth, the bright pink paint making me want to drop to my knees so I can worship her from the ground up.

I cut a glance to Noah, who is sitting across the aisle from me, reading the financial section of the *New York Times*. A big part of me wishes he wasn't here so I could spend the next several hours coaxing the truth from her.

I nod, looking down. "Your book. Is it good?" It must not be. I haven't seen her turn a page in the last ten minutes.

"Very." Short. Curt. Bordering on antagonistic. It's irritating. Very fucking *irritating*.

"That's it," I bark. I throw the papers in my hand to the empty seat next to me and unbuckle my lap belt. Scooting forward, I dig my elbows into my knees and lace my fingers together. If I don't, I may very well drag her over me and redden her ass until she spills whatever she's bottled up inside.

Maybe I've taken the wrong tactic with her all along. Maybe a strong hand is what she needs to break through that fucking wall, not coddling and patience. Something I'm almost out of.

I've spent the last hour discreetly poring over every document that Jack Hancock couriered over yesterday, trying to find a needle in the haystack that will give her and her mother their rightful due. But that goes to the wayside for the moment because this woman coils me into knot after knot with that sharp, sarcastic tongue. And it's time for her to have a little taste of her own medicine.

She eyeballs my every move, her breaths picking up.

"What's it?" She hits that word "it" hard, like a punching bag, now holding that damn book like a shield. As if she needs anything else to keep her from me. I reach out, pluck it out of her hands, and toss it so it joins the papers next to me.

"I want you to tell me what's going on." Her eyes flick to Noah, then back to me. I'm well aware Noah's attention is 100 percent on us, even if he's pretending to read the stock report. "Don't look at him. Look at me. I asked you a question and I'm waiting for an answer."

Those eyes. Those beautiful fucking eyes that would make nations fall turn hard and flinty.

She. Is. Pissed.

Good. It's a reaction, at least. Better than this silent bullshit she's been pulling for the last fifteen hours.

Her jaw clenches and unclenches a few times before she spits, "It's a good thing we're thirty thousand feet in the air right now, Drive By."

I bark a short laugh. "It's a good thing we're not alone right now, Goldilocks. If we were, your ass would be on fire."

She sucks in a sharp hit of air, her gaze going back to Noah's. Staying there. If he's looking at her, I can't tell. I don't give a shit, anyway. I'm done playing. I'm done being soft. She's going to answer me. I stare at her until her eyes find mine again.

They're fire and ice.

It's a fucking turn-on.

"I don't know why you're holding back. Isn't that your thing?" Her voice is piqued and she cocks her head in that challenging way that makes me rock hard.

My eyes narrow, replaying her cryptic words again. I have no idea what the hell she's talking about, but whatever it is, it's why she's suddenly so cold to me. She's not stepping foot off this plane until we get to the bottom of it. I may be new at this relationship stuff, but there is one thing I know: if we don't communicate, we may as well throw the white flag now.

"Is this the part where you give me some vague female rhetoric I'm supposed to decode? Because if it is, I gotta tell you, sweetheart, I may excel at a lot of things, but I don't mind admitting mind reading is *not* one of them. Passive-aggressive isn't your style, so why don't you just say what you want to say and we can move past it."

She draws her bottom lip into her mouth and looks away. This time she stares out the small porthole, and I know it's time to back off. I've done what I set out to do. Make her mad. Make her think. Make her understand I am not going anywhere she doesn't go, too.

Then it's my turn to suck in a breath when she says without looking at me, "I ran into one of the conquests you and Noah shared on the way back from the ladies' room last night."

"Oh fuck," I hear Noah mutter.

Yeah. My feelings exactly. Guess I have my answer as to why she's shut me down cold.

Of course she'd eventually hear about Noah and me. It was the reason I hired her in the first place. It was foolish to think she wouldn't find out, but to hear it from some scorned one-night stand who wanted more than we would give her isn't the way I would have planned it. Not that I would have planned it, ever.

I juggle my options. I could feign ignorance, but that would only belittle her and she is worth far more than petty lies. Besides, all of that is past tense anyway. Meaningless. So I cop to the truth.

"Who?" I ask, but it was the sound of agony on a cloud of regret instead. First Annabelle, now Willow. More and more I'm wishing I could undo all my past indiscretions when it comes to Noah and me, even if it was consensual and every one of them predates her.

Willow turns to Noah. Noah—not me—and a feeling I can't even describe wallops me. I am insanely, irrationally jealous to the point I am not thinking clearly.

Does she want *that*? Him? What if she does? Would I give that to her? *Could* I?

No. Oh *hell* to the no. He won't lay a single finger on her. Jesus, I feel utterly sick. I swallow the bitter bile creeping up my throat.

"Voodoo Eyes," she answers softly, again not to me but to Noah. If I didn't think we'd all be sucked out and plunged to our death, I'd muscle open the emergency exit and throw him out. The only person I want her attention on is me.

"Who the hell is—?"

"Lianna," Noah answers before I finish punching out my question.

Now it's my turn to curse. I hang my head, squeezing my

eyes shut. What an absolutely fucked-up situation this is. "Did you know she was there last night?" I ask Noah.

"I saw her briefly, yes."

My head snaps his way. "Then why the fuck didn't you say anything, asshole?"

Noah throws his hands up. "Jesus, Merc. Because she wasn't causing any waves and I didn't think she was worth mentioning. She runs in our circles, man. She was bound to see you with Willow at some point. Hell, she's surely seen you two in the papers by now. This day was inevitable."

"But at least I could have managed the situation instead of it turning into the clusterfuck of the month. I could have talked to her, prepared Willow."

His mouth turns up, his smile wry. "Right. That probably would have done the trick."

"Fuck you, Wildman."

"I'm still here," Willow says, her quiet voice raw with hurt. I am gutted. Utterly gutted. I can only imagine the bullshit Lianna filled her head with.

"She meant nothing," I tell her adamantly, looking deeply into her lustrous eyes, her hurting soul. Christ, I hate myself. I want to take away her pain, not add to it.

Her gaze bounces between Noah and me. Every fear she has is front and center. So damn easy to read. "Yeah. She made that pretty clear."

Lianna. That fucking bitch. I think of the many ways I can ruin her, but none of it matters if I don't have Willow at the end of this. I see no one before Willow. Nothing after her, either.

In a flash, I'm kneeling on the carpet in front of her, her face between my palms, my lips on hers. My sorrys pushing into her with every sweep of my tongue.

Her tiny palms land on my chest. She pushes. Reluctantly I break our kiss, but lean my forehead to hers, panting, gasping for a chance, praying for a life with her. Why is it people are trying to rip the only woman I've ever coveted from my hands at every motherfucking turn?

"You are not her, Willow."

I feel a tear roll over my thumb. Hand to God himself it takes everything in me not to weep like a baby. Her pain is mine. Hundredfold.

"You are not like anyone. You have changed me. You are *all* mine, you understand that? All fucking mine. Tell me you believe me."

Believe that I wouldn't let Noah touch one hair on your head, let alone hear the way your breath hitches when you unravel.

"I'm trying," she whispers. Her hands now come to my forearms, curling around them. "I really am."

"We are stronger than any force working to tear us apart, Willow. Unbreakable."

Mergen. Lianna. Fate.

Fuck them all.

We are airtight. I *have* to believe that. If I don't, how can I convince her?

When she nods, I pull back. It takes a few seconds, but when her eyes—full of unshed tears and doubt—reach mine, I have to bite back my confession of love. If I tell her I love her now, what will it mean? Will she believe me?

Again, it pisses me off that those three important words will be trivialized if I say them right now, just like after her little lunch with Mergen. But I push that anger aside, wanting only to focus on making Willow *feel* loved and special instead. I may not be able to say it yet, but I will show her. Actions speak louder than words anyway, and the time will be right eventually.

Needing closeness, I undo her belt and sit back down, bringing her to my lap, glad she's not fighting me for once. The seats in our Gulfstream aren't terribly big, but Willow is small and she wiggles around until she wedges into me perfectly.

Edging a finger under her chin, I tip it up. The water has subsided but isn't yet gone.

I love you, I silently tell her. *So fucking much.*

I'm trying to believe you, I'm sure she says back.

Believe, I assure her. *Please, believe in me.*

I smile. She forces one back. Never in my life have I felt this conflicted about what to do. I'm heading to a Podunk town in the middle of nowhere USA to track down a scared, recovering drug addict, hoping she helps me put one threat to rest, when I have another fucking one pop up.

The words poised on my tongue should be said in private, not in front of Noah or anyone else, but we're not landing for another two hours. I can't wait two hours. I lower my voice, murmuring, "Trust that what I have with you is unlike anything I've had before, Willow. With anyone." When I see her listening—*really* listening—I continue. "I've been moving toward you my entire life. I just didn't know it."

Those tears—each one like tiny razor-sharp splinters stabbing into me—flare up again. Her palm touches my cheek. It's soft and warm like her lips, when she leans up, pressing them tenderly to mine, sighing my name.

"There's no one in here but you." I grab her hand and place her palm flat, right over my heart. It's racing. Beating for her. "No one else has *ever* been in here before. No one will be again." I didn't understand that crushing loneliness took up that space, but it's noticeably absent now, replaced with the only woman I'm convinced can breathe the very life into me.

She smiles. It's shaky. She needs reassurance I'm happy to give.

"You and me. That's it. That's all it will *ever* be, Goldilocks. Just you and me." And I don't just mean no other man will ever touch her, including Noah. I mean I want to commit everything I am to her and her alone. I'm surprised at the desperation I feel to tie her to me. Make her my wife. Beg her to carry my name, my heart, my children.

My fucking God, I'm lost to her.

"Thank you," she mouths so damn sweetly I want to carry her back to the bedroom and spend hours showering her with pleasure. I think about it. For a couple of seconds, it's *all* I can think of, actually, but the thought of Noah hearing even one of her sexy moans deflates the swelling happening inside my dress pants.

"You look tired." I noticed the whites of her eyes were bloodshot when I picked her up early this morning. She said she hadn't slept well, and it's entirely my fault. I can't imagine what's been going through her head since she ran into Lianna.

"I am a little." Her lids fall low as if it's suddenly too hard for her to keep them open.

Palming her head, I rest it against my shoulder, telling her, "Close your eyes, beautiful. I'm not going anywhere." *Ever*.

I stroke her hair until I feel every muscle of hers loosen. In minutes she falls asleep soundly in my arms and I can finally relax. Taking in a long pull of air, I blow it out and lean my head back against the headrest wondering what the next few hours will bring me. Answers? More questions? Relief, or a plunge directly into a hell of my sister's making?

I wish I knew what I was going to walk away with here. I want it to be Willow. I *need* it to be her. I need it to be Annabelle, too.

Christ almighty.

Out of the corner of my eye, I see Noah watching us. I roll my head and look at him but his eyes are on Willow. Instinct makes me tighten my hold. She snuggles and sighs contentedly, even in slumber. It's as if she knows her place is with me. I watch him watch her, this inscrutable look on his face but at last, when our gazes connect, his whole face lightens and the corners of his lips turn up just a bit. "It's all going to work out."

"This whole thing is fucked," I say back, quietly. "Mergen. Annabelle. Now Lianna. Jesus, I can't seem to catch a break here." I let my eyes run over Willow's incredibly gorgeous face, fresh and innocent in sleep. Her eyes move fast behind her closed lids like she's dreaming. I can't help but press my lips tenderly to her forehead before I give my attention to Noah once again. "I haven't wanted anything this much in my entire life, Noah."

He purses his lips and gives me a clipped nod. "She's not

going anywhere, Shaw." He's filled with conviction I seem to be missing. I'm glad one of us believes.

"I hope you're right."

The fact she's worried she'll end up like every other woman before her—naked between my best friend and me—would be valid if she were anyone else. It will take work on my part to convince her otherwise, but it's work I won't mind putting in. I'm not worried about that in the slightest because it will *never* happen.

No…there is a far bigger issue at play that's causing the acid in my gut to eat away at my lining.

If this little meet and greet with Lia Melborne today goes south, I have no fucking idea where that will leave us. Or if there will even *be* an us anymore.

Chapter Fourteen

THAT DREAM.

Noah patiently lingering.

Chest heaving.

Cock straining.

Crisp hazel eyes so feverish I may blister under them.

A gentle swipe of his thumb against my forehead, silently reassuring me.

Shaw grunting: "I want to watch you swallow his cock."

Me asking: "Would that turn you on?"

Him responding: "Is it wrong if it does?"

It was...

Good God, what was it?

A turn-on? Repulsive? A little of both, maybe?

On the plane, in the comfort of Shaw's hold, I fell into a twisted, fitful, hedonistic sleep about Vegas and black-tie balls and ringing in the new year with Noah's tongue lashing me to orgasm. Hours later, most of the details may have faded but sharp remnants still cling fast.

Part of me knew it was odd; not actually real the entire time I played the starring role in a fantasy that was never mine to begin with, but one that was subconsciously planted by a lovesick ex who only wanted to hurt me. Regardless of what Voodoo Eyes said, she wasn't doing womankind a favor by "warning" me. She stuck a rusty, jagged dagger in, twisted it, and soaked in my pain, fueling the flames of jealousy burning clearly behind her black corneas.

Shaw doesn't want to share me with Noah. He made that clear on the plane. *You and me. That's it. That's all it will ever be, Goldilocks. Just you and me.*

I believe him. But what if…

Yeah. What if that small, insecure part of me whispers. What. If.

What if this is all a momentary thread in time?

What if I can't let him in all the way?

What if he changes his mind?

What if he decides he can't commit?

What if he needs these twisted activities between him and Noah more than he thinks he does?

What then?

I'll admit that for a single solitary second, I contemplated walking away. From the contract. The money. My commitment. *Him*. All of it. For a single solitary second, I wanted to forget I ever met the man who made me burn with life again.

But then that second passed.

The simple fact of the matter is even if it's what I *should* do, I don't *want* to. I am desperately, foolishly, irrevocably in love with the billionaire playboy of Seattle who has never been in love with a woman in his life. While he may well be like the wind—uncontrollable and wild—Shaw Mercer is an inescapable force of nature.

He kissed my soul, leaving an indelible stain behind.

I am his.

I fully realize I could end up like Voodoo Eyes and every other one of his relationships. I may. It's entirely possible. But I may *not*. Maybe I'm his anomaly, too. Maybe he's risking as much by loving me as I am by loving him.

With a deep breath in, I let the hot spray of the shower pound into my back, wishing my insecurities would slide off me and disappear down the drain.

Shaw and Noah dropped me off at the Ritz a few hours ago before they took off by chauffeured car for their meeting. Shaw said they'd be back by dinnertime, surprising me with a day full of spa treatments. The works. Mani, pedi, facial, wrap, massage. I skipped the hair and makeup, sick of being pampered after five straight gluttonous hours.

Water beads on my skin, the oils acting as a repellant. I suds up a washcloth with vanilla-scented body wash and start to scrub. Minutes later with mundane tasks complete, body clean, hair washed and conditioned, and a razor smoothing the important parts, I feel slightly better but linger under the water longer than usual, trying to pull my thoughts together. Convincing myself what I learned about Shaw and Noah last night, despite my disturbing dream, is ancient history.

Now the fact he needed a fake girlfriend makes all the sense in the world. And this has to be the reason why Reid has been trying to cast shadows on Shaw. Of course he knows. Noah and Shaw have a sordid past together, and it likely doesn't bode well for Preston's campaign if any of their escapades were to leak to the press during election season.

There's more to it than that, though. I feel it in my gut. Just as I haven't let Shaw in all the way, he hasn't returned the favor. I know other dynamics are at play with his family. Annabelle is one bad decision away from making headlines. Gemma and her husband's relationship seems strained. And his brother Lincoln? I don't know his backstory, but I'd bet money Shaw is trying to protect him from something, too, because that's the way he is.

Fingers starting to prune, I switch off the water. Quickly drying with a plush, oversized towel, I take care to squeeze excess moisture from my hair. I finger comb it best as I can, intending to do a better job after I've dressed.

Grabbing a thick white robe from a hook on the wall, I slip

my arms through and cinch the waist as I pad to the bedroom to grab my toiletry bag.

It's only then that I notice a dress the shade of fresh winter snow lying on the comforter. Other than a few well-placed sequins, it blends in, which is why I must have overlooked it when I came back from the spa awhile ago.

Shaw. God, that man.

Voodoo Eyes' threat whispers in my mind, warning he'll ply me with gifts only to break my heart, but I ignore it and run over to examine the silky fabric.

Reaching to pick it up, I spot a vanilla linen notecard with only my name on the front. With shaky hands, I open it and read the neatly penned inscription in his handwriting. By the time I'm done, my heart has swelled with so much love the seams of me feel stretched to the max.

Willow,

Somehow, someway you have managed the impossible. You have captured every shred of my heart, every piece of my mind, every bit of my very soul. Everything I am belongs to you.

Yours,

~ Shaw

Goose bumps erupt everywhere. I find myself smiling ridiculously, like a teenager whose boyfriend told her he loved her for the first time. And in a way, I think he just did.

My attention goes back to the gift. I run my fingers gently over it, top to bottom. It's short. Sexy. Sheer. Revealing. *Too* revealing to wear out. The translucent fabric doesn't even meet in the middle of the structured lace cups. It will leave me exposed straight down to the juncture of my thighs. That's when I realize it's not a dress at all, but a nightie with intricate matching panties.

It's exquisite and downright sinful. I rub the silky material between my fingers, excited to feel it lay against my skin for the briefest of seconds before it's hopefully ripped from my body.

Knowing I should wait for Shaw but not wanting to, I drop the robe to the floor, slipping the delicate piece over my head. It flutters against my damp skin, tickling along my belly. I forgo the panties, striding to the full-length mirror to examine myself. I twist, gauging myself from various angles. I adjust my boobs for maximum push-up effect.

I look virginal in the color he chose. The way the gown frames the trimmed patch of curls between my thighs, I'm a virtuous sacrifice. An offering for his whims, his use. His, period.

An image of him returning to the suite with me draped over the baby grand in this, sans the panties, sends tingles of longing ghosting across my nipples. I'll order in champagne and chocolate-covered strawberries. Put on soft music. We'll stay in all night as I let him feast on every part of me until we pass out from exhaustion.

We were supposed to go out for an elegant dinner. I bought a new little black dress for our reservations at eight, but now all I can think about is secluding ourselves away in this tiny corner of the world where I can have him all to myself.

I'd love nothing more than vegging on messy sheets and eating junk food until crumbs stick to the backs of our thighs. I want to kiss, pet, cuddle. Be normal. Boring. Just the two of us. I need to solidify the connection between us. It's taut, fresh with reservations that threaten to snap us in two.

Hopeful he'll forgive the abrupt change in plans when he sees my wet pussy on display for him, I scurry down the hall to the living area of the spacious suite Shaw reserved for us. It's ridiculously large for only two people, and at 2,900 square feet, it's bigger than many people's single-unit homes, mine included.

I intend to grab my cell to call him only I jump straight from my skin when I see a broad figure slumped in one of the velvet chairs, facing me.

"Jesus Christ," I half squeal, half yell.

It takes a second or two for my brain to catch up to my sprinting heart. As the adrenaline that's flooded my bloodstream wanes, I squawk, "Shaw? What are you doing here? You scared the *shit* out of me."

And how long has he been here? Was he here when I came in? No. The room was dark. Why didn't he tell me he was back? My questions morph into immediate concerns, the scene feeling off. *Way* off.

"I'm sorry," he offers, monotone. Disconnected from the moment. His body is present but his mind is absent.

I take one step forward, my eyes adjusting to the low light. He looks completely disheveled. A one-eighty from his usual crispness.

The tails of his button-down are pulled haphazardly from the waist of his dress pants; the top two buttons are broken apart. His tie is askew, undone, hanging in a mess, which now that I'm looking closer matches his chaotic hair. Deep grooves are clearly evident as if he's repeatedly raked through it. Under normal circumstances, it would be sexy as hell. Now, though, it's unsettling.

Dangling precariously between his middle finger and thumb is a tumbler, a splash of brown liquid sloshing in the bottom. He's been here long enough to pour himself a drink, then. He watches my eyes track to it and back to his. They're dark. Severe. So intense I squirm, shifting my body weight to my other foot.

"What's the matter? Did your meeting go badly?"

Instead of answering, he brings the glass to his lips and tosses back the entire contents in one swallow. Gently he sets it on the table next to him, so quietly no noise registers at all. When his gaze finally pops back to mine, the air in my lungs freezes.

He looks…*desperate.*

My palms start to sweat. I have no idea why but every cell in my being cries out his mood is about us, not his business meeting. Which is crazy. *Right?*

Forgetting I'm barely covered I walk toward him with purpose. "Shaw, tell me what happened."

I stop between his spread legs and drop to my knees, the soft carpet cushioning the abruptness of my move. Setting my palms to his thighs I stare up at him, cowardly on the inside but trying to remain stoic on the outer edges. I have the distinct feeling he needs that from me now more than anything.

Unconsciously, I glide my fingers up slowly, dragging the smooth fabric with my upward trek until his hands on mine halt me. It's then I'm sure my heart will beat from my chest.

He's *trembling*.

Fear is a living, breathing thing taking me over. I'm *not* crazy. What the hell happened today?

"Shaw, please. You're scaring me."

With his attention securely on his lap, he gently picks up my hands and brings one to his cheek. He closes his eyes and rubs back and forth. Coarse day-old whiskers abrade the thin skin on top.

The act is tender, sweet, and wrought with such intimacy I can hardly breathe through the thickness of it.

I'm kneeling at the feet of the man I love in barely a wisp of silk covering my nakedness but it's not my body he needs right now.

"Talk to me."

His eyes are still shut. He squeezes them so tight it looks painful. Placing his lips in the center of my palm, he whispers brokenly, "There is not a single person in my life more important than you."

The declaration makes me gasp more than the physical contact, but I'm not going to deny that electricity prickles the length of my arm as he slides his lips up to my wrist. "How did that happen?"

I'm pretty sure his question is rhetorical. I murmur back "I don't know" anyway. And it's the God's honest truth. Neither of us expected to be here; the professional turned so personal we both ache with uneasy, uncharted emotion.

His lids pry open and penetrating murky irises fasten to mine. "I would do anything to keep you, Willow. To make you mine. Christ, I want you to be mine more than I've ever wanted anything before."

I'm utterly confused at what happened over the past few hours. He left a note telling me I was essentially his. In fact, he's been telling me that for days. Now his tone holds an edge of fear that I don't understand. "I am yours, Shaw."

"Are you?"

"Yes," I tell him with every ounce of determination I can muster. "Nothing will change that." *Unless you want it to.*

"God, how I want that to be true."

What he said was mumbled, but I heard it clearly anyway. Only weeks ago, he was preparing me for the end. Now he sounds as if he couldn't go on if I'm not in his life.

Clawing terror like nothing I've ever felt scorches a path from my belly to my rib cage. Invisible threads that feel more like bony fingers of impending doom clutch my chest, squeezing.

I never understood the depth of true love until I met this man. The way it crowds your whole being. Consumes your soul. Implants itself straight into your bones, your marrow until your DNA changes to match his. I'll never experience another thing like it as long as I live.

And something is threatening it. I feel it in every molecule.

This is a defining moment for me. Right now. This very second.

I could withdraw. Curl back into my protective little ball and play out the next few weeks with the practiced veneer I've mastered for the past fifteen years. I could hide this insane love I feel for him behind a fortress built of fear and unworthiness.

Or I can harness those feelings. Use the energy I expend for self-protection to flay myself until I'm raw and exposed, searing past wounds closed in the process.

Could I get hurt? No question, the answer is yes.

But is he worth it? A million times over.

That's it then. Decision made.

"You're in."

"Huh?" he asks absently.

You're in, you're in. You wanted in and you're there.

God, my stomach hurts.

"I'm in love with you," I tell him softly. In fact, it was so soft I'm not even sure he heard it. I'm not even sure I said it out loud, but when his eyes, which had fallen back down to our joined hands jerk to mine, I know I did because the lines in his cheeks turn sharp. His nostrils flare when he fills his lungs deeply. He parts his full pink lips slightly as if he's going to say it back. But he doesn't. He closes them again and swallows.

I offer a small smile, though nerves are causing my lips to shake furiously. He doesn't return it, simply continues to stare at me. Into that closed-off place I ripped open just for him. Even telling Reid I loved him the first time didn't feel like this.

He's quiet for so long I start running at the mouth, trying to defend myself in case this isn't what he wanted. "I know it wasn't supposed to happen. I know this is just a job and that it will be over soon, but—" He cuts me off by pressing his thumb firmly against my mouth.

"Stop," he growls.

Oh shit. Oh crap. Did I misread everything that's happened over the last few days? Maybe I got the cues all wrong, the words he wrote me all twisted into what *I* wanted them to mean.

Panic winds me up. My face goes hot. My lips feel dry as dust and even though his finger is still there, I dart my tongue out to give them some relief. I can't help but taste him in the process. He jolts, his eyes even more hooded.

"Say it again." It's a command. It's dark and gravelly. Pure need. Straight sex. He's *telling* me to tell him I love him again and I close my eyes in sweet relief that I wasn't wrong.

Taking in bravery through my nose, I whisper, "I love you," when I blow the breath out.

Then my face is between his strong hands. He tugs me toward him, and he looks wild and brutal and so, so beautiful I want to weep. "All of it. Say all the words again, Willow. Every last of them."

All the words. Okay. I can do that.

"I am in love with you, Shaw Mercer."

He never looks away.

"Fuck." He blinks slowly. Breathes deeply. "Again."

I start to smile at his bossiness. Those clusters of angst in my belly loosen. I bring my hands up and place them over his, resting my small fingers between his larger ones. "I am in love with you, Shaw Andrew Mercer."

I push myself to my feet, bending over at the waist because my face is a hostage in his hands. I crawl into his lap, straddling his thighs. He moves with me the whole time, leaning back as I lean forward, but he never lets me go, doesn't even loosen his hold on me an ounce.

"I am in love with you." This time my voice may be buttery soft, but I hit each syllable with purpose.

I dip down to kiss him. We both moan at our first touch. He tastes of chambered power, smoky liquor, and sheer awe, if that had a flavor.

It's gentle, my kiss. Different from others before it. It's jam-packed with every raw emotion I now want him to feel. For the first time since I was a little girl, I'm completely see-through.

We move languid and light against each other. For once he lets me lead. I nibble and play, letting our mouths break often before coming back to a different spot to do the same. I whisper, "I love you," over and over, feeling more powerful and sure each time it leaves my mouth. The last time I say it I pause and wait for his eyes to open so he understands how much I mean it.

He sees it. His jaw muscles jump. His fingers flex against my cheeks briefly before sliding back to wind through my still-damp hair. Tilting my head, he tugs me back to him. He deepens our connection but doesn't take over while our tongues slow dance and our souls blend into one.

I want to strip his clothes and sink down on him. I want to

look into his eyes the entire time he's moving inside me and let him take stock of everything that's there. The good, the mistakes, the fears, the guilt, the past. It's all his now. Every raw part.

But innate habits die hard. I'm insecure and I've just told Shaw I love him for the first time. Where does that leave us now? I desperately want him to say it back, but I want him to say it because he means it not because he feels he has to. Tearing away, I lean my forehead against his, panting a little, and I give him an out.

"I know you said what you feel for me is new and I know you don't do relationships—"

He grunts and puts his lips back to mine, shutting me up. This time the kiss brims with passion. He owns it, controlling me. He grows hard beneath me, kissing me senseless, and when he tells me, "It's madness how much I love you, Willow Blackwell," quietly against my wet mouth I can't hold back my sob. "Utter fucking madness."

"You love me?" I mumble, frantically trying to hold my shit together.

"You know I do." He looks up at me from under heavy lids. Those blue eyes of his soften and clear. They bounce all over my face, landing on my watery eyes, my swollen lips, the cheeks that I'm sure are stained pink. "I have never felt anything like this before. I didn't know it was possible."

"Me either," I confess thickly.

A corner of his mouth ticks up and he sobers. "Yeah?"

I nod, feeling choked up all of a sudden. I heard the real question behind his charming insecurity. I need to tell him about Reid. That we were engaged, practically married. How I left him. I need to tell him a lot of things, actually, but not now. Reid doesn't belong in this moment with us.

"Are you going to tell me what happened today?" I ask, following the line of his thick eyebrow with my thumb. The ease on his face is instantly replaced with sharp edges and a flinty stare.

"No," he snaps.

I'm taken aback, the bark of his denial smarting like a slap. "Why not? Something upset you."

"Willow, I just..." He sighs not once, but twice. He's choosing his words carefully, I can tell. "I don't want to talk about that right now. Please."

"You can trust me, you know." I sound surly. I am.

"I know." A soft smile curves that insanely sexy mouth. I start to melt against him again. Damn him. How can he do that to me? "You have no idea how much trust I've placed in you, Goldilocks."

"Really?" My sarcasm snaps him like a wet towel.

"Please, Willow. Please, just let it go. For now," he adds quickly.

I don't want to let it go. I want to push him. Drag the truth out about what had him in a state I've never seen him in before. He was practically despondent when I walked into the room not twenty minutes ago. But he seems borderline desperate for me to let this go and I don't want to get into a fight. For now, I will let it go. Reluctantly.

"Okay." I wind my hands around his neck, lacing my fingers. "But we're not done talking about this."

He nods curtly, visibly relaxing. A few beats pass and the mood in the room shifts once again when he finally realizes what I'm wearing.

"Holy fucking shit," he breathes. Both hands on my hips now, he pushes me back slightly to get his fill.

His gaze stretches over me, slowly. Purposefully. Starting from my neck, it caresses every exposed inch of my collarbone, kissing the swell of my breasts. His eyes flare, banked fire roaring back to life when he notices for the first time that I'm wearing the gift he left.

"God, you're sexy," he tells me, sounding dumbfounded.

Bringing his index finger to my shoulder, he traces the thin strap down to the cups that hold me high, running it over the edge of the material from one breast to the next. He dips inside.

A low rumble leaves the back of his throat when he finds my nipple hard as a jewel. I feel his eyes tracking even lower and he lets loose a long string of creative profanities when he sees I'm sans panties.

"Stand up," he demands. It's needy and feral and leaves no room for my usual play at defiance.

I flex my thighs and slide off of him. Curling my toes into the carpet, I rise on unsteady legs and present myself. My chest heaves. My heart pounds against my breastbone. The insides of my thighs are slicked with visible want.

"Turn around."

I can barely move with the way he's consuming me, but I manage to spin in a full circle without falling.

"You are divine grace, Willow," he says when I'm facing him again. His fingers wrap around my slim hips, short nails biting into me. It stings. It burns. It feels fucking amazing. "A goddess I am not worthy of."

He scoots forward until he's balanced on the edge of the chair. Legs spread on either side of mine, he tugs me until my knees graze the leather. His gaze walks back up me. I let him drink me in, feast on my mutual need.

"Please touch me," I urge.

I'm washed in warm breaths only a half second before his hot mouth presses to my lower belly, right above my pubic bone, and he whispers while looking into my eyes, "I love you, Willow. I am madly, deeply, irreversibly in love with you."

Oh God. I break out in chills.

"Do you know how many women I've said that to?"

My legs give a little. Setting my hands on his shoulders to hold myself steady, I lick my dry lips and shake my head. In my heart, I know, though. *I know.*

His mouth starts moving, placing tiny kisses along an imaginary panty line. His hands start wandering over my ass. A finger runs down my crack. It dips inside me, easily finding its way; then it's wandering back up the way it came. He rims me. Watches my reaction. I can't keep my head up any longer and it falls back on my shoulders, feeling so damn heavy.

Then my feet are parted from the floor. I'm in his arms. A shock of cold hits my butt as he sets me on the edge of the baby grand—its top is closed and flat. He spreads my knees and lays me back. He draws a finger through me, front to back, right before his mouth closes on me.

My spine arches.

My pussy burns.

My hands grip the short strands of his hair and pull as he licks me, moaning this unholy moan, unlike anything I've heard from him before.

"None," he growls before thrusting his tongue into my channel. I'm dripping. On fire. My legs wrap around his neck. He grabs under my thighs and tilts my pelvis up, driving in farther.

He's relentless. Manic. Starved. I'm dying. *Holy shit, I can't think.*

I'm teetering, my whole body clenching in anticipation when the bastard stops, leaving me to balance on orgasm's sweet edge.

"No," I whine, strung tight enough for it to physically hurt. I would rub my legs together to set myself free, but they're locked open in his impassive grip.

"Look at me." Not a request.

I manage to pry open my lids, but they only go halfway up. I'm panting. My fists clench by my sides as he stands over me, looking all exotic and wild and feverish. "Outside of family, not one woman, Goldilocks. You're it. You'll only *ever* be it."

"Shaw." I sigh, an amazing fullness pulsing in the center of my chest. That pain of denied release ebbs and I reach for him, but he grabs my hand and presses the palm flat to my stomach. He slides it down until the pads of my fingers touch my clit, which is hard and pulsing in mutiny.

"Touch yourself while I finger you. I want to get you off together."

Good lord, this filthy man.

One side of his mouth tilts up like he heard what I'm thinking. With that wicked smile still in place, he slides two fingers through my slit and into me, palm up. He curls them precisely, tuning in to that secret spot only he seems able to find.

I gasp, "Oh fuck." My chin lifts and my eyes find the ceiling when he caresses it just so. My hips move, seeking more. With each plunge inside I lift to meet him, needing more.

"You're not doing your part." I hear the smirk in his tone, and he slows his rhythm considerably until I'm forced back upright. I realize my fingers remain exactly where he set them, but they're not moving. "Watch us. Watch how good we are together, Willow."

I want to disobey. I want him to stare into the soul I just sliced open for him and challenge him the way I always do, but it's such a dirty directive, I have to comply.

My legs are open, heels resting on the closed fall. I'm at the edge of the lid, spread so wide my thigh muscles scream a little. I push myself up all the way until I'm sitting, spine straight. An arm is anchored behind, holding me up.

Circling around the most sensitive part of me, I watch us. I start slowly at first but pick up pace almost immediately. My arousal is abundant and runs down into his palm. It may be about the most erotic thing I've ever watched: his glistening fingers disappearing between my tight walls again and again.

"Christ, look at you."

"I'm looking," I whisper. My bare folds are puffy and pink, the inner lips two shades darker. The veins in his wrist bulge and I grind on his hand while I work my clit faster and faster. It's hedonistic and...

"So wet. So greedy. I have never seen anything sexier than this, Willow. Fucking ever."

Neither have I.

With the thumb and forefinger of his free hand, he holds my

outer lips open making every wicked move more visible. "This pussy is mine. This orgasm is mine. *You* are mine."

Shit, I'm shaking. Heat builds, the intensity of it multiplying so fast it's making me dizzy. My fingers fly. So do his.

"Oh yeah, that's it, beautiful," Shaw coaxes. "You're there."

Then and only then do I tear my eyes away from the sight we make. Shaw does, too. Our gazes click. Our souls align. And only seconds later I'm gone. My eyes slam closed. Electric currents fire through me, one after the other. My body shudders and shakes with the force of them. I open my mouth to wail, but it's merely a strung-together mess of soft *yeses* that comes out instead. I clasp Shaw's wrist and keep him steady inside me so I can savor every second of my orgasm until it's gone.

I collapse forward, panting into his chest. Drained and happy, I silently weep.

Shaw Mercer loves me. *Me*. I can honestly say I have never trusted someone with my heart more than I trust the man currently wrapping his arms around me, now whispering in my ear how I'm his forever. And maybe that should worry me, yet it doesn't.

I think he'd do anything for me.

Absolutely anything but break it.

Chapter Fifteen

WHAT THE FUCK ARE YOU doing, Merc?

I laid Willow on the bed like something fragile, something rare to behold. I peeled that silky sexy-as-fuck sliver of fabric from her body as if she were ripe fruit I couldn't wait to sink my teeth into. I shed my clothes and came over her as if the thought of diving inside her warmth was singular and fundamental to being able to take my next breath.

She loves me.

I'd hoped it. Like a pussy, I'd prayed for it, even. But to actually *hear* it? That truth rumbled so goddamn deep inside me I felt the Earth split in two. Instead of apathy when other women have said it, I felt pure, undiluted elation. Like I was wide-awake, born again.

And I love her so goddamn much I am beyond reproach right now. If I wasn't, I would let her go. I would hurt her now to save her later. I would do what needs to be done behind the scenes to protect her, to secure her financial future and leave her the hell alone.

I should have done it earlier. I beat her back to the room and I heard her come in. I watched as she strode to the bedroom oblivious to my presence in the dark. I listened to her shower. I waited for her, the lies all prepared. *Thank you for your help, but I no longer need your services.* Sitting in the dark, I practiced them over and over until I thought I could say them without choking. I even briefly thought of inviting Noah back to our suite and into our bed, fucking bastard that I am.

But then she was there, her aura wholly surrounding me. She brought this unfettered peace and tranquility with her into the room without even trying. And it broke me. My misery leaked out. The lies evaporated. I don't even remember what I said when she dropped at my feet, looked up at me with those brilliant eyes of hers, and told me she loved me.

When she knowingly stopped me from telling her I was in love with her the other night, I was angry. Mostly I was hurt. But after today, I thought maybe it was fate. Maybe she was never meant to know how deep my feelings run or how I can't even stomach the thought of touching another woman again who isn't her. When she told me I was in, though, that was it. Game over. The idiotic thought I'd had of pushing her away vanished. She was officially mine.

But the fact still remains that professing our love only adds layers of complexity to this already convoluted mess and for once, I don't know what to do about it. I had hoped today would clear Annabelle, but…fuck. *Fuck.*

It didn't.

If Lia Melborne is to be believed, Annabelle was there. They were *all* there. Hell, they're all as guilty as Annabelle in my opinion, yet no one came forward or did a goddamn thing. But it was my baby sister who…

Shit. I run a hand through my hair, letting my mind drift to earlier when I slid into Willow without a single barrier between us—no latex or false pretense or those fucking blockades she throws.

"Where are you?" Willow asks quietly, sliding her tiny hands over my cheeks.

The tender move snaps me back to her and I realize I'm

hovering over her, lost inside this hell I've found myself submerged in. How will I live my life without her in it?

Unfathomable.

She's waiting for me with such yearning on her absurdly beautiful face, my cock rages. "I'm home," I spill truthfully, laying my cheek to hers. I gather her close, shove my face in her neck, and inhale her.

"Shaw," she breathes. "I love you."

Christ. Why do they call it falling in love when it feels like you've jumped out of a plane headfirst without a parachute? "Not possibly more than I love you, Willow." Not possible.

I needed her with a desperation that bordered on wild. So I shoved away the sickening news, lined up my length, and sank deep, slowly making love to her until we were sweaty and our lips hurt from kissing. I treated each second with her as if it were my last. I feared it might be.

We ordered in, ate naked in bed, talked and kissed and touched. We made love countless times. I did anything she asked. Every kinky thing she wanted. Sweet-talked her into a few of my own. It was the most glorious night I've spent with anyone.

The pads of my fingers trace up and down her arm lightly so as not to wake her. She's been asleep for hours, yet I'm lying here unable to close my eyes, wishing we could freeze ourselves into this place and time while the world goes on without us.

Sun spills around the curtains, its rays usually welcome. I love the sunrise. The dawning of a new day, new possibilities. But today I curse Mother Nature herself as unearthly panic thickens and multiplies. Tomorrow is almost here and with it brings a million questions I'm not ready to answer.

What the fuck am I going to do?

How am I going to get us all out of this mess unscathed?

Is that even a possibility?

Honestly, the answer is no. Every one of us loses here.

"Fuck, Annabelle. What have you done?" I mutter into the soundless room.

A knot forms in my throat. I can't go there yet. Not yet. Instead, I focus on Willow. I listen to her light breaths, drowning in the perfect sound of her serenity. I let the warmth of her body snuggled against mine burrow into me so far, I'll feel her for a lifetime. I memorize the feel of her fingers twitching against my chest and the unique scent of her I take in with each deep inhalation.

For the first time in my life, I feel heavy and vulnerable. The infamous Shaw Mercer is not invincible or impenetrable after all. The proof is sprawled on me, her hot pussy pressed tight to my leg, her knee tucked a little too close to my well-used cock. I actually tear up at the thought of not having this. Of not keeping her or waking up feeling as if I've finally found my place in life.

Pressing my lips to the crown of sex-and-sleep-mussed hair I leave them there. Wrapping my other arm around her, too, I find my eyelids too weighted to stay open.

Just a moment, I think. I'll rest them for only a moment because I can't waste a single second I have left with her in the haze of sleep.

I wake to pounding.

I pry open my eyes to find it fully light in the bedroom of our hotel. A glance at the digital clock on the stand to my right tells me it's after nine. Shit. I did more than close my eyes. I dropped into oblivion.

Thud thud thud.

The dull noise comes from the door to our suite and irritation sets in. I was positive I put out the Do Not Disturb sign last night to avoid this exact thing.

Carefully, I extricate myself from Willow, who is still sound asleep, and grab my dress pants from the floor beside the bed. I shove one leg in first, then the other. I do up the zipper but leave the button undone. The knocking resumes but I pause, gazing at the love of my life. So sweet and innocent when she has that harpy mouth of hers closed.

She didn't push me the rest of the night about my mood, but that's only temporary. She will, likely the second she opens her eyes. Then what? How will I divert her this time without outright lying? And that I just can't do. Lying will erode this fragile trust she's placed in me, and I won't do that no matter how tempting it may be.

With a sigh, I reluctantly leave her and make it to the door right as the loud noise resumes. I throw it open, not even bothering to check the peephole, sure it's housekeeping. I'm preparing to bite an innocent's head off when the face of my best friend appears in my vision.

"What the fuck? We aren't scheduled to leave until noon."

"This couldn't wait." He brushes past me, uninvited. Asshole.

I don't want to deal with Noah right now. I don't want to deal with what's waiting for me back in Seattle, either. I want to crawl back into bed beside Willow, peel back the sheet covering her, and tongue my way down her perfect curves until I reach her center. I want her to wake up panting, clawing at my hair, begging me to let her come. I don't want to leave and a big part of me wishes we never came here in the first place because at least then I could still be living behind a cloak of denial a little while longer.

Quietly shutting the door behind me, I follow Noah into the living room of my suite. "You could have called."

He gives me a look of pure annoyance. "I tried your cell a dozen times. You didn't answer. You think I wanted to get my ass out of bed this early?" Noah is an early riser. The only time he stays in bed past six is if he has a naked beauty twisted in his sheets. "I didn't."

I smirk. Yeah, I was right.

I spot my cell on the end table as I walk across the room but leave it. "Then why did you?" I ask sinking into the same armchair I was in last night where Willow told me she loved me.

Noah scans the room before he hands me a tablet. "Because you need to see this."

"What?" I grab the device and swipe so the screen comes to life, and in under a second, I wish I'd never answered the door. My eyes are drawn first to the grainy picture, and while it's not crisp, there is no mistaking what is going on in it. "What the fuck?"

I cut my eyes up to Noah's to see they are hard as steel. "I'm sorry." His tone is filled with repentance. The night this picture was taken flashes in clicks across my vision. I knew it. I *fucking* knew this would come back to bite me.

Swallowing the bile burning like the fires of hell up my throat, I drop my attention back to the short article that came out in this morning's *7-Day*. And the kick in the balls is that it's right below a picture of my father reading to a class of preschoolers. An intentional play, clearly.

Motherfuckers. I am seething with fury.

"Is monogamy overrated?" I spit, scanning the black letters that seemingly mock me. It takes me less than three minutes to finish the asinine exposé that's nothing but suppositions and lies. "What is this?" I toss the tablet to the sofa with disgust. "A goddamn witch-hunt?"

"Appears like it," Noah responds, voice gravelly.

The gist of the brief bullshit story is that I cheated on Willow. And the picture they somehow got their hands on is certainly incriminating.

It shows Gina, the lovely waitress that served Noah and me that night, with her eyes squeezed closed and unmistakable ecstasy lining her face. Her fingers are cinched in my shirt, conveniently covering her bare breast from the side shot. Noah's long fingers are wrapped around her hip and that's all you see of him.

But you can see me plain as day. And the worst part? My fingers are holding her chin still and my lips are touching hers in a tender kiss as she rode out her orgasm.

Fuck. Me.

I didn't participate in anything that night other than this simple, chaste kiss, but I might believe this drivel if I didn't know the truth.

Willow might believe it, too, because while the picture is real, everything else in the article is a lie. And, of course, that's likely the desired outcome, isn't it?

I have so many goddamn questions, but the only question that matters is, "Who is responsible for this?"

I want to find them and crush them. This will kill Willow, seeing me with another woman this way. Especially after what happened at the party the other night with Lianna. What we have is still fragile. It needs to be nurtured. It needs time to grow and root and this...*shit*. This could blow what we're building to bits if we let it and that's even before the devastation of the other news I'll have to eventually tell her.

Why does it seem as though the entire universe is working against us?

Noah plops onto the couch and throws an arm over the back. "There are a lot of candidates."

True.

Restless, I push myself to stand and start pacing. My mind immediately goes to Mergen. He knows this would gut me in the worst possible way but not only will it hurt Willow, it could possibly hurt my father's campaign. Would he do that to serve his own end game anyway? I wouldn't put it past the bastard.

Then there's Lianna. What's worse than a woman scorned? Not much, in my experience. But how would she get this? If she had been there that night, I would have seen her, right? It sure is convenient timing, to say the least.

And of course, let's not forget my father's competition. Hell, *anyone* could have taken this and sold it to the *7-Day* for a mint. It could have even been Gina herself setting us up, but why?

Fucking fuckety fuck. My father was worried something like this would happen from the beginning and I just gave Harrington live ammunition. I may as well have hand delivered the grenade with the pin pinched between my teeth.

Suddenly the screen on my cell lights up. I had set it to silent last night, unable to stomach the thought of talking to anyone after we left Annabelle's friend. Noah reaches over and picks it up, eyeing me from his seated position. "Your father."

Of course it is. I wonder how many times he's called already. I shake my head and he shrugs and sets it back down. "You're going to have to deal with him sometime, Merc."

I ignore Captain Obvious, going straight into problem-solving mode. The picture is out there. As much as I'd like to think differently, there's not a damn thing I can do about it now.

"We need to do damage control." The first step being, how am I going to break this to Willow? If I thought there was a way I could sweep it under the rug so she'd never find out, I would. I'm not that stupid, though. Mergen will be all over her like flies on shit hoping this breaks us and he can thieve her out from under me.

"Do damage control for what?" a soft voice that does *not* belong to Noah asks.

Of course.

"Uh-oh," Noah murmurs. I follow his gaze and stiffen when I see Willow and what she's wearing. Her golden hair is still mussed and she has this satisfied, sleepy look on her stunning face. A fluffy white robe, cinched at the waist, is wrapped around her small frame and I just know she's butt naked underneath.

My mind blanks.

"I thought you were asleep," is all I can think to say.

She smiles. It blows my mind the same as every other time. "I heard voices." Then she walks toward me. She saunters slow and sexy, but in my head, she may as well be stripping for me along the way. Her arm coils around my side when she reaches me and I release a pent-up sigh at having her plastered to my side. That lasts as long as it takes for her to ask again, "What damage control needs to be done?"

I look to Noah and simultaneously our eyes fall to the iPad.

Willow being Willow doesn't miss a thing. She steps out of my hold and tugs the lapels of her robe tight around her chin. It's not sexy in the slightest, that stupid robe, but because it's on her it's a work of art.

"What's wrong?" she demands in that vixen tone of hers that means she's gearing up for battle. Even her raised brows punctuate her seriousness. "And this time you're not going to get away with not answering me."

"I think maybe it's time for me to go," Noah announces, shooting to his feet.

"Chicken shit," I mumble under my breath. Though I don't blame him for wanting to hightail it out of here. I don't want to see the devastation and censure on Willow's face either.

Noah strides toward the door but diverts and stops right in front of Willow instead. He throws me a strange glance, almost as if asking silent permission first, before putting his hands on her shoulders.

The atmosphere, already tense, takes a header as Noah makes his blatant move, touching her like that in front of me...especially when I know a little flick of the fingers will part the two halves hiding her sleek perfection.

Willow straightens and tips her head toward me. She knows it's serious when she sees me making no move to break Noah's fingers. Her mouth presses into a thin line and the worry forming wrinkles in her forehead slays me. I want to soothe her and tell her everything will be okay, but I'm not sure it will be. And it's not only the picture. It's everything.

"Hey," Noah says softly, commanding Willow's attention back to him. "Don't believe a word of it."

"Of what?" She's quiet. Nervous.

Noah doesn't answer. He takes a few long looks at her before drawing her into his arms, and while the act bristles me all over, I understand what he's doing. It's his way of apologizing. But I don't blame him for that night or for the picture. I blame *me*. I should have stopped him the second he slid his hands under Gina's tiny skirt.

He dips down and whispers something in Willow's ear. Her eyes close. She squeezes him tighter. So does he. My hackles are starting to cramp when he releases her and is gone before I can throat punch him. Good move. My patience was wearing pretty thin.

Willow takes a deep breath and faces me. She fortifies her spine and winds her arms around her slim waist, all strong and ready. She's magnificent. Christ, how I love her.

"Tell me. I can take whatever it is."

I hope so. *I fucking hope so*, I want to tell her. *Because if you can't take this, we don't have a shot at surviving far worse shit that's patiently waiting for the right time to end us.*

With tension wrapped like a vise around every muscle, I pick up the tablet Noah left and hand it to her, simultaneously throwing a plea up to any divine being listening that she'll still look at me with love in her eyes two minutes from now instead of pure repulsion.

Willow

Chapter Sixteen

I'M SICK. LITERALLY, SICK TO my stomach. The fruit we ate late last night sits whole and undigested and threatens to rematerialize in a very ugly manner as I stare at what is obviously a sexual escapade meant to be private but was captured and put in print for the world to see and judge.

Like a masochist basking in the pain, I don't read the article. The intent of it is painfully clear. Instead, I study the nuances in the crude photo, wishing beyond all wishes I could simply put it down and erase it from my memory bank. But a masochist, by definition, derives some sort of sick gratification from being humiliated, so I keep gawking.

Shaw's eyes are open. They are lidded but heated and intense as he keenly watches the woman's reaction, his lips barely on hers. The woman—only her profile shown—is young and beautiful and obviously bent over a table in the throes of pleasure. She isn't naked, but the important parts are on display for her suitors. And while it's Shaw shown in the picture, with the five long male fingers wrapped around her bare hip there's no question who the third is in their public tryst.

Now Noah's cryptic, "It was before you," whispered shallowly in my ear makes a lot more sense.

The grave concern on both their faces was evident when I walked into the room. The sincerity of what I now understand was remorse in Noah's eyes spoke volumes to me. The fear I noted all over Shaw's posture when he handed me this hot potato was palpable. So I believe Noah and I'll believe Shaw when he tells me this didn't happen while he was with me, regardless of what this reporter probably said otherwise.

Yet still, every deep-seated insecurity I have about Shaw—about us—rears its ugly head once again. Without even thinking, the expensive piece of equipment in my hand falls to the carpet with a thump and I tear off to the bathroom, barely making it in time before the contents that's been churning for the last few minutes violently explodes out of my body.

"Jesus Christ," Shaw's voice, dark with concern, growls next to me. He winds my hair in his hand, holding it back from my face as I throw up twice more. I don't want him to see me like this, but I can't force myself to tell him to leave either.

"Are you okay?"

I wipe my mouth, my head now hanging limply over the toilet bowl. I'm sweating, utterly drained. I manage to reach up and flush my embarrassment away, asking hoarsely, "Can you bring me some water?"

Shaw hesitates. I can tell he doesn't want to leave me, but when I add, "Please," he scrambles away and returns within seconds with a glass half filled. I drink it all. On shaky legs, I walk to the vanity and brush my teeth until the taste of regurgitated strawberries is mostly gone. Disgusting. It will be a cold day in hell before I touch another strawberry.

Taking a few tentative sips, I fight with the cool water as it tries to find its way back from where it came. I lean over the sink and breathe slowly through the nausea, barely winning the battle, and wonder why I'm reacting so strongly to this when I already knew this about them.

"Jesus, Willow. You're scaring me here," Shaw says from

behind me. He's standing close, the pull of our bodies magnetic and undeniable, yet he doesn't make a move to touch me.

"I'm fine," I lie. I wasn't feeling the greatest when I woke but now I truly feel like shit warmed over.

"Do you still feel sick?"

"It's passing." It's not.

He steps into me now, palms landing tentatively on my shoulders. His touch is a calming balm I desperately crave and need right now, regardless of whether he's the one who caused my current state to begin with. I raise my head and catch his pained reflection in the mirror. He's filled with anxiety and somehow it makes me feel a touch better.

"You look pale."

I try to muster a smile. "I'll be okay."

The gut-wrenching feeling of actually seeing *your lips on another woman you shared with Noah will fade. Eventually. Maybe. I hope.*

His mouth tries to curl up but, like mine, falls flat.

"I'm sorry." He's sincere and contrite. A man who fears he has everything to lose.

I wet my lips while my stomach churns. I'm riding the world's largest emotional roller coaster and I want off the mother.

"I know," I eventually say back. I don't know what else to offer. *It's okay* would be a lie. It's *not* okay.

His eyes fall shut slowly. When they open after what seems like forever, that trademark determination I fell in love with is firing on all cylinders, but it rubs my already raw nerves bloody when he states vehemently, "None of it is true, Willow."

Oh really? I can think of *one* goddamn thing that was true.

The burn of hurt and humiliation still sits square and flat on my heart, squashing the nausea I've been fighting. "None if it?" I spin and face him, gripping the counter behind me. My legs wobble like wet noodles. "So the picture was a lie, too?"

He has the decency to look ashamed. Good. He should be.

"That's the only thing that isn't," he confesses on a wafty

breath of remorse. "It was before we started dating. Please believe that."

Dating.

Laughable. What a lie we are.

I'm shaking. God, this hurts. Bad.

"Willow—"

I talk over him. "When?"

His brows pull together briefly. "When what?"

I'm sure he thinks I'm asking him about the girl, but I don't give two craps about her. It's not his honor I'm questioning. It's his proclivities. I know he said he loves me, but insecurities are a cruel bitch that sometimes becomes impossible to wrangle, and if Voodoo Eyes is to be believed, he's shared every woman before me. So why *not* me?

"When do you start sharing *me* with Noah?"

His hands snap to my face in a fury. I'm held tight in his iron grip as eyes that are now hot as melted steel bore into me the same way his calloused voice does. "I would never share you with him. Never."

My thoughts stray to that stupid dream where Shaw *wanted* to share me. I know it was my overactive imagination, not real life, but that uneasy feeling it left inside me has been stirred up again.

"Why? What makes me so different from her?" Now I *am* referencing the woman in the picture because God. Damn. I *do* give two craps. I give dozens of craps. My jealousy is a raging fire, singeing every brain cell I have.

He squeezes and shakes me a little. "Are you fucking kidding me, Willow?" When he sees I'm not, his entire demeanor tones down. "Everything. Every single thing about you is different, Willow."

"That's lame." I blink, fully aware I am fishing for compliments just as he likes to do, but I need that selfish soothing right now. My ego is shattered. Publicly, I might add. I deserve more than generic platitudes.

His eyes search mine forever as if he's running through the

right words to say. I love it when he takes his time instead of blurting out the first thing that comes to mind.

"You want to know what makes you different?"

"Yes." I'm breathy, hanging on his every word.

Shaw clamps my chin between his thumb and the knuckle of his forefinger, tips my head just right, and places his lips on mine. His eyes stay wide open the whole time his mouth barely touches mine. It's soft and purposefully demonstrative.

Just like the picture.

"You already know what makes you different, Goldilocks, but since you need the words, you'll get them all."

Slowly he turns me around until I face the mirror once again. He tugs on my robe until it hangs off both shoulders and reaches around to pull my long hair behind me, out of his way. His eyes hook mine and I'm stuck in his gravitational pull until he decides to cut me loose.

He places his mouth at my ear and starts, "In them, I saw no depth. In you, I see a complex mystery that will take me a lifetime to solve."

He kisses me on the neck and I shiver, barely suppressing a moan.

"In them, I saw bland clichés. But you—" He shakes his head. "You, Willow, are a fascinating woman who has an unquenchable thirst for life but needs the freedom to live it."

His hands come to the knot on my robe, his nimble fingers working it slowly as he continues, "In them, I saw a means to an end. In you, I only see the beginning. Even when I was with them, they were already the past, but since the first time I sat across from you at Randi's, I couldn't stop envisioning the future, and in it, all I saw was that smart mouth of yours that keeps me on my toes."

With the belt now undone, the two halves covering me are open, exposing a one-inch slip of flesh down my middle. His chest expands, pressing into me with his long inhale. Leaving aches in his wake, he lazily grazes a finger from my collarbone downward while he keeps talking.

"In them, I could lose myself for a short time, but in you, Willow Blackwell, I'm not lost at all. In you, I have finally found my reason for existing. You epitomize graceful strength and quiet courage. You are different because I'm in love with every last piece of you. The scared, the scarred, and the *sacred*. I think I love those the most, the sacred parts you haven't shared yet because I know when you eventually do they will mean even more to me than the extraordinary gift of your name."

With reverence, he peels the fluffy garment from my body and lets it fall to the floor, leaving me bare and exposed, craving his next touch, his next word.

"In them, I saw absolutely nothing." My nipples bead when he runs my lobe through his teeth and breathes, "But in you, Willow, I see a blank page I want to fill with color and memories, light and laughter. I want to pack page after page with the story of our life, and I've never wanted that before."

My eyes well up and goose bumps blanket me. Shaw Mercer weakens every part of me but strengthens me in equal measure.

He pauses and quirks his lips. "I could keep going if you want."

"I'm—" Speechless. Reduced to a blubbery mess. I expected him to talk about my eyes or my breasts or maybe even our explosive sex, but instead, he cast the net deep and wide. He went where I needed him to go. I swiftly get rid of a couple of tears leaking from the corners of my eyes. "No. That was pretty good."

Shaw chuckles before nibbling along my shoulder now. "I would see him six feet under before he laid a finger on your soft skin." Two pads now set lightly over my carotid. "Or felt your pulse as it speeds up like this." He runs his thumb along my jaw. "Or heard that broken pant you make right before you let go."

His other hand slips between my belly and the granite, then between my wet folds. Spreading my arousal around before driving two fingers inside, he clamps his teeth to the curve of my jaw and growls, "He'll never feel the walls of this hot little cunt squeeze the life from his dick. I promise you that."

I whimper when he backs away, but when I see him practically ripping his pants from his body, I tell him to hurry. He does and with a gruff command to brace my hands in front of me—which I do—he cocks my hips back and drives all the way home.

"He doesn't get this pleasure, Willow. This fucking gift you give me every time you let me inside your body."

He presses a thumb under my jaw and forces my attention back to the sight we make in the mirror. My boobs bounce. My skin flushes. My fingers curl, nails scraping the slick surface as I try, but fail, to find purchase, an anchor against his merciless assault. I've never felt so base or so damn needy in my life.

"He'll never taste the salty flush of your skin or treasure the candied flavor of your orgasms."

Strumming my clit, he drives me higher. Works me harder. He's relentless in his quest to show me his truth.

"God, Shaw," I pant. I push back against him needing more, wanting it all, trying to get him deeper.

"No man will have that right again besides me, beautiful. Not Noah. Not Mergen. No one."

His artistry is gone. He's pure power. Raw grit. He pounds into me like a man possessed. And when he takes my fleshy nub between his fingers and pinches to punctuate his point, I ignite. I break apart, spiraling under his skill and devotion. I float endlessly in my own paradise of bliss and satisfaction and barely register his teeth holding fast to my neck or his fingers bruising my hips as he growls long and broken. Holding himself still for only a couple of beats, he moves furiously against me again to drag out his own pleasure.

"I am so sorry for hurting you, Willow. If I could take it back, I would in a heartbeat. I see nothing before you. Please believe that."

He tells me this quietly after we've both caught our breath. His lingering remorse hangs thickly between us, even with what we just shared. He hasn't moved an inch, made a move to withdraw or clean up or leave me in any fashion. His face remains buried in my neck, and he's mostly hard, pulsing every few seconds with the aftereffects of his climax.

He's asking for forgiveness, but is there honestly anything to forgive? We both had lives before the other and though having his former conquests shoved in my face is bound to sting, won't mine feel the same to him when I tell him about Reid? In fact, in many ways it may sting worse because there were real feelings involved between us and if Shaw had had feelings for this woman, that would have cut me to the quick even deeper than his physical display of dominance did.

I reach around his head to hold him to me. To reassure him. His relief encases me like his arms do when I say, "I believe you."

I have no choice but to believe him. I'm in this far too deep now and let's be honest, I was in too deep the moment I gave him my real name.

Shaw

Chapter Seventeen

"WHAT IN THE NAME OF Jesus Christ Himself were you thinking?" Preston Mercer's voice booms loud enough to rattle a nearby lamp.

My father is standing in front of me, face beet red, shaking a copy of Sunday's *7-Day* at me the same way he did when I brought home a C– in Algebra the first quarter of eighth grade. Though I refused to admit it, I was more fixated on the way Penny Wilmer's lips silently moved when she worked her math problems than the lessons Mrs. Gremer was trying to teach.

The following Monday I asked to be moved to the opposite side of the room from Penny Wilmer and I brought my grade up to an A the next three-quarters straight. I fixed that. I'll fix this, too, though it's far more complicated than putting a few desks between me and a pretty redhead who got me hard by biting her lip.

"Do you know what your careless actions have caused?" He doesn't even wait for my response. "A shit show, Shaw, that's what. A goddamn fucking shit show!"

Oh boy. Profanities galore. My father is upset. I get it. I

deserve it even, and I'll take his wrath like a man. I fucked up. I'll own it exactly the way I did in the eighth grade.

"I'm taking care of it," I announce evenly.

"Taking care of it? And how are you taking care of it, exactly?"

The *7-Day* is a political outlet but they have bordered on more of a gossip rag the last year and their credibility is starting to come into question. A fact I'm particularly pleased that John Whelan, the president of Lock Media, agreed with me on during our brief conversation yesterday.

I wasn't too surprised he took my call. Seemed that little stunt the *7-Day* pulled made it all the way to his desk before I did. He agreed they would print not only a retraction but an apology and assured me the reporter responsible would be fired. Then he assured me heads would roll if they slandered one of the most prominent businessmen in Seattle again. And when he extended that courtesy to my siblings I told him I wouldn't pursue legal action.

"I have it under control, Dad."

I lean back on the couch and place my left ankle on my right knee. My arm hangs loosely over the back and my fingers tap against the soft fabric, masking the sheer rage boiling in my veins at this second. And this time, it's not because my father is treating me like I'm a prepubescent who got a bad mark that may soil my chances at an Ivy League education.

No...it's because Reid "fuckface" Mergen is sitting a little too comfortably to my right. Slightly out of choking distance. Enjoying my verbal lashing if I had to guess.

I haven't talked to my father since the incident broke two days ago. I've had more important things to deal with, such as repairing the damage some dumbfuck did and keeping Willow close and out of her own head. And away from Mergen. But Noah was right. I had to face him sooner or later and since I knew this could get ugly, I insisted I meet him at his house instead of his office.

Now I'm not so sure that was a good idea.

"You had a minor dip in the polls. You'll be back up by the end of the week," I say easily.

"That's not even the issue." It is. "Do you know how your mother reacted when she saw this trash?" I wince a little at that one. My parents don't want to picture me having sex any more than I do them. "How the hell did this happen?" Still yelling. Still shaking that damn paper.

Sliding my gaze over to my father's campaign manager, I address him when answering, because honestly? This is the basic question I've had for days now. "I don't know," I sneer. "Why don't you ask campaign boy over here. Isn't it *his* job to keep this shit from the press in the first place?"

Mergen's eyes glaze over in a flurry of black hate. If he grinds his molars together any harder, I'm sure he'll break a tooth. I pray for pain. "My *job*"—he punches—"would be a helluva lot easier if you'd keep your fucking dick in your pants."

"Where I put my dick is none of your business," I toss back nonchalantly. "Keeping it out of the papers is." Besides, my dick is not in question here. It was nowhere near the waitress. Except for that brief second she palmed me over my jeans, which I barely remember.

He leans forward. It's meant to be threatening and I want to castrate him on the spot. I'm plotting where I can find the dullest kitchen knife when he slams me front and center, no contact necessary. "And what about Willow? Is where you put your dick *her* business or are you plotting so far ahead you've already forgotten she's the woman you're *supposedly* in love with?"

This fucker's nuts are mine. They'll be hanging in my trophy case by sundown. I shoot up at the same time he does, and the only thing that stops me from throwing a punch is the fact my father has stepped in between us as a buffer.

"You won't do this in my home. Sit down. Both of you."

My father is about my size, about my weight, but with a twenty-seven-year difference between us, moving him out of the way so I could take down this prick on the other side wouldn't be a hard task. I think about it. For a blistering second, it's all consuming. Mergen would be on the ground bleeding before he could do a damn thing to stop me.

It's tempting. So damn tempting. But I'd have to listen to my mother's reprimand for the next year and this piece of shit isn't worth it. Instead, I stab my finger in the direction of his chest. "You say her name again, I won't think twice about laying you flat."

His smug smirk fires up the intense hatred I have for him and all he's trying to do to my family. And my father is clueless.

"You don't deserve her," Mergen says with fiery heat.

"God help me," my father mutters. He walks over to pick up the drink he abandoned earlier so he could berate me.

"You're right. I don't," I surprise him by answering. I am so over my skis with Willow it isn't even funny. But by some divine miracle, and despite all of my shortcomings, she loves me and I'll take it. "You sure you didn't have your sticky fingers in this little debacle? It seems awfully coincidental given the fact you've made it clear you want her back."

Mergen doesn't say a thing. He doesn't breathe. He doesn't even blink. A weighty silence falls over the room. I gaze at my father who is now staring at Mergen, an unreadable expression on his face. It's as if he's finally seeing the real snake in the grass for the first time in weeks. About fucking time.

"Is this true?" he asks him.

For the first time since I walked in, Mergen looks uncomfortable. My father likes Willow. He likes us together and though he knows as well as I do there is history between the two, I'm betting he's as much in the dark about the details as I am. If he thinks his campaign manager has nefarious intentions toward his son's girlfriend, which in turn may hurt his campaign, maybe Mergen will write his own ticket out of town. One can only hope. For all our sakes, that's the best possible outcome.

"No," he answers my father, not daring to look my way.

"No?" My incredulous rebuttal morphs into a harsh laugh. I

cross my arms and widen my stance, then go in for the kill. "So, when you told me over our little chat recently, quote unquote, 'I'm the one she'll marry, the one she was always meant to marry,' you were just what? Trying to goad me? Get under my skin? Be a fucking prick? Is that it?"

His chest expands slowly. I note his fingers have curled in slightly and his jaw muscles tick with fury. I let my lips turn up into a cocky grin.

"I haven't asked you this before because quite frankly I don't think it's any of my business, but what exactly is the nature of your relationship with my son's girlfriend." My father punctuates the last word nicely.

Boom. Go Dad.

Mergen's eyes cut from me to my father, who is now standing straight and tall. Waiting. My father doesn't like to be kept waiting.

"Preston—"

He interrupts, "I don't have time for bullshit, Reid. I'd like a straight answer if you please." He pauses only briefly. "You were more than cast mates, I take?"

Silence.

So much silence it's suffocating me from the top down.

Maybe he sensed the subtle step I took toward him or maybe it was my father's shaggy gray-tipped brows that are now touching his receding hairline. Either way, at last he reluctantly answers, "Yes."

My gut clenches. Hard. *You already knew this, Merc. Man up.*

"And?" my father prods gently. It seems counterintuitive, but that's the innate politician in him. Getting anyone to talk about anything. He makes them actually *think* they want to get things off their chest that are weighing them down. It's a gift I wish I had inherited. It would come in handy with Willow, that's for sure.

Mergen turns back to me, and when I think about this night for months and years to come, I'll remember every frame of it with sick accuracy.

I won't forget the dark pit in my stomach I thought would swallow me whole. Or the hateful thoughts clouding my mind as he spoke the truth with conviction. The piercing in my chest is akin to a swift, serrated knife being driven in farther with each syllable from that one fucking word...

"I was her fiancé."

Fiancé.

And all that shit swirling inside me was bad enough, wasn't it? What could be worse than standing face-to-face with the man who had my woman's life entwined in his before I did?

I didn't think it possible, yet there was one thing.

What would stick with me most wasn't how *I* felt, but how *he* did. The obvious anguish present in his voice, visible on his now sober face said it all. Once upon a time, he had someone so precious, beyond extraordinary, and she slipped through his fingers. He wanted her back with such desperation he would do anything. *Any. Thing* regardless of morality, but everything he did was an effort in futility because she didn't reciprocate his feelings any longer. She belonged to someone else now.

It was a foreign feeling. One I hoped to hell I would never experience.

But with the twisted trajectories our lives unknowingly took years before we met, with those poisonous secrets I now hold from Willow my worst fear is I will end up exactly like Reid Mergen once she finds out.

Alone and pining away for the woman I will love until I die.

Willow

Chapter Eighteen

"HI, MOMMA." I KISS HER on the cheek and visually examine her. Millie has a bunch of errands to run so this afternoon it's just me and my momma. Times I both relish and dread with equal measure. "You look good today."

"Hi," my mother replies tentatively, staring at me like a stranger.

It makes me sad. I miss her so much. I miss how she used to sing me to sleep and tried hopelessly to teach me to sew. I miss being able to talk to her about anything and everything. And after these past few days with Shaw, I need my mother more than ever. I need a nonjudgmental ear to bend. Someone to be happy for me. Someone to simply listen, a skill Sierra is incapable of. And my friend, Jo, would just as soon scold me if I told her I went and fell in love with a client than go with me to pick out a bridesmaid dress.

Patting her on the arm, which is cool to the touch, I grab the water glass by her recliner and head to the kitchen to refill it.

"How are you feeling?" I ask, setting the drink on the table beside her before sliding onto the couch.

"Fine, I think." She pauses, contemplating. "Yes, I feel fine."

"You seem cold. Do you want a blanket?"

Sparse brows twist in as she thinks. "Yes, I suppose that would be nice."

I hop up and grab one from the wicker basket sitting by the bay windows and settle it around her legs. "Feel good?"

She nods. I don't think she's sure but I'm glad she's playing along.

"Can I get you anything to eat?"

"No, thank you," she answers politely.

"Do you want to watch *Jeopardy*?"

"Oh, yes. That would be lovely." I smile at the excitement in her voice. The one thing that hasn't changed in all this time is how much she loves *Jeopardy*. Grabbing the remote, I flip on the TV and settle in for a marathon of the world's toughest trivial pursuit game. She even surprises me a few times by getting the answers right.

Alzheimer's is a confusing disease. Useless random facts can be recalled on a dime, but the faces of your loved ones often remain elusive.

About an hour in, I'm nearly stunned silent when she looks over at me and says completely out of the blue, "I miss your father."

My eyes water. Hers do, too. I don't know if she thinks she's talking to me or to Violet, but if she's having a moment of lucidity, I choose to believe it's me. "So do I." That was hard to get out.

"What happened?"

"To Daddy?" I ask, my voice shaky. As sad as it is to say, most of the time I'm glad she doesn't remember losing her husband of thirty-two years because when she remembers, I can tell the wound is as fresh as the day it happened. Though the steps I'm wading through feel like sludge sometimes, at least I can try to move forward. She's just stuck in some sick time warp where she's constantly treading water.

She nods slowly, confusion furrowing her forehead. "I...I know he's gone, but..."

"It's okay." I reach over and take her hand, stopping her before she becomes agitated. "He…" Jesus, this is hard. I swear if I look over at the stairs right now he'll be lumbering down them, his hair all disheveled from spending hours raking through research. "He got into a car accident," I lie.

She will never know the truth about what happened that night. It will absolutely kill her like it does me.

She presses her lips together, and her gaze falls to her lap. She's quiet for such a long time I'm sure she's slipped away from me again, but then she asks the same question she always asks when we talk about him in the present tense. "Was anyone else hurt?"

She wants details. I don't have them.

She wants answers. I don't have those either.

The ever-present guilt I'm married to rears her ugly head. Are we both living without my father because I was too caught up in my own life and missed something? I can't bear the answer.

"No. No one else was hurt."

Her lip quivers. "I get scared sometimes. I forget things. Why can't I remember? I don't understand what's happening to me."

I don't understand either.

I slide from the couch and kneel in front of her, my heart clogging my throat. I take her hands in mine and give her all my strength. "I know, but I'm here. I'll *always* be here for you, Momma. I promise. I love you." *I'll never leave you like Daddy did.*

Her trembling lips turn up. She strokes my cheek, pinching it at the fullest part like she always used to do when I was little. Then she blinks, drops her hand, and I watch our precious moments together evaporate. She studies me blankly for several beats and turns her attention back to the TV. I head to the bathroom and take the next few minutes to pull myself together before spending the rest of the afternoon bingeing on *Jeopardy* while she naps.

Later that evening, I'm back home cooking dinner when

Sierra makes an appearance. No doubt the smell of food drew her out of her cave. I swear she'd starve if it weren't for me. I'm not sure how she survived those few months I lived with Reid.

"How's the hot toddy?" she jibes. Picking up a stack of pancakes with her fingers, she drops them onto an extra plate I already set out. *Don't like breakfast for dinner? Uh-huh, right.*

It's been almost a week since I've last seen my roommate. I've been spending more and more time at Shaw's, but tonight he's visiting with his dad. He asked me to wait for him in his bed and while it was more than tempting, for some odd reason I wanted the comfort of my own house. And my friend.

"He's fine." I hand her the syrup, which she generously pours and I wait with bated breath. Sierra's not much of a paper reader and I'm not about to bring up the article in the *7-Day* if she doesn't. I'm still trying to mentally bleach the lingering vision from behind my eyeballs. The last thing I want to do is talk about it.

"Really?" Her eyes find mine. They challenge.

Dammit, she knows.

"Really." I shut my mouth. Try to keep cool.

"Hmmm." She licks the stickiness from her fingers, and I wait for it. Unapologetic Sierra. "So…how was your trip?"

I watch her cut a perfect triangle through her pancakes and stab them with her fork. She swipes them in the syrup spreading on her plate before bringing her fork to her mouth and her gaze back to mine.

Well, let's see: I had a hedonistic dream about a threesome with Noah and Shaw. Later there were professions of love (minus Noah), damning pictures made public (including Noah), and a life-altering connection against the bathroom vanity where Shaw made it perfectly clear there would be no Noah. So, yeah…it was weird and exciting then devastating all in a span of twenty-four hours.

"Uh…it was fine."

She observes me while she finishes chewing a huge bite. "Fine?"

"Yeah. Fine." I shrug, going for nonchalant. The mound of pancakes in front of me is enough to feed an army. I flip off the griddle. I may have gotten carried away.

"Lots of fines," she says impassively.

I laugh, setting the large bowl still filled with batter in the sink and turning on the water. "Yeah. Lots."

"Mmm."

This is so not over. Not by a long shot. I give her five seconds, tops.

Five.

Four.

Three.

Tw—

"So, that picture of your boy toy and his slutty friend doing the blonde didn't bother you then?"

"Jesus Christ, Sierra," I scold. That barb she threw jabs and wounds me deep.

"What?" She shrugs. She can be utterly clueless sometimes.

"What? That was a little harsh, don't you think?"

"You know, I told myself this morning I was turning over a new leaf. That I was going to test run this 'filter' thing that everyone is so goddamn convinced makes this world a better fucking place because God forbid we hurt someone's feelings by saying what we're really thinking even if it's the truth."

"Well, I think you need to try a little harder."

She smashes her bee-stung lips, the color of them like ripe strawberries even without any tint. She stands and dumps her half-eaten contents in the garbage, then puts her plate in the dishwasher. "Back to your hot coffee and the bimbo in the pic."

"Stop," I tell her firmly as she takes her next breath. "It's not what you think, Sierra."

"Not what I think? He was with another woman when he was supposedly with you."

He wasn't, though.

I finally made myself read the article earlier today when my mother was napping. It basically insinuated that Shaw had been caught cheating on his "girlfriend" with a waitress from an exclusive club. True, the date time-stamped on the picture was mere days after he rear-ended me, but it was before we started "officially dating," only that's not how the reporter portrayed it because that's not what we told her when she interviewed us last month.

We essentially dug our own hole with the lies we've spun, and while I'm not happy with the whole situation, my guess is this reporter thought she was doing me a weird sort of favor since she thinks Shaw cheated.

"That's not how it was, Sierra. It was all lies."

"Says who? Him?"

Irritation crawls on me like bedbugs. "Says me," I pipe back, irritated. "It was before we started seeing each other."

She snorts. "He's *paying* you to be his girlfriend, Low."

But everything has changed, I want to scream. We love each other. I'm a blank page he wants to write our life on. But none of that will matter to Sierra. She sees what she wants and she's stubborn as hell about it.

"Nothing happened with that woman while we were together."

We stand on opposite sides, a chipped counter between us. She crosses her arms over her ample chest, her protective stance almost comical. Her unerring love for me shines as bright as a diamond. Her approach is harsh and direct but her friendship is limitless.

"But it's happened with plenty others, I bet. This is the reason he had to hire you in the first place. Am I right?"

Bull's-eye.

I feel sick. "It's different now."

"Is it?" she challenges, head cocked.

"Yes." I pick up the remaining pancakes and place them in a Ziploc bag, my appetite ruined.

"Willow." She sighs. "I'm not trying to be a negative Nancy here. I'm just worried about you. I'm worried he'll hurt you."

I set down the bag with a huff. My heart's pounding. I'm

angry with her and where this conversation has gone. Her concern is valid, but the more I think about it, the more I'm convinced she has the shoe on the wrong foot.

It's *me* who could hurt *Shaw* and it's not that I don't love him. I do, with everything in me. But I'm still holding critical pieces of myself back. I said he was in, but…*is he*? Really? Am I keeping certain parts to myself because I'm unconsciously preparing for the worst and when that happens, at least I won't have handed over *everything* I am? Is that why I haven't told Shaw about Violet or the fact I was engaged? Have I conditioned myself to be so emotionally secluded I'm completely incapable of a real relationship and don't realize it?

What we have is unconventional and beyond complicated, but regardless of his past womanizing or trysts with Noah or the fact he hasn't loved another woman before me, I don't think he'll be the one to hurt me. I think *I'll* be the one to hurt *him*.

I sit down on a stool, all the fight leaving me. She slides next to me, and I stare ahead silently while she stares at me.

"What if it's the other way around, Ser? What if I hurt him the way I did Reid?" I ask, turning my head her way.

"So it's too late then, huh?"

I laugh, sort of. "That train has left the station." I unzip the plastic bag and zip it back up again. "What if I can't love him the way he deserves?" There. I said it. My deepest, darkest, biggest fear caught wind.

"You have a big heart, Low. I don't think that's the problem."

"No. I have a guarded heart, Sierra. *That's* the problem."

Her head moves back and forth. I don't even think she realizes she's doing it. "God, woman. You have the biggest heart of anyone I know, and I don't want to watch you sink back down into that pit of despair again. You're finally happy and content."

And apparently I am an even better actor than I realized. I've fooled the one person who's known me since I was eight. The one person who knows me better than anyone else in the world.

I am not happy.

I am not content.

I am lonely. And reserved. And worst of all, I'm a giant poseur who has everyone snowed. Except for Shaw. He didn't fall for my act for a minute. He challenged me on this very fact after our first date when I told him I'd managed quite well without him my entire life. He always saw my lies for what they were.

"That's the thing, though, Sierra. I never crawled out of that pit until Shaw gave me his hand. And now that I have it, I'm not sure I know how to hold on to it."

Blowing out a long, stoic breath, she gauges me. "Know what I think?"

The edges of my mouth lift. "I think I can't stop you from telling me."

She barks a short laugh. "You know me so well. It's simple, really. If you love him and you think this has a real shot at working, hang on to that hand like your life depends on it. Just don't let go. Not for any reason."

If only it were that easy.

Maybe it is. What would I know?

"I haven't told him about Violet yet. Hell, I haven't even told him how serious Reid and I were. Every time I go to do it the words kind of get stuck."

Sierra lays her hand over the top of mine, squeezing. "It's a gritty process to lay yourself open, Low, even if that's what you want."

It is.

"It's terrifying," I agree.

"It doesn't have to be all at once, babe. If he's the right one, he'll wait as long as you need. One step at a time."

"It's uncomfortable."

"Trying new things usually is," she says as the doorbell rings.

We exchange knowing looks. My belly flutters. The only person ringing our doorbell this late would be—"Your boyfriend's here," she singsongs sarcastically.

Pushing herself up, she pulls me in for a quick hug. "If you're happy, I'm happy. Sincerely. I know I'm a mother hen and cynical, but—"

"I get it. I do," I interrupt. "If someone tries to fuck with you I am the same way. I appreciate it, but I need you to cut him some slack." The bell chimes again, this time twice. "I love him, Sierra."

Her reply is slow and resigned and maybe a little sad. "I know." With a kiss to my cheek, she takes the stairs up to her room, two by two, leaving me to let in our impatient visitor.

I cross our small living room in a few strides. My hair is a mess and I'm wearing lounge clothes. I didn't expect to see Shaw tonight, but I don't care how I look and I doubt he will either.

Excitement replaces anxiety with every step I take. A smile splits my face by the time I turn the knob, only it falls flat the second my gaze lands on him.

"What's wrong," I ask, opening the door wider to let him enter.

But he doesn't. He stands there looking all twisted up, his face a mixture of shock and...*hurt*? No. It's not hurt. That's too mild. It's devastation, and it's a mirror of the other night.

"Shaw?" I reach for him. Fear pinches my chest when he flinches away and utters four words no woman wants to hear from the man she loves.

"We need to talk."

Shaw

Chapter Nineteen

JESUS, SHE IS BEYOND BEAUTIFUL. So breathtaking it makes my heart weak.

I watch the smile fade from her lips and feel like a piece of shit for making that happen when all I want to do is put it there.

I'm upset. Fine, I'll admit it. I realize she is not an open book and I accept that about her. Or I thought I did until tonight. The part of me that uses reason and logic in my daily business ventures knows I have no right to be a gnarled mess of emotions because she was practically married and didn't tell me. But the possessive man in me who is in love with her *is*.

It would have been a blow to hear it from her lips but the reality is this news should have come from her, not him, and tonight I need more from her than I ever have before. I need her to strip herself to the bone. I need her raw and real and more open than she's ever been. I need it all and I fucking *need* it like air.

You can't beat your enemy if you don't know your enemy and all I know is his weakness, but that's not enough. His weakness is *my* weakness, too.

She reaches for me, but before I can think better of it I draw back.

"We need to talk." Fuck, that felt like acid crawling up my throat.

I brush past her. It shreds me up inside not to take her into my arms and kiss her senseless or quell the worry I now see in her eyes. I take a seat on the couch, my jacket still on. She stands by the open door, considering me for long seconds.

Wordlessly she shuts it and slowly walks my way. She eases into an armchair right across from me, sitting on the edge, silent, as if she's waiting for a bomb to drop.

I have a bomb, all right. But I'm not ready to drop it quite yet.

"Tell me about Mergen." It's a rough command. Leading but chock-full of knowledge she'd be a fool to miss.

She begins twisting her fingers but never looks away from me. Point to her. But I swear by all that's holy if she starts beating around the bush, I am going to fucking lose it. And I'll be taking it out well and good on her hide.

"Well," she starts—sassily I might add—"by the look on your face, I'd say you already know the answer to your question."

And a fool she is not.

"Don't fucking play with me, Willow. I am standing on razor's edge right now."

She drops her head, eyes going to the floor. Her chest expands deeply before she stands and paces to the opposite side of the room. She looks out a small window that faces the front yard, that sexy nose ring of hers winking at me from the rays off the streetlight.

Oh, how I want to march over there and drag her back over my knee, spanking her ass until she spills every goddamn truth she buries inside. But I do that...she shuts down. She has to do this on her own. It's an excruciating process to watch and even more so to be on the receiving end of. And I can't even say I get it, why she's like this. I simply have to accept it if I want to be with her. Which I do.

"Nothing I've told you has been untrue," she says softly.

I bite my tongue hard enough to draw blood. I'm trying to keep from spewing caustic words, but...

"Except for the fiancé part. You conveniently left that out."

Okay, so I am being a giant fucking bastard, but no one can rile me like she can. No one. She causes every emotion I have to be intensified by a thousand.

At my snarky comment, she twists her head my way, not even bothering to turn her whole body. I expect her eyes to be alight with fury and that signature fire embedded in her DNA but the only thing they're full of is sadness.

I'm crushed all over again. My hand goes up to my chest. God, it aches.

"Yes, Reid was my fiancé and yes, I probably should have told you when he showed up out of the blue at your father's house." She faces me fully now. "But in all fairness, Shaw, up until this past weekend, I didn't even know what you and I really were. Our contract ends in a little over a month now and I just..."

Ah. Her mistrust in us rears its ass-ugly head yet again. I wonder if I'll go to my grave fighting for every single scrap of her. I have her body, I know I have her heart and soul, but the one thing I want most I don't even deserve right now.

Her trust.

I'm sitting here accusing her of being dishonest when I have done the same damn thing. I kept the real reason I hired her in the first place a secret, and I'm doing the same thing with this devastating news about Annabelle and her father.

Yeah. I suck. I know it.

Yet that doesn't stop me from claiming her, here and now. She is mine. It's barbaric and primitive and wrong on so many levels, but at the moment, I don't give a million flying fucks.

"We will never end, you and I. Never. That piece of shitty paper doesn't hold any power over us and honestly, I'm not sure it ever has. You've had that from day one, Goldilocks. Day one." What I don't tell her because she'll balk is that contract is already gone. Destroyed. I'm taking care of her. Of everything she and her mother need. Money will never be an issue for her again whether she ends up wanting me or not.

Her lips slip up. It's brief before somberness returns, but I watch her muscles visibly ease in relief.

Satisfied we've resolved that issue, my eyes travel over her lush curves for the first time since she let me in. She's wearing a pair of crazy multipatterned leggings and a loose-fitting gray top that slides down one shoulder. Her feet are bare, still painted that blinding pink from the other day. She's casual, yet chic. She looks like royalty.

My slow trek back up her body ends at her face. My breathing slows. We hold each other's eyes, tied together with this invisible string neither of us will be able to sever. I *have* to believe that. I'm aching with the need to pull her onto my lap and cup her face in my hands. I want to eat her up. I want to kiss her and love her until she curls into me, warm and sated. I'm not sure I've been in her presence this long without touching her in...ever.

I hate it.

She runs her tongue nervously over her teeth before coming to sit back across from me. She inhales deep, then starts.

"We met during a play we were both in." That, I knew. "He asked me out a dozen times before I finally said yes." Stubborn. Sounds familiar. "We dated a little over two years before he asked me to marry him." Not feeling any better here. "It wasn't love at first sight like with..."

She stops cold, throwing her glance to the floor nervously. Those fingers she rubs together when she's nervous are going fast and furious. When her cheeks pink up, despite having to endure this horror story, I smile. I want to hear what she was about to confess. I should let it go...

"Like with who?" I prod her to finish. Like with *me?* Is it egotistical to think I would be the one she'd fall head over heels in love with on sight? Yes. Do I care? Not one fucking bit.

She cocks her head and throws me a brilliant, glowing grin. "Been awhile since you've gone fishing, hasn't it, Drive By?"

I laugh. Under the circumstances, nothing is laughworthy, except when I'm with her. Always her.

"Anyway," she goes on, skirting around my expedition, "do you want me to continue?"

My teeth snap together. Want? Hell no. I want her to tell me that when she stood outside my Rover and haughtily dumped pieces of her fender in my lap, she fell in love with me instantly. Because when I look back, I know that moment was it for me.

"Go on," I growl instead.

Her lips curve and flatten back out again. "I knew he was going to do it. He had been acting all weird and nervous. He took my father out for coffee since my father didn't drink alcohol and I knew it was to ask for his permission to marry me."

Everything in me falls at that statement and a firestorm of emotions bubbles up to take the empty spot. Empathy. Fear. Regret. *Hate.* But sorrow probably trumps them all. I'll never have the chance to ask her father for her hand in marriage because, in some cosmic impossibility, our lives are unwittingly entwined in tragedy.

One life lost.

One life saved.

I blow out a long breath. Clasping my hands together, I drop my head and absorb it all for a minute. I don't look up when she continues. I just can't.

"Reid was—is—a great guy, Shaw." I snort. That's the furthest thing from the truth. If only she knew what a low-life fucker her former *fiancé* is. "I know you don't want to hear this but he treated me well, and he really did love me. I just…" I do look up, then. My gut twists. "It didn't work out is all."

I chew on my lip, an uncharacteristic trait for me. Do I ask the question burning my tongue or do I swallow it back? She told me that night in my parent's bathroom that he hadn't hurt her, she had hurt him. She's told me more about Mergen than she ever has before, so I decide to go for it. "What happened between you two? Why did it end?" *Does he have a chance in hell at getting you back?*

That small laugh that usually sounds adorable is ripe with pure pain tonight. "After my father died..." She stops to swallow. Her eyes tear up. Fuck, I am dying here. She clears her throat and begins again. "After my father died, I kinda went on autopilot. I had Momma to take care of and a funeral to plan and paperwork to deal with that I didn't understand because I was now power of attorney. I didn't know crap about life insurance or pension plans or filing for death benefits through Social Security. I honestly don't even remember those few months after he died. I had to shove aside my own grief, as usual, to make sure everyone and everything else was taken care of."

She sniffles and wipes away the water running down her flushed cheeks. That's it. I can't keep my hands from her a single second longer. I grab a tissue to my right, pop up, and go to her. She tilts her head and the mourning I still see bobbing deep in her soul shreds me.

Without thinking I grab her and switch places. Now she's sitting on my lap, legs hanging over the arm of the chair. Her head is tucked into my shoulder and she's making a good effort to stem her tears. It's not working, so I just hold her as she sobs softly, feeling each tear as if I share in her pain. And I do. A million times over.

"I'm sorry," she says sometime later.

"Don't be. I'm sorry I pushed you." I stroke her hair. I kiss her forehead. My insides turn brittle at the thought of not being able to do this with her daily.

She looks up at me through red-rimmed eyes that glow like starlight. I want to crawl inside her and live there, bathing in her rays of purity. "Don't be. I should have told you sooner."

"If I could take away your pain, Willow, I'd do it in a heartbeat." *If I could bring your father back, I'd give my life for his.* Jesus, what the fuck am I supposed to do?

"I don't talk about my father much. It's hard."

"I understand." *More than you think.*

She lies there with her head back, glassy eyes searching my face. Can she spot the secret I'm hiding? "I left Reid two weeks before the wedding." She ducks back into the crook of my neck, hiding from me. I let her, mulling over her words. "We'd gotten into another argument that night. He wanted me to hire someone to take care of my mother because of the toll it was taking on me. He was right, of course, but I was defensive and unreasonable. I accused him of being selfish. I barely had time for him. He accused me of not letting people love me. Again, he was right. I lay awake that night while he slept next to me. It was four in the morning and I still hadn't been asleep. When I looked over at him, I couldn't breathe. All I could do was associate the pain of losing my father with him. It was wrong and unfair. He didn't do anything to cause his death. But I couldn't shake it and I just knew I couldn't marry him."

My stomach folds over, contracting violently as if ten thousand volts of electricity were just pumped into me. I can't breathe at the thought she'll soon associate *me* with her father's death instead of *him*.

"Like a coward, I left him a note, along with his ring, and walked out. I refused his calls. I refused to see him. For months he didn't give up and then he finally did. He moved and I didn't hear from him until that night at your father's."

Christ, my fate was just painted, a mirror of his. Except mine will be justified.

I press my lips right above her forehead, on her hairline, and leave them there, breathing in the smell of her citrus shampoo. Fear burns like fire ants through my veins. These precious minutes together are now sands in the hourglass, rapidly depleting.

"My father would like you, I think." I look up at the ceiling and bite back the sting behind my lids. "I know I don't have to say this"—her head falls backward again, those blue irises piercing me—"but I never loved Reid the way I love you."

My traitorous eyes well. I don't hide. I let her see how weak I am when it comes to her. How only she has the ability to make me crumble. Palming her nape, I bring her lips to mine. I kiss her slow and thorough. Gentle and sweet. I taste the salt in her mouth. I'm betting she tastes mine.

"Thank you," I whisper against her lips, sincere. "Thank you for trusting me with this. I know how hard it was for you." *I don't deserve it.*

"I trust you more than I've trusted anyone, Shaw."

Gut punch. Right there.

I should do it now. She's led me there, a horse to water. The longer I hold on to this, the more upset she's going to be and the more unforgivable it becomes. Yet being the selfish man I am, I'm not ready to give her up. Not yet. I know I can find a way to save every one of us from devastation. I simply need a little more time.

"You tired?"

"You staying?" She draws back and cups my face.

"Try making me leave." I don't have a thing I need with me, and I have a six-thirty breakfast meeting, but that won't stop me from holding her in my arms all night long. Will it be our last?

That smile of hers eats me alive. Every time. I scoop my arms under her legs and behind her slender back and easily stand. I make my way to her bedroom, depositing her gently on her bed. We undress, quietly. She's drained. So am I. After we both perform our bathroom duties, she slips into bed and pulls back the covers, patting the empty side, that sweet grin my undoing.

I slide in beside her and tug her close until our bodies could be one.

"Will you be gone when I wake up?"

I don't want to be. My fingers drift up and down her bare arm. "Unless you get up before the sun rises, yes."

"That's cruel and unusual punishment," she replies with a smile in her voice, twisting her fingers in my chest hair. I'm growing hard.

"It's why I make the big bucks."

Laughing, she places her lips on my chest. The muscles under her mouth flex involuntarily. "You have a big ego, you know that?"

I need her.

Grabbing her hand, I slide it down my stomach, wrapping it around a dick that is now excited at the prospect of being sheathed in anything of hers. Hand. Mouth. Pussy. Tits. *Ass.* So many possibilities. I want them all. Tonight. She's not getting any sleep. "Right now I have a big cock, Goldilocks."

Her tiny hands flex around the fabric of my boxers, making me moan and jerk. "That you do, Drive By." She pushes the sheet covering us aside before sliding down my body, settling between my legs. "Need help with something?" she asks, her impudence as endearing as her hot little mouth lingering inches above me.

Not waiting for my response, she dives her fingers under the waistband and pulls my underwear midway down my thighs. I'm butt naked yet Willow's still wearing the tiniest, sexiest tank and shorts known to man. I'll never forget them.

She hovers over my straining length, fist wrapped around the base, warm breaths torturing me with each exhale. Looking up my body under thick, dark lashes, those mysterious eyes of hers sparkle with mischief and unadulterated love.

I reach down to run a lock of hair through my fingers, memorizing the silky feel. Wondering how many more times I'll be able to touch it.

"Fuck me with your mouth, Willow." It's more than a demand. It's a supplication, a prayer for her to wash away all my sins. This secret has spread like black mold on my spirit. I need to atone.

Sliding those perfect full lips over me, she blows my mind. She teases at first, then gets down to brass tacks trying to make me come in record time, which the vixen accomplishes. No woman's mouth has ever felt as good wrapped around my dick as hers. No one's ever will.

After I return the favor, I tuck her now naked body back over mine and tell her to sleep for a while. In a few short minutes her breaths even out. I know she's out like a light because of that little twitch thing her body occasionally does.

I lie awake for a long time, unable to shut my brain off.

Tomorrow I need to stop putting off the inevitable and figure out where we go from here. Tomorrow I need to see Annabelle. Tomorrow I need to have a hard conversation with Willow. Tomorrow everything I love in this world could be destroyed.

Everything.

I've never felt this fucking helpless in my life.

Dread sits like a lead mass in the pit of my stomach and I begin to pray, fervently. With the desperation of a man who sees his world crumbling down around him and knows he needs help. If there is a God or higher power that hears the cries of tormented souls, I'm hoping mine screams the loudest. That my prayers are answered first.

Please protect my baby sister.

Please, by some miracle, let me keep Willow.

Pleasepleasepleasefuckingpleasehelpadesperatemanout.

Please.

Chapter Twenty

"I'M SURPRISED TO SEE YOU here."

Glancing up, I see Noah in my doorway. I'm reviewing the final pages of Charles Blackwell's documents but I'm doing it from the comfort of the couch versus my desk. I couldn't stomach watching Red getting railed from behind today.

I toss the papers and pen in my hand to the low table in front of me.

"Yeah. I, ah"—palming the back of my neck, I rub the tense muscles there—"I couldn't do it."

Noah walks to my wall of glass and stands silent a few moments. The trajectory of his gaze tells me who has his attention. Letting loose a big sigh, he makes his way back over, plopping down beside me. He throws his stylish caramel Mantellassi loafers onto the table and crosses one foot over the other. The thick heel thuds dully against the wood. "Can't say I blame you."

I met Annabelle for lunch. Actually I had lunch catered in my office, and I'd planned to tell her what I found out in a place that was relatively safe and neutral, with Noah down the hall only a holler away to help me subdue her when she freaked out. When, not if.

But when she floated in she looked so damn happy, as if she was walking on air and free of the demons that plague her, if only for a bit. And I just couldn't make myself do it. I couldn't be the one to drive her directly into a pit of self-hatred. How will I ever be able to do that?

"She asked me if I'd found anything out. I lied. I told her it was all a big misunderstanding."

She had no idea we were going to see Lia Melborne. I didn't want her worried at what I truly thought would end up being nothing. "I don't know what I'm going to do, Noah. You know as well as I do that when Annabelle finds out what happened, we're going to lose her."

He whispers a curse. "Why not wait until after the election to figure it out."

"Mergen's just waiting for me to do that. All I'm doing is putting off the inevitable."

"Maybe. Maybe not. Maybe he'll never call your bluff. But it will give us time to figure out a strategy."

"He's not bluffing. He's biding his time. Waiting for when this little explosive will cause the biggest blast." It's what I would do if I were in his shoes.

I cross my arms and rest my head against the back of the couch, letting my gaze drift to the high ceiling. My mind whirls, working overtime to find a solution. It has for days. All I come up with are blanks. Big. Fat. Fucking. Blanks.

Even if I wanted to call her a liar, I can't. I believe Lia Melborne was telling the truth. An award-winning actress couldn't fake the kind of remorse that's been eating her up.

She didn't know the name Reid Mergen and didn't know how he would have found out but none of that matters at this point anyway. Facts are facts.

According to Lia, Annabelle was hysterical and had jumped out of the back of the car on Schultz Bridge—while they were driving. By the time they stopped, she'd already climbed onto the ledge and was talking about how her life wasn't worth living and how everyone would be better off without her.

One of the girls was passed out in the back and didn't know what was going on, but Lia and another one were trying to talk Annabelle down when along came a good Samaritan to save the day.

Charles Blackwell.

Only in saving my baby sister, Charles Blackwell lost his own life. And while I don't blame Annabelle for not remembering, neither of the other two girls came forward to save the victim's family unfathomable grief. Makes me sick.

"Besides…I don't think I could live with myself if I didn't tell Willow." I sit up and lean forward. I push my thighs out with my elbows. "The thought that her father committed suicide has done a number on her for more than four years. She deserves the truth." Every ugly detail of it.

I'm ill. Utterly fucking ill.

Noah copies my position. "Even if that means you lose her?"

I can't swallow the acid rising in my throat fast enough. It's pungent and tastes of wrong choices I want to make but can't.

Mergen holding this over my head is unconscionable, but I'll be damned if I'm going to take a page out of his book and keep it from Willow, no matter the consequences. That would make me no better than him.

All I can do is nod.

"You know what's ironic?" I say almost absently. "We have Annabelle today because of Charles Blackwell's selflessness." I glance at him. "And Willow is suffering without her father because of Annabelle's selfishness. It's so fucked up."

"She was lost, Shaw. I know it's hard to see that through everything that's happened, but you need to remember how bad of a place Bluebelle was in at the time. Self-destruction was her middle name."

"I know." I scrub my hand over my face.

"It's an unconscionable accident, but that's all it was." He sighs. "There has to be a way out of this. There's *always* a way. We just have to find it."

There's no way out. I appreciate his friendship and optimism, but we are all royally fucked.

"I talked to Bull earlier," Noah announces quietly.

I stiffen and my head snaps back his way. "You did *what*?"

"Calm the fuck down. We had to know the extent of what we're dealing with here, legally."

Before I do something, like say break his pretty boy nose, I push myself to stand. I walk ten paces away and breathe long and slow until the urge to throttle him passes. Mostly. "Did you tell him—?"

"He's not stupid," he breaks in, unrepentant. He eases back, laces his fingers together, and places his twined hands behind his head. "I didn't mention her by name but I couldn't very well get the answer I needed without giving him a rundown of the facts."

"Fucking hell, Noah."

A fear parallel to me losing Willow is what happens to Annabelle once this all comes out, outside of her obvious road back to drugs. Is there a legal requirement for a witness to come forward in an accidental death? Will the district attorney bring charges against her, even though she can't remember most of that night? Will *Willow* want charges brought against my sister and her friends? Would I blame her?

I slide my hands into my pockets and stalk over to the windows, the urge to draw blood greater than it was a few seconds ago. The sun sits low in the sky, a blaze of bright orange. It's now the middle of October. The election is a mere three weeks away.

Three weeks.

Is that all the time I have left with Willow? More? Less?

When does my life become barren and cold? Not worth living?

It should be today but I can't force myself to tell Willow any more than I could Annabelle. Putting this off will bite me in the ass. Mark my words.

Pinching the bridge of my nose between my fingers, I squeeze my eyes shut. A massive headache is bearing down on me and I haven't been able to take a full breath in days that isn't laced with despair except when Willow is wrapped around me.

"What did he say?" I finally ask. My voice feels scratchy and sounds like shattered glass pieces scraping against each other. These are answers we need and I've been trying to prepare myself for the worst. I haven't been ready to hear what my sister's future will look like. I already know what mine does.

"Well, *hypothetically*"—I hear Noah shift to stand—"if the victim was trying to prevent a suicide and an accident ensued as a result that claimed the victim's life, then the most the witnesses could be charged with is hindering an investigation. An accident is an accident, according to Bull. Regardless of past priors or incidents."

Relief is as sharp as a lightning strike but it's short-lived. It's only one worry allayed. One hurdle overcome. The rest seem insurmountable.

My best friend sidles up beside me. Instead of enjoying our favorite Wednesday afternoon show, though, he turns his back to them and sets his butt against the window ledge, facing me. "It's a slap on the hand, Merc. Charges likely won't be filed. Bull said if it was his case he wouldn't even bring it to the ADA."

I hate how his words are as clinical as if we're discussing a plot on CSI instead of Willow's father and my sister, who was so fucked up she wanted to take her own life.

Jesus. H. Christ. If my father thought the picture in the paper was a shit show he has no idea what's about to hit him.

My eyes cut to Noah. "I'm pissed you did it without consulting me first, but...thank you. It's a relief to know at least she won't go to prison."

"Yeah," he agrees. "So what are you going to do?"

"I don't know yet. Not doing anything isn't an option, though. It's just...the timing could not be worse for my family."

"I know."

"This leaks to the press, my father is finished. Harrington will have a field day dragging us all through the mud."

"That he will."

I take up position next to him, leaning against the cool windows. We both stay quiet for a while before I share the one golden nugget I've found throughout this entire disaster. It's the only thing that's made me smile since I left Willow alone, sleeping in bed this morning.

"CJ had himself covered with a patent."

Noah doesn't say anything. When I look at him, though, he has this goofy smile on his face and at that moment I could not be more grateful for my friend. He cares about Willow and even though I'll likely lose her, I know I can count on him to keep tabs on her so I can feed this unhealthy obsession I'll always have for her.

He eyes me from the side. "Her wealth will put yours to shame," he says with a giant grin on his face.

True. When the FDA grants their final approval for Zytin to be manufactured, her mother, and Willow by extension will be wealthy beyond their wildest imaginations. Granted, it may be up to a year yet, but the financial security I'd wanted to make sure she had was always there. She just didn't know it.

I half chuckle, rubbing my hand through my hair. "That it will. She obviously has no clue."

"I imagine something like that is easy to overlook if you don't know what you're looking for."

"I imagine."

"Everything else on the up and up?"

I nod. I did find one other thing that needs to be rectified but it's something I want to keep to myself for now. It will take a bit more digging and I have no idea the steps I'll need to take to make it happen.

"I'm going to lose her." My voice is thick, strained.

"Have more faith in her than that, Merc. Have more faith that the infrastructure you've built can sustain this goddamn earthquake that's about to hit. Because if you don't, how can she?"

"I'm trying."

"Try harder. I went to a lot of work to get you two together." He clasps my shoulder. "It was an unimaginable, unintentional, unthinkable accident, but her father did a brave thing saving your sister. I think once the shock wears off she'll see it the same way I do."

He pushes himself straight and strides toward the door. Hand on the knob, he glances back. "Say, think you can sweet talk Sierra into attending your dad's fundraiser with me Saturday night?"

After I get over the surprise of his request, I begin to laugh. Really, really laugh. I laugh until tears gather at the corners of my eyes. It feels good letting the pent up out.

"Some inside joke I'm unaware of?"

At the seriousness of Noah's face, I laugh even harder.

"What the hell? Did she hate me *that* much? Did she say something to Willow?" Now his arms are crossed and his face holds a frown.

I howl.

"Forget it."

He spins and stomps out of my office, giving me a middle-finger salute, and somehow I feel lighter. Stronger. And a little more optimistic that maybe, just maybe I can contain the chaos when it implodes because I know I won't have to handle it alone.

Noah is right. It was an unimaginable, horrific accident. But an accident it was. I only hope both Annabelle and Willow can see it that way and we can all move forward together, a happily ever after secured with everyone I love beside me.

Willow

Chapter Twenty-One

"ARE YOU SURE EVERYTHING IS okay?" I ask him again as the chauffeur-driven car comes to a slow stop. He's been acting strange all week. In fact, he's been acting weird for weeks now. We've spent the last three nights at his place, and I've woken two out of the three to find him sitting in a tobacco-colored Chesterfield chair watching me sleep.

Picking up our entwined hands he brings them to his lips. They're warm and soft when they touch my palm. It tingles. "It is as long as you're by my side," he tells me with a quiet reverence that makes me breathe a tad easier. Bringing his free hand around the back of my head he draws me close, placing a light close-mouthed kiss to my red-stained lips.

"You're going to get my lipstick all over you," I tease.

He growls and cups my chin. "I think that color would look splendid smearing my cock tonight, don't you?"

I go instantly wet. "I'm not really sure it's your shade."

"It's my shade, beautiful. Trust me." I laugh when my eyes drop to the nice big bulge in his sleek gray suit pants.

I want nothing more than to go home, crawl into bed, and make love to him all night long, but we're already running late from the against-the-wall orgasm he gave me before we left. "Your father's probably waiting for us."

"Probably. I love you, Willow Blackwell," he whispers, lips grazing mine.

"I love you more, Shaw Mercer," I tell him.

"I doubt that, Goldilocks."

With one last lingering look that says so much but leaves me with this gnawing feeling at the same time, we exit the car. He wraps an arm around my waist, drawing me close as we start up the sidewalk to the Four Seasons where this all started.

It's surreal. One of the worst nights of my life turned out to be one of the best. If I'd never met Noah that night, I know I wouldn't be with Shaw now.

Minutes later we're striding into the grand ballroom where I had my "date" with Paul Graber. I shudder. I hope Shaw never finds out about that. I'm sure I'd have gotten an earful by now if he knew.

"Shaw!"

His name is yelled the second we step into the oversized space. His father, who is waving us down, is about ten paces away, standing next to a very elegant Adelle on one side, Reid flanking him on the other. In front of them are a couple of well-dressed older gentlemen, one of them who looks to be… "Is that the governor?" I ask Shaw in a whisper.

"None other." He beams. He's so incredibly proud of his father his entire being radiates.

Shaw twines our fingers and makes quick work around the throng of people waiting in line to shake Preston Mercer's hand until he steps to his father's side. He pats him on the back twice with his free hand. "Hey, sorry we're late. I got buried in something important."

He says this with sheer deadpan as he pretends to rub an itch on his nose but glances at me with this transparent smirk tilting his lips. I feel warmth crawl from my chest up my neck and into my cheeks as I fight to bite back a smile. He was buried, all right. Three fingers deep. The same ones he discreetly smells.

Good God almighty, that wicked man.

"You all right, dear? You look flush," Adelle's sweet voice sings.

"Oh, yes, fine." My eyes are filled with reprimand as they land briefly on Shaw, who doesn't care in the least. That smirk has now turned into a full-fledged grin. Bastard. "It's just a little…warm in here." I pluck at the loose neckline of my dress for effect.

"That happens with so many people in an enclosed space," she easily agrees. I hear Shaw lightly chuckling as his mother pulls me in for a hug, followed by Preston. After my introduction to not only Governor Malcolm Presley but the state's lieutenant governor as well, I stand dutifully beside Shaw, his arm snaked around me once again, while he makes small talk look easy.

I feel Reid's eyes on me, burning through the thin skin of my cheek but I refuse to turn. I haven't acknowledged him once. He's tried calling me five times over the past week. Ever since the article broke. He's left five voice mail messages and sent three text messages. All relatively vague, but with the same message, the same urgency: "I need to talk to you about something important."

Well, I don't want to talk to him. I don't want to listen to anything he has to say. In fact, I'm pretty damn mad at him for telling Shaw about our engagement when it should have been me, no matter the circumstances. Shaw had every right to be upset I hadn't told him about it, but the time never felt right. Kinda like the whole threesome fact he kept from me, I suppose. But I think until we both knew where we stood with each other, we were each holding secrets in reserve.

I still have one, though. The hardest one yet: *Violet.*

My sister's memory is hallowed to me. It's surprisingly harder to talk about her than my father's death. For some stupid reason, I want to keep her all to myself.

Maybe it's because I'm the only one left who actually carries her whole memory. Maybe it's because I don't want her judged for how she died and as soon as you mention "drug overdose" there's a certain stigma attached that most people can't see through to the person underneath.

It took me over a year to tell Reid about Violet and even then, I didn't tell him outright. He followed me one day to the cemetery. He thought I was cheating on him because I'd disappear for hours at a time and I wouldn't tell him where I was going.

My fingers automatically go to my throat. A month after he followed me, he gave me the abstract silver willow he commissioned a friend of his to make. *"So your sister is always with you,"* he told me, misty-eyed. I broke down. Regardless of what is between us now, I've treasured it ever since. I always will. It's weird, probably imagined, but I *feel* her in it.

Shaw's deep laugh blasts me back to attention. I glance up at his profile, so strong and beautiful. I love him *so* much. This final barrier needs to go. I need to tell him. I *want* to tell him. And I plan to tonight. I also plan to use that opportunity to talk about Annabelle. To see if he'll share anything about her with me. I just know I saw the same haunting in her eyes as I did Violet's. Only I recognize it for what it is now, when back then I didn't have a clue.

As if my thoughts conjured her, Shaw's little sister appears right in front of us, along with a rather nerdy-looking young man about her height on her arm.

"Annabelle," Adelle coos. She air kisses her cheek before hugging her warmly. "You look absolutely breathtaking, sweetie."

And she is. She's an undeniably sophisticated stunner tonight in a mint green, floor-length, two-piece ball gown. It's slightly daring because of her bare midriff, but the high neck and high waistline are overall conservative. Her raven hair is twisted into a simple updo and her makeup is subtle. Utterly perfect.

She looks happy. Those shadows I'm sure I glimpsed a few weeks ago seem noticeably absent. Maybe I was wrong about her after all?

"I almost didn't recognize you," Shaw quips, giving her a quick peck on the cheek.

I hug her quickly. "You look gorgeous," I whisper. She smiles and blushes at my compliment.

I turn to the governor who called my name, debonair in his charcoal suit. "Did you say your last name was Blackwell?"

Saliva floods my mouth. All the happy feelings that were fizzing pop, one by one. I nod, whispering a yes.

"Any relation to the late CJ Blackwell?"

I was prepared for it, yet still I suck in a sharp breath at those words strung together. Shaw's muscles stiffen and his hold on me noticeably tightens. Heart pounding in my chest, my eyes glide over Reid. His gaze is stone hard. But it's not on me and it's not on the governor. It's on my boyfriend. And Shaw's is on him.

"Yes. I'm his daughter," I answer, my voice wobbly. I lean on Shaw for support.

The corners of his mouth turn down in sympathy. "I thought so. I didn't know him well, but we were both members of the Rainier Club. He talked about you and your sister often and with pride. I just thought you would want to know he was well respected and is very missed."

Oh fuck. The only thing that's worse than him talking about my dead father is him talking about my dead sister. Especially since no one here knows about her besides Reid.

"I didn't know you had a sister, dear," Adelle innocently states.

My eyes go to her. I can't find my voice. Perspiration breaks out on my forehead and my heart kicks violently in my chest until it hurts. I'm acutely, painfully aware that everyone is waiting to see what I'm going to say. "I—"

I don't. Not anymore. She's dead and gone, just like my father.

My ears start ringing and the noise drowns everything else

out except the faintly spoken words that trickle down from above me on a waft of wounded air. "I didn't either."

I am so sorry.

"You look pale," someone says. It sounds far away. "Are you all right?"

I'm dizzy. Sweating everywhere.

"I—"

My legs are heavy, my knees soft.

"She needs some cold water on her face."

I think I might faint.

Someone grabs my elbow and guides me forward. I'm aware of Shaw's arm slipping from me but not much else. I'm cold, numb, and so fucking sorry that Shaw had to find out this way.

My feet move automatically, one in front of the other, each step shaky and uneven. I don't know who has me or where we're headed but soon the noise fades away and I'm being pushed down onto a cushioned bench.

I stare at the creamy tiles beneath my heels, my body weighing two tons. My eyes blur until someone squats in front of me with a wad of wet paper towels. They're pressed to my forehead. They feel cool. They feel good. I grab them and pat my whole face.

After a few beats, the ringing in my ears subsides. My heart slows. The constriction in my lungs abates. I'm so embarrassed I could die.

"Better?"

My eyes raise and connect with ones that are a mirror of her brother's.

I nod.

Annabelle blows out a long puff of air and visibly relaxes. A dry grin crosses her pretty face. "I thought for a second there you were gonna take a header."

I huff a short laugh. "Me too." I run the damp towels down either side of my neck, enjoying the cool sensation.

"I mean that would have been one way to make headlines, I guess."

My smile is forced. I feel more clear-headed with each passing moment. "I don't think it takes much where your brother is concerned."

"The press does love him," she says with a fair amount of mockery.

So do I.

The door to our left pushes open and a woman with a phone pressed to her ear stands there. She looks frazzled. When she sees us, her eyes scan the rest of the ladies' room lounge before she turns and walks back out. Just as the door closes I spot Shaw. Our eyes connect briefly before he's out of sight. He looks concerned. And hurt. Very, very hurt.

Shit.

My head falls against the wall in defeat. I suck.

"You like my brother, huh?"

I roll my head toward Annabelle. Her eyes are big and blue and look otherworldly. "Very much."

One side of her mouth kicks up. She watches me quietly. She's choosing her words. It reminds me of Shaw. A lot about her reminds me of Shaw. "He watches you like a hawk."

"He's very attentive," I agree.

"I don't mean Shaw. I mean my father's campaign manager."

Wow. Uhhhh…what the hell am I supposed to say to that? Do I agree? Deny? Play dumb? "Oh, ah…it's complicated."

"He loves you."

Holy balls. Straight to the point, this one. "Well, I don't—"

"Shaw. Shaw loves you." She's changing subjects so fast my neck's getting a kink. "I mean so does the other guy, but it's obvious you only have eyes for my big brother."

I'm not quite sure what I'm supposed to say so I keep quiet.

She slips off nude sandals and slides her feet to the cushiony leather beneath us, pulling the fabric of her long skirt over her bent legs. Wrapping her arms around her knees, she lays her cheek on them and stares at me.

Those shadows I thought were gone are back. Maybe they

never left and she simply hid them like an expert. Like Violet. Like *me*. I want to pull her down into my lap and stroke her hair. Tell her she has a whole life ahead of her of her own choosing and not to give in to them. I want to beg her to not end up like Violet, breaking everyone who ever loved her into invisible pieces they'll never find again.

"Do you love him?" I'm trying to figure out which *him* she's referring to when she adds, "My brother. Do you love my brother? If I had to guess I'd say you do but I want to be sure."

She's a miniature Shaw. Fierce protection must be a Mercer trait.

"Yes," I reply. "More than I thought possible."

"Will you love him no matter what?"

I shake my head at her Spanish Inquisition. It's sweet. "We all have flaws, Annabelle. When you love someone, you love the whole package. The good and the not so good. You don't get to choose which pieces you want. You take them all."

Moving her chin to knees, she stares ahead in our small space. "What if he did the worst thing imaginable but he did it to protect you? Would you still love him then?"

I roll her strange question around for a few seconds. Does she know something I don't or is she only trying to determine how deep my love for her flesh and blood goes? "I can't imagine he could do anything that would make me stop loving him," I tell her truthfully. "But if he did, you can't just turn love off with the flip of a switch. It doesn't work that way."

"I know," she mumbles before falling quiet. Two more women who are chatting excitedly about meeting the governor enter, barely acknowledging us as they pass by and head through the swinging door into the restroom. I make it a point not to look for Shaw this time.

I think the twenty questions are over when she asks, "Have you ever done anything you regret?"

She can't see my sardonic grin but it's there. "Too many to count," I admit quietly. Take now, for example. I should be out apologizing profusely to the man I love that I kept such a big part of my life from him, yet here I am—hiding in the restroom like a coward instead.

"Do you think some mistakes are unforgivable?" Her question is softly spoken, almost inaudible.

I study her. She's still staring forward, eyes barely blinking as if she's in a trance. My gut screams this is no longer about Shaw. "Nothing is unforgivable."

She lays her cheek on her knees again, eyeing me. "Do you really believe that?" The skepticism in her tone makes me think that's not what she expected.

"Yes. I really believe that. What kind of world would this be if we didn't forgive each other for our mistakes?" Blue eyes blink back at me. They hold mysteries and a deep well of darkness she fights falling into. "Do *you* believe that, Annabelle?"

I haven't spent a lot of time with Annabelle, but it's easy to recognize she works overtime trying to convince everyone she's happy and fine. I know the tactics. In this moment, though, she seems young and fragile and incredibly vulnerable. I think about asking her a few questions of my own, wondering if she'd trust me enough to answer me, but the moment comes and goes in a blink and that cocky attitude she dons like a second skin is back and in my face.

"Do you want to marry him?"

I laugh before I realize she's serious. "I—" I pause, contemplating how I'm going to field this one. There's no other answer but yes, yet I certainly don't want Shaw thinking I'm planning a wedding with his sister behind his back in the ladies' room of the Four Seasons the same week I told him I loved him. "He would have to ask me first."

"If he asked you, what would you say?"

This is like having a conversation with Sierra. They would get along splendidly, a modern-day Thelma and Louise.

I inhale deeply and consider my next words carefully. "*If* he asked, I suppose I would say yes."

"You suppose or you know?"

I toss the now warm paper crumpled in my hand into the garbage can beside me, chuckling. Shaw failed to mention his sister is a Rottweiler with a bone. I eye her and go for it. "Yes. The answer would be yes."

Her smile reaches her eyes. She pats my leg. "Good to know."

"Did I pass?" I ask as she slips on her shoes, one by one.

"With flying colors."

With her hands pressing on the bench, she stands, turns, and gazes down at me. "My brother is probably five seconds away from storming in here to check on you himself."

Yes. Then I'll have some explaining to do. Will he ever believe I meant to tell him about my sister tonight? I wouldn't blame him if he didn't. "I'm sure he is. Can you…"

"Yeah. I'll tell him you need a minute."

She holds out her hand and helps me up. "Thanks, Annabelle."

"Thank you for making my brother crazy. It's…" she pauses as if swallowing a snarky comment. "I'm glad he has someone."

My lips turn up gently. "Thank you." I'm making my way into the restroom when I hear my name called softly behind me. "Yeah?" I turn around.

Annabelle throws her gaze to the ground quickly, then back to me. She presses her full lips together in a nervous gesture. "I'm really sorry about your dad…and whatever happened with your sister to make you look so sad."

A lump grows in my throat. Pinpricks bite behind my lids. "You remind me of her," I croak.

A weird look crosses her face. "How?"

I swallow, stalling for time. I don't want to tell her how I see the same caverns I saw in Violet and I'm worried about her falling into one, so instead I say, "She was musically gifted, like you. She was funny and gregarious and outspoken. Spontaneous and sensitive. Observant. Misunderstood, I think. And smart. Incredibly smart."

She looks away but not before I see her eyes glass over.

Smiling a tight, quick smile, she mumbles something and exits, leaving me standing there, alone.

I walk to the mirror and take stock of the woman looking back. The blood has returned to her face, though she still looks a little sallow. Faint red streaks the whites of her eyes. A lifetime of sorrow pulls down the corners of her mouth. She looks like she could end up sad and alone with twenty-three cats, crocheting tiny hats for tiny newborns if she doesn't cut the shit.

When I talked to Shaw about my father, it was a relief of sorts. When I let everything out about Reid, I felt the same way. So why I've been holding back the most impactful loss of my life, I don't really know. Change is hard, even if it is needed.

After a few minutes of putting myself back together, I step into the hallway. My heart pounds when I see Shaw pacing, stabbing a hand through the side of his hair. His attention zeros in on me and he freezes. A few people pass between us but he never takes his eyes from me. He's breathing hard. His lips are pressed in a hard line.

"I'm sor—"

"Not now, Willow." His gruff demeanor makes me want to bawl. "My father is giving his speech any minute."

"Oh."

In three strides, he's at my side. Gently taking me by the elbow, he walks quickly. With his long legs and my heels, it's hard to keep up but I'm not going to complain or slow him down. We're here tonight, two-and-a-half weeks from the election, to support his father's last fundraiser. With the latest poll results, along with the outpouring of support Preston Mercer has tonight, I'd say there is no way he's not winning this race.

But all I care about right now is mending fences with Shaw.

"I'm sorry," I tell him before we spill from the relative quiet of the hallway. Regardless of the fact he just told me he doesn't want to talk about it, I can't keep my apology inside. "My sister…it's, she's—"

He stops so abruptly I run into the back of him and stumble. His fingers wrap around my biceps, steadying me. Once he's sure I'm not going to fall flat on my face, he walks me backward until my spine bumps with a coarse wall. He comes flush with me.

Palming my nape, he hooks his thumbs under my chin and holds me prisoner in his power. His blue gaze grips me hard. It's intense, a little scary. The dark stubble he left on his jawline only serves to add an extra edge of sharpness to him. He's magnetic. I'm soaking.

"She's one of those sacred secrets it's hard to share," he says in an oddly even voice.

My exhale comes out in a rush. Blinking fast, I nod, not feeling as if I deserve his understanding but glad I have it anyway.

"I'll wait as long as you need, Goldilocks. Whenever you're ready, say the word and I'll drop everything."

I breathe his name in relief and the mixed emotions I'm grappling with start oozing out of their lockbox. "I was going to tell you about her tonight. I swear. After…" My gaze flits to our right where all the activity abounds.

He clamps his jaw together and moves his head in agreement, though I'm not sure if he believes me or not. But I don't get an opportunity to ask because in the background we hear someone announce Preston Mercer a second before the crowd goes wild, clapping, cheering, whistling.

"We need to go." His lips settle on my forehead a brief moment.

"I love you," I whisper before letting him step back.

His thumb comes under my chin, pressing up until my head tilts all the way back. Resolve burns into me. "I'm not going anywhere, Willow, okay?"

I sag in relief and let him drop a sweet kiss to my mouth before we're off once again.

When we ease in at the front of the crowd beside Shaw's siblings, Noah is there, seemingly without a date. He gives us both a questioning once-over before wrapping me in a quick hug. He asks me if I'm okay. I tell him yes.

It's so loud all I can do is wave to Lincoln and Gemma who are to Shaw's left. Shaw's younger brother looks uncomfortable in his snazzy vest and fitted pants and is standing next to a handsomely dressed man several inches taller than him who is paying him all kinds of attention. It appears Gemma is trying to wrangle three unruly children by herself, her husband nowhere in sight. She hands Eli off to Annabelle so she can pick up Cora, who is tugging relentlessly on her skirt. Shaw scoops up Nicholas and sets him over his shoulders allowing him to clearly see his grandpa. He beams and starts bouncing up and down until Shaw tells him to sit still.

It's utter chaos and I love that I'm part of it.

"Thank you for coming," a loud voice booms over the melee.

My attention goes to Shaw's father who is standing on the main stage, which is raised a few feet above us. He's behind a makeshift podium grinning, waving, letting his supporters go wild. Just to his right is Adelle, hands clasped demurely in front of her. Reserved pride is written on the fine lines of her face as she gazes at her husband, knowing it's his time to shine but also knowing she's the invisible backbone behind a great man's success.

And off to the mayor's left stands Reid. He's clapping along with the group, but he's not looking at the crowd or at his candidate. His hawklike stare is homed in on Shaw. If hate had a color, he'd be wearing it.

As if he feels me, his eyes flick from Shaw to me, and the air in my lungs freezes. The hate quickly dissolves but he has this look about him that's hard for me to decipher at first.

But then I see it. Clear as day. He wants me back. He's told me as much. But now it appears he doesn't care who knows anymore. It's dangerous, what he's doing. Not only is it dangerous, it's not at all welcome or appropriate, given his station with the Mercer family. He's supposed to protect them from scandal, not create one.

People continue to clap. Reid continues to stare. Sheer determination is mixed with unmistakable proprietorship. A triple dose of barefaced yearning is thrown in for good measure. It's there, simmering. A noxious combination that's ready to boil over and scald everyone around him.

It's coming. Fast. Without warning. And when it does, no one will be sheltered from the damage it will cause.

No one.

Chapter Twenty-Two

"SMUG BASTARD. IF I COULD rip off his balls and feed them to him one by one without going to jail, they'd already be sliding down his throat."

Taking a swallow of my Lagavulin, even the smokiness of the pricey aged Scotch does little to wash away the tang of rage lining my mouth. I don't take my eyes from him for a split second. Standing next to my father like he belongs there. Shaking hands with businessmen, housewives, the people of Seattle like they are *his* people. Fucking pompous prick.

"Did you see the way he looked at Willow when my father was giving his speech?"

"I saw it," Noah replies tersely. He's as indignant as I am. "Fucker's getting bolder and bolder."

Fierce protectiveness fires every neuron inside me until they're pinging violently against the walls of my veins. I scan the room for Willow. My mother dragged her away more than a half an hour ago to parade her around. Don't think I haven't noticed Mergen tracking her every move, either. As much as I've not taken my eyes from him, he's barely taken his eyes from her, though the last few minutes he's been engrossed in conversation with a US senator and one of my father's closest friends.

"She's over there," Noah's low voice drawls.

I follow his line of sight, and sure enough, spot Willow with a small group of my mother's closest friends. My mother apparently says something that brings blood rushing to her fair skin because even from this distance I watch her cheeks redden. That gorgeous, sassy mouth I love sinking my cock into breaks into a sheepish smile, and she quickly throws a glance around the immediate vicinity as if she doesn't want someone to overhear their conversation.

I wonder what made my girl blush so beautifully.

"So, you two were arguing earlier."

I slip my eyes to Noah for a moment and go back to watching Willow. He wasn't around for the awkward scene. One guess as to who filled him in. Bluebelle is like *his* baby sister, too. "First a dead father I didn't know about, then a fiancé, and now a mystery sister."

"*Ex*-fiancé," Noah clarifies.

"Whatever. Ex-fiancé. The point is I'm beginning to wonder if I'll ever extract all of her secrets or if they'll just blindside me when I least expect it."

"Isn't that part of the fun?"

"Is it? It doesn't feel fun sometimes." It feels like extreme sports, actually. One brutal hurdle after another, wondering if I'll ever make it to the finish line or be forced to tap out. And with the way Mergen's blatantly displaying his feelings for her—publicly now—I don't think I'm too far off the mark. Hence why I'm keeping him in my crosshairs.

My time's almost up. I feel it vibrating in every cell in my body. And that means I have to make my move before he does. That means every second with Willow is more precious than the one before it.

That means I have to tell her tonight. *Fuck.*

Noah draws in a gulp of air and blows it out loudly. He swallows a mouthful of his rum and Coke and turns to me. "I don't know, Merc. Sometimes I think I wouldn't mind finding someone like her to twist me all up."

I should be more stunned than I am, but the truth is I've seen a change in Noah since I started dating Willow. A good one. My lips slide up. "Really? Is that why you wanted me to talk to a certain statuesque brunette who wouldn't give a second thought to pulling out your short hairs with sharp tweezers?"

He shrugs but the gleam in his eye gives him away.

I thought it would be fun to set the two of them up, watching sparks detonate like the Fourth of July, but Noah surprised me. He's clearly taken interest in Willow's best friend and roommate, though I'm not sure she reciprocated. And I'm not sure she's the woman he should be fixated on.

"I thought you were kidding the other day."

"I wasn't," he says, testily.

"Wouldn't let you in her pants, huh?"

"Fuck off, Merc. That's not it."

"I think maybe it is."

"It's not, okay? She's...*God*." He scratches his stubble, contemplating. "So fucking wild all I can think about is taming her."

"She hates men," I tell him, throwing back the last of my drink.

Another lift of his shoulders. "No. She hates the *thought* of men. Big difference."

I bark a laugh. "She thinks you're a manwhore."

He simply grunts and slams the rest of his drink, too. "A leopard can change its spots."

"I think you have that phrase backward, my friend." I set my empty on the tray of a passing young waitress who can't be more than twenty, tops. She gives me the once-over and smiles. It's flirty and forward. A blatant invitation for a ride on my cock later.

"You didn't," he says rather casually, handing our waitress his own dry glass. He doesn't even bother to look at her. She stands there for long seconds, hoping for something more than blind dismissal. When she sees she's not going to get it, she walks away.

"I didn't what?" I scrunch my forehead, confused.

"Have it backward. You set your sights on her." He nods toward Willow. "You fought for her and now you have her."

But for how long, I'm getting ready to ask when commotion and a familiar voice screeching behind me shift my attention.

I spin around to see Annabelle storming toward us, the boy she brought in tow close on her heels. She's carrying her shoes in one hand, holding up that long skirt of hers with another as she powers forward.

She's yelling obscenities behind her at...*what was his name again*? Drew? Dan? Whatever. Doesn't matter. What *does* matter is the scene she's making. While most of them are gone, a few members of the press still linger, probably hoping for this exact moment. Something juicy to print alongside a picture of my father doing something philanthropic. Bloodsuckers. All of them.

I snag her by the waist as she walks by and flatten her to my chest, my arm banded tight. She fights me, barking at me to let her go and when I don't, she tries hitting me with those spiked heels that could be lethal weapons if they hit a vulnerable spot on a man.

"Fuck, Bluebelle. Calm the hell down," I hiss, working like mad to control her. Raging river, right here.

"He's an asshole!" she shrieks, kicking her legs out at her date like a child. She connects with his shin and he lets out a grunt, bending over to rub his wound. Pussy.

Drew or Dan or whoever he is grits, "I didn't do a fucking thing, Annabelle."

She growls. Actually growls. "You've been looking at her all night. Don't even try to deny it." She stabs her finger somewhere toward the sea of people in power suits and fancy dresses. Many of whom are starting to pay too much attention to our little spectacle.

Drew or Dan lets out a frustrated huff. "I didn't. I *wouldn't* disrespect you like that. I swear. I don't even know who you're talking about! Tell her." His eyes land on me, desperate for help that he's not getting. Regardless of if he's 100 percent right—which he probably is—there's no talking sense into Annabelle when she's like this.

"Lying sack of shit!" she throws back hotly. "You did the same thing at that party last weekend when you were talking to that slut Patty Collins."

He rolls his eyes.

This kid has a lot to learn. Even I know that's the kiss of death.

"You'd better just go," I tell him.

"But—"

"Get her out of here," Noah says. "Camera, two o'clock."

Christ almighty. My eyes latch on to my father's, about halfway across the room. His entire face is hard.

"Take care of him," I direct Noah, nodding to junior.

"Don't touch me," I hear the kid say as I set Annabelle on her feet. Keeping my grip tight, I usher her in the opposite direction, her date's words drifting behind us. "I'm outta here. You two can deal with her crazy."

Yep. Kiss of death. Loser. Good riddance.

"Let me go," my baby sister demands, attempting to yank her arm from my implacable rule.

"Not on your life."

I make a sharp left and drag her down the thankfully empty hallway until we come to a set of meeting rooms. I try two doors before I find one open.

As soon as we're inside, I let her go. She takes several steps to a rolling chair, pulls it out, and plops down. She sets her elbows on the table and her face in her hands. I stand by the door, thwarting any attempted escape.

For several minutes the only sound in the room is her harsh breathing. When it finally evens out, I take a seat beside her.

"So," I start, "this party last weekend. Tell me about it."

Her head shoots up, her bloodshot eyes fisting mine. "*That's* what you want to talk about?"

"Yes," I tell her plainly.

Annabelle's a recovering drug addict. A party is the last place she should be. Even tonight I kept my eye on her. She's legally old enough to drink, but a recovering drug addict shouldn't have a drop of alcohol either, even if that's not what she was addicted to in the first place. Addiction is addiction. And it runs wild and uncontrolled in her blood.

"You're an asshole."

"Duly noted. Now…the party." I cross my arms, my directive clear: Answer. The fucking. Question.

Her spine straightens—that Mercer strength and stubbornness I admire ever present. I watch a hot blaze smoke up her sky-blue eyes. "You're not my father."

"Then don't make me be, Annabelle," I answer, softening my tone a touch.

"I'm a grown-up. I don't owe you an explanation."

I breathe deep, my patience quickly waning. Annabelle needs my attention but that leaves Willow unprotected from a predator otherwise known as her ex. The sooner we deal with this so I can get back to her, the better. "Then start acting like it. You don't air your personal crap in a public venue like this. You know better than that."

She sighs, glancing away before answering petulantly, "It was a twenty-first birthday party for a friend of mine, okay?"

"And I don't suppose this twenty-first birthday party took place at Chuck E. Cheese?" I respond drolly.

That earns me a cantankerous glare. Not really caring, though. I'm immune to her theatrics.

"I have to learn to be around it sometime, Shaw."

"You're not even a year sober, Bluebelle. It's a bad idea."

"I can't just sit in my apartment and watch my life pass by."

"I never asked you to," I tell her somberly. "But you need to make smart choices, or…"

She leans back in her chair, crosses her arms. Her hair is a mess. Her cheeks are red from anger. She looks older than her young years. "It was hard. I'm not saying it wasn't. But I did it. I turned down every offer. I left completely sober."

Her chin goes up in her personal brand of defiance. All she wants is to be acknowledged. "I'm proud of you, Bluebelle. That couldn't have been easy."

"It wasn't, but Dean…"—Dean, *that's* his name—"he didn't drink anything either, so it helped." She looks down to her lap and starts smoothing her pastel skirt. "I overreacted," she confesses softly.

"I assumed," I reply, knowing she's referring to the debacle in the ballroom. "Do you like him?"

She peeks at me under lashes caked with black mascara. Her nod is small but unmistakable. "He's right. I've been acting crazy." I'm anxious to get back to Willow and call it a night, but I wait patiently, letting her gather her thoughts. "I've just been on edge ever since…"

She doesn't finish her thought but she doesn't need to. I know exactly what she's referring to. I knew she didn't believe me the other day.

I breathe a heavy sigh and stand, unable to sit any longer. Scrubbing my hands down my face, I open my mouth to tell her the truth. I *have* to, even though this isn't the time or place. In fact, I can't think of a worse place to do this but I can't keep putting it off any longer. It's not fair to anyone. Right as I'm trying to push out words that could send her into a tailspin, my cell buzzes.

I reach into my pocket and slide out my phone, gazing at the message.

Noah*: Where are you? I can't find her.*

There's only one *her* he'd be referring to.

Willow.

That motherfucker. I'm gone for all of five minutes and he pounces. "I have to go," I tell my sister, pocketing my phone again.

"What's wrong?"

"Nothing." My heart races. I've no doubt Mergen is with her and it's not a stretch to think he's spilling his guts but will twist the facts to his advantage. "Go back to the party and stick by Dad. And behave yourself." I'm at the door, turning the knob, not looking behind me to make sure Annabelle's followed instructions.

For some reason, instead of heading back toward the party I continue down the hallway to my left where more conference rooms are. I force myself to walk slowly with purpose, straining to hear voices. This part of the hotel is not occupied this evening so if there happens to be unusual activity I should hear it.

After about fifty feet I come to a fork where I need to choose. Right or left. Going purely on gut instinct I pivot left, taking me farther into the guts of the posh lodge. Catching a faint whiff of the floral perfume I inhaled on Willow earlier, I know I'm on the right path. Still, I pass room after room in the extra wide hallway, hearing nothing.

Until the last one.

Low voices draw me to the final room on my right. The door is cracked and as I near, Willow's voice becomes quite distinct. I loiter outside, eavesdropping.

"This is completely inappropriate, Reid," she hisses. She's angry. Good girl.

"You didn't leave me any choice, Willow," he replies with a bite. "You won't return my calls or my texts."

Fucker.

"Because there's nothing to talk about."

"Oh, there's plenty to talk about. What are you doing with a guy like Mercer in the first place? He's a philanderer, Willow. You deserve better than a yuppie who fucks random women in public places and ends up in the goddamn newspaper!"

That's it. My hand automatically comes up to shove the door open but instinct makes me pause when Willow spits, "Don't say another word. For all I know *you* had something to do with that whole thing."

A slow smile creeps across my face. I love this woman with everything in me.

Mergen's laugh is bitter. "I only wish. I had to work overtime to clean up his shit." He didn't lift a fucking finger. *I* did it all.

"This is not you, Reid," she says sadly. "Why are you acting like this?"

"Do you know how excruciating it is to wake up each day knowing you're not mine anymore? It's hell, Willow. Every second of every day of the last four years has been pure, utter fucking hell."

My jaw clenches tight. If he wasn't trying to tear apart my family, I'd almost feel sorry for the asshole. *Yah, no.* That'll never happen.

"Reid." She stretches out his name, her tone hemorrhaging sympathy. "I…I don't know what you want me to say."

I know what I want her to say.

"Say that this…whatever you're doing with Shaw Mercer is temporary."

It takes her a long time to answer. *Too* long. Frankly, it takes her so long I'm beginning to wonder what her answer will be, but when she finally speaks, I realize it's not because she doubts us, it's because she's trying to let him down as gently as possible. As much as I want her to tell him to fuck off, I love that caring side of her.

"It's not, Reid. I'm in love with him. I told you that. I know I left you hanging all these years and for that, I am incredibly sorry. It was wrong of me. I don't want to hurt you but that doesn't change the fact that what I have with him is real. He's…it for me."

"He doesn't know you like I do. He never will," he protests.

"You're wrong."

"What does he give you that I can't, huh? Money? I have money, Willow. Maybe not as much as he does but enough that I can help take care of you and your mother."

"Now you're just insulting me," she tells him hotly.

There's a long moment of silence. "He will never commit to you."

I'm done. I've heard enough. I bulldoze my way into the room with such force the door slams against the wall, nearly nailing me before I have a chance to step out of its recoil. "I already have committed to her, asshole," I announce, taking in Willow's shocked face for all of a breath before I'm in front of her. Then she's in my arms, my eyes falling shut momentarily when she slides hers around my waist.

"How did you know where I was?" she mumbles into my chest.

"I followed your scent," I say into her hair, inhaling deep.

She tilts her head up and smiles brightly. Her whole face is lit up, and I fall further and further into her. Feathering my thumbs along her cheekbones, I drop a kiss to the tip of her nose.

"Let's go." Sliding my palm down her arm, I take her hand in mine and start walking toward the exit. We're two steps forward when Mergen's smug chirp halts us in our tracks. "He's using you. Did you know that, Willow?"

I feel her whole body stiffen beside me. "Don't do this, Reid."

"Don't do what?" he mocks. Leaning one butt cheek against the long executive table, he crosses his arms, stretching the shoulders of his fitted gray suit. "Tell you the truth? Don't you want to know what kind of man you're committing yourself to? Because he's not an honorable one, that's for damn sure."

"Right." I snort. "Says the moral prick who's trying to steal my girl."

Mergen barely acknowledges me, his entire focus on Willow. "Did you know this"—he nods back and forth between us—"*arrangement* is a hoax? That he singled you out to be his girlfriend for a few months with every intention to cut you loose the second Preston is reelected?"

"Stop Reid," Willow pleads quietly. Her grip on me increases.

"Stop? Fuck no. I'm not stopping until you know everything. You're choosing a man who built what you *think* you have on a bed of lies. He doesn't love you. He's *using* you!"

I go to drop my hold on her, one foot already forward, intent on annihilating this motherfucker but Willow tugs me back. Rather forcefully I might add. "Don't," she tells me, lowly.

That spine of hers snaps straight. She locks eyes with her ex. Her shoulders are set back and that obstinate chin juts out. I recognize this stance. That's my girl: battle born and combat ready. Magnificent.

"And I suppose I should be thanking *you* for that, shouldn't I?" The indignation Mergen's been steeping in for weeks falls flat. When he doesn't answer, Willow adds, "It *was* your idea, wasn't it?" She waves between us. "This?"

I want to smile but don't. No, I want to get us the hell out of here before the room burns down around us because when Mergen sees he's not getting anywhere with this little revelation, he's bringing the big guns.

Setting my hand to her back, I try to push her forward, but she digs in her heels.

"No, just a minute," she tells me without taking her stare from Mergen. "He told me everything so whatever it is you think you're doing isn't going to work, Reid. It only makes you look desperate."

The flash of hurt is unmistakable but then a vile grin snakes across his mouth as his eyes slide to mine. "He told you everything, did he?"

"Yes," she answers at the same time I give her a little shove forward, telling her, "We're out of here."

I smell the smoke. I feel a curl of blistering flames lashing my blackened soul for not confessing this the second I found out. And if I don't get her the hell out of here right now, I'll be completely swathed in third-degree burns.

This time we make it to the door. We're nearly home free when Mergen's slimy voice slithers behind us, "So I suppose he told you that your father didn't commit suicide then, right?"

She freezes.

"Let's go," I say, barely leashing my anger. I try nudging her forward but she's stiffer than a corpse. With one hand she pushes me away and pivots back around.

"What did you say?" she whispers harshly.

Mergen stands up and drops his hands to his side. He looks almost contrite. Fucker. I want to murder him where he stands.

"Willow, let's go," I plead. I need to be the one to break this to her. Not him. *Me.* I wind my fingers around her bicep but she pushes me away again, taking two steps toward Mergen.

"Tell me what you just said." Now her voice is sour and cutting.

Mergen looks tense, yet he keeps going. "So he didn't tell you everything then."

"Willow—" I reach for her but she brushes me off, moving another step away.

"Don't," she says, tone razor sharp. I'm not sure if she's talking to him or me but that's soon put to rest. "Don't you dare bring my father into this. What kind of sick game are you playing, Reid?"

"Me?" he snarls. "*He's* the one you should be asking."

"*He* has nothing to do with this. How could you say something like that?" She chokes out the last few words and I so badly want to wrap her in my arms and protect her from this but I can't. And in under two minutes, she'll never let me again.

"He has everything to do with this!" His hot gaze flashes to mine. "Tell her, Mercer. Go ahead and tell her about your sister's involvement in her father's death."

If I thought it would do a lick of good, I'd beat the ever-living shit out of him. I'd face assault charges. I'd gladly spend days on end in a six-by-six cement jail cell. But that won't change a damn thing. It won't erase the confusion plastered on Willow's face. It won't wipe away the horror when she realizes Mergen's not just being a dick. It certainly won't change the truth.

"What does he mean?" she mumbles, her dainty brows knitting tightly together. She eases back toward Mergen. I'm not even sure she knows she's doing it. I want to fall at her feet and beg her forgiveness. "Shaw, tell me what he means." This time she's found that inner strength I revere.

"I—" Fucking hell. I set my hands on my hips and drop my gaze to the floor, keeping it there for several seconds. I draw in a breath of fortification and pray God is merciful when I raise my eyes to her, hoping beyond all hope we can weather this. "It was an accident."

"An accident?" Her legs give but it's not me who's there to catch her, comfort her. It's *him*. "I don't understand. My father committed suicide. It's in the police report. It's on his death certificate. There was no one else there. No witnesses. It *wasn't* an accident."

"It was." I take a step toward her but she shrinks away, back into *his* hold. She's looking at me like she doesn't know who I am. I want to die. "Willow, let's go somewhere and talk about this. Alone."

"We're not going anywhere until you tell me what happened."

"I'm not doing this with him here."

"Goddammit, Shaw! Enough! Just tell me already," she fires back. She shirks out of his hold, thank Christ, but she stands there, so damn regal next to the man who wanted to marry her. The man who still loves her fiercely and will be there for her when she kicks me out on my ass.

If there's a worse hell than this one, I don't want to know.

I make my throat work to force down the saliva that's pooled in my mouth before launching into the only facts I know.

"My sister—"

"Annabelle?" she asks, clarifying.

"Yes. Annabelle," I tell her. "She was out of sorts that night—"

"Out of sorts?" she interrupts again.

Sighing heavily, I know now is not the time to hold back. "Drugs, alcohol. You name it. She did it." Her lips turn down. The lipstick she glossed them with earlier is nearly gone and what's left she's chewing off. She already sees the path I'm laying, and it's fraught with hairpin turns and vertical falls. If we survive, it will be a fucking miracle. "She was in a really bad place, Willow, even before that. She was reckless, careless, thoughtless. But that night some really bad shit happened and she broke. She didn't care if she lived or died."

"What happened?" Willow asks, her voice a hoarse whisper. There's both a softness and edge to her question.

She deserves the entire story, but not now. Now she'll get the condensed version because I'm not airing all of my family's crap in front of someone I don't trust. I flick my attention to Mergen, whose features are stone hard. I have no idea if he knows everything I do but I'm not giving him any more ammunition to use against me.

"Somehow, she ended up on Schultz Bridge with her friends, every one of them drunk or coked out of their minds. She..." I hesitate, this part still grueling for me accept. My little sister wanted to die and had it not been for her father, I believe she would have succeeded. "She had climbed up onto the railing and was threatening to jump when your father came along."

Tears immediately flood her eyes. They spill over, running in thick rivers down her cheeks. Desperate to feel her, I close the three feet between us but she holds out her hand, forbidding me from touching her.

But not *him*. She's leaning against the table for support, flush to his side. Mergen's arm is now around her slumped shoulders and she's just looking at me, looking through me. Blinking, water flowing. Disbelieving. No doubt feeling as though she's locked in the same nightmare I am, no escape in sight.

"He saw what was going on and he stopped. He climbed up onto the railing with her when she refused to come down." She brings a hand up to wipe her face. It's shaking. I lick my dry lips and continue, trying like hell to ignore these thousand pinpricks of raw agony battering my heart because she's leaning on *him* for strength. "She tried to jump. He lunged and threw her to safety but…" I can't finish it. I can't fucking say it.

The air thickens around us, curdling with the stark realization that all these years she's lived a lie. Her father did not take his own life. He didn't leave her. He didn't leave his wife. He gave his life selflessly to save my baby sister.

"How do you know this?" she croaks. "How *long* have you known this?"

Unable to meet her turmoil head-on any longer I turn toward the bank of windows on my right. I think, given time and introspection, she would be able to come to grips with this horrific scenario. She's compassionate and forgiving that way. But the fact I've known about this for weeks and didn't say anything? Inexcusable.

"Long enough," is all I say.

"Long enough," she repeats, her voice shaky. Her chest heaving. "The whole time? Have you known this the whole time?"

"No," I tell her adamantly. "No, Willow. If you believe nothing else, *please* believe that. I should have told you the second I found out but my only excuse was I was trying to process it all myself. It was wrong. I'm sorry. So goddamn sorry."

She blinks. "Is this why you've not been yourself lately?" I nod once. It hits deep she knows me well enough to know I was off. "Is this what was wrong in Charlotte?" Again, I nod. "Is this why you *went* to Charlotte?" I don't respond. She knows.

"Oh my God. Oh my *God*." She grabs the fabric covering her chest, balling it into her fist.

"Willow." I lean toward her, slowly bleeding out on the inside that she's hurting so bad and I can't do a damn thing. She looks pale. So pale.

"Don't. Just…don't say another word."

"Fuck." I jab my hand in my hair, tugging the strands until I pull a few out. The sting feels good. Right. I do it again. And pace. Three steps one way, three the other. I keep my eye on her the entire time. She's far, far away. None of us speak. None of us dare. Hours pass, only I'll later know it was mere seconds. Horribly short seconds before she'd walk right out of my life.

"I…I need to go." Her eyes are unfocused. Glazed over. Her face is streaked, makeup smudged under her eyes. She's a mess, yet she's the most exquisite creature I have ever laid eyes on.

"I'll drive you," Mergen and I say at the same time, closing in on her.

"No. I'm driving myself."

She pushes herself to stand but wobbles. I'm there to steady her. "You don't have a car," I remind her. She slaps my hand away. Damn stubborn woman. She can be pissed all she wants—she has a right to be—but she's leaving here alone over my dead body. "I'm driving you, Willow. End of story."

She snaps out of her zombie state and her glare is so hot and stifling a ring of fire surrounds me. "You're right about one thing. This is the end of the story."

"Jesus, Willow," I plead, my voice strained. "Please don't do this. Let me explain the whole thing. Please."

"And you," she spits, turning that death glare on Mergen as she ignores my plea. "How dare you. Did you honestly think this was going to win you any favors? How long have *you* known?"

At least the fucker has the decency to seem repentant. Willow may never forgive me for this but at least she's smart enough to know that Mergen tipped his own hand while trying to make me look like the bad guy.

He was with Willow when her father died. He witnessed firsthand her pain, her confusion, her debilitating grief. Years later it remains fresh and raw. He had to have known how not only the loss, but the *way* that loss occurred was devastating to her. If he cared about her one iota, he would have told her the second he found out. Not used it as means to hurt *me,* but as a way to ease *her* suffering.

"Willow, you don't understand," he starts hoarsely.

"I don't understand?" Her eyes are wide, her voice dripping venom. "Oh, I understand perfectly."

Mergen moves toward her, his arms out, still trying to save himself. "I—"

Throwing a hand up; she cuts him off. "Don't. Don't say another word. I'm leaving. Don't follow me. Don't call me. I don't want to see either of you ever again."

Her words are a switchblade at the edge of my wrist, the heaviness of them sinking the sharp metal into my flesh, nicking an artery.

And that's that. Mergen and I remain frozen, both watching the woman we love walk out of the room and out of our lives.

It's the single biggest blow I've taken in my thirty-six years.

Chapter Twenty-Three

I'M NUMB. DEAD INSIDE.

My father didn't commit suicide.

"What are you still doing up?" I hear the sound of keys hit solid wood, then footsteps. "In fact, what are you doing here at all? Shouldn't you be with your hot coffee trying to make that fake baby?"

I don't answer. I can't. I'm numb.

My father didn't commit suicide.

Out of my peripheral vision, I see Sierra walk around the kitchen island. I've been sitting in the same spot since the second I walked through the front door. How long has that been now? Minutes? Hours? I'm not even sure I've blinked. Can you keep your eyes open for hours on end, not blinking? Is that possible? I think it is.

"Why are you still wearing your coat?" She opens a cupboard.

I don't answer. I can't. I'm numb.

My father didn't commit suicide.

"What's the matter? Your prince charming a little less shiny today?" she says sarcastically, laughing. She's kidding, but oh, how right she is.

But I don't answer. I can't. I'm numb.

My father didn't commit suicide.

I hear the fridge open and liquid being poured. Orange juice. Sierra's nightly ritual when she gets home from work. Orange juice and a snack-sized Baby Ruth. It's surprisingly comforting to be part of her odd routine tonight.

"Lowenbrau, what's up? Why are you not answering me?"

Because I can't. I'm numb.

My father didn't commit suicide.

She comes up behind me and spins me around to face her. My head is frozen at a thirty-degree angle, gazing downward. She slips her hands around my cheeks and lifts so I'll meet her eyes.

But I don't. I can't. I'm numb.

My father didn't commit suicide.

"Okay, now you're freaking me out. This is the same way you acted when..." She lets that thought trail. "Willow." She says my name with force and urgency. She shakes me. "Willow, look at me."

But I don't. I can't. I'm numb.

My father didn't commit suicide.

A sting on my cheek brings me out of my trance, and I realize she slapped me. I latch on to her scared eyes and the dam I've worked tirelessly to erect weakens. Cracks appear at the fragile base first, rapidly worming their way up and soon the entire structure heaves and groans under the mounting pressure.

"Tell me what the hell is going on or I'm calling Mercer."

That's all it takes. His name. That's all I needed to break into thousands upon thousands of tiny little pieces that I watch float aimlessly around me, names clear and visible on each minute shard.

Shaw

Charles

Annabelle

Shaw

Reid
Annabelle
Charles
Shaw
Annabelle
Annabelle
Annabelle...

They swirl, slow at first, speed increasing, sound deafening, until they all intersect, crashing with electrifying violence. They fall, landing in a heap at my feet, the reverberations thundering and terminal. Fragments embed in me so deep I'm bleeding everywhere. Inside and out.

I am *not* numb.

I am *not* dead inside.

I am in so much fucking pain I can't breathe.

I stare into my best friend's eyes crammed with worry and creeping anger, and I crumble into nothing.

My father didn't commit suicide.

Shaw's sister was responsible...and Shaw knew.

Shaw

Chapter Twenty-Four

"SHE OKAY?" MY CHEST HURTS so goddamn bad I'm sure someone is squeezing it. I'm oxygen starved, already slowly suffocating without her.

"She didn't say a word the entire way. She seemed pretty out of it. I got her inside and was going to stay until Sierra got off work but she told me to leave, so I stayed in my car instead until Sierra came home."

"Did you talk to her?"

"Who?"

"Sierra."

"No. I didn't talk to her. She didn't see me."

"Thank you," I reply dully. "For taking care of her."

"Don't do that. Don't thank me." Noah takes a seat beside me on my sister's thrift store, vomit-green couch. The cushions are pilled, matted, and stained, the shitty décor straight from the seventies. It's ancient. Eclectic. It fits her. "How's Bluebelle?" he asks.

"How is Bluebelle?" I echo.

Well, let's see. After I texted Noah and told him to get Willow home safely, I decided to get my ass in gear and go after her myself. But the moment I stepped into the hallway, I saw Annabelle, slumped against the wall in a stupor. The brat had followed me instead of going back to the party as I'd instructed. She overheard everything. Every sordid detail of a night that intersected the futures of two families in a twisted, horrific way. So, not only did I lose the chance to tell Willow on my own terms, I couldn't break it gently to Annabelle either.

The entire evening has been a clusterfuck of epic proportions, and I have no one to blame but myself.

"She's too calm. I'm worried about her."

"Is she asleep?"

I breathe out a heavy sigh. "Pretending to be."

Noah's been gone for hours. It's now after four in the morning. I'm surprised he showed up here, yet not. I'm not sure I want him here, though I don't tell him to leave.

I stare at the hideous piece of art on the wall directly across from us. It's a picture of a woman's body, seated, but the head is a single giant eyeball with a white turban wrapped around the top and draped over her shoulder. The eyeball watches you, follows you around the room. It's bizarre and disturbing.

Annabelle was so excited when she bought it at a garage sale for five bucks she could hardly contain herself. I told her she should have been paid to take it. She replied in her usual flippant way, "You should see it when you're high." When I attempted to rip it off the wall, she laughed, telling me, "Relax. I've never seen her when I'm high." She stepped back and stared at it thoughtfully. "I know you see something disgusting when you look at her, but I see a reminder to stay the course, you know. Eyes open. One foot in front of the other. Be something more than everyone thinks they see." She's not only smart; she's insightful, too. I love that introspective side of her.

Now what? Now what happens after all the hard work she's put in? I'm terrified. Absolutely fucking terrified. She knows I stayed and she knows why. Neither of us said it, but this is a suicide watch, plain and simple.

"I could use a stiff drink," Noah announces.

"Yeah. Me too." Only I worry I'll fall into the bottom of the bottle if I get started. Plus, I can't have that shit anywhere near Annabelle right now. No telling what she'll do when I fall asleep. Which is why I've had three Red Bulls since midnight. I plan on keeping vigil right here until morning. Then I will drag her kicking and screaming to my house so I can watch her like a hawk until I'm sure she won't go off the rails.

"Did you tell your folks?"

"No. I just played it off as boyfriend trouble. Wasn't too hard to convince them."

"And Willow?"

"Told them she wasn't feeling well and I had you take her home since I was dealing with Annabelle." Not a *total* lie.

"They're going to find out."

"I know. I plan to talk to them in the morning. Time to air all the dirty laundry, I guess. Besides, we're all going to need to pitch in." I scrub a hand over my face. "Bluebelle's going to need therapy for years to deal with this. My parents aren't going to be able to bury their heads any longer."

"I don't think they mean to ignore it, Merc."

"Doesn't matter. It's hard shit to deal with. I get it. But if they don't open their eyes, we will lose her."

Noah matches my position, sinking into the couch in a slumped position, legs spread wide. We're both still decked out in our designer suits. Still wearing our high-priced loafers and $10,000 watches.

I am a man with immeasurable wealth, yet in this moment, you won't find a single soul poorer than me.

The only woman I will ever love doesn't want to see me again, and my baby sister is balancing on a high wire and if she makes one misstep, she could fall to her death.

"Give her time, Shaw," he says quietly after I think he's drifted off.

I blink back the burn behind my closed lids. I want to weep.

"Which one?" I ask. *The woman who hates me or the woman who knows what she's taken from me?*

"Both." He sets his hand on my thigh and squeezes once. "Both."

Noah scoots back, wedging himself in the corner and we fall quiet, nothing left to say.

I know he's right, but I'm here to tell you…as each second ticks by without Willow, without hearing from her, without talking to her, without knowing what she's thinking, I fall a little further into despair.

Only months ago, my life was easy and uncomplicated. I did what I wanted, when I wanted, how I wanted, why I wanted. I dated and fucked countless women without guilt or a yearning for more. I was free and content. I had it all, or so I thought.

Then along comes this hellfire named Willow Blackwell, who tested my patience and hypnotized my soul. In her, I found what was lost in me. She's color, she's sun, she's rain, she's earth, she's breath, she's warmth, she's salt, she's sweet.

She's life.

She's mine.

Without Willow, I am nothing.

A ghost of the man I thought I was.

I can't give her up. No matter what she says or how many roadblocks she puts in my path, I won't be like Mergen and walk away from us. It's not in my makeup. Never gonna happen. My life was on pause before her and will be again without her.

I've always considered myself a fairly selfless person but with Willow, I am beyond selfish. I want it all. I want every second, every day, every year, every decade with her until death do us part. I want to build a life with her that other people envy and I won't give up until I have it.

I'm desperate to go to her and force her to listen to me, make her accept my apology. Convince her we can weather this, somehow, someway. Never in my life have I been this torn. The more time I give her, the farther away she'll get.

But I can't leave Annabelle. I can't. Not for a second. Willow may be mad and confused and distraught but I know Sierra will take good care of her until I can.

As hard as it is, I need to stay here. Annabelle is in a perilous place, and no matter how much I ache for Willow, this is where I need to be. I'd never forgive myself if I weren't here and she did something irreversible.

If there's a hell, this is it, right here. I am balls deep in its blistering heat.

Hearing Noah's even breaths, indicating he's nodded off, I jerk my phone from my front pocket and pull up Willow's number. She said she doesn't want to hear from me again? Tough. She clearly doesn't grasp how persistent I can be when I want something.

I type out a short message, my finger hovering only momentarily over the send button before telling the woman I love with every fiber of me in no uncertain terms I am not giving her up. I tell her the same thing I told her when I had her underneath me at the hotel after I swept her from the dance floor at Skyfall.

I'll give her time and space. I know her. I know she needs it, but the clock is ticking because this isn't the end of us. Not by a long shot.

You are worth fighting for.

Nothing has been worth fighting for more.

Chapter Twenty-Five

"WHAT ARE YOU DOING?" SIERRA asks, standing at the mouth of the living room, staring.

"What does it look like I'm doing?" I reply sweetly, not bothering to look up. Fine, sweet may have been an exaggeration. *Whatever*. I'm a little short on sleep these days.

She stands there, waiting patiently until I can't stand the sight of her bare feet anymore. I gaze up from the mess I've made on the carpet and latch on to dark eyes filled with worry.

"It looks like Shutterfly threw up in here."

She may be right. My entire heritage is laid out before me.

Pictures are scattered everywhere, over every available surface. I took every tote stuffed with photo albums and loose prints I could find from my mother's attic and brought them all home. Five plastic storage bins full of thousands upon thousands of memories. My parents' wedding, Violet's birth, my first birthday party, my fifth-grade graduation, Violet and me building a snowman outside the Breckenridge condo we stayed at for five days when I was eight. My parents couldn't get me to come inside except to sleep. My cheeks were chapped for a week after we returned home.

"I've been meaning to organize them," I tell her, going back to business. Once upon a time, my mother loved to snap candids and she didn't believe in digital storage. She wanted something she could hold, touch. "A picture should live in your sight, not in the bowels of a piece of plastic," she would say.

After Violet died, picture taking became less and less frequent, mostly at special events or holidays, so the majority of what's in these boxes is from the first half of my life and that of my parents' lives. Some are already organized. Most are not, living dark, dank lives tucked away in stuffy shoe boxes.

I glance at the picture in my hand and pause, stroking my daddy's handsome, youthful face. Thick glasses made him seem much older than his seventeen years. But even then, he was stoic and handsome. You could tell he was destined for great things by the flicker in his eye and the determination in his smile.

Much like another man I know whose name I can't even bear to think of right now without hyperventilating.

"This your dad?" Sierra asks, now standing over my shoulder.

"Watch it," I say, tugging on the edge of a print she's crinkling with her size-ten hoofs. She lifts her foot and sighs, then bends over and scoops several snapshots to the left, making enough room for her to squat down beside me.

"Hey," I berate. "I had those in order."

"In what order?"

"In chronological order. What other order is there?"

Her gaze floats around the room and she laughs. Quicker than I can react, she snatches the thick pile of photos from my hand and holds them away when I reach to get them back. Since Sierra's arms are a good six inches longer than mine, I quickly decide my effort is fruitless and give up until she says her piece.

"I think you're drowning yourself in crap that doesn't matter to anyone, including you, so you don't have to face whatever it is that's had me fending off the posse for the last few days."

I snort. *Posse.* The only one she's fended off has been Reid. He's shown up at the house every blessed day. Sometimes Sierra's boorish behavior comes in handy. She makes a good guard dog.

"Why don't you mind your own business," I snap, gritting my teeth against the fact I'm so transparent.

"Come on now, you can do better than that, Low."

She thinks she's one-upped me but she hasn't. I abandon the group of pictures she's holding hostage in favor of another one next to me. I pick it up and start the same process I've been working on for hours.

Anything to keep the pain at bay.

Only she grabs the next set of snapshots from my hand, too. *Bitch.* I'm starting to get irked. Can't a girl wallow in her pity party without interference?

I pick up another pile, sit up, and face her. "I can do this all day."

"So can I," she retorts, snatching that group, too. Lifting one eyebrow high, she smirks and waits for my next move.

"What do you want, Sierra?"

"What I want is for you to stop acting like a cunt and tell me what's really going on."

Damn. That was harsh, even for tactless Sierra.

"Now you're just being a bitch," I say.

In a huff, she tries tossing the three stacks she's confiscated to the floor in front of her, but because they're slick with gloss they start sliding everywhere and suddenly her lap is covered in hundreds of photos. And when a rather large daddy long legs darts out from between two pictures and starts crawling across her bare foot, she screams as if the apocalypse has descended. All four limbs start flailing and I duck to the side to avoid an unintentional right hook.

She's squealing, jumping, thrashing around. Pictures are stuck to her feet and hands and backs of her thighs and those that aren't are flying everywhere.

The situation is so ridiculous, so comedic I start to laugh.

And I laugh and laugh and laugh until the tears finally come. And then I cry until Sierra is once again sitting beside me, holding me through my racking sobs.

"You're starting to piss me off, you know that? You're going to make me call him if you don't start talking."

"Don't," I wheeze. I forbid her from saying his name again seven nights ago. At least she's respected that. "I'll hate you forever if you do."

"No, you won't. You're going to make me your fake baby's godmother, remember?"

That only makes me cry harder. A tissue appears in front of my face and I snatch it up, wiping my dripping nose first. I free myself of her hold and scoot back a few inches so I can lean against the couch. Sierra follows, throwing her legs over the coffee table.

I've cried more since I met Shaw Mercer than I have in a lifetime. I wonder what that means?

"You need to talk about it sometime, Lowenbrau. Confession unburdens the soul," says the hypocrite.

But I can't. I won't. I can't think about him. I can't talk about it. *I can't I can't I can't.* I'm not strong enough to deal right now.

I pluck a picture Sierra missed from her calf and hold it out.

Johnny Hankins. My junior prom date. Out of all these pictures, *that* one had to be stuck to her.

"Oh my God, let me see that." Sierra sneaks it from my fingers and studies it. "You had the most hideous dress. I told you not to wear something that basically looked like a cotton candy comforter."

"Hey." I rip it back. "It was fashionable." It *was* hideous. I don't know what I was thinking. I looked like something straight out of *Beauty and the Beast,* except in bright, neon pink. And not nearly as elegant.

Her face screws up. "It's a bed warmer."

"It was Violet's favorite color," I say softly. Mermaid hues were in that year. Blues, golds, greens. Pink dresses were hard to come by, and my junior prom happened to land on what would have been Violet's twenty-second birthday. I wanted to do something for her, I guess. It was stupid.

Now Sierra's mouth turns down and the mood in the room takes another nosedive. I tear up again. Sierra runs a finger under one eye, catching the first drop of water to leak. "Oh, Low…haven't you learned after all this time that you don't have to shoulder all your burdens alone? Doesn't it wear you out?"

Yes. I'm so fucking exhausted every muscle feels atrophied.

"My father didn't commit suicide," I blurt. "He was trying to save Shaw's sister Annabelle from committing suicide and he fell."

"What?" Her brows scrunch. Her voice is pitched in disbelief. She's as confused by this sucker punch as I was.

I tuck my knees under my chin and wrap my hands around my shins, staring at the mess I've created. It's incomprehensible that fate is such a cruel, cruel bitch.

I had a decent life before Shaw came along. Hard sometimes. Lonely, perhaps. But I got by. I'd accepted where I was, who I was, flaws and all. I'd even accepted that a man or a family of my own probably wasn't in the cards for me.

That is, until an infuriating, gorgeous, godlike man rammed his way into my world. Literally. Shaw has taken me over completely, and after only a few short months I already don't know where I end and he begins. He's so tangled in every thought, every action, every decision, I can't fathom never hearing him groan my name as he drives inside me or waking in the middle of the night just to watch him sleep or mouthing back when he turns up his power to ten.

But how can I move past this? How can I accept it? All these years I've been living a lie and the grief that consumed me when my father first died rules me once again. I'm back to square one. How can I ever look at Shaw or Annabelle again without replaying what I lost? How can I forgive her, even if I believe it was an accident? How can I ever trust Shaw again after he kept this information hidden from me for God knows how long?

How?

God, I don't know.

"How do you know this?"

I open my mouth to answer, ready to unburden my soul at last, when she yells, "Wait. We need alcohol for this. Lots and lots of alcohol."

It's two in the afternoon, but it's five o'clock somewhere, right?

Not a minute later she's back with two shot glasses and a full bottle of Patron. This could get ugly.

"You aren't messing around."

"I have a feeling Bud Light isn't going to cut it, do you?"

My smile is thin, barely there. "Good point." I'm not sure anything will help me through this. She pours us each a shot, which we down quickly. Then she immediately fills our glasses once more. I slide her a look but she simply raises it and holds it there until I clink and drink. I savor the warmth burning a path down my chest. It's the first time I've felt warm in a week.

"So..." she prods.

I take a deep breath, "So..." and launch into what Shaw confessed to me a few nights ago. I realize as I'm rattling off details to Sierra that there are holes in the story because I didn't stick around to listen to it anymore. Like, what had a sweet sixteen-year-old so distraught she wanted to take her own life? Did Shaw know she was in such a bad place? Did her family? Had she tried it before? Has she tried it since?

And what did my father say to her that night? Why didn't he call the police? Why didn't anyone else stop to help them? And why—*fucking why*—didn't one of those girls come forward and put my momma and me out of our misery?

There's also the obvious connection to Violet. If I thought it, so, too did my father, because there wasn't a day that went by he didn't wish he could have saved her. Just like me. I can only imagine what went through his mind when he pulled around that corner and saw a girl his dead daughter's age perched on the ledge of that bridge.

Would it matter if I knew answers to the hundreds of questions bobbing around in my head? I think maybe it would, though I'm not ready to do what it takes to get them yet. Because that means talking to Annabelle, and I'm not sure I can stomach looking at her.

I've been trying to push away the distraught look on her face when I ran into her outside of the conference room, but the second I close my eyes at night she's there.

Her eyes were haunted. She looked lost, destroyed. Completely shattered and I can't understand why. This is not new news to her. She was *there*, for fuck's sake. All this time...all this time she knew. She *knew* who I was. She *knew* what happened. She *knew* and she never said a fucking word, so she doesn't get to be devastated. *I* do.

"That's fucked."

"Ya think?"

"Where does your ex fit into all this?"

"I don't know exactly, but he knew. He knew and he never said anything either. How could he do that?" I feel so betrayed. So incredibly betrayed. By everyone.

"I don't even know what to say." Sierra's speechless. That doesn't happen often.

"I need another one." I hold out my hand, too wrung out to lift the bottle that's now close to a quarter gone.

Sierra obliges and we decide on a fourth, too. Pretty soon, my brain is fuzzy and my fingers start to tingle. It feels nice, numbing up. I slump down and lean my head back against the cushion, letting my gaze float upward. Sierra settles in beside me.

"What are you going to do?"

"I honestly don't know," I confess. "I love him so much, but I...I don't know how to move past this, Ser."

Sierra grabs my hand, holding tight and for once she has nothing biting or sarcastic to say. We sit in silence, as we've done so many times before when life took a giant crap on one of us.

I may not know what I'm going to do yet, but I do know a lot of other things.

I love Shaw Mercer to the dark depths of my being. I can't breathe without him. I ache everywhere, and the thought of never seeing him again makes me physically ill. My skin even hurts. But how can love be enough to get us through this? I'm not sure it's possible, though he apparently disagrees.

He's not called me. He's not showed up on my doorstep like Reid, but he's also not respected my wishes to never contact me again either, and I haven't come to grips with how I feel about that yet.

Every day I receive the same simple text. Just one: *You're worth fighting for.*

And every day I delete it without responding like I did the day before. Exactly the way I did with Reid all those years ago.

Can I really let Shaw go the way I did Reid? Though the situations are totally different, my actions are exactly the same. Run, hide, suffer alone. It's a technique I've practiced and I've mastered it well.

"Here." Sierra shoves another full shot into my hand I take it without complaint. We spend the next few hours just like this, repeating the same process until the bottle is gone, the sun is down, and I can't feel my limbs any longer.

Between shots and small talk, we manage to eat a little something and avoid any more depressing conversation before we pour our drunk asses into bed, knowing we'll curse the harsh bite of the smooth-talking liquor in about six hours. Sierra snuggles in beside me without being asked and I'm secretly grateful even though I know she's a cover whore.

I switch off the lamp, throwing us into darkness. I'm blessedly letting the alcohol drag me under when I hear it...

The soft ping of my phone.

I lay still, breathing fast, knowing it's him. I don't want to look but I won't be able to fall asleep until I do either. My hand trembles as it hangs over the cell, which has now pinged a second time.

"Look at the damn thing, for Christ sake," Sierra mumbles, turning away from me, already dragging the blankets with her.

"I'm just shutting it off," I tell her, ignoring the *uh-huh* she mockingly voices under her breath.

Picking it up, I squint against the bright light in the darkened room, staring at the text message I know awaits me on the screen.

You're worth fighting for.

I stare at it for a while. I run my fingers over the words, feeling the smooth edge of each syllable. I hear his raspy voice whispering them in my ear as he moves over me. I let the resolution of them sink in a little more. With a long sigh, I power the device down, fully aware I didn't perform that one last step in the ritual I've executed flawlessly for the past seven days.

I know at some point I'm going to have to face this, face *them*, talk about it, think about it, wrap my head around this new reality. Shaw is bullheaded and persuasive. It's why he's been so successful, how he got me into bed. It's why I love him so much. I don't believe he'll give up on me anytime soon, if ever. He won't just leave me behind like Reid did. He won't *let* me leave him behind. This I already know.

So here's the decision I'm going to have to make: Is *Shaw* worth fighting for? Are *we* worth fighting for? Am I willing to gut my way through this inconceivable hell to find out what we could be on the other side? That's the real question because it doesn't matter if Shaw wants us. It matters if *I* do.

And as I finally allow myself to drift into the void of nothingness I truly wish I had the answer to that question. But I don't.

Not today I don't.

Willow

Chapter Twenty-Six

"HOW THE HELL DID YOU get my number?" I hear Sierra bark.

The sound of her voice is like screaming bullets ricocheting off the inner walls of my ears. God almighty, that hurts. In fact, as I roll around and take stock of my surroundings I notice everything hurts.

My lips are chapped. My tongue feels like an overstuffed sausage. The back of my throat is as dry as if someone shoved a spoonful of fine sand in my mouth when I was sleeping. As I mentally move my attention down my body, I notice a tightness in my chest and then I get to my stomach.

Sweet mother of all hangovers.

My stomach. It's rolling over on itself like I'm riding out thirty-foot waves on an inner tube. The half bottle of tequila I drank pushes its way up my esophagus. I push back. Tequila has more muscle than I do this morning, though. Tequila's been working out.

Oh *shit*.

I draw in a long breath, concentrating only on air filling my lungs and not the roil of liquid sloshing in my middle when I feel the bed dip beside me as Sierra sits up.

For the love of all that's holy! I mentally scream at her. *Don't fucking move. Don't breathe, don't talk, don't let me do this again.*

"What kind of friend are you?" I groan, gently placing the pillow I'd been cuddling with over my head. I want to die. No, first I want to brush my teeth, then I want to die.

"I don't give a simpleton's scrawny white ass why you're calling, Wilder."

Wilder? The only Wilder I know Sierra knows is Noah. Why is Noah calling her? Did Shaw ask him to intervene since I'm ignoring him? That's when another thought hits hard and fast. It steals my breath.

Oh Jesus…what's happened? Is Shaw okay? Is Annabelle okay? Something has happened. I feel it heavy as a bag of rocks in my bones.

Panic now joins the get-together in my stomach. I chuck the pillow that was over my head to the floor and pop an eye open, unable to move for fear of losing the war with tequila. Sierra wears her usual scowl but it's overly pronounced as she listens to the male voice on the other side of her cell. As he talks, her scowl deepens. She looks at me, her eyes widening as she listens to the voice a few more seconds before handing me the phone. She immediately snags my iPad from the nightstand and my stomach sinks.

Now what?

"Don't beat around the bush, Noah. Tell me what's wrong," I croak. Those rocks in my bones have moved to my vocal chords.

"Willow?"

But it's not Noah's voice that filters through the speaker. It's Shaw's, rich and heady. My heart stutters. An actual skip of a beat. A rush of relief runs through me that he's all right but it's quickly snuffed out, replaced by the memories of everything he's put me through. I glance up at Sierra to cut her with my invisible shank for tricking me into thinking I was getting Noah but her eyes are racing over the iPad screen.

"What do you want, Shaw?"

He sighs, clearly dejected over my harsh tone, but answers me regardless. "There's an article in this morning's *7-Day*."

Of course there is.

"What does it say?" I manage to ask, this time not sounding quite so gravelly.

"Fuck, Willow," is all he says back. I hear the pure frustration and implied apology in his deep voice when he adds, "I don't know how yet, but I promise you I will fix this."

"Fix what?" A fire of anger boils the witch's brew in my belly to toxic levels. I push myself to a sitting position and secure the phone between my shoulder and ear. I swallow a few times until I'm sure the bad decisions I made the night before will stay put for now and yank the iPad from Sierra's hands. "Did another one of Noah's and your *mistakes* end up on page one?"

A sharp hit of air, followed by a soft, "I deserve that," reach me but I can't respond. I'm frozen by the damning article in the *7-Day*.

A CAMPAIGN PARLOR TRICK?

A week shy of Election Day and a potential scandal has rocked Mayor Mercer's campaign.

Early on it was clear there was no love lost between Seattle's current mayor, Preston Mercer, and his seat's rival, Wicklow Harrington III, a lifelong resident of Seattle and an esteemed, respected entrepreneur. Mayor Mercer acquired his current position when Mayor Thurston passed away suddenly from a stroke in April 2015.

While both parties have turned up the heat as Election Day draws near, both camps have managed to keep typical campaign mudslinging to minimal levels. Until recently, that is.

In an interview with Mayor Mercer last week when asked about the accusations from his opponent that he was a roadblock to enticing new businesses into Seattle, he candidly told one of our reporters, "My record speaks for itself." When pressed to respond to Harrington's allegations, Mayor Mercer said, "I want to run a clean campaign based on my leadership merit, not my ability to one-up my opponent. Instead of rhetoric not based on merit, we need to stay focused on the issues that matter to Seattle's residents, such as reducing our homelessness, providing affordable housing for everyone, and implementing civilian oversight for the police department. My eye is focused on my obligations to the people of Seattle, as it always has been and will be while I'm blessed to serve a city that I love. Anything else is simply not worth my time."

Interesting, then, that the 7-Day *has learned Mayor Mercer's campaign may not be as squeaky clean as he would lead us to believe and that he may be using his eldest son's recent and conveniently timed relationship with Willow Blackwell as a good old-fashioned parlor trick to demonstrate picture-perfect family stability when that's also recently been questioned by the Harrington campaign.*

I gasp, dropping the phone as my eyes continue to scan the article.

Blackwell, an audiobook narrator for LLK Publishing, began dating Shaw Mercer, co-CEO of Wildemer & Company, just days before Mayor Mercer's official campaign kicked off. It's speculated Blackwell also works for an exclusive entity that provides companionship in exchange for strict confidentiality and a hefty price tag, which, according to the 7-Day's *confidential source, is actually how they met and not via a car accident as the couple claimed in an interview with the* 7-Day *a few weeks ago.*

Oh. My. Fucking. God. I can't breathe. There's a sharp pain piercing my chest.

Blackwell, along with her mother, Evelyn, survives scientific researcher Charles Blackwell. Charles Blackwell, better known as "CJ" by his colleagues and friends, took his own life in November 2012, leaving both Aurora Pharmaceuticals and the scientific community in a state of shock and disbelief. In an interesting twist, Wildemer & Company, a global management consulting firm, is assisting Aurora Pharmaceuticals in their IPO launch, planned for early next year.

I scan the rest of the article for one name and one name alone, and blessedly not finding mention of Randi, I drop the iPad to the mattress, unable to stomach reading the last half. The only good news is tequila has decided to give me a reprieve for the moment.

How in the hell did this happen? Who knew? What kind of blowback will this have on Preston's campaign? And, oh my God, what will Randi do once she finds out?

Jesus, Mary, and Joseph. This is devastating. And no matter what Shaw says, there is no fixing this. This is far worse than him pictured with that woman. This is career destroying. For all of us.

I need to do something. Anything. I realize Sierra is no longer here and neither is her phone. I snap mine off the nightstand and power it up. Just seconds later the notifications pour in.

Shaw (7:32): Missed call
Reid (7:33): Missed call
***Shaw (7:33)**: I know you're still mad, but call me, please. It's urgent.*
***Reid (7:34)**: I need to talk to you. It's not about the other night. Pls call right away.*
Randi (7:44): Missed call
***Shaw (7:44)**: Willow…I'm not kidding. I need to talk to you. It can't wait.*
***Randi (7:45)**: we need to talk…now*
***Reid (7:46)**: Now is not the time to dig in those stubborn heels. It's critical I talk to you ASAP.*

Jo (7:53)*: girl, what the hell did you do?*
Millie (7:59): Missed call
Shaw (8:01): Missed call
Reid (8:03): Missed call
Randi (8:05)*: call me or you're fired*
Shaw (8:10): *I promise you, Goldilocks, you won't be able to sit for a week if I don't hear from you in 10 min.*

And the list goes on and on, each text progressively more urgent and threatening. Each missed call more and more frequent. My gaze lands on the digital clock. 8:35.

I rank the urgency, quickly deciding Randi is most critical. Forget about me. What's done is done. I'll fade into the background with the next headline tomorrow. It's *her* ass on the line. The "anonymous" source certainly knows about Randi, about what she does, and intentional or not, if some greedy reporter starts digging further this could spell big trouble for her.

Heat prickles my skin in a slow, painful roll. I want to talk to her like I want to be escorted to my own beheading. And I have nothing to offer. I have no idea what happened.

Fuck.

Fuck. Fuck. Fuck!

I am dead. She's going to kill me. I knew this was a bad idea. I knew I should have walked out of her office and away from the one man who made me feel vibrant and teeming with life. Even if I didn't intend on returning to La Dolce Vita, I certainly didn't want to go out this way. Baked in scandal. Possible criminal charges brought against her.

Crap on a cracker.

In the few seconds it's taken to run all this through my mind, my phone has buzzed six more times. It's ringing now. And as if her ears were itching, it's Randi.

I send it to voice mail and immediately pull up the number of the only person I can talk to about this. The only one who will shoot it to me straight.

The phone rings only twice before he answers.

"I was wondering if you would call," he says, his tone not holding any of the lightness I've become used to. The edges of my mouth drop, though he can't see.

"Guess you don't have to wonder anymore."

"How are you doing, doll?" His voice is low, full of concern. I want to cry. I wonder if Shaw is standing nearby. I imagine him pacing, becoming more and more agitated the longer we talk.

I lie back down and try to forget the sloshing in my belly and the heaviness in my limbs. "I'd say on a scale of one to ten, I'm at about a negative three."

Noah makes a hum in the back of his throat. "I'm sorry, sweetheart."

Yeah. Me too. Then I get to the point. I can't do small talk right now. "I don't suppose you know who did this?" For some reason, this all feels a little personal, though I know it's probably just dirty politics.

"Not yet, but we'll find out. Trust me on that."

I have no doubt Shaw won't stop until he knows who to burn at the stake.

"Okay then." I sigh, moving on to the next most important question. And while I shouldn't care anymore what happens to Shaw or the rest of the Mercer family, the simple fact of the matter is I do. I'm pretty sure I always will.

"Tell me how I can help."

Shaw

Chapter Twenty-Seven

THE LAST FOURTEEN DAYS HAVE been a trip straight to hell and back.

Every last fucking second of them.

Starting first with the fiasco at my father's fundraiser, not only have I spent fourteen nights in my bed alone, I've pretty much made a full-time job out of babysitting Annabelle and trying to clean up the nuclear fallout that resulted from the article in the *7-Day* last week. On top of that, I've had to work side by side with my nemesis to accomplish the latter.

I want to slit my wrists about now. I'm exhausted, I'm angry, and I'm ravenous for a woman I'm not sure I'll ever get a genuine taste of again.

Within an hour after the exposé broke, Mergen had come up with a game plan, finally demonstrating the value he brought to my father's campaign. I had to reluctantly agree it was a good one, but it required Willow's cooperation, and I wasn't sure if she would go along with it. I wasn't sure I blamed her.

I wanted to be the man to reassure her. The one she leaned on. So when I realized Noah was talking to Willow—that she had called *him* back to get details and not me—I may have lost it.

My father, Mergen, Noah, and I were in my home office at the time, which now is short one bottle of very pricey Hennessy 250. Even though I later had the entire carpet steamed twice, I can't get the stench of liquor out of the air. And the dent it made in the wall where I chucked the full bottle still needs to be repaired.

But after that minor blowup, I had to look past the agony gradually eating its way through my soul to the immediate problem at hand. I sat not so patiently while Noah calmly explained to *my* girl the steps we needed to take to mitigate the damage.

Surprisingly, she agreed, though for some inexplicable reason, Willow will do anything for Noah. If I'd asked, I can only imagine the expletives she'd have filled my ear with.

In the past six days, Willow and I have given an interview to the biggest and most respectable daily paper in Seattle, the *World Herald*, along with on-air interviews to each of the major news stations in town. We refuted the *7-Day* article, of course, citing their past behavior as demonstrative of their blatant support of Harrington, along with an obvious bone to pick with me.

We've subtly called the *7-Day's* editor-in-chief's integrity into question when Mergen uncovered she conveniently happens to be the second cousin of Harrington's wife. I wish I'd known that.

And between all this, we've made it a point to be seen out together often while Mergen anonymously tips off reporters where we'll be.

Leaving city hall hand in hand.

Cozy dinners on the water.

Taking my niece and nephews to the children's museum.

We've somehow convinced the outside world we are stronger than ever when we are anything but. After a torturous week apart, Willow spent time with me not because she wanted to, but because she was forced to. She jumped in to do what she does best. What I'd originally hired her for. She played my girlfriend to a very fucking pointy T, and by played, I definitely mean acted.

She pasted on that dreamy smile she's flashed me countless times.

She let me touch her, lavish attention on her for the cameras.

She grazed my jaw with her lips and batted her eyes with practiced shyness when I told her how she took my breath away.

But when the flashes ebbed and we were alone, I saw it. It took me months to find the bottom of those hidden blue depths, but now a murky, impenetrable darkness blocks my view.

It's what I've feared most.

She's shut down thoroughly. Shut *me out* completely. She is right next to me yet a world away, and I don't know how to get her back.

It's a truth that burns me to my core.

It's burning me right this second, in fact, with her warm body plastered to mine, her arm around my waist.

It's D-day. Election evening, actually. The day I've been dreading since I walked out of Randi Deveraux's office with Willow's signature still wet.

My entire family is here, waiting. And it would look odd if my girlfriend weren't by my side, wouldn't it?

"Can I get you anything, beautiful?" I ask her. I set my lips to her temple and inhale the coconut scent of her shampoo. Her breaths come faster. My dick twitches. He misses her as much as I do.

"No, thank you. I'm good," she replies curtly.

The corner of my mouth lifts up, but it's a far cry from a smile.

I am done with this. The evasion. Her stubbornness. I've put up with it for two weeks now and my patience is rubbed completely raw.

"You and I are talking tonight after this is over."

"We're talking right now."

Christ almighty. I want to bury my face between her legs until I have her so worn and weary she'll listen to every goddamn word I have to say.

Instead, I tilt my head to the ceiling and pray for patience. I haven't prayed this much since I wanted a golden Labrador at the age of twelve.

"I'm tired of this bullshit, Willow. Of all this surface crap you've given me this week. We need to talk like adults, without the cameras. Just you and me." She stiffens beside me but keeps that false fucking smile planted on her lips. I lean down, whispering in her ear, "You owe me this, Goldilocks."

Her smile wavers. Just a bit, but she schools it in record time. Looking up at me she beats those long lashes lovingly but her voice drips with incredulity. "*I* owe *you*? That's rich. I distinctly remember *you* telling *me* you wouldn't be anything less than honest with me. And I foolishly believed you."

The day after the *7-Day* story was printed, my father's lead dropped by five full points, narrowing his lead with Harrington to within a statistical margin of error. A week later, it's crawled back up three points but it's still too close for comfort, and what should have been a landslide is now too close to call.

I should care more than I do if my father wins or not. After all, that's the only reason this beauty is glaring at me with barely veiled icicles dangling from her eyelids. But the only thing I can make myself care about is her and how I can win her back.

I pivot and press my body fully into hers. Her breath skips in warning, but she doesn't make a move away from me because that's not what a doting girlfriend would do.

We're tucked toward the back of the packed room and no one is around us at the moment. All eyes are focused on the updated polling results scrolling along the bottom of a giant screen on the wall. Not that I'd care if we were in the middle of a circle with everyone's attention on us anyway.

It wouldn't stop me from doing this...

Cradling her face in my hands, I don't give her a chance to deny me as I press my lips to hers in a gentle, tender kiss. It's real, not for show. I move my mouth slowly against hers, with purpose, the way I did the first time I kissed her. I run my tongue along the seam of her pillowy lips. I nip at her lower one until she stops resisting and her moans turn into a sweet symphony of submission.

I lock my muscles tight forcing her to stay flush with me. She hasn't let me kiss her this way all week and I am greedy. Insatiable. I'll never get enough. I keep kissing her until her hands crawl up my back and, whether she means to or not, she pulls me closer.

I allow my heart to soar with hope.

She doesn't want this to end any more than I do. She simply doesn't know how to move through it. I don't have the answers either. All I know is we have to do it side by side.

"I love you," I tell her adamantly against her swollen lips when I break away and lean my forehead to hers. Her eyes close as I talk but I can't close mine. I need to watch every single reaction. "And you deserved the truth from me the second I found out. I'm sorry. I was wrong. I was scared. I've never been more scared of losing anything in my life, Goldilocks. You, Annabelle. Everything I loved was on the line."

Her hold loosens. Her hands drop to my lower back and now she's barely touching me, only her fingertips making contact. I am bereft.

"I don't know how I'm supposed to do this, Shaw," she tells me lowly. She's still hiding her eyes from me, though they're open. They're downcast as she moves her hands from my back to my sides and curls them around the fabric of my dress shirt. Now I don't even feel their warmth. "I love you, but I'm not sure that's enough."

The wind puffing my sails a minute ago is suddenly still and stifling. I'm dead in the water.

What do I do? I try not to panic. To think logically, strategically.

In my experience with Willow, begging won't work, but maybe the truth will. It's my last play.

"Some bad stuff happened to her that night, Willow. Even I didn't know the details until recently." I pause, the next part hard to think about let alone say. "She was almost raped by some druggie asshole boyfriend of hers and...yes, she was impaired, but she was in a bad place mentally even before that."

I shouldn't be doing this here, only I may not have another chance after tonight. If she decides this is over, it's quite possible I may never see her again. She's stubborn and determined and steadfast in her decisions. Like me.

"I'm not making excuses but Annabelle doesn't remember what happened that night after she fled. She doesn't remember trying to jump, or your father coming along, or...the accident. None of it. She didn't even realize there was a connection. None of us did until Mergen threatened to tell you about it if I didn't back off."

Those bewitching eyes pop open now. A myriad of emotions runs through her and I see every one of them transition to the next. Confusion, realization, sadness, then concern.

"I wanted you to know the whole story, not the shady version your ex was trying to peddle. I wasn't trying to keep anything from you, Willow. I was just trying to figure out how to deliver the blow with the least amount of impact. To everyone. But I always intended to tell you. Please believe that."

"Annabelle was outside the room when I left. She looked..."—she pauses, thinking—"distraught."

I nod. "She learned at the same time you did. She followed me and was eavesdropping. I'd been trying to find a way to tell you both without..." I scrub a hand over my face, wanting to lay it all open. *How selfish I've been.* "Without losing either of you."

Her face is scrunched in disbelief as she quietly understands what I'm telling her. "Oh my God." She breaks from my hold and steps to the side, running her gaze over the room.

I've intentionally stayed away from my mother and father tonight. Per my instructions, Annabelle is attached to their hip, with Noah watching guard. I didn't think it would be a good idea for either Annabelle or Willow to have to interact tonight. Wounds are too fresh.

"Is she okay? I mean, is she…you know?"

Oh, how I love this woman. She's so damn selfless. And the fact she's even worried about Annabelle *means* something. I refuse to believe it doesn't.

I wrap my arm around her. "She's been staying with me." Though she's bitched about it all hours of the day and night. "She started seeing a counselor last week and I have her sponsor on speed dial. She's not spending much time alone these days. I'm making sure of it."

She lets out a long, measured breath. "Good. That's…that's good."

"That night." I have to clear my throat and start again. "That night, the police picked her and three of her friends up about a quarter mile from the accident site. I've never been more scared in my life when I walked into that holding room and saw a ghost of my sister sitting there. We immediately put her in rehab and I'll be honest, she's struggled. She slipped last year and voluntarily went back again and…" I blow out a ragged breath. "Terrified doesn't even touch the surface of how I feel about her falling back into that again, Willow. This is a lot for her to handle. For *all* of us to handle."

Quiet falls on us. I wonder what she's thinking. I'm getting ready to demand she go somewhere private with me after the results are announced when she grabs her pendant between two fingers and starts running it back and forth along the silver chain, saying quietly, "My sister, Violet, died from a drug overdose when she was seventeen."

I suck in a hard breath. Jesus Christ. Her entire family has been decimated. No wonder she's this closed off. She's clutching that necklace as if it's giving her strength. Suddenly I don't care if Mergen had anything to do with it. I don't care about anything but her.

"Willow, baby, I am so, so sorry." I draw her closer and let my lips linger at the top of her head.

"I was twelve. She was my best friend and the best big sister anyone could ask for." I physically feel her pain seeping into me. I can hardly bare it. "She was a musical prodigy. She played the piano like no one I've ever seen before."

"Like Annabelle," I find myself whispering. My eyes happen to connect with my baby sister's and she offers me a forced smile.

"Yeah, like Annabelle. Your sister reminds me a lot of Violet. She's gifted and smart and beautiful. She has unlimited potential."

"She does," I agree, wishing Annabelle would see all the good bits in her that others do.

Willow tilts her head up, meeting my gaze. Her blue eyes are soft and sad. "She's also volatile and haunted and teetering on the brink. She has the same look my sister had before..."

It takes a few beats before I can respond, "I know." Hence why someone is with her 24/7.

"She needs you right now. Your *family* needs you right now."

I don't like the feeling that benign sentence leaves behind. I shift her body to mine, pressing us together, knees to stomach. "What are you trying to say?"

She tenses as if she intends to pull back. My grasp becomes implacable.

"This isn't over between us, Willow. It will *never* be over. *You* are family. You're meant to be mine. My lover. My wife. The mother to my children. I know it won't be easy to get through this, but I'm not letting the love of my life walk away from me."

She opens her mouth right as the entire room erupts in cheers. I automatically release her to see what's caused the chaos and, glancing up at the screen on the wall, I see that the race has been officially called.

With 52 percent of the popular vote, my father has won.

My father won.

Sweet relief runs through me. I catch my father's eye from across the room and grin when he gives me a brief acknowledgment of thanks. My mother is beaming and Annabelle is trying to act happy but she's edgy. I'm torn between going to her and staying with Willow, but when I see Noah throw an arm around my sister's shoulder and she playfully punches him in the gut, I know she's in good hands.

I ignore Mergen staring at us and turn to Willow at the same time she turns to me.

She smiles, but genuine happiness isn't blanketing her face right now. Ending and closure are. It almost knocks me on my ass. "Congratulations. You did it."

"*We* did it," I retort, wrapping my arms all the way around her again. She puts her hands to my chest, keeping distance between us. I loathe those inches. Every blessed one of them.

Shaking her head, she says, "I had nothing to do with it. In fact, I think maybe I almost cost him the win."

"That's not true. You had everything to do with it, Willow. Everything."

You've changed my life. My world. My focus. Me.

Willow balls my shirt in her fists, pinching a few hairs in the process but I don't balk. She rises on her tiptoes and places a chaste kiss on my cheek. It feels final. I close my eyes. They're already watering.

"I have to go," she whispers, her mouth still lingering against me.

"You need to stay." I tighten my hold. "Please," I beg her. I'll grovel, throw myself around her ankles, sell every possession I own. I have nothing without her anyway. "Please, Willow. I'll do anything you want. Please don't walk out that door without me."

If she does, we're through.

"I just can't." She brushes her lips along my jaw, up to my ear. "Tell your father congratulations and that I'm sorry I couldn't tell him myself. And take care of your sister. She needs you now more than ever."

"I need *you*, Goldilocks. Now more than ever." But if she heard me she doesn't react because she's already walking way. As if the clock struck midnight and her coach was morphing back into a pumpkin, she's walking away.

With each clipped step she takes toward the exit, another piece of my soul is violently ripped from me and I know...

This is good-bye.

Chapter Twenty-Eight

I RING THE BELL, THEN turn toward the driveway as I wait.

It's chilly today, with temps in the upper forties. And it's dreary, even for Seattle. A perfect mirror of my temperament.

Dark skies opened up an hour ago and it hasn't stopped pouring since. Cold rain slices through the air at a thirty-degree angle and I scoot closer to the house to keep from getting even more drenched than I already am.

My jeans are plastered to my legs. Water drips from the tips of my hair, all from a quick run from my car to the front stoop. I reach up to wipe underneath my eyes in case my mascara is running. One look at my finger shows it is.

I try my best to make myself presentable, cursing the fact that the umbrella I usually keep in my car was taken along with my Fiat when Shaw had it hauled away. I haven't gotten around to replacing it yet.

I stare at the black Audi and remember the day in his office when I tried to return it. The fierce look of possession that sharpened his jawline and darkened his eyes. The feeling of weakness when he demanded I strip and the feeling of power when I drew a long groan from him as he bent me over his desk. The sense of being owned and revered and consumed when he fell over me, replete.

I remember things I don't want to remember but can't force myself to forget.

Why can't I get him out of my head? Why can't I find that damn splinter and pull the fucker out so the wound will heal? When will I wake up and not ache without the feel of his arms surrounding me?

I think maybe never.

It's been nearly two weeks since I left him to celebrate Preston's win with his family and yet I'm no better off than I have been since day one without him. In some ways, I'm worse.

He texts me daily, even calls now. All of which I ignore.

I hate myself. I hate the way I run and hide. I hate the fact I feel more broken inside than I ever have before, and it's because I'm nothing without him. I did the exact thing I swore to myself I wouldn't do.

I let go of his hand.

Once again I ask myself the same question I've been asking day and night: Am I making a mistake? Is there a way we can move beyond this? Do I have it in me to forgive Annabelle? That's the question I've been trying to answer.

My heart and mind are at war and I'm not sure who's going to win.

"It's considered good manners to call before showing up on someone's doorstep, especially on a Sunday."

I spin at the sound of Randi's brusque voice, surprised she answered the door herself. And by the look of her in a plain white tee and ragged jeans, both splattered with paint, I caught her completely off guard.

"I'm sorry," I sputter, noticing splotches of red and yellow dotting her face and blond hair, which is thrown up in a messy bun. I'm stunned. Randi is always polished perfection. Relaxed this way she's casual and fresh. Approachable. Almost like a real person instead of someone who has struck the fear of God in me. "Uh, this couldn't wait."

Showing up unannounced is not the smartest idea I've ever had. Randi was furious when I finally plucked the courage to call her, though I wasn't sure if she was mad at me or the situation.

Her gaze floats down my sodden body and briefly over my shoulder. She purses her lips, and for a few seconds I think she'll send me packing, but she moves to the side and waves me in, holding the door open with one hand.

"Stay there," she barks the second my feet touch the throw rug. "You look like a drowned rat and I don't want you tracking mud on my clean floors."

"Okay," I mumble as she saunters away. I don't have mud anywhere on me but whatever. I'll deal with her wrath if it means she'll see me. She returns a full minute later with a bath towel. I've already hung my raincoat on the coat rack and removed my shoes, sans the invisible mud. I take the towel and wipe my face, running it over my hair a couple of times until she seems satisfied.

"Just drop it there." She points to the floor beside me, turns, and walks away. I assume I'm to follow, so I do. I expect she'll head to her office but without a word, she leads me through a part of her house I've never seen before, not that I've been given the grand tour the two previous times I've been here.

When we arrive at our destination, I stand still in complete and total awe, seeing a whole new side to Randi Deveraux, Queen of Hearts.

We're in an enormous room with exposed wood beams on the ceiling and a wall of glass sliders that overlooks her spacious backyard. Every other wall is lined with mismatched, eclectic built-in work tables covered with what I imagine is every paint supply known to man. Several easels are spread throughout the middle of the room, each holding various sizes of canvases. All are in different stages of completion, but the theme is consistent.

They're nudes.

Randi paints nude women.

Tastefully nude women. And she's...*good*. Really good. Like she could sell these and make a living *good*.

She strides over to the largest canvas, probably nearly two feet wide, and picks up a brush from the table beside it. I quietly come up behind her for a better look.

A naked woman is lying on a pastel comforter, her back to us. Her arm is thrown over the back of her head and her fingers have disappeared in her long chestnut hair. There's a berry-colored throw over the tops of her thighs, but it doesn't cover her heart-shaped butt. Her spine is pronounced, her lower back curved in as if she's pleasuring herself with the hand we can't see.

It's stunning. And sad. And uniquely erotic.

"Wow. You did this? It's so good."

She dips the tip of her brush in a touch of black paint and mixes it with bright red to create rich maroon. Then she brings it to the painting and taps lightly, shading along the blanket thrown over the woman.

"What's so life shattering you forgot your manners?" she asks tersely, not acknowledging my compliment.

I take a couple of steps back, not wanting to crowd her.

I've thought nonstop about what I need to do, the cords I need to cut, and the next steps I need to take. Working for Randi was a lot like crossing a bridge. The structure is there for a reason. To move over rough terrain with ease. But I'm at the other side now, and while I'm grateful for her support, going forward is the only option.

Besides, we both knew when I took the job with Shaw this was coming.

"I wanted to thank you for all that you've done for me, for taking a chance on me. I don't know what I would have done without you,"—*I don't know what I'll do without you now*—"but I can't work for you anymore. So I guess I'm giving you my notice."

Her eyes slide to mine briefly as she picks up her brush from the canvas. "What makes you think I'd let you continue working for me after what happened?"

Damn. That slap smarted. I unconsciously bring my hand up to my cheek and rub. "You're right. I'm sorry."

She doesn't respond. She just goes back to painting. She hasn't said and it's probably none of my business, but, "Is everything…I mean has anyone found out about you because of this? Because of me?"

She scoffs and reloads her brush. "Don't worry about me, Willow. It's going to take a hell of a lot more to bring down my kingdom than one measly insinuation in a disreputable newspaper. You don't think I've been threatened this way before? You do what I do long enough and this sort of shit happens."

Threatened? Her?

This wasn't about *her.*

"But this was about the election and—"

"This was about someone getting his entitled dick in a twist because he couldn't have what he wanted."

I am so confused. Who wanted what? "Which was?"

"You."

Say what? "Me?"

"Yeah, you."

I shift my weight to the other foot and slip my hands into my front jeans pockets. The damp denim abrades the back of my hands. "I don't understand," I say when it's clear she's not going to offer more.

"Of course you don't," she mumbles, concentrating on her art. My brows scrunch together and right as I'm about to ask another question she offers, "Powerful men with God complexes don't like being denied."

"I'm sorry, Randi. I'm not following at all."

She drops her paintbrush into a cup of muddy-looking water that's stuffed with other paintbrushes and faces me. "Paul Graber."

Paul Graber? "What about him?"

"He wanted you. I said no. He didn't like it and tried flexing his small dick the only way a man like him knows how."

My hand goes to my throat as I digest what she's telling me. "Paul Graber did this? He was the *7-Day's* anonymous source?"

Her nod is clipped.

Whaaat? This makes no sense. He did all of this because I wouldn't sleep with him? I knew the asshole gave off a bad vibe the second his hand touched mine, but I never expected a man of his stature would be so petty.

I think back to the cryptic conversation between him and Noah that night long ago. He seemed peeved at Preston for something. Even if he was the culprit, it seems entirely political, not personal. "Are you sure?"

Snorting, she answers, "Very."

"But—"

"I know what you're thinking. Trust me. This was about me, not the mayor."

"How do you know that?"

She snatches up the cup, spilling a few drops of dirty water in the process and saunters over to the sink, telling me, "It's not important. What matters is I've dealt with him. He won't be a problem again. I promise you that. And I'm sorry. I take pride in vetting my clients, and in this case, I clearly failed you."

Wow. An apology from Randi. Mark the date.

She keeps her back to me as she washes paint from the synthetic bristles. Part of me suspects she's ignoring me because she wants me to leave, but she's not getting rid of me that easy. I have one more thing to do so I breathe deeply and confess the other reason I'm here.

"I want you to return the money in my account to Shaw Mercer."

I haven't touched a penny of the two hundred fifty thousand dollars Shaw has paid me. As we backed out of Preston and Adelle's driveway on the first night I met them, I already knew I'd return it at the end of this even though I desperately needed it. It didn't feel right keeping it when I was no longer playing a part but falling in love.

She throws a glance over her shoulder, halting her task. "You come into some inheritance I'm not aware of?"

I look away and shake my head. I hear her inhale and blow it back out. The water shuts off.

"Nothing happened to your mom, did it?"

"No," I mumble before I remember I've never talked to her about my momma. We've never discussed anything personal, actually. My gaze zips back to hers. She's leaning against the counter, wiping her hands with a black towel, watching me. "What do you know about my mother?"

She ignores me. "I'm not your go-between, Willow. You're a grown woman. I personally think you're making a mistake but if you want to return the money, then you can do it yourself."

She looks cool and collected while that fire that Shaw has unearthed in me burns wild and erupts. "I have never asked you for a thing," I bite. "You owe me this."

She cocks a perfectly coifed brow. In any situation, that one little muscle movement would have me shrinking in my seat, but not today.

"You asked me for a job," she says coolly.

"I didn't ask you for anything. You offered."

"Semantics." She drops the hand towel and crosses her arms. "You needed help. I gave it, no strings attached."

She's right. Damn her.

"I—" My heart pounds. *I can't do it,* I want to say. I'll crumble like a fall leaf the second my eyes land on his. I'll let his very presence convince me we'll be okay and if that's even remotely possible, which I don't see how it is, I have to reach that conclusion on my own. "Please, Randi," I plead quietly. "I can't keep it. I can't send a check for two hundred and fifty thousand dollars in the mail, and I can't see him. I just can't."

Her lips thin. A few moments tick off. "I know what happened," she announces evenly.

Right. Of course she does. She's like the all-seeing Oz behind the curtain.

I fight to swallow past the ball of conflict in my throat. "Then you know why I'm begging."

Her gaze falls to the floor and a weird sort of look comes over her face. She pushes off the table and when our eyes connect again, I see a totally different person than the aloof, unfeeling one I've always encountered. The thick, intimidating lines on her forehead are gone and the edges of her mouth have softened considerably.

"Follow me," she orders as she walks by. Once again I'm on her heels like a puppy. This time we end up in her office. She waves for me to sit. I do, expecting her to pull out paperwork I'll have to sign, authorizing the transaction. She tosses a plain manila folder on the desk instead.

And when she opens it, I stop breathing.

I volley between the upside-down photographs and her, the blood in my veins icing over.

"Why do you have pictures of my sister?" I snap. A swarm of bees has invaded my ears. "What? Do you have a whole dossier on my life in there?"

How dare she.

Sick to my stomach, I snatch the folder, spin it around, and begin sifting through dozens of old four-by-six snapshots. I expect to see creepy candids of me taken from afar by telephoto lens mixed in but as I flip through picture after picture, I realize they are all of Violet.

Some are of Violet alone or with other people, but most feature my sister with an arm thrown around a petite stringy-haired brunette with sunken cheekbones and protruding ribs. At first glance, she's unfamiliar but the longer I stare, the more I see it: big brown eyes that look troubled instead of confident and sure. Everything about this girl in the picture is different from the one I know.

I lift my eyes to ones that are now older and wiser. They are much the same yet so incredibly different years later. The ones in the photos mirrored Violet's in those last few months before her overdose. Red, glassy, strung out. The ones I'm looking into now are experienced and wise. They're brimming with remorse.

My mouth tastes of fury and utter disbelief when I ask, "You knew who I was all along, didn't you?" There's some massive stinging happening behind my eyelids. I try to blink it away. It's not working.

Randi runs her tongue along her lower lip and sucks it into her mouth as she shifts in her wing-back chair. She looks uneasy, her tough-as-shit exterior cracking from the ground up.

The air suddenly thins. It's hard to take in.

"You knew my sister?" She moves her head in what could be considered a nod, I suppose, but it's not enough. It's not nearly enough for the crap she just laid at my feet.

Randi Devereaux knew my dead sister.

Un-fucking-believable.

"She was my best friend," Randi confesses, her tone hushed and wistful, her eyes teary. I'm having a hard time feeling sorry for her when anger crowds everything else out.

My head is spinning. I came here to give my resignation and to twist Randi's arm into returning money I need but can't take when suddenly the doors were ripped off the past, and I'm staring straight into the mouth of hallowed space. Afraid to fall into it. Unable to turn away.

I reach for a picture half-hidden under another. In it Violet and Randi are floating on a lake in inner tubes, in skimpy bikinis, holding hands and squinting against the sun. They're laughing at water being splashed on them from someone who's not captured.

I remember the bright yellow bathing suit Violet is wearing. My mother helped her pick it out before we went to Cannon Beach the summer before she died. The first time she wore it my dad nearly blew his lid. He told her it was too revealing. She told him he didn't like the fact she was growing up and it was the only suit she'd brought. He grumbled and told Momma to get her something else. She didn't. He let it go.

I run a fingernail over Violet's smile, over the space between her front teeth that most people would hate but she said gave her character. She once told me the French believed those blessed with a gap are said to have good luck follow them through life. I used to wish we were French after she died.

She looks young and healthy. Like she's having the time of her life.

"We met at the pier the summer I moved here." She nods to the ghost in my hand. "I didn't know many people. Violet was friendly and fun and her bubbly personality was infectious." It was. How I envied that about her. "We clicked immediately."

I clamp my lips together and stuff the sob that wants to escape back down my throat. Violet's face turns blurry. I don't want her to say another word but I'll choke the life from her if she doesn't.

"Then we met Brock. He seemed like a nice guy at first. Fun, wild, a little hippieish. But he turned out to be a piece of shit with a quick temper and a fondness for hard drugs." She stops, a wry grin on her face. "We both were lured into the illusion that we could escape anytime we wanted, and after a while Violet wanted to walk away, but I…I fucking went and fell in love with the asshole and she wouldn't leave until I did."

I'm lost for words. My face feels hot.

"I feel responsible for her death, yet her death was the only thing that saved my life."

I break from my sister's soulful face and look into glassy chocolate hues. I see so much lurking in them. Self-reproach. Suffering, still, after all this time. The agony of loss that never goes away.

I was twelve years old when Violet overdosed on cocaine.

I hadn't started my period yet. I hadn't been kissed by a boy. I still liked Saturday morning cartoons and was a book nerd. I have no rational reason to feel guilty about her death, yet I do. I didn't know the signs of drug use. What normal twelve-year-old would? In retrospect, it's clear, but at the time all I knew was she had changed. Her light had been cast in shadows. She was anxious instead of carefree. She locked her bedroom door. She fought with my parents. There were secrets between us that were never there before.

It would be easy to sit here and blame Randi for it. In reality, I'd always wanted someone else to blame besides Violet herself. Because it's easier to think someone else did it to her than holding her accountable.

But that's *not* reality. Randi is no more to blame for Violet choosing drugs than I am. She's no more to blame for Violet overdosing than I am. It's a black hole called martyrdom we'll both stay trapped in if we let ourselves.

And I've been there long enough.

"I'm sorry," she offers. It's genuine and heartfelt and completely unnecessary.

"It's not your fault."

"I introduced them. Got us caught up with that crap in the first place."

"No," I disagree. The change in Vi started well before they met. It was a storm that had been brewing for months. I think back to the "cigarettes" I found in her drawer once. Now I know that for the lie it was. No. Randi isn't to blame. "Violet was pulling away from us before that, Randi. My mother pushed her hard. She pushed back."

She shakes her head. "We were best friends. I was supposed to look out for her."

"I was her sister. Don't you think I feel the same?"

"You're not the one who left her at the party. I am," she says in a faraway voice that breaks. "She told me she'd be right behind me and when she didn't show up at our friend's house, I got worried and came back, but by the time I got there she was already unconscious and everyone else was too coked up to notice. I performed CPR the best I could while someone drove us to the ER, but..."

But it was too late.

"It's not your fault, Randi," I repeat. "It was an unfortunate accident." It's true, and for the first time, I honestly believe what I'm saying.

Eyes that had lost focus now sharpen, zeroing in on me.

"I know firsthand what it's like to be weighed down by the burden of someone else's death, Willow. To hate your reflection, your very existence. It's a daily descent into the pits of hell you can't possibly fathom." She pauses and smiles sadly, adding, "Well, I imagine you think you can but you're wrong."

I know what she's getting at and I don't know how to respond, so I blurt, "I'm pretty fucking pissed at you. Why not just tell me this?"

She doesn't acknowledge me and I honestly don't think she cares if I'm mad or not.

"And this whole situation is not on Shaw. He was put in an impossible spot, you understand this, right?"

My head hangs in shame. My heart understands this doesn't belong on Shaw's shoulders but tell that to my brain. One second I want to run to him and beg forgiveness for being selfish and shortsighted, but then I know I'll have to see Annabelle and I can't make myself do it. I don't know if I'll ever be ready for that.

And one doesn't come without the other. I would never ask that of him.

"If you don't love him, that's one thing, but I don't think that's the case. Is it?"

I manage to swallow and whisper, "I don't know what I'm supposed to do."

There's a long gap where the only sound in the room is the second hand from an artsy clock hanging over Randi's head.

"I don't know Annabelle Mercer. I've never met her and I have no vested interest in her but what I do know is that when your father came upon her that night, he would have seen an opportunity to spare another father, mother, or sister that same hell he was living in without *his* daughter."

She stands and comes to sit in the chair beside me. She sets one warm hand over mine, squeezing. I'm not breathing. I'm crumbling away.

"You're processing all this, I get it, but once you do that you have a new reality to face."

Numb, I can only nod in agreement.

"And regardless of whether that new reality includes Shaw Mercer, you need to forgive Annabelle. Your father would have wanted that, Willow. Your father was an intelligent man who would have weighed the dangers. He knew what he was doing when he climbed up on that ledge. He knew the risks and he did it anyway."

I know that.

"He saved her life, and while he lost his in the process, you should be proud of him."

I am. I'm so incredibly proud of him. Not everyone would do what he did. It knocks my breath away that Shaw could be the one grieving his sister's death the way I have my father's. I couldn't bear it.

My teeth find my lip. The sting biting my eyes starts up again but I force them back.

"She needs your forgiveness to deal with what's happened, Willow. Even though it was an accident, she'll take this on herself. She won't be able to heal without you. Trust me on that. I couldn't move forward until I knocked on your door at two o'clock one morning nearly a year after Violet died and begged your father for *his* absolution."

My lungs seize. She met my father, too?

"He said I didn't need it but he didn't hesitate a single second to give it to me anyway." She reaches up to wipe a single tear away, her hand shaky. "In fact, he sat and held me for an hour while we cried and grieved together."

That's the final straw that breaks me down completely.

Every shard of agony I've tried to bury comes violently storming to the surface. It feels like 10,000 needles scraping the inside of my skin.

My body shakes.

My spirit bleeds pure anguish.

Without even thinking, I throw my arms around my former boss, my sister's best friend, and grieve the people I miss.

My sister.

My father.

The mother I used to know.

...and Shaw.

I miss them all so much, but the harsh reality is—it's the man I'm denying myself who I miss the most.

Chapter Twenty-Nine

GRAVEL CRUNCHES UNDER THE TIRES of my car.

I've gone over this same patch hundreds of times throughout the years. I have the same anxiety when I make the turn. The same nettle in each breath. The familiar, ever-present ache that no amount of time we have with those we love will ever be enough.

Only this time it feels different from all the other times before it.

My lungs feel slightly less constricted. My heart a little less heavy. I feel, I don't know, lighter, I suppose.

I ended up staying at Randi's until early morning, talking mostly about Violet. It was cathartic for both of us. And eye-opening. Randi knew a whole different side to my sister, and it was nice to reminisce with someone who misses her as much as I do.

I haven't talked about Violet—*truly* talked about Violet—since she died. It was a taboo subject under my mother's roof. It wasn't a much better one with my father because it caused him pain, too, and while I know Sierra would have listened, it's not a burden you want to saddle your friends with either.

With each story Randi and I traded, the fog of grief that's kept me trapped since I was twelve was driven further and further away. By the time I dropped into bed at five o'clock this morning, exhausted, an entire lifetime seemed to have been lifted from my shoulders.

And with all that weight gone I found something within myself only *I* ever had the ability to find: peace.

I thought I'd spent all these years searching for me, but what I've actually been desperate to find is the hush that comes with accepting we're just along for the ride.

The truth is we control very little in this life. And accepting that, finding peace within after we've mourned and closed ourselves off for a while so we can heal is the only control we *do* have.

We all love and lose. It's a sad fact of life. But we can choose to hold on to the loss itself or to the love that came before it. All this time I've chosen wrong.

I realized something about myself yesterday at Randi's. My entire family would be disappointed with how I've lived my life up to this point. Or not lived it as the case may be. And I want them to be proud.

As I arrive at the eternal place my sister and father rest, I notice a black Jeep parked in my usual spot. Not giving it a second thought, I slow to a stop and push the gearshift into park before exiting the car, careful to leave enough space between our vehicles.

I scoop fresh flowers from the passenger seat and step out into the chilly November day. Tugging the edges of my coat against my chin with my free hand, I'm almost to the willow tree when I see her.

My feet freeze, along with my breath.

She's kneeling, her back to me. Long raven hair, streaked turquoise in spots, blows in the cold breeze as she traces my father's name carved in gray limestone. She draws a finger down the last "l" before she starts over again.

My eyes instantly water.

I don't know how Annabelle found my father's grave and it doesn't matter, I guess. Watching the reverent way she goes over his name for the third time since I walked up breaks something loose.

I knew I needed to talk to Annabelle, only I didn't know how, or when, or what I was going to say. What does one do in a situation like this?

But her being here today, at the same time I am, is not simply divine intervention. My *father* brought me here at this very moment for this very reason. I'm convinced of it.

If this had happened yesterday morning, before I talked to Randi, I would have turned and left, hoping she didn't see me. But you don't look divinity in the face and walk away from it.

Nervously, I command my feet to move, each step deliberately quiet. When I come closer, I realize she's talking. A word or two caught by the breeze floats my way, and although my sheer presence is an intrusion into an incredibly private moment, I continue forward until I'm within a few feet.

As if she feels me, she snaps her arm to her side like the rock suddenly shocked her. Her shoulders square and her back stiffens, though she doesn't turn.

"I can go."

She starts to rise but I set my palm on her shoulder. "No. Stay." I notice she's shivering. She must have been here awhile.

She hovers in indecision but eventually sinks back to where she was. We stay like this, her kneeling, me standing behind her until she breaks the awkward silence.

"I remember events about that night I'm desperate to forget but I'm desperate to remember the ones I can't. Why is that?" Her voice is small, childlike, and horribly torn.

Three shuffles and I'm next to her. I bend down over my sister's tomb, the cold from the ground sucking the warmth from my shins. Noticing a fresh bouquet of flowers in the holder that she must have brought, I set my own bundle beside me.

I wish I had something philosophical and insightful to say that would ease her personal hell. But to some degree, she's got to come to terms with this on her own, as I have. Instead, I try to channel my father's wisdom and what he would want me to say.

"I think the mind works in mysterious ways."

She bows her head until her chin burrows inside her jacket. "I need to remember. I *need* to." Her voice cracks. A single drop of water drips down her cheek.

That's the last thing she needs, but I don't say it. Remembering that night would be the worst form of torture. Truthfully, I'm glad she doesn't remember because I would beg her to recount it second by second and those are details I don't want stuck in my head either.

"When I was little I used to have nightmares. Bad ones. Nightly for a while. I'd wake up in a cold sweat, screaming and shaking and Daddy would hold me until I calmed down. But every time he asked me what they were about, I couldn't remember. The only thing left was the feeling of panic and being powerless."

"Sounds familiar," she murmurs.

I stop to bite my lip and steady my voice.

"One night after a particularly bad nightmare, I asked him why I couldn't remember."

I see her head turn, sense her staring at me but I'm staring ahead, lost in the feel of my father's strong, comforting arms. I swear they're wrapped around me now.

"He said because bad memories take up too much space and you need that space for good memories."

Why didn't I remember that until now? He was trying to placate his scared little girl but what he said was so profound. And so true. Bad always overshadows the good if we let it. And I've let it.

"I need more space," she says on a hush.

"Me too," I reply the same way.

The soothing rustle of leaves is the only sound for a while. I watch Annabelle, wondering what kinds of horrors could possibly be buried in her young psyche already.

She bends her knees, drawing them up to her chin. Her usually bright eyes are dull and lidded. Her porcelain skin carries an unhealthy hue. She reminds me of me when my sister died, crawling into herself for protection. She looks as if she could splinter into the earth below her and be fine with it.

Guilt eats me up. If she ends up like Violet, I'll never forgive myself. But I don't know how to help her either.

"Your sister was a Metallica fan, huh?"

My gaze falls to the musical notes on Violet's headstone. I brush off a couple of dried leaves sitting on top. "My sister was a music fan, period. Metallica, Blink 182, Grieg's Piano Concerto in A Minor." I chuckle to myself, recalling the inside joke I shared with my father. "You name it, she loved it." I turn to her now. "Like you, I imagine."

Her eyes dart to Vi's memorial and back to me. "She died young."

"Yes, she did," I agree. It doesn't hurt quite as much this time when I say it.

"That's…I'm sorry."

I swallow and nod.

"How?"

A bold question but I'd expect nothing less from Annabelle.

"She overdosed on cocaine."

Her head jerks in shock as her mouth flies open as if either the idea is preposterous or it hits a little too close to home.

For days I've questioned my ability to put this entire tragedy into some sort of perspective that makes sense, but something my father said once pushes its way to the front of my mind, almost as if he's whispering it in my ear now.

"Our lives unfold a certain way for reasons that aren't always apparent to us until the time is right."

Quite frankly at the time, I thought it was bullshit he made up to make me feel better about my sister dying but now that I understand it, I realize the burden I've carried about Violet's death, or his death for that matter, weren't actually burdens at all. The gifts of empathy and compassion simply can't be understood through anything other than life experience.

I was set straight on a path to love Shaw Mercer for more than one reason and she's currently staring at me as if I'm possibly the only one in the world who can throw her a lifeline.

"It's uncanny how like you she was. In every way."

She presses her plum lips together, drawing in air through her nose. "You mean the drugs?"

"I mean everything," I reply, straightforward, taking Sierra's approach for once. While Annabelle looks precious and breakable, through her shadows I see grit and tenacity and a belligerent spirit she'll need now more than ever. "How are you handling all"—I wave around—"this?"

She slides her heels to the ground, angling her legs to the side. She turns her attention back to my sister's grave, fingers absently plucking the dead grass beneath us.

"I want to numb myself against it all, if that's what you're asking."

"It's what I'm asking. Have you?"

She half laughs, half huffs, throwing the blades in her hand to the wind. "I'm under house arrest. Not a lot of drug deliveries to the gated mansions on Yarrow Bay."

So she's still staying with Shaw. I want to ask her about him. How he is. If he got the new fancy treadmill he was researching for his home gym or if he's been up in the middle of the night eating Eleanor specials like he does when he's stressed.

Instead, "That's probably a good thing."

A noncommittal humming noise leaves her throat. I shift to push my legs out in front of me when my knees start to ache.

"So how are you here, unguarded?"

The smile she gives me is droll and mocking. She quickly looks behind us as if she's confirming she wasn't followed, but we're all alone. Suddenly I'm checking her more closely. Are her eyes glassy? Is she extra fidgety? Do I even know what I'm looking for? I decide she seems perfectly fine. Sad, lost, but physically okay.

"You escaped yet you came here instead of a drug dealer. That's a good step."

She starts twisting the ends of her hair around her finger.

"Don't let them win, Annabelle," I say. "The drugs. The monsters inside. Fight them with everything in you. Don't let them win."

"I don't want to," she replies softly, her eyes filling to the brim with water. "But I don't know how I'm supposed to live with what I've done."

Knife straight through the heart.

I reach out and smooth stray hairs stuck to her cheek back behind her ears and tell her the same thing I told Randi, meaning it. "It's not your fault, Annabelle. It was an accident."

Her gaze, which had fallen to my lap, slices to mine. "Accident? How can you say that?" She shoves herself to her feet. I follow, worried she'll bolt. "I killed your father, Willow. I *killed* him. If I hadn't been a fucked-up mess that night, he would still be alive. You would still be with my brother. I wouldn't be shaking with the need to do a line like my next breath right now so I could drown out the guilt that feels suffocating. Even if for a little while."

I don't tell her I'd never have been with Shaw if my father *hadn't* died and she lived. I'd be married to Reid. "No. My father *saved* your life. You didn't kill him."

"Same thing."

I take a step toward her. She takes a half step back. I lower my voice and will her to hear what I'm saying.

"It's not the same thing at all, Annabelle. I know what happened earlier that night. You were distraught." Her face blanches. Another dance. Me forward, her backward.

"You don't know anything." Her voice is quiet torment on a wisp of air.

A bad feeling swarms me. Call it woman's intuition. Could more have happened that night than she told Shaw?

"Then tell me."

More shuffling. Her head moves left to right. She's not ready. She may never be ready.

"I know you have your family, but if you want to talk, I have a good ear. And I don't judge."

She nods once, kicking her right foot back and forth over the top of the grass.

"I don't blame you, Annabelle. For anything," I tell her sincerely.

"You should."

"I don't. In fact, I think we're standing here together for a reason."

"And what would that be?" She's brusque but I don't let it get to me.

"I don't know yet," I tell her truthfully. "But I know there is one." I reach out and take her hand. "If you don't hear anything else I'm saying, please hear this: I don't feel I have anything to forgive you for, but if you need it know that I do. I forgive you."

Her head bobs up and down. She swallows hard.

"Then why aren't you with Shaw?"

"I needed time. This is…" I blow out a long stream of air until my lungs are completely empty. "Hard. For all of us."

Her gaze doesn't waver. "You told me you would love him no matter what."

It's not that easy, I want to say. I'm fucked up. This is what I do. But there's a part of me that knows that's an out-and-out lie. A cop-out. My usual, tired MO. I want to be with Shaw more than anything. Be part of his life and their crazy, imperfect family. I want to help his sister heal. *Really* heal, from the inside out because, with the little I've been exposed to Annabelle, I already know she's taking my well-treaded path to keep to herself.

"I do love him, Annabelle. That hasn't changed. That will *never* change."

"Then why did you run off at my father's party? Why have you been M-I-A for the last two weeks? Why is he behaving like a fucking asshole, running around biting off the dicks of every man, woman, and child he comes into contact with?"

I can't help it. It's so inappropriate in this situation but the picture she's conjured is too realistic. And damn funny since I can see Shaw doing exactly that.

I try to bite it back but I lose.

I smile.

She's confused at first, then the corners of her mouth begin to curl, too.

A giggle escapes my closed lips. One escapes hers.

And pretty soon, we're both full-on laughing with tears of joy and sorrow streaming down our faces.

"Biting off dicks, huh?" I squeal through hiccups.

"Yeah," she agrees, her tone shrill.

We laugh until we're all laughed out, but our tears don't stop. They don't stop when my arms come around her shoulders or when hers wind tentatively around my waist. They don't stop when she buries her head in my overcoat or when we hear a car roll by.

In fact, they don't stop for a long, long while.

Together we grieve a man who was honorable and selfless.

Together we thank the man who gave her another chance at life.

Together we begin a healing process that wouldn't have been possible without the other.

And sometime later, when she walks away after we're talked and cried out, I call after her, "Annabelle." She turns around and I tell her what my father would say. "Don't squander the gift Charles Blackwell gave you. Make my father proud."

Face red and eyes swollen, she lifts her trembling lips and whispers, "I'm trying."

It's not until I head back to the gravesite to say my private good-bye that I notice them.

Thin, red-hued branches sprinkled throughout the pure white arrangement.

They're willows.

Red catkin willows.

My heart gets so big I think it's going to bust clean through my ribs.

There's no way Annabelle brought these flowers.

Shaw did.

Willow

Chapter Thirty

THE SUN HAS ALREADY SET BEFORE I turn down Court Way toward home.

I'm utterly exhausted. Even my bones are tired.

After I left the cemetery, I needed to pick up Momma's medication for the month, stop by the post office for a week's worth of mail, and buy a few groceries for Momma and myself.

It's now past eight in the evening and I contemplate calling Shaw, desperately wanting to hear his voice, but I know he'll insist on seeing me in person and I need one more day to process my jumbled thoughts. After only a few hours of restless sleep last night, I'm looking forward to a bath, a glass of wine, and my bed.

That plan goes out the window, though, when I see a car halfway down the street idling at the curb right outside my house.

I slow and contemplate my options. He's facing this direction. If I turn around and speed away, he'll likely give chase. Just as well, I decide.

It's time.

In truth, it's time to face everything head-on.

I'm ready to live, even if it hurts.

Our eyes meet as I take a left and creep to a stop in my driveway, making sure to stay to the left so Sierra has a place to park when she gets off work. I swoop up the bundle of mail held together with a thick rubber band and throw my purse over my shoulder. When I push the door open he's already outside, waiting, a mixture of determination and awkwardness radiating from him.

"Grab the groceries from the back," I tell him, heading toward the house. I unlock the side door. He follows behind five seconds later. I throw everything down on the kitchen table. Snagging a glass from the cupboard, I fill it with lukewarm water and down the entire contents before refilling it. I keep my back to him a few more ticks before spinning around.

He's not even a foot away…on the edge of my comfort zone.

He knows it.

"What do you want, Reid?"

I set my left hand on top of my right bicep, pulling the glass across my chest, using it as a barrier. His eyes drop to my movement then back to my face. He presses his lips together and swallows as he shoves his hands in his front pockets, dragging his faded jeans low on his hips.

"I wanted to see if you were okay." His mouth twists up but his eyes never avert from mine.

He's nervous. The vengeful part of me is glad.

I reach around and set the cup on the counter behind me, skirting around him. "Well, you've seen."

That doesn't mean I'm not still peeved with him, though, and I don't plan on making this a cakewalk. I have a lot of questions he's going to answer, first being how he found out about my father, second, why he was using it as a bargaining chip instead of telling me like he should have. No matter his motive, it was wrong.

Shaw was equally wrong by not telling me, but now I understand it was out of love and concern. His intense devotion to his family is one of his most attractive and endearing qualities, and as I've worked through a gamut of emotions the past few weeks, I've come to realize he deserves to be forgiven. He said he was being selfish, only I think it was the complete opposite.

If he still wants a future with me, I want to see where this could go.

For most of my life, I've wondered if it's better to have loved and lost than never to have loved at all. After I lost my father, I was firmly in the *never to have loved at all* camp, but after meeting Shaw, I see the flaw in that logic.

I pick up the mail and tear off the binding, cursing when the rubber band breaks and snaps my fingers, stinging. I begin sorting the junk from the bills, anxious when the bills pile grows higher than the junk one. My attention zeros in on my monthly bank statement. I'm afraid to open it. I toss it to the side, pulling a Scarlett O'Hara.

After all, tomorrow is another day.

Reid comes up close enough behind me that I feel his body heat. I almost forgot he was here. "You don't seem okay."

I whirl on him, snapping. "Really? What would make you think that, Reid? The black circles under my eyes your first clue?"

He takes a step back. "Willow..."

"Don't Willow me. You're going to tell me everything you know, and then you're going to leave and never come back."

He looks crestfallen. There's no other description for it. His eyes droop, his mouth falls, his shoulders slump. I want to feel sorry for him but I don't because now I have confirmation he was hoping to slip into Shaw's vacant slot. Only it's not vacant. It never was.

"There is no good reason you kept this from me, Reid. Not one." I lean my butt against the table behind me.

"And *he* has one?" he sneers as he crosses his arms and spreads his stance. Such a male thing to do. It must be ingrained in every stupid chromosome.

"We aren't talking about Shaw. We're talking about you."

And yes, he has one, I don't add.

After a five-second stare-off, he huffs and shoves his hands through his hair. He turns from me and paces to the counter where I left my glass. He faces me once more, gripping the edges with both hands, his elbows bending backward. It's as if he's holding himself away from me. Maybe he is.

"Several months ago, there was a threat against Preston that would expose all of this to the media. That's why I was brought in to begin with."

"What?" My knees suddenly feel like overcooked noodles and I grab for a chair, lowering myself. I think back to our conversation a few weeks ago about the governor of Minnesota's mistress and how Reid dug up information he used to bury her before the story came to light.

"Preston knew about this?"

"No," he says quickly. "I mean, at first it was a vague demand, but enough to be concerning given Annabelle's history. The campaign manager Preston originally hired was young and inexperienced. It was his first big campaign and he had the foresight to know he was in too deep, but he'd heard of me and my...skills."

He goes silent to see if I'll say anything. I don't.

"I'd heard good things about Preston Mercer, so I took the job."

Question after question whirls through my mind, all of them at lightning speed. "What was the threat?"

"Extortion, obviously."

He lowers his gaze to the floor for a second, before looking at me underneath long lashes I used to stare at as he slept. "I admit you crossed my mind when I accepted. I thought...well, you know what I thought."

I push my lips together, sad for him.

"Anyway, it wasn't until I got here and dug into the threat further that CJ's name popped up and then I knew I was called here for a reason, Willow."

I'm stunned. Processing all this is a bit of a challenge.

"Who made the threat? Was it..." I gulp. Could it be? "Paul Graber?"

"That's confiden—"

"Oh, can the fucking excuses, Reid. We're way past that."

The corners of his mouth edge up slightly as if he's amused with me. "No, it wasn't Graber. It was Annabelle's slimeball ex, Eddie Lettie."

My heart falls. Her ex. Is this the same guy who tried to violate her? Who may have succeeded?

I have a hard time swallowing against the angst building in my chest.

"I don't understand any of this. How did he know what happened that night? Was he there?"

Reid comes back over and takes a seat beside me, the legs of the chair scraping the floor. Leaning toward me, he plants his elbows on his knees and spreads his thighs wide. His clasped hands fall between them. "No. Got half a story one night from one of her druggie friends who was there and thought he had an opportunity to capitalize. Stupid fuck thought Preston would just roll over and pay to shut him up."

I breathe again, not realizing I was starting to get dizzy from lack of oxygen.

"When did you find all this out?" I ask, my voice rough, my heart heavy.

He waits a few beats before answering. "In an ironic twist, the day I saw you again at Preston's house."

I don't know why it hurts that yet another person was in on this secret. "So Preston knew all along."

I didn't realize I'd said it out loud until Reid chimes in, "No, he didn't."

That catches me off guard. "But—"

"I never mentioned you or CJ. He never knew. Just told him the threat had been neutralized. It's better for the candidate if they don't have details anyway."

"So they can play dumb?"

He smiles softly. "Something like that."

"Is he still a threat?" I'm sick that this guy is walking around, waiting for his next chance to make trouble for Annabelle or the Mercers.

"Let's just say karma is a bitch." He picks up the broken rubber band and starts twisting it around his index finger. "Drug trafficking charges tend to keep a man in orange for a good long time."

"Drug trafficking?" I remember our conversation about him burying threats to his candidate. "Did you..."

"I wish I could take the credit, but I'm afraid I can't."

I crack a small smile, relieved that a dangerous criminal is behind bars regardless of how it happened. We look at each other quietly for a long time as I let everything he told me sink in. His gaze is sad and tender. Mine probably is, too.

"Why didn't you tell me this when you found out?"

He shifts away from me, leaning against the back of the chair. He hooks one elbow on the corner of the table, letting his hand dangle over the edge. "You know why." One edge of his mouth pulls up. "I'm not saying it was the right decision, Willow. But I was..."

"Jealous," I offer after he fades off.

"Yes. Incredibly fucking jealous. He had you and I didn't. I've always wanted you, Willow. Even when you broke my fucking heart, I still wanted you."

I know and I'm sorry.

"And you thought what? That Shaw would drop me like a bad habit if you threatened to expose all this to me?"

His eyes shift away apologetically. Yeah, that's exactly what he thought.

"Do you know Annabelle was almost raped the night of my father's accident? Probably by that guy? I don't know, maybe she even was."

The color drains from his cheeks. I keep going, the anger building.

"Did you know she doesn't remember anything about

trying to jump or about the accident or that my father was even there? That this is news she learned at the same time I did? Can you imagine how that felt for her?"

His Adam's apple bobs as he swallows. "No. I didn't know any of that."

And right here is the problem.

"Of course you didn't because you defused a threat without understanding the threat in its entirety and you used half a story as a bargaining chip against the man I love. You saw what I went through, Reid. You listened to me cry myself to sleep for months. You *knew* I felt responsible for my father's death. What you did was far worse than Shaw trying to figure out how he's going to help his sister deal with this without either turning back to drugs or trying to commit suicide again. Why would you do that?"

"I'm sorry. I didn't think it all the way through. All I could think about was you."

Before I can reply he's on his knees at my feet. His palms warm my cheeks. His fingers feel strong wrapped around the back of my neck. It's the same possessive hold Shaw has, only when Shaw does it I mold like warm clay. It's as if his hands could single-handedly shape me, smoothing out every one of my rugged, honed edges.

"What I did was wrong but my only excuse is I am blinded by desperation to win you back. I love you, Willow. I've never stopped loving you. Not for a second, a minute, an hour, or a day."

"I..." This is brutal. "I know."

His eyes drop to my lips and before I know it he's tugging me toward him and placing his mouth gently to mine. His lips are warm. They taste familiar. The kiss is chaste and brief. Wrong and final.

"You're going back to him."

Even though I'm angry with him, his pain hurts me. I keep my eyes closed, whispering, "There was never a question." And I realize as I say it that it's true. Buried under the agonizing pain, I knew I couldn't live without him. "He's more than me. I don't know how to explain it."

His cheek presses to mine, lips resting against my ear. "You don't need to." His voice is grieved, dejected. He angles back out of my space and waits until I open my eyes. When I do, emotion closes my throat. The first tear pushes its way over his lid when he hoarsely whispers, "It's the same way I feel about you."

Words are weapons even when you don't mean them to be. Sometimes they wound, and sometimes they kill.

"I'm sorry. I'm sorry I hurt you then. I'm sorry I'm hurting you now."

"Don't be sorry. You've finally let somebody see your soul. Don't apologize for that."

All I can do is nod, biting my lip hard to keep from losing it completely.

He flexes to stand. Pausing, he gazes thoughtfully down the plane of his body at me. He reaches out and lightly strokes a thumb along the edge of my jaw. His hand falls away, taking our past with him.

"If you ever need anything I'm a phone call away, okay?"

"Are you leaving Seattle?"

"I think it's best I do." He starts toward the door without a good-bye. I let him get as far as turning the knob before I run and throw myself around him and hold fast. His breaths are heavy, his desperate grip on me overflowing with love and finality.

"You're different with him than you ever were with me. Not gonna lie, I really thought with his sleazy past and inability to commit I would win you back, but the second I saw you look at him in a way you never did me, I knew it was over. I just had a hard time accepting it." He runs a hand down my hair. "Be happy, Willow."

I nod against his chest. "Thank you."

Kissing the crown of my head, he releases me and leaves. He walks to his car with sure strides. He slides inside;

the whoosh of the door closing reaches me almost instantly.

As I watch him disappear from view and from my life, a part of me is incredibly sad. But I'm also incredibly proud. I've exposed myself more in the past two days than I ever have in my life. Instead of avoiding, I'm conquering. It feels good. Empowering. Liberating.

I opt for a shower instead of a bath. I eat a light snack of cheese and crackers before dropping into bed around nine thirty. I turn out the light, sans the wine, right as the chime on my cell goes off.

I don't bother to look because I know who it is and I know what it says and the repose it brings me is indescribable.

You're worth fighting for.

More than the words themselves, the steadfastness behind them smashes through my walls. It took months of repetition but his gritty, patient hard work has paid off.

I finally believe.

I believe *in* him.

In love purely for love's sake.

I finally believe in living again.

I believe I *am* worth fighting for.

But so is he.

And tomorrow, if he'll have me, I'm going to grab his hand and never let go again.

Chapter Thirty-One

MY DREAMS RUN WILD WITH her, night after miserable night.

Starlight illuminates her flaxen hair. Her creamy skin shimmers with lust. Her eyes dance with love and levity. The sound of her sultry voice chanting my name in the throes of ecstasy runs rabid through my blood. It pools in my cock, stiff and throbbing every fucking morning for her.

And when I open my eyes morning after miserable morning, I reach for her. Only her side of the bed is cold and deserted. I stare blankly at empty space for several minutes, positive if I wish hard enough she'll magically appear wearing nothing but an impudent attitude and a shy smile that begs for me to take her from behind. To show her who's boss.

But she never appears.

She never calls.

She never texts.

She doesn't knock on my door or show up unannounced at my office with the fires of retribution in her eyes.

No.

She doesn't respond to a single, solitary outreach and I'm ready to fucking snap. My patience is gone, especially when I got the message from Noah last night that Randi had, at *Willow's* request, returned every red cent of the money I paid her.

Part of me knew she would do it and that part of me respects the hell out of her. The other part, however, the primal one with needs to shield, protect, and care for his woman is so livid he's practically morphing into a barbaric animal ready to take matters into his own hands.

She walked away from me the night my father was elected, but I *let* her, knowing she needed space. Respecting that that's the least I could give her and if I pushed her too far with my sometimes-overbearing attitude, I could lose her for good.

But enough is enough. The last two weeks have been unbearable.

She's not ready, that sensible side reminds me.

I loathe that side of me these days. The logical one who uses strategy, finesse, and patience to vet and exploit the opponent's weakness for the win. I've finally met my match. There is no chink in her armor. No ace up my sleeve to use against her. Willow is not weak in any way, shape, or form. She's thundering strength inside quiet courage.

I have no choice but to dig deep yet another day and wait for her, which goes against every male instinct I have. It's excruciating.

With a heavy sigh and a perpetual boner I refuse to handle, I swing my legs over the edge of the mattress. It's far too early but since I swear each rough thrust inside of her could be real, it's almost more torturous to dream of her, so I don't get much sleep these days anyway.

I throw on a pair of blue plaid pajama bottoms and head into the kitchen, pouring myself a cup of coffee that brewed at four this morning. More out of habit than anything, I open the freezer but the first thing I spot is the box of frozen waffles. I slam it shut again, unable to think about anything but how Willow soothed my soul the night she caught me eating my Eleanor special.

I yank the freezer open again and chuck the waffles into the garbage.

Snagging my mug, I head back into my bedroom. I'm careful to avoid gazing at the leather armchair I can no longer sit in because it belongs to her.

Even though it's just after four in the morning, in under ten minutes I'm showered and dressed and settled in my home office where I spend a lot of time these days, especially if there's no one to monitor Annabelle. She cannot be left to her own devices. She's too fragile. Too depressed. Her attempts to put on a strong front are laughable at best. I've never seen her like this.

Needing focus, I force thoughts of Willow and Annabelle to the back of my mind, making myself dig into the acquisition briefing report Dane had couriered over last night. Pretty soon I'm immersed and half my morning goes by in a blur, conference calls and contracts blending together in a mass of blasé detachment.

I used to love my work. It's all I lived for. Now it's an endless chore with no reward at the end of the day. The passion I once had for this company has been overshadowed by my unexpected love for an incredibly stubborn woman.

Go figure.

"Yes, Mr. Mercer?" Dane's cheerful voice pipes through the speaker on my phone. Every fucking shiny syllable he speaks rakes down already exposed nerves, leaving a trail of hot fire in their wake.

"I'm missing the Ramsey file. I thought I asked you to include that with the M&A paperwork you sent over yesterday."

"It was. I mean"—he stutters—"I thought I did."

Poor Dane has taken every opportunity to avoid me for the past several weeks. I am hell on wheels and pretty much everyone around me has taken ten steps back to avoid the venom from my bite. But because Dane can't run too far, he's taken the brunt of my verbal lashes like a champ. I'm surprised he hasn't resigned. I've been an absolute, epic bastard. I make note to up his bonus at fiscal year-end.

"Well, you didn't."

A shadow catches my peripheral and I glance up to see Annabelle standing at the mouth of my office. Her crazy hair is tousled. She's wearing a simple pair of plain teal leggings and an oversized Seahawks sweatshirt that hangs midthigh. Red-rimmed glasses are perched on the edge of her freckled nose. She saunters in and silently makes herself at home in the chair across from me.

"Are you sure it's not there?" Dane's voice wavers as if he's about to get in trouble for something he didn't do. That may or may not have happened last week. "I marked it with a bright blue Post-it Note."

Of course he did.

"Not blind, Dane," I snip.

I sift through all the papers scattered on my desk, the bright blue Post-it Note elusive because it's not fucking here. Annabelle nonchalantly reaches across my desk and plucks a paper-clipped packet from underneath a pile and hands it to me.

Pasted to the front is a bright blue Post-it Note.

"I'm sorry, sir. I can copy them again and get them to you immediately."

"Never mind," I mumble. Asshole. Yup, that's me. Annabelle rolls her eyes and sits back. She seems more relaxed than I've seen her in weeks.

"Are you sure I can't get you extra copies—"

I growl, ready to move on with the rest of my day, "It's fine."

"Anything else I can—"

"No."

"You'll have to ignore my brother these days, Dane," Annabelle pipes in. "It's not you, it's the blue balls talking."

Dane starts chuckling.

"What the hell?" I punch the speaker button and abruptly end our call, staring her down. "You can't say things like that to my assistant. What the hell is the matter with you?"

"You're being a dick. He has the right to know why."

"He's my employee. With the money I pay him, I can be Dick Cheney if I want to be. And he doesn't need to know shit about my personal life, so knock it off."

She shrugs, not the least bit sorry.

"Did you need something or can it wait?"

She takes her sweet-ass time answering, her dawdling intentional. I drag in a lungful of air, my patience ready to shatter.

"You were never like this before her, you know."

My teeth clamp together. "Like what?" I ask, knowing she's referring to Willow.

"Emotional. I don't mean to say you were some prick with a block of ice in the middle of your chest but you were always so calculated and reserved. And now"—she waves two fingers up and down me—"you're acting like me during Shark Week."

Why that little...

"Don't even try to deny it."

I open my mouth; the immediate need to refute the brat weighing heavy on my tongue, only she's not wrong. Willow has taken the cool, calm, methodical man who didn't want anything beyond shallow sex and turned him into an emotional, pansy-ass wreck no one can stand to be around. Even I can't stand me right now, and that's saying something.

Funny thing is, though, I wouldn't change a damn thing about it.

"Back to my original question."

She simply smiles. Not the fake one she's been giving me but a genuine one that makes her eyes light up, and I see something in her I haven't seen in weeks: a flicker of sunshine. God, I've missed that in her.

"What's going on, Annabelle?" I lean forward now, forearms flat on my desk, fingers clasped.

"I'm leaving."

"I thought you didn't have class today?"

She sits up straight, scooting to the edge of her chair. Uh-oh.

I know this look. "I don't mean school. I mean I'm leaving, leaving. I'm moving out."

"No," I tell her, voice even and firm. I grab a pair of readers I only need when my eyes are tired and slip them on. "You're not."

My attention drops back to my desk, dismissing her. I expect her to huff and puff and threaten to mutilate critical male reproductive parts in the dead of night as she has several times over the last month that she's stayed with me. I always ignore her. I also lock my bedroom door when I sleep now.

"I'm moving in with Mom and Dad."

Nothing moves on me but my eyes. Over the top edge of my spectacles, I catch her gaze, fully expecting a satirical smirk on her lips. Just the other day she told me she'd rather sleep in a tent on my lawn for the rest of her life than move back home, something my mother, in particular, has been after her about since I dragged her here.

Only she's not kidding.

I reach up and take my glasses back off, folding them up before setting them down in front me. *What the hell has changed in two days' time?*

"Why?"

"Isn't that what you wanted?"

One brow sneaks up my forehead. "That's not what I want, Bluebelle, and you know it. What I *want* is you safe and healthy and happy." I pick up the glasses and start to play with the temples, crossing them back and forth.

"And sober," she offers. And yeah, I heard her hint of sarcasm.

"That goes without saying."

She draws her feet to the seat, tucking them up to her butt. Her arms come around her shins, her chin to her knees.

On the outside, my baby sister has all the appearances of youth. Smooth skin, fresh face, everything in its right place, even a hint of innocence, though I know that not to be true. But underneath her petite, wrinkle-free face resides an old soul who has seen too much and knows how seedy the underbelly of our streets can be.

I've always thought of her as a tortured old soul stuck in a young person's body.

"Burying whatever plagues you got you into trouble in the first place, Bluebelle. No matter what you say to the contrary, you are not fine. This accident with Charles Blackwell has to be messing with you big-time as it would anyone, and I'm just concerned about you, as is everyone else."

She chews on her lower lip and starts playing with a hangnail on her thumb. I expect her to dodge around this subject the same as she does every other time I try to bring it up. She surprises me, though, confessing quietly, "It is."

Some of that tension I've been carrying for weeks abates, ever so slightly. Finally, we're making progress.

Her eyes lift to mine. "I went to his grave yesterday."

That surprises me, but I don't have time to dwell on it because her next revelation knocks the wind from my lungs.

"Willow was there."

"Willow was...?"

Uh...Oh. *Fuck.* Willow was there? What happened between them? What was said? Did they even talk or did Annabelle simply leave without Willow knowing? I know that space is sacred to her, as evidenced by the way she meticulously takes care of their plots and I don't know how she'll feel about Annabelle being there. I have no idea where her head is since she won't fucking talk to me.

As if she senses my turmoil, she adds quickly, "It was cool. She was nice. Nicer than I deserve."

Of course she was. She's a caretaker, compassionate to the core. Even if she were bitter, she'd shove it down for the betterment of someone else because that's what she does.

Suddenly, I'm exhausted.

"So you talked?"

She nods.

"What did you talk about?" My voice cracks. *Did she mention me?* I selfishly want to ask. The need to know is a vat of boiling acid blistering my gut. It pains me.

"Just stuff."

"Just stuff," I parrot.

"Yeah. Stuff." She slides her feet to the floor and stands up. Quietly, she pads over to the window on the far wall. The urge to rapid-fire question after question is a blade biting my tongue.

How did she look? Happy? Miserable? Is she getting too thin? Getting enough sleep? Was she alone? Please fucking tell me she was alone.

Instead I let her organize her thoughts while mine whirl wildly. Eventually she turns around and leans against the jam of the glass. "I'm going to take a semester off. Maybe two."

"Annabe—"

"I'm talking and I need you to listen without interrupting, Shaw. Please. This is important."

I swallow and set the readers back down. I'm not sure I've seen her this somber before. Or determined. I cross my arms. "Okay, I'm listening."

"There's something not right inside me." On instinct, I open my mouth to refute her but she holds up her hand, stopping me. "It's true. I don't know what it is or why it is or how it is but I need to figure that out or I'm going to end up on either the bad side of a needle or the bottom of a river."

"Jesus, Bluebelle."

She ignores my loud outburst.

"I need more space."

My house is nearly ten thousand square feet. We could probably go days without bumping into each other, not that I'll let that happen. "I'll give you my room, then," I tell her, frustrated.

"Not real estate, Shaw. In here." She points to her temple. "I need to get rid of some of the bad so I have more room for good."

I shake my head, dizzy from the circles she's taking me in. "I'm lost."

She gazes at me thoughtfully. "Willow gave me a new perspective on things."

"Willow?"

Her entire being softens like a valve has been released and everything she's held inside releases with it. "Yeah. She's kind of amazing. I can see your draw to her."

My eyes are suddenly on fire, burning like a bitch. But my heart? Jesus, that swelled so much it's going to bust right out of me.

"I don't want to blow my second chance, you know? I owe Willow's dad that. I need to get to where I believe it, too. So Mom and I found this place in Colorado. Intense inpatient psychotherapy for a minimum of ninety days, then we'll see how I'm doing and decide what's next."

The surprises keep slamming into me, one by one. She's going away for three months? And my mother helped her?

"You and Mom?" I ask, stunned. She and my mother mix like oil and water.

Her lips tilt up. "You're pretty shitty at this listening thing."

"Sorry. Continue."

"Anyway, they don't have an opening until after Thanksgiving, so I'm going to up my therapy sessions to every day until I go. I'm going to hit at least one NA group every day and my sponsor already said he'll go with me. And I'm going to give you back your own space."

Again I try to speak. Again she stops me.

"I know you're going to tell me you don't need your space, but you do. And so do I. But I also can admit I need a support system and that's my family. I won't make it without you guys. Without you or Linc or Gemma...or Mom and Dad." She pops off the ledge and walks toward me. "I'm already packed, and you can't tell me no. Mom is on her way to pick me up."

She stops in front of me and I realize that at last, my baby sister is taking accountability for her life.

"Thank you for all you've done, Shaw. I know I've been a brat about it all but not for one second have I been ungrateful. I couldn't have made it this far without you."

I don't know what to say.

"It's okay to talk now," she jibes, a light curve on her mouth.

"I'm proud of you, Bluebelle. I don't mean to sound trite or patronizing, but I'm..." I choke up. "I'm so fucking proud of you."

The moment I'm on my feet she launches herself into my arms. I hug her, my sweet, infuriating, melodramatic baby sister who's caused more hell than my other siblings combined. We've been through this before, this declaration of hers, but this time feels different. This time I believe she finally wants to find out who she is.

"I'll visit as often as I can," I tell her.

"I can't have any visitors for the first thirty days, but after that, you'd better make sure your ass is there at least every other week."

"Count on it," I promise, kissing her cheek.

I let her go, feeling thankful but sad at the same time. I will sincerely miss her.

The chime from the front gate sounds.

"That'll be Mom."

A few swipes on my security keypad show a powder-blue Mercedes at the front gate instead of the black Audi I long to see. I try not to let myself be disappointed as I buzz my mother in.

"I'll go get my stuff." She heads toward the exit but turns back at the last second. "Can you do me a favor?"

"Anything for you, Bluebelle."

"Will you tell Willow thank you? I'm not sure I did and I want her to know if it wasn't for her and everything she said I... Well, just tell her thanks."

I don't have time to tell her I don't know if Willow will ever speak to me again so I'm not sure I'll be able to pass along her heartfelt message. I can only watch, intensely conflicted, as she bounds from the room.

I'm glad she's finally taking initiative. I'm thrilled to see a genuine fire lit in her belly. And I'm overjoyed she's letting my mom close instead of pushing her away. Annabelle needs this.

But the truth of it is, having Annabelle here was as much for me as it was for her. Taking care of my sister has given me this sort of sick purpose that still ties me to Willow somehow. Without her, that tie is broken and I'm flapping in the wind.

Alone.

All.

Fucking.

Alone.

The peace of solitude I once craved I now despise with a passion.

At that moment, something in me snaps apart. The thread of patience I've balanced on for three weeks solid frays and gives way and I hit the proverbial wall.

I'm done.

Fuck this distance she's insisted on putting between us. Fuck this situation. Fuck it all. I love Willow. I know she loves me. And that's the only truth that matters. The rest is noise we have to figure out how to turn up or down when we need to.

She's had enough space. Enough time. *I'm* taking the reins back like I should have from the beginning. No way on God's green Earth will I let her leave me behind like she has everyone else.

Not gonna happen.

I'm going to be her husband, her future, the man she wakes up to every morning and battles over the covers with at night. I've told her she's worth fighting for every single day since she left me. Now I need to prove it.

If I have to drag her stubborn ass back here and tie her down to make her talk to me, I have no problem with that. In fact, the thought of it makes me hard as stone.

Scooping up my phone, I deviate from the plan I promised myself I'd stick to steadfastly. I pull up her number and, knowing she won't pick up if I dial, I pound out a text.

You have thirty minutes, Goldilocks. Then I'm coming for you.

"Shaw? A little help here," Annabelle calls cheerily from halfway across the house.

The weight of power finally tilted back my way, I shove my phone into my pocket and head toward the front door, every footfall now pure determination. I snag one of Annabelle's suitcases sitting on the floor and step out onto the stoop, my head down.

And that's when I hear it.

That voice. That sexy, sultry, hard-on-inducing voice hits me with the force of a thousand suns.

In slow motion, I raise my head to catch Annabelle in my line of sight. She has a gentle smile on her face. "Don't fuck this up, okay? I like her." With a peck to my cheek, she grabs the bag from my hand and lugs it down the stairs herself.

My heart is racing so damn fast I feel every jarring beat against the back of my ribs. For a second I think I'm hallucinating but when her seductive vibrato reaches me again, I know she's not a mirage.

Willow is here, in the flesh. In my driveway. Talking to my mother. Hugging Annabelle. Smiling, waving good-bye as they fold themselves into the car and leave.

Then she's turning around, staring directly at me.

And she looks less than happy to see me.

In fact...she looks downright pissed.

In an instant, my cock grows painfully stiff.

Jesus, I have missed her and this impudence that fuels the flames of my incessant thirst to own her soul and worship at her feet.

Crossing my arms, I casually lean against the jamb and wait, the throbbing in my balls intensifying the longer her glare singes me.

I allow a slow grin to spread across my face, which brings the scowl on hers down even farther. The more relaxed I become, the wilder she burns.

She's magnificence epitomized.

Strength and beauty.

My fiery girl is here in all her brilliant fucking glory.

And it doesn't matter why or how or that her looks could drop a lesser man cold.

Now that she's brought herself to my doorstep, she's not leaving.

Ever.

Chapter Thirty-Two

SHE FLOATS TOWARD ME. A goddess dipped in gold, all blinding and hypnotic.

Something has her madder than a hornet and I'm betting all I own it's what's inside the envelope she's waving around like a madwoman. This isn't necessarily the reunion I envisioned, though it's the one I should have expected.

Angry or not, she's so majestic I fall under her thrall as she stalks toward me. Those sinfully wicked hips sway back and forth, taunting me, tempting me. Making my mouth water for a taste of what's between them.

"What is this?" she barks, angrily waving said envelope pinched in her hand.

I have an idea what has her so riled up but I say nothing.

My grin grows.

Her brows knit closer together, wrinkling that cute little nose I want pressed against the root of my dick as she swallows me down.

The wind catches her platinum hair, picking it up as if she's free-falling from the sky in answer to my prayers. In a huff, she winds her mane around her free hand and holds it to the side. She reaches the steps, stomping up them, one by one.

God. Damn. I love it when she gets like this.

"Well?" she demands cutely.

I can smell her now.

Passion.

Intensity.

Fortitude.

That sweet vanilla she sometimes washes her succulent body with.

Fucking hell. Her unique scent fuses to the air surrounding me and I breathe deep, briefly closing my eyes as I let it permeate my blood, invigorating me, strengthening me.

"I am not keeping this," she bites out. Halting a good foot from me, she shoves that envelope right in my face. "I am not a damn charity case, Shaw."

Her head is tilted up, blue eyes blazing hotter than twin volcanos. Those luscious lips part with every angry pant. She is glory and grace. My dick pounds against his confines to get to her.

She flattens the object of her ire straight to my chest. "I mean it. I am not keeping this."

I want to both revere and throttle her right now.

I circle her wrist and keep it taut, preventing her from moving away from me. I want her. All of her. Every stubborn inch of her. But I want her to admit she's here for *me*, not out of some sort of pissed-off confrontation that will only end in her walking away again.

"Is this why you came?" I grit, tightening my hold.

Her eyebrows lift but she can't hide behind the many fronts she's put up any longer. I'm onto her. "Why else would I be here?"

My lips twist up. So fucking bullheaded. I have a lifetime of this to look forward to.

My hand goes to her hip. I yank her into me with force and resolve. "Because you can't live without me any more than I can without you, Goldilocks."

Her eyes dart from mine but I'm not having it. I release her wrist and gently pinch her jaw between my fingers, drawing her eyes back to me.

"I'm sorry," I say, tone pitched low. I'll tell her I'm sorry every fucking day for the rest of my life if that's what it takes. "I'm sorry I kept the truth from you when I found out. I should have told you. If I could do it differently, I would."

That fire in her eyes dampens considerably and her muscles begin to relax.

One thing I've come to learn about Willow is she's an extremely emotional being. She puts on a good fuck-you face but that's all it is. She feels deeply. Love, guilt, joy, anger, hurt, indignation, pride. Every emotion she has is exaggerated because as soon as the sharp edge of one pierces her, she bolts it back down, faking apathy because that's easier. But over the past few months, she's changed. She can no longer keep those feelings under lock. *I* have the key. And I'll use it every chance I get.

"I understand why you didn't." The slight wobble in her voice is the only indication I get that no matter what pretense she used to talk herself into coming, we both know the real reason behind it.

So I wait.

I wait while she fights through that internal battle to push words out she wants to say but has a hard time voicing. The show is spectacular as always.

"I'm sorry," she whispers. "I'm sorry for so many things. For being in my own head too much. For being scared. For pushing you away when I needed you most. For being a complete idiot when it comes to relationships. But mostly"—she stops to swallow, and I appreciate how hard this is for her—"I'm sorry I let go of your hand because it's the only thing that gives me the strength to crawl out of a place I've been stuck in for too long. I'm sorry I hurt you, Shaw. I'm so, so sorry. Please forgive me."

Relief is harsh and violent, slamming into me from all sides. "No forgiveness necessary, Willow. It's been brutal for everyone. I'm just glad you're here now. Please tell me you're here to stay."

"Do you still want me? I mean...after everything?" Her voice is small and unsure and it blows me away she'd even question that.

"Want you?" I ask incredulously, squeezing her chin between my fingers. "I want nothing *but* you, Willow. I'm not letting go of you again. Ever."

She draws in a deep breath and says, "I love you," with so much heartfelt emotion I nearly sob.

I lean in, lips grazing hers. "I love you more." I wait a beat and add, "Annabelle told me you two talked."

The tips of her mouth turn. "We did."

"Everything okay?" I ask, nervous even though I saw the two of them hugging.

She turns thoughtful. "It is."

"Will you tell me about it sometime?"

She nods. "Yes."

My entire demeanor lightens considerably and I take a full, deep breath. We're going to make it. "You're not leaving. Not even to get your things. You know that, right?"

Her gaze drops to the forgotten envelope between us, then crawls back up to my face. She blinks a few times in quick succession, the smile on her mouth evening out. "I want you to take it back."

It takes me a second or two to understand what she means but when I realize she's talking about the money, not my profession, I laugh. Loud and boisterous. She's going to be the death of me.

"I mean it, Shaw." Her tone is harder now. No nonsense.

Oh, Willow.

My smile is so big my face hurts.

Game over, sweetheart.

I press her lower half to mine until she can't miss what her cheeky attitude does to me. "Know what *I* want, beautiful?" I drop my head, our noses nearly touching. "I want your breasts heavy, your pussy drenched, and your heart knocking violently against your ribs when I unbutton those sexy-as-sin jeans."

I glide my palm over the curve of her supple ass, my fingertips grazing between her cheeks. Her eyelids flutter. The rise and fall of her chest quickens.

Oh yes, that's it.

"I want your nerves awakened, your flesh tingling, and your blood to rush while I finger-fuck you to orgasm against the door in about six seconds." Not giving her a chance to respond, I pull her inside. Slamming the door shut, I push her back against it, take her face in my hands, and look straight into already lusty eyes.

"And I want every muscle of yours quivering with unchained desire by the time I finally sink slowly inside the home you've denied me for four long fucking weeks now."

I slant my mouth over hers and take. I drive my tongue between lips that cling to mine, though not only in desire. She's brawling, battling. Vying for the win. Fat chance, that. She's back under my tutelage now. My safekeeping.

My rules, my whims.

"Shaw, I'm serious," she groans, breaking our kiss. Her hands sneak between us, the paper in her fist crinkling. She tries elbowing me. Pathetically ineffective.

I shackle her wrists between one hand and shove them over her head. The envelope falls to the ground beside us. "I want you naked, Willow. I want you wet and bent over, legs spread wide so I can see just how fucking much you missed me." I exhale every word of this between harsh nips up her neck, along her jaw. Jesus, I'm so hard it hurts and every ragged pant of hers wraps its way around my cock twice, driving me closer to losing my load prematurely.

"Stop."

It's the same plea she made the first time I had her against this door, only her hips follow the dance of my fingers beautifully this time, belying her protest, so I don't stop. I skim inside her silk panties, over the bareness of her smooth, warm flesh. A pained whimper escapes her throat when I run a finger right down her center.

Her clit is already firm and pulsing and she's so wet. So fucking wet. A fantasy, alive and breathing in my house.

I push one finger inside, then two. Her need drips onto my palm. It's nirvana, the way she reacts to me.

"You sure that's what you want, Goldilocks?"

"I'm not letting you"—pant, pant—"take care of me and my"—pant—"momma."

I know exactly why she's full of piss and pride but what she obviously doesn't know is that I had little to do with the five mil now sitting in her account.

It's not *my* money. It's hers and her mother's.

All I did was help right a wrong.

"That money belongs to you," I tell her firmly.

The smooth patch I'm seeking comes into focus, causing her pussy to clamp and her pelvis to kick forward. Her fingers curl, manicured nails deliciously cutting into the webbing connecting my thumb and forefinger.

Her eyes glaze and her neck relaxes. She lets her head fall back to the door. I watch the reins on her mulish will gracefully slip while I pump in and out, reveling in the feel of her squeezing me like a boa constrictor. She's so tight and so hot and so damn wet I want to strip her and fuck her where we stand until my legs won't hold us up.

But I need to watch her come once first. I crave it.

"I don't want your stupid money." Her voice is rough, and her hips roll with every plunge inside her honeyed channel. My thumb rotates repeatedly over the nub that will set her off like the Fourth of July in about ten seconds.

She's close.

So damn close.

I trap her in my gaze and don't let go. And I don't address her comment either. "Jesus, I've missed the feel of you, the smell of your need, the fucking taste of your nipples, the sweetness of your release."

"I'm not taking—" Ecstasy gets the best of her. Her lids close. "God, Shaw."

Yeah, that's it, baby. Submit.

"Did you get yourself off thinking about me, Willow?" The thought drives me wild.

Her back bows, her neck arches.

Five.

"Did you cry my name? Beg for my cock when your climax was empty and unfulfilling?"

Her mouth falls open.

Four.

"Did your soul ache for mine every fucking second of every fucking day?"

Her eyes pop open. Grab me. Dive straight into my core.

Three.

"Because mine did, Goldilocks. Mine has bled for yours until it bled dry. You are mine, Willow Blackwell. Mine. You hear me?" I set my cheek to hers and whisper, "Now come for me, beautiful. Come hard and long and loud enough to piss off the neighbors."

My good girl does as she's told. That pussy strangles my fingers sweetly as she lets herself go. She convulses and weeps and is so goddamn radiant it brings tears to my eyes.

I sweep her limp, still-clothed body into my arms with ease and carry her through the house. She weaves her hands through my short hair, pressing kisses to the base of my throat.

I'm one walking mass of pure, male need. I want to glut myself on her for a straight month.

Eat her. Fuck her. Feed her. Pet her. Bathe her. Hold her. Own her. *Love* her.

"We should talk."

"We will," I assure her softly. I'm single-minded. "But I need to be inside you and I can't wait another second."

I take her to *the* chair. The one I envision her pressed over. Stretched over. Impregnating her in. I'm obsessed with her and that goddamn chair.

I set her on her feet and begin removing her clothes but she bats my hands away.

"Let me," she says.

I'm wound up tighter than a top, ready to come unglued if I'm not making love to her in the next minute. Only I see she needs this, so I reluctantly take a step back to give her some space.

Smiling softly, she sheds her yellow jacket and throws it to the side. I expect her to continue undressing but she steps into me instead. Eyes fastened to mine, she grabs the hem of my maroon Henley and drags it slowly up my body. Her fingers skim over my ribs. Her thumbs intentionally nick the edges of my nipples, hardening them instantly.

The tease.

Smirking, I lift my arms and let her divest me of it.

"I missed you," I say, my voice muted and scratchy. I run a finger along her jaw, still not believing she's here. "I missed you so much, Willow."

Her eyes, they melt. "I missed you, too."

"You're not leaving." She pops the buttons on my jeans. I stop her, gently circling her wrist. "You're staying, understand?"

"Always so bossy."

Jesus. That brassy smile renders me useless every time.

"Always testing me," I retort.

Rising on her tiptoes, her lips whisper against mine. "But it turns you on, doesn't it?"

"Fucking right it does."

I flatten her hand to my stomach and guide her inside my boxer briefs to show her exactly how hard and thick her saucy mouth makes me. Helping her palm my cock at the base, she squeezes hard, and *fuck me,* nothing has ever felt so damn good. I can't keep my head up straight.

Eyes shut, head back, every other sense is magnified by ten.

The warmth of her skin on mine.

Her lips traveling over my chest, her breathing labored.

The thundering of my heart inside my chest cavity.

The agonizing tightening of my balls.

It's torture. Sweet, sweet fucking torture.

She slides up my shaft leisurely and deliberate, and when her thumb sweeps over my weeping head, my whole body shudders. The buzzing at the base of my spine gathers incredible speed and every ounce of control I've been exercising disintegrates in a flash of voracious hunger.

I'm going to come and I'll be damned if it's going to be because of one swipe up my dick. When I explode, it's going to be deep inside her womb where I belong.

I shove my pants and underwear down my legs. She tears her blouse off. Her jeans are gone next. I see a glimpse of a pale blue bra before it's gone. I snap her panties clean from her hips.

Our movements are rushed and frenzied. I grab her by the back of the neck and smash my greedy mouth to hers, lifting her up and over my cock at the same time with my free arm. The feel of her taut nipples scraping my chest is utter bliss.

I coat myself with the remnants of her orgasm, then not wasting another second, I slam my hips forward and drive my aching cock inside the only place it was meant to be.

"Jesus, fuck." I suck in a sharp breath and go to war with my dick, ready to release. "God, Willow. Being sheathed inside this pussy is like nothing else." A broken moan is her only reply.

Forget the chair. I won't make it five seconds if I have her on top of me. Bending my knees, I lower us to the plush rug below, the first place I made love to her. But this time I don't restrain her.

I want her hands to roam, her eyes to roll. I want her mouth all over me, sucking, biting. I want her wild and feverish.

Bracing on my forearms, I twine my hands in her soft hair. Her legs wind around my back. I start to slide in and out, gritting my teeth against the tingles racing up my legs.

"You're moving in," I announce, laying kisses along the creamy expanse of her delicate throat.

"That sounds like an order," she breathes, clamping those hot, silken walls around me with purpose. Her nails scrape my back. I pinch a beaded nipple, hard, before taking it in my mouth to bite down even harder.

Her gasp is a familiar song I've missed listening to.

"You're marrying me." My hips move faster, my control unraveling at the speed of sound.

"I don't like being told what to do."

Oh, Willow. Willow, Willow, Willow.

Such a little liar.

I felt that smile against my cheek.

"We're having four kids. All boys."

She sucks my neck so hard I may have a hickey. I start fucking her in earnest now. She grabs my ass, fingers flexing in time to each uneven thrust.

"Three. Two girls and a boy," she counters on ragged breaths.

Palming her ass cheeks, I push her pelvis toward the ceiling and rise on my haunches. Our gazes, heavy and thick with this inconceivable love, stick to each other.

"You can have whatever you want, Willow. Anything. Name it."

Happiness radiates from her. Actual beams of it pour from her eyes. I've never witnessed her like this. If I weren't already madly in love with her, I would have fallen in love with her right at this moment. To see every facet of her so clearly is stupefying.

"I already have everything I want. Right here. I'm sorry. I'm so sorry."

Water builds in her eyes. It slices me up and down.

"Shhh. Baby, don't cry." I slow my pace, my need to comfort her overpowering my need to come.

Her fingers fly to my thighs, her grip strong and bruising. "If you stop now I'll sic Sierra on you."

Almost a sure way to shrivel a man's junk, but I don't let her idle threat affect me in the least. I withdraw almost all the way, then ram back inside so forcefully her breath catches. "You drive a hard bargain, Goldilocks."

"You taught me well, Drive By."

I impale her hard, rough, completely, through moans and breathless entreaties. She comes first, pulling me close behind. I can't take my eyes from her, even through the rip-roaring intensity of my own climax. When I've wrung every drop of pleasure I can from us both, I collapse on top of her, our slick skin pasting us together.

Minutes later, our breaths caught and the edge taken off, I snag a pillow and throw from the couch and get us settled. I don't bother to clean us up because in less than ten minutes I plan to have her bent over that chair, ass glowing red from the spanking she's going to get for not only staying away from me but for the dangerous situation she put herself in with Paul Graber. I've never been more grateful for Noah than when I found out about the events of that night and how he protected her.

"This is a little like déjà vu, huh?" she says, staring at the fire I kicked on.

"It is," I agree, fingering the goose bumps on her arm. Except now I can admit I'm in love with her. I grip her chin between my fingers and tip it up until her eyes lock on me. "The money is from your father's life insurance policy. It's yours."

She pops up, the blanket covering her incredibly sexy and very naked body slipping down. Her pretty pink nipples immediately tighten to points that beg for my teeth. I fight the urge to tweak one. Fuck, my restraint is incredible.

"What do you mean it's from my father's life insurance policy? I told you they wouldn't pay because..." A pause. The pieces are clicking together but I see she's still confused. "I don't understand."

"It's quite a process to get the cause of death changed on a death certificate."

"You—*What?*" She shakes her head in disbelief.

I sit and pull her into my lap, not wanting to have this conversation separated. She wraps her legs around my waist, her pussy snug and tight to my groin. My dick is already readying for round two when I feel our combined fluids drip on me.

"The coroner changed the cause of death from suicide to accident and someone at Aurora worked with the life insurance company to make sure the claim was expedited. The only thing missing was your account number but Millie was kind enough to give that to me."

She cocks her head. "Millie? You saw Millie?"

"Yes," I tell her simply.

"You...? Millie gave you my bank information?" The incredulity in her voice makes me laugh.

"What can I say?" I shrug. "I'm pretty persuasive. I spent a couple of hours with your mother as well. She has quite a sense of humor."

"You did?"

"Of course. She's important to you, Willow. What's important to you is important to me."

It's a few beats before she smiles. Her shoulders drop, relieved. "Is this real?"

I run a few strands of her hair through my fingers. "As real as it gets."

I know my woman. Her pride is worth as much as her stubbornness. Not that I wouldn't have given her every cent I own but after she returned the two-fifty, I knew the financial burden would return with a vengeance. I'm just glad she'll never have to worry about money again.

"His policy was worth five million dollars? Really?"

She's having a hard time with this.

"Two point five, actually, but...an accidental death pays double."

That brilliant smile falls away. I stroke her bottom lip and lean in to press a kiss to it. No matter how much time goes by, this will always be a bitter pill to swallow.

"So you see, the money is yours."

And that's not all. I want to tell her she'll be rich beyond her wildest dreams when Aurora starts production on her father's patented drug six months from now, but I have a feeling she can only handle one thing at a time. I'll save that news for another day.

"I'm still confused. I mean the coroner wouldn't just take your word for it. Would he?"

She wiggles around. I harden to full mast. I clamp my hands on her hips to hold her still or she'll be riding me instead of getting answers.

"No. It wasn't quite that easy. I accompanied two of the girls involved that night to the police station so they could tell their story and the police report could be augmented."

I swear her eyebrows are stuck together. So cute.

"Who?"

"Lia Melborne, the one Noah and I visited in North Carolina, along with Annabelle." When I originally approached Lia about it, I wasn't sure she would agree, but the years of guilt over keeping this secret had eaten her up. She jumped at the chance to right this wrong.

"But I thought Annabelle didn't remember anything?"

"Not about the accident, no, but she remembers enough about earlier in the evening. Lia corroborated that story and filled in the blanks."

I see the questions she has fly by at a hundred miles an hour.

"They went to the police? Are they in trouble?"

"No, baby. It was an accident. No charges will be pressed against either of them."

"Thank God," she replies. "How is she doing? Annabelle?"

I tuck a few hairs behind her ear, relishing in the softness of her skin. I can't stop touching her. "She's leaving for Colorado after Thanksgiving for three months of therapy. It was her idea."

She breathes in slow then blows it out. I try not to get

distracted by the way her breasts just brushed my chest. "I'm glad. I hope it will help her."

"Me too."

She shivers and I reach for the blanket to drape it over her shoulders. My gaze drops to her throat where that pendant always lies in the hollow. Only…it's noticeably absent. It's the first time I've seen her without it in four months.

Is it wrong I want to pound my chest in victory?

It is.

Right?

Out of habit she touches the empty space and smiles this smile that tells me she knows what I'm thinking. I can't help but smile a smile that says *I don't give a fuck. You're mine. Only mine.*

"Vi is with me. She's always been with me, necklace or not."

"It's from him, right?"

She purses her lips. The answer is in her eyes.

"You can wear it, you know. I don't mind." I do. Sort of.

Her smirk tells me she heard my unvoiced thoughts. "I don't need it anymore." She runs a fingernail along my stubble and squirms so much I clamp my fingers around her hips to still her. "I have your hand, remember?"

"Damn straight you do," I murmur, leaning in to tongue my way up her neck.

Her fingers tunnel in my hair. She scrapes her nails along my scalp as she tilts her head to the side. "Did you know Randi was my sister's best friend?"

Talk about a small, small world. "That sort of makes sense. She seemed very protective of you when I met with her."

"Yeah. She always was."

I force my lips from her skin and tell her, "You're done there," just in case it needs to be said.

"In this one instance, I won't argue."

"Well, that's progress at least." I chuckle when she smacks me playfully.

We both grow somber and gaze at the other.

"Are you really here?" I ask her, still in utter awe she came to me.

"I'm here." Her smile hits me square in the chest. "It won't be easy, Shaw. I can't change overnight. You'll have to push me out of my comfort zone and be patient with me when it's hard for me to talk to you about my feelings."

"I never do anything easy, and I'm pretty damn good at pushing," I assure her, falling a bit more into arresting eyes that are so clear I can see to the bottom.

"You know, I've avoided complications my entire life. After Violet died, I..." She stops to swallow. "I kind of went numb. Not kind of, I *did* go numb. It was easier that way. I was okay with my life, though"—she starts drawing light circles around my collarbone, down my chest—"until some asshole who couldn't drive ran into the back of my death trap of a car."

Her body heats. She shrugs. The blanket falls. Sorry (not sorry), but my cock starts to riot. Willow's body is in-fucking-credible and round two is far overdue. And my Goldilocks, God love her, is perceptive. She doesn't miss a beat. Her fingers, which were absently playing with my smattering of chest hair, now start trekking south. Waaaay south.

"Willow," I warn. If she wants to finish our talk, she'd best not move another inch. She does. She fucking does.

Lesson time.

Oh, how I *love* lesson time.

Before I know it her ass is in the air, already a warm pink from my palm, and her fingers are wrapped around either arm of her throne. I'm driving into her, thrumming her clit, both of us halfway to orgasm when I start making my demands.

"You're marrying me."

I'm a businessman at heart. It's been ingrained in me since birth. I know when to use strategy, when to use tact, when to be a hardass, and when to walk away. I know how to use every single tool in my arsenal to achieve the desired outcome.

So it's with zero shame I release her clit and slide a thumb through her abundant wetness, going in for the kill. I rim her puckered flesh once before slipping it inside to the hilt. Instead of pulling away, she sinks into me with a hiss.

Fuck, how I've missed her.

"Say yes, Goldilocks," I demand, voice thick and coarse.

"You're not..." Her knuckles turn white as I pound her relentlessly. She's almost there. "...playing fair."

Breathless. Exactly the way I like her.

Draping over her, the ridges of her spine pressed to my front, I slow my tempo considerably. "Marry me," I whisper against her ear.

"Faster."

"Marry me."

"Harder."

"Marry me," I repeat, moving at a snail's pace.

"You're bullying...me." The last part comes out as a whine.

She's going to come.

I pull her face toward me. Kiss her swollen lips. "Wrong. I'm loving you. I love you with every square inch of me, Willow. Hopelessly. Forever. Be my wife, beautiful. Don't let go of my hand now. Marry me. Please."

Her walls flutter. Her body tenses, but her eyes...those soul-sucking lakes that have me forever trapped in their fathomless bottoms stay on me as the first wave of ecstasy crashes over her.

"Yes," she whispers. "Yes, yes, yes, yes."

And I know her mantra isn't in response to the pleasure coursing through her limbs. It's for me.

Only me.

I sigh and let myself follow, allowing unequaled serenity to settle in my bones once my orgasm wanes.

Six months ago, I thought I had it all, but I realize now I had nothing. I found the man I was meant to be in the most unexpected of places. In her softness. In her tenacity. In her strength and twisted labyrinths.

Although Willow will always be a patchwork of her tragic past, I have a lifetime to unravel her complexities, one by one.

And I will celebrate each victory, no matter how small.

It's going to be a ride, of that I'm sure.

"Can we do that again?" she pants. Her cheek rests on a forearm. Her lids are closed and there's a soft, dreamy grin playing on her lips. I put that there.

"Which part, beautiful?" I ask, pushing back sweaty golden strands stuck to her forehead. Sweaty and sated look very fucking good on her.

Her eyes open and slide to mine, accompanied by a vixen's smile that turns me upside-down. "All of it."

But I gotta say, it's a ride I wouldn't take with anyone else.

"I thought you'd never ask, Goldilocks."

Willow

Epilogue

"WHAT ABOUT THIS ONE?" I spin the iPad around and push it her way. "I think it's perfect."

She barely gives the screen a passing glance. "This is a joke, right?"

"Sierra," I scold.

"No." She shoves the device across the table. I barely keep it from falling off the edge, almost spilling my iced tea in the process.

"You're being impossible, you know that. You have to decide." I click out of that website and move on to Nordstrom's, trying not to freak out about all that's on my plate.

The last three months have been a whirlwind. I moved in with Shaw. We set a wedding date for early summer that's rapidly approaching. I was selected by a number one *New York Times* best-selling romance author who wasn't happy with her previous narrations and wants me to rerecord most of her backlist. Plus she's put me on retainer for her future works. Between trips to Colorado every week to see Annabelle, who is like night and day from when she left, my momma was in the hospital for five days last month with pneumonia. Luckily she's completely recovered.

Oh, and I'm apparently going to be as rich as Warren Buffet since the FDA approved production of Zytin, which my father held the patent to.

But none of that trumps the most exciting development of all.

I'm pregnant. Ten weeks.

I can't believe this is my life.

"Can't you just elope? This wedding thing seems like a lot of work." Sierra slumps in her chair and begins picking at her black nail polish.

"I plan to get married once and I'm not going to let some bad Elvis impersonator sign my marriage certificate. Besides, whether or not my momma remembers it, I want her there."

"Fine," she grumbles loudly. "Show me something else."

"You have to help me out here, Ser. You haven't even *told* me what you like."

She shrugs. "I prefer leather over lace."

I ignore her. We've already had this conversation. Four times. "V-neck? Sweetheart? A-Line? Strapless? Floor-length? Knee-length? Dusty rose?"

She snorts at that one. She hates pink in any form, except in her hair.

"How about this?" I show her a midnight-blue short V-neck dupioni cocktail dress. "Look…it has pockets," I offer excitedly. What woman doesn't like pockets in dresses?

"Hard pass."

"You're killing me, Smalls." I sigh. "This is like the hundredth dress you've shot down."

"Because you have terrible taste. Need we revisit junior prom again?"

"Another Coke, ma'am?" the waitress, who has approached our table asks Sierra before I have a chance to remind her that her velour sweat suit phase in the eighth grade wasn't exactly her finest hour either.

"Let me ask you something." Sierra hooks an elbow on the

back of her chair and cocks her head at our young, perky waitress named Azalia. *Uh-oh.* "Do I look like a ma'am to you?"

Azalia's wide eyes pop my way for help. I offer her an encouraging smile and sympathetic shrug. She's on her own.

"Uh…" A mouse caught in a snare is exactly how I'd describe Azalia right now. Poor thing.

"Don't look at her," Sierra snipes. Man, she's in a mood. You'd think she was the one with hormones ravaging her body instead of me.

Our clearly Southern server, bless her innocent soul, is saved from whatever scathing remark Sierra was about to swallow her up with because Shaw and Noah choose that moment to arrive for lunch.

I stand to wrap my arms around my fiancé's neck.

"I missed you," Shaw purrs a half second before kissing me on the mouth. It's long and lusty and far too inappropriate for a restaurant. I go wet instantly, my craving for him never satisfied.

Mouth still devouring mine, he buries a hand in my hair and leverages it to his advantage. He kisses me senseless, breaking away right as I turn liquid. My lids are heavy and the throbbing between my legs begs me to take him somewhere dark and private so he can relieve it.

"You seem hungry." He smirks, the gleam in his eye telling me he did that on purpose.

"That was mean."

"That was an appetizer, beautiful." His eyes sweep down my body, heating me up. "I'm looking forward to dessert later."

"For the love of Christ," Sierra bemoans. "You're ruining my appetite."

"Funny. Mine seems to be growing," I hear Noah say with a chuckle.

"Oh my God," Sierra mumbles. I laugh.

"Uh, I'll just give you all a moment." Azalia scurries away, probably to find someone else to take her crazy station.

"Hey, doll," Noah breathes, lips skimming my cheek. Shaw shoves Noah away, who is now laughing. He's lightened up considerably with the brotherly affection Noah shows me.

Shaw ushers me back to my seat and takes the one to my right, while Noah pulls out the only remaining chair at our four-person table.

"Sierra," Noah's dark voice greets her. The way he elongates her name feels the same as ribbons of silk being drawn across your naked flesh while blindfolded. Sensual. Erotic. Even I have goose bumps.

But my coldhearted former roomie remains unaffected. Or at least that's what she wants everyone to think. She makes a big production of rolling her eyes and clucking her tongue in annoyance.

Noah sits, never taking his eyes from her. An amused smile sits on his lips. I think he knows Sierra's act is just that. When she looks away, I barely keep myself from asking why she doesn't let him bang her and get it over with.

Comical, these two.

"Why is he here again?" Sierra spits, crossing her arms. Noah, so lighthearted and easygoing, throws his head back and chuckles. He sets his arm on the table and leans as close to her as he dares.

"I'm the best man. You're the maid of honor. And in a wonderful twist of fate, we're going to be godparents. Afraid we're going to be glued at the hip for quite some time, pet. And I, for one, can't think of anything sweeter."

She gasps, affronted. I'm sure there were numerous things in that sentence that set her off, but when his heated gaze falls to her hips, an honest-to-God flush creeps up her collarbone and doesn't stop until it reaches her hairline. Satisfied, Noah leans back and casually picks up his menu.

Uh, okay then.

"So," I ask, closing the cover of my iPad. "How was your morning?"

Shaw and Noah had some clandestine rendezvous planned

this morning they refused to disclose in advance. "Guy time," Noah had said.

They exchange furtive glances.

"Good." Shaw, too, picks up his menu and opens it, glancing over the list of appetizers.

"That's it? That's all you're giving me?"

"How are you feeling?" he asks, side-eyeing me. "Nauseous today?"

On a short laugh, I call him out. "You're not as smooth as you think you are, Drive By."

He winks. Dammit, he knows what that does to me. "I beg to differ, Goldilocks." His eyes go to my nipples, which stand at attention for him.

"Just show her, Merc," Noah says. "She's going to see it anyway when you bump uglies later."

"See what?"

I rake over Shaw's body to see if anything different stands out, but he has on the same fitted black tee and dark-washed jeans he left the house in this morning. He is sexy as fuck. Those honed muscles, his long, lithe fingers, that talented...

Concentrate.

"Tell me." My gaze volleys between them.

Shaw glares at his best friend but Noah shrugs it off. "Probably not smart to rile a pregnant woman. Didn't you say her temper was on an even shorter wick these days?"

Shaw curses under his breath.

I don't even have time to get mad because Sierra jibes, "What'd you do, Mercer? Get her name tattooed on your ass cheeks?" She slips her straw in the corner of her mouth and drinks, the other corner curled into a grin.

"Good guess," Noah interjects, laughing.

Sierra says something to him I don't hear. All of my attention is now on Shaw, our two jesters forgotten.

"You got a tattoo?"

He nods, slow, tentative.

He's nervous.

I'm quite sure I've never seen the confident and all-powerful Shaw Mercer so worried before. It's adorable.

"Where?" When he doesn't answer, I ask on a teasing laugh, "On your ass cheek?"

He throws Noah and Sierra both a quick glare. "No." They shriek in laughter.

"Ignore them." I scoot my chair closer to him, taking his hand in mine. "Tell me."

"I wanted to tell you in private." Another glower in Noah's direction. His eyes search mine for a good few seconds. Then he slides his hand out from mine and lifts his shirt, exposing sinewy abs that make my mouth water.

I immediately zero in on a piece of clear plastic film that covers a patch on the left side of his ribs, right over the puzzle pieces I traced with my tongue this morning in the shower before I made his knees weak. The skin underneath is red and irritated...and freshly inked.

My breath catches in the back of my throat. "What is that?"

I reach out to touch it but he grabs my hand, stopping me.

"Here. It needs to come off anyway." He peels back the film, exposing the angry skin below, and with the covering gone I clearly see what he did.

I start to cry. Ugly cry. Snot and everything.

Damn you, hormones.

"Baby. Willow, don't cry."

He drops his shirt and reaches for me, but I push it back up to study the symbol of love he'll carry forever.

Weeping branches hang over a weathered trunk.

The leaves are intricate but obvious. Most are filled in, some are left empty.

Roots spread from the base, thick and plentiful. Deep and established.

The willow tree fills the empty space perfectly.

I raise my head to find him smiling, tender and warm. He frames my face, brushing my tears away. He moves close enough to whisper against my lips, "You once told me my tattoo was unfinished, remember?"

I'll never forget.

"I finally found something I love enough to complete it," he tells me hoarsely.

Have you ever felt your heart balloon? Inflate with so much love and happiness your chest physically expands to the point you're sure it will rupture?

I hope so. Because everybody deserves to experience an emotion that's pure and flawless and untainted at least once in their lifetime.

Raising his shirt one more time, I trace around the reddened skin, my breath watery. "That's permanent, you know."

He chuckles, kissing my lips hard. "So they warned me."

I feel gooey inside. "Thank you for not giving up on me." I throw my arms around him and squeeze. "Thank you for fighting for me, Shaw."

"You're a tough opponent." He extracts me from his arms and cups my face. "But a worthy one. Incredibly worthy."

What woman wouldn't melt at that? Sierra, maybe. "I love you."

His lips drop to mine and he whispers against them, "I love you, too."

"Uuugh. You two are really making me sick," Sierra laments, loudly slurping the last of her soda. One look at her, though, and I know she's lying. She's happy for me.

"I think in this case I must agree with Sierra," Noah adds, scrutinizing her with intent. She purposely avoids his rapt gaze.

Snickering, Shaw flips his menu open right as the waitress returns to take our order. The conversation quickly turns to everyday stuff. The wedding. The damage to our roof in last month's hailstorm. Annabelle's highly anticipated visit home next weekend. Her first.

The conversation is light and relaxed and I allow myself to

sit back and take stock of my life and the people I've allowed myself to love. To truly, fully love without reservation, without fear. My circle may never be big, but it will be stronger than ever because of one link.

Years ago when I was at the lowest point in my life I ran across a quote: *Sometimes getting lost is how we find ourselves.* It stuck with me, all this time, even though I wasn't sure I could ever be found.

Only now I understand I never was lost. I was simply hiding in plain sight, waiting for someone to take notice, to have the fortitude to fight their way through every obstacle I put up as if their life depended on it.

I was waiting for someone to take my hand.

I was waiting for Shaw Mercer.

~ The End ~

Babbles...

I know what you're thinking. I already know what will show up repetitively in reviews. Willow, for the love of Christ, what is wrong with you? JUST TELL SHAW YOU LOVE HIM ALREADY! Tell him about your sister. Vomit every single thing inside you because it's rotting there! You could have avoided all this drama!

I felt your frustration, believe me. But I also get where Willow was coming from. I more than get it, actually.

There are those who have a hard time expressing their true emotions for whatever reason, whatever scenarios life has put them through. ***I*** am one of them. My husband likes to talk everything out. I don't, even though I genuinely want to most times. It's a constant frustration for him, even though he is the person I trust most in the entire world.

So if you think I'm trying to create drama for the sake of drama, I can certainly be guilty of that sometimes. But not in Willow's case. Not how she felt or her inability to get things out that she desperately wanted to. Sometimes it's **not** just as easy as opening your mouth—ask my husband.

On a side note, the Eleanor special is real. My grandma used to eat waffles that way so my husband nicknamed them Eleanor specials. To this day he, too, likes to eat waffles with jam.

Finally, I took some liberties around the drug approval portion of my story. Getting a new drug approved by the United States Federal Drug Administration is complex and drawn out. There are multiple phases and clinical trials that can take eight to ten years to wade through. As you can imagine, only a small percentage of drugs even make it to phase three clinical trials, an even smaller percentage approved. Anyway, my point is I sped up the process a bit for the sake of the story, but know I did my homework.

Thanks for sticking with me through this very long book and series (roughly 206K words in all). I happen to love long, intricate stories where we can delve several layers into the complexity of the human character, because let's face it: not one of us is just one-faceted. A longer story allows me, as the author, to take that journey with you, so if people complain about the length, I won't apologize. This is the story I wanted to tell and I'm beyond proud of it.

Now to my thanks. As always, thanks to **Nikki Busch**, my editor, for smoothing my manuscript and making me look good. Special thanks goes to my sister, **Tara**, and my author bud **KL Grayson,** who both gave me honest feedback that helped me make this the story I wanted. I hope you both now know what a sacred cow is because no one else will since I took it out! (cries tears). THANK YOU for taking time out of your busy schedules to help me! **Heather Roberts**: I cannot express how appreciative I am of your tireless work, availability at all hours of the day or night, and your endless support of all the things. I truly think I'd have given up this writing thing by now if not for your help and guidance. Last but never least, thanks always to my **husband** who loves everything I do. *Everything*. Even my snoring. You're my biggest fan and I love that about you, even if I don't always tell you.

Friends, family, bloggers, authors, betas, pimpers, Kreig's Babes, and most importantly MY READERS: if you supported me in any way, shape, or form, you know who you are and you know I thank you from the bottom of my heart. I am nothing